CLAIR M.

DON'T CRY WOLF

POULSON

CLAIR M.
DON'T CRY WOLF
POULSON

A NOVEL

Covenant Communications, Inc.

Published by Covenant Communications, Inc.
American Fork, Utah

Printed in Canada
First Printing: August 2008

14 13 12 11 10 09 08   10 9 8 7 6 5 4 3 2 1

ISBN 13: 978-1-59811-596-3
ISBN 10: 1-59811-596-0

To my brothers and sisters: Alma, Stan, Lynn, Leesa, Kent, and Marsha. I love and appreciate all of you. Your support and encouragement over the years mean the world to me.

PROLOGUE

Tires screeched on the wet pavement. Screams filled the minivan as it careened wildly, slid sideways, and then overturned. It rolled again before coming to a stop on its top at the edge of the road, amazingly, still clinging to the pavement. Steam rose from the broken radiator, and oil and gasoline spewed onto the pavement, gliding over the watery surface. One headlight was still shining, lighting a large pine tree near the road. In the eerie semidarkness, the silence after the crash was broken by a single sound—a sobbing child within the demolished vehicle.

For several minutes the sobbing continued. Then the boy began wiggling his way out of his car seat. The sudden stillness terrified him, and he clawed at his safety restraints. When he finally managed to escape from the seat belts, he began crawling through the broken glass, tangled metal, torn fabric, and blood. He touched a still, twisted body that was enveloped in an inflated air bag.

"Mommy!" he cried. But Mommy wasn't moving. Mommy wasn't answering. "Sarah," he tried as his hands touched another body. She didn't respond either. Tears welled up in his blue eyes, and his body shook in spasms.

An old pickup truck pulled up beside the van. A door slammed and an angry voice called out, "Get back in the truck." A dog barked in response, and a minute later the same voice said, "Looks like they all bit it. Nothing I can do for them. I better get out of here before the cops show up. What happened here ain't my fault, but they'll blame me. Come on, dog, get in. We're gettin' out of here."

Jimmy could make no sense of what was being said. But whoever that man was, he didn't sound like a nice man. And, as Jimmy peeked at him past his mother's lifeless body, he didn't look like a nice man. In fact, standing there in the rain on the dark road and glaring at the crumpled van, he was a terrifying figure. Jimmy felt his teeth rattle, and a numbing fear almost smothered him.

Opening the door to his truck, the man ordered, "Get in!"

The dog approached the jagged opening through which Jimmy was peeking. "Either get in or I'll leave you," the man shouted. "I ain't waitin' around for the cops to come."

Jimmy watched in relief as the man climbed into his truck and drove away. The dog remained. It stood for a minute, peering into the dark interior of the van. Then it too turned and disappeared into the blackness and rain.

A minute or two passed, and Jimmy's trembling subsided. It was almost totally black inside the van without the lights from the man's pickup. The darkness itself was frightening. Somehow, his traumatized brain recognized that he was alone now, and that too was frightening. The laughter he'd heard before was gone. It had turned to screams as blinding headlights had suddenly veered toward the van. Those screams repeated themselves inside his head now. He clapped his hands over his ears. But it didn't help. He didn't know where those blinding lights had gone. He had ducked and shut his eyes. But he remembered the screeching tires and then the van rolling over and over, bumping, banging, and making horrible grinding noises. But mostly Jimmy remembered the screaming. He too had screamed.

He had to get out of the van. He was afraid to stay in there— afraid of the darkness, but also afraid that the terrible man would come back and find him and . . . His mind couldn't quite find words for what the man might do. He forced his way past the still bodies and slowly pushed his way through a window.

Once out of the tangled wreck, he stood on the wet pavement and looked at what was left of the blue van—Big Blue. The rain continued to fall, and the darkness was menacing. He had to get away from here! Something cold and moist touched his bare little arm, and he stiffened.

Just then he saw headlights in the distance. And he remembered the ones that had shone on the van just minutes before. He also remembered the voice of the man who had left without his dog. His muddled mind remembered that the man who was coming was the reason he'd crawled out of the van. He forced his short legs into action and fled from the road and into the nearby trees, stumbling as he went. He looked back when the vehicle stopped, but after a shadowy figure got out and approached his family's crumpled van, he turned and struggled farther up the slope. He didn't want to be there.

After a few steps he discovered that he was not alone. The man's dog was following him. He tried to run, fearing the dog as much as he did the man who had left it behind. The dog kept coming after him, and Jimmy finally did what he'd seen his brother and father do when they had been followed by an unwanted dog. He picked up a rock and threw it.

The dog stopped in its tracks. Feeling safer, Jimmy hurried on, thinking he'd scared the animal. Finally, the boy sank down by a large pine tree and hugged his knees to his chest. Tears came again, mixing with the drenching rain. He cried for his mother. He cried for his sister. He wished his dad were here. And then, without realizing it, he prayed—just as his parents had taught him to do. It was a short, almost incoherent prayer. Then he closed his eyes and tried to pretend that the terrible things had not happened. Again something cold touched his bare arm.

Jimmy froze, wondering if the dog was about to bite him. When it didn't, he slowly looked up. He could barely see the outline of the dog's face near his in the darkness. An unexpected calmness settled over him. His fear subsided. Together, the young boy and the dog waited near the terrible place where Jimmy had lost his mother and sister.

* * *

Sergeant Matthew Prescott got the first call for a serious accident a few miles south of Gallatin Gateway on U.S. 191. As a deputy with the Gallatin County Sheriff's Department, he investigated very few accidents, but that night the nearest Montana Highway Patrol trooper was nearly thirty miles away, working on another accident. So the dispatcher asked him to respond and secure the scene while she called for another trooper.

He flipped on his lights and siren and left town. The dispatcher said the person reporting the accident over a cellular phone had been hysterical, that it was a bad wreck. Matt drove as fast as he dared, his knees trembling slightly as his truck approached eighty miles per hour on the rain-slicked highway. An officer never knew what he might face when he first arrived at an accident. And that always worried Matt.

Of course, the wreck might not be nearly as critical as reported. People have a tendency to exaggerate. They often cried wolf, and though that usually made him angry, this night, he prayed that they had. He didn't feel like dealing with a fatality.

His family would be home soon. Maybe they already were. He had missed them the past few days while they were visiting his wife's parents in Jackson Hole, Wyoming. Only his oldest son, Keith, had stayed home with him. Keith had a job at a local grocery store and couldn't get time off. They'd both grown tired of Matt's cooking. He had three specialties—from a can, from a box, or, infrequently, takeout. His mouth watered at the thought of Carol's cooking. He'd always felt especially lucky that she had agreed to marry him, not only because of her cooking—although it was terrific—but because she was sweet and gentle, intelligent and lovely. That was a good start on the list. But even more, for reasons he could never figure out, she loved him.

The radio crackled again, and Matt was informed that an ambulance was en route. It was only minutes behind him. A trooper was also responding now, but it would take him a while to reach the accident. If Matt would just secure the scene and tend to the injured, he was told, the highway patrol would handle the investigation. It didn't sound like anyone had been exaggerating on this one. His palms began to sweat.

The rain had let up, and although it was not much more than a drizzle now, the road surface was still dangerous. That was probably part of what had caused the problem just a mile farther up the road. Someone was in too big of a hurry and had lost control.

He rounded a long, gentle curve and could see a cluster of lights ahead. He let up on the gas pedal, slowing as he approached the accident scene. He pulled to the side of the road, behind the wreckage, and stopped his vehicle, leaving his emergency lights flashing. His stomach lurched as he climbed out of his truck. As he surveyed the mangled remains, he wondered if anyone could still be alive in that wreckage. Someone would be crying this night.

"There are people inside that van," a burly truck driver told him as he approached the wreckage. "I can't see anyone stirring. Looks like they're dead to me. You better have a look."

Matt shifted his gun belt nervously and bent down, shining his light through a very tight space and into what remained of the van. He gave a strangled cry, and his stomach erupted as he fell back from the wreckage. His light had illuminated a face.

He knew that face.

And he loved that face!

Sergeant Matt Prescott cried.

The big truck driver asked gruffly, "This your first bad wreck, deputy?"

Matt looked up from where he now sat in the water and oil and gasoline. "It's my family," he choked.

Later, after the bodies were removed, one of the EMTs put an arm around his shoulder. Carl Davis was a member of Matt's ward in Bozeman, and they'd been friends for years. "We got them both out," he said. "I'm so sorry, Matt." His voice was choked with emotion.

Matt leaped to his feet. "Both?" he cried.

Not understanding, Carl said, "Yes, I'm so sorry. Carol and Sarah are both dead, Matt. I thought you knew that."

"What about my little boy?" Matt demanded. "Jimmy was with them."

"There are only the two of them."

"That can't be! Jimmy went to Jackson with them. Where's my son?"

Everyone who was acquainted with Matt Prescott knew he was a serious, dedicated officer. If he said his five-year-old son had been in that van, it was so. They began a frantic search, first in the wreckage, then in the tall grass and shrubbery along the highway.

Matt tried to help, but his mind was numb. He wandered up and down the highway, calling Jimmy's name and shining his flashlight around—looking for him but not expecting to see him. Had he been able to unravel his twisted thoughts at that moment, he probably would have admitted that he didn't know exactly what he expected.

Carl approached him. "He's got to be here somewhere, Matt. He must have been thrown farther than we thought at first."

"He wasn't thrown from that van, Carl," Matt said woodenly. "Carol never let him go anywhere without being belted into the car seat."

"The seat's still in there," Carl said.

"Then where's Jimmy?"

As Carl started to respond, he was interrupted by a mournful howl that came from somewhere in the trees beyond the road. "Sounds like a wolf," he said.

Chills raced up Matt's spine. He sprang toward the trees. "It might have my son!"

Carl followed him. The men had gone only a hundred yards when Matt's light fell on a pitiful heap on the ground near the base of a tall pine tree. A large dog resembling a wolf stood next to it. As Matt began to run toward the little figure, the dog raised its muzzle into the air and filled the murky night with its melancholy howl.

"Gotta be part wolf," Carl muttered under his breath as he too ran toward it and the boy, a large stick in one hand.

The dog sat calmly, and Matt gathered his sobbing little boy into his arms. As he started quickly back toward the accident scene, the dog followed close behind them. Jimmy clung tightly to his father, his face buried against his father's chest.

No one took particular notice of the old pickup truck moving slowly by the accident scene as Matt loaded his son into his truck. And no one, not even Sergeant Prescott, noticed the large, wolflike dog jump into the back of the sheriff's pickup.

1

One Year Later

Matt glanced around, searching for his boys. They always met just inside the west door of the church after meetings on Sunday. It was a habit Carol had started when Sarah and Keith were small. Even now, after a full year, he still felt an uncomfortable lump in his throat whenever he spotted the boys without their mother and sister.

"Hi, Dad," Jimmy said as he hurried to his father. Matt was still grateful to Dr. Lubek, the psychiatrist who had helped Jimmy emerge from the pain-filled silence after Carol and Sarah died. Matt remembered only too well the weeks that went by without Jimmy uttering a single word.

"Hi, son," Matt said, trying to conceal the catch in his voice. He guessed he'd never stop missing Carol and Sarah. Every single day there were things—sometimes very little things—that reminded him of one or both of them.

"Where's Keith?" Jimmy asked.

"I'm sure he'll be along in a minute," Matt said. "We'll wait here for him."

"Brother Prescott," a voice called from behind him. "I'm glad I caught you before you left. Jimmy has a talk in Primary next week. He says he thinks he's ready to try it."

"Great. I'll make sure he's prepared," Matt said as he looked at the slender young woman who was speaking. Lately he had found himself looking more often and more closely at her. He pulled his eyes from her attractive face and looked down at Jimmy. "Don't let me forget to help you get it ready."

"I won't," Jimmy said as he pulled a wadded paper from the front pocket of his pants. "Sister Flemming told me to be sure to give this to you."

As Matt accepted the paper from Jimmy, Sister Flemming said, "Thanks, Jimmy. I hope your dad can come into Primary next week and listen to you give your talk."

Matt looked her way again and swallowed quickly. Something about the way Lindsay Flemming said Jimmy's name reminded him of Carol. Perhaps it was the affection in her voice. She seemed to be genuinely fond of his son. For that matter, Jimmy liked Lindsay a lot too. He often said she and her father, Noah Flemming, were the best Primary teachers in the whole world.

His eyes met Lindsay's bright blue eyes and held them for just a moment. It was hard for him to talk to single women. Matt felt it was somehow a betrayal of his love for Carol. And with Lindsay Flemming that was especially true. Lindsay was as attractive in her own way as Carol had been in hers. Carol had been almost as tall as Matt's five-foot-ten, with green eyes and very blonde hair, always worn short and never a hair out of place. On the other hand, Lindsay was petite, not much over five feet. She had long, light brown hair, and Matt guessed she spent as little time as possible on it. Usually she wore it simply tied back in a ponytail, like it was today. And yet it somehow managed to look really good.

Finally, Matt said, "I'll be there to hear him."

"I knew you would be, Brother Prescott," she said with a smile.

"Any more trouble with wolves?" Matt asked awkwardly when Lindsay appeared in no hurry to walk away.

"Not recently," she said, "but Dad and I worry about them all the time. They're such beautiful creatures, but we just can't afford to keep losing calves the way we did in the spring. If they'd just stay in the park, it would be great."

"I have a wolf," Jimmy said proudly, just as his seventeen-year-old brother joined them. "His name's Claw."

"He's not a wolf," Keith reminded him. "He's a dog."

"Sometimes he howls like a wolf," Jimmy argued.

"Okay, I guess he might be part wolf," said Keith.

"But he doesn't hurt calves or lambs," Matt added quickly.

"I've seen Claw. He's a gorgeous creature." Lindsay smiled at Jimmy. "Well, I better get going," she added as her eyes once again met Matt's, causing him to squirm. "Dad was ill again this morning. He hated to miss church, especially our Primary class, but I insisted that he stay in bed. I better get home and see how he's doing." Noah and his daughter had been called just a few months ago to teach Jimmy's class together, and Matt was grateful to them for the special attention they gave his son.

"I hope he's feeling better soon. Give him my regards," Matt said.

"Thanks, I'll do that." Lindsay smiled at Matt, turned toward Jimmy and patted him on the head, and left.

"She's a nice lady," Keith said as the three of them piled into their silver Chevrolet Silverado pickup a couple minutes later.

"Who is?" Jimmy asked.

"Lindsay Flemming," Keith said. "You know, I'd ask her out if she wasn't so old. She's probably twelve or thirteen years older than me, but she sure is good-looking."

Matt was surprised at his son's comment, although he agreed with him.

No one spoke for the next few minutes as Matt and his sons headed for their small farm outside Bozeman. At the edge of town a group of cars had pulled off the road. A young man with long, stringy hair was holding a sign while two more pounded a steel post into the ground behind it. Others, both men and women of varying ages, clustered near the cars. They were a motley-looking crew, not the kind that left a positive impression.

"What did that sign say?" Jimmy asked.

"Save the wolves," his brother answered. "Those people are trying to stop ranchers from shooting wild wolves that have drifted outside Yellowstone Park."

"I hope their being here doesn't start trouble," Matt remarked, as much to himself as to the boys. Such activists were occasionally a problem for the local law enforcement. Not because they intentionally started fights, but because their presence stirred up the local farmers and ranchers, and now and then trouble erupted. They were not bad people, just misguided, in Matt's judgment.

"We had an assembly at school on the very last day," Keith said. "One of those guys was there talking about how it was everyone's responsibility to save the wolves from the *big bad ranchers*. They got booed, and it made the principal mad. I think he's on their side."

"I suspect he just wanted the fellow to be shown some respect, Keith. In this country everyone is entitled to express their views. That's what they're doing. I think most people like wolves. They just like them in their proper place," Matt noted.

"But these people think ranchers shouldn't shoot them," Keith protested.

"Well, Keith, I don't think ranchers like to do that either, but to them it's a matter of economics." Matt slowed up as a couple of deer jumped the fence and crossed the road ahead of them.

"They're pretty," Jimmy said. "When can we go into the park again and see the animals?"

"Soon," his dad promised.

"I've never seen a real wolf," Jimmy added. "Think we can see some of them when we go?"

"Maybe."

"Best place to see a wolf is on one of the big ranches north of the park," Keith said. "Like at the Flemmings' place."

"We hope not," Matt said. "I know that wolves got three or four of Flemmings' calves early in the spring. But it sounds like they haven't lost any for a while. I hope they don't lose more. I'm sure they can't afford that."

"If the wolves eat calves, why are those people back there trying to save them?" Jimmy asked innocently.

"It's just their cause," Keith said. "They don't seem to have anything else to do, you know, like get a job and work." He was on his soapbox now. "They also think the ranchers ought to feed the buffalo, even if they have to let their cows and sheep starve in order to do it. The wolves and buffalo need to stay in the park where they belong."

Matt glanced at his oldest son. He hadn't realized he felt so strongly about the issue. "Hopefully, the conflict will be resolved without a major problem of some kind," he said to Keith.

"They won't bother us," Jimmy said after a thoughtful pause. "Claw will keep them away."

Matt and Keith chuckled, and they began to talk about other things.

* * *

When Matt drove into the sheriff's office on Monday morning, he noticed that the SAVE THE WOLVES sign had already been taken down. He assumed it was the Bozeman police who'd removed it. Permits were needed before posting signs, and activists didn't usually bother with such mundane regulations. Of course, it was also possible that an angry rancher had removed it. This had become a contest of wills lately as the activists stepped up their campaign against the Montana ranchers. He thought no more of it, and as soon as he reached the office, he began work on a report he hadn't finished before he'd left for the weekend on Friday.

Although Matt still held the rank of sergeant, he'd struggled with his job after the death of his wife and daughter. Eventually, the sheriff had asked him if he'd rather be a detective than a patrol supervisor. He agreed to give it a try, and that was what he'd done ever since. Those first few months had been difficult for Matt. He hadn't worked for several weeks following the accident, partly because of his own grief, but also largely because of Jimmy's emotional upheaval following Carol's and Sarah's deaths. With the help of Dr. Lubek, an excellent child psychiatrist, Jimmy eventually came out of his shell and began to speak again, suffering only occasional relapses, which were increasingly less serious. After that, Matt finally went back to work full-time and began his new duties. He found that he quite enjoyed doing investigations.

That morning, as Matt was entering the report on his computer, Sheriff Ethan Baker came into his office and sat down. They visited for a few minutes before the sheriff got to the point. "This wolf protest thing is worrying me, Matt. I was on the phone just a few minutes ago with the sheriff over in Park County. One of his men obtained a copy of an e-mail from an anonymous informant that makes me a little nervous. It made him mad."

"What did it say?" Matt asked with obvious interest.

"The identity of the writer and the intended recipients weren't revealed in the e-mail. Well, I guess technically they were, but they were code names. The writer referred to himself as Avenger. The ones it was sent to were called Enforcer, Protector, and Guardian. The names may have meaning to the activists themselves, but they seem a little strange to me. It's the tone of the communication, though, that sounds like there could be trouble brewing. The writer said something about taking stronger measures against any rancher who shoots either a wolf or a buffalo. He was calling for some kind of meeting."

"Did he say what was meant by stronger measures, Sheriff?" Matt asked. Like his boss, he too disliked the sound of this. It was not something that had happened before.

"No, but we need to be prepared for whatever happens," he answered. "Whoever these people are, one thing's for certain—they aren't your run-of-the-mill activists. They could be dangerous. Most of the folks who picket aren't violent."

"Hope this group is small then," Matt said.

"I agree. Anyway, Sheriff Newton has assigned one of his investigators to handle all calls relating to wolf problems. He suggested I do the same. I agreed, and that's why I'm here. You're the man for the job."

"Okay Sheriff, I'll handle it. But what exactly do you mean by wolf problems? I thought wildlife officers take care of most of those things," Matt said.

"I'm talking about any crimes committed, either by activists or ranchers, that are related to wolves being where they don't belong. You'll be investigating any complaints of criminal activity that seem even remotely related to the dispute," Sheriff Baker said. "And you'll be working closely with Detective Reese Bogart of Park County. You've worked some cases with Reese before, haven't you?"

"I have. He's a good officer. So, when do we begin?" Matt asked.

"As soon as you've finished that report you're typing," the sheriff said with a smile as he heaved his hefty frame from the chair. "I believe Detective Bogart lives in Corwin Springs. Sheriff Newton said that if you'll give Reese a call, he'll meet you sometime today. Then the two of you can decide how you want to proceed."

"Glad to do it, Sheriff. I just hope it doesn't get too serious."

"I do too. There's enough for you to do without this business."

Matt stopped by his small farm before heading east to meet with Reese Bogart. His sons were not at home. Jimmy was at his grandparents' house, where he spent most of his time when Matt was on duty. Keith was at the grocery store stocking shelves. Claw came from somewhere in the corrals behind the house. "Come on, boy. You can go with me if you'd like," Matt said, patting the tailgate of his unmarked pickup.

That afternoon the two officers compared notes and discussed strategy for keeping the lid on the activists' activities and making sure the ranchers and farmers of their counties didn't aggravate the situation.

"It looks like you've had more problems than we have," Matt commented after Reese filled him in on the recent problems in Park County.

"Yeah, but I'm guessing yours will pick up," Reese said gravely. "The wolves seem to be expanding their range again. By the way, that dog of yours looks like it could be part wolf."

"Yeah, I suspect he might be a wolf-dog cross," Matt agreed.

"Where did you get him?"

Matt told him.

"I still can't believe what a terrible thing happened to your family," Reese said after hearing Matt's story. "And I'm surprised someone didn't ask about the dog when you advertised. He's a beautiful animal. He's surely been missed."

"There could be a reason," Matt said. "My little boy saw the man the dog belonged to. He came back to the wreck while Jimmy was still inside the van. I may never know for sure, but I think it's possible that the man caused the accident. If he did, that would explain why he didn't come forward and claim Claw. I spent weeks after the accident checking with cities throughout southern Montana to see if an animal meeting Claw's description had been licensed. I came up empty-handed. None of the local animal shelters had any information either. I just haven't been able to come up with any leads."

* * *

"Good heavens, where is he?" Lindsay Flemming said in exasperation. She was talking to herself. It was a habit she had developed over the years from frequently working alone on the ranch. She was worried. She'd tried to dissuade her father from riding out on the ranch late that morning.

Even if he is feeling a lot better than he felt yesterday, he's been gone for more than four hours. Oh, I know, I know, the ride and fresh air could do him some good. But he's been out there way too long, Lindsay thought.

She had placed a sandwich in her father's saddlebag before he left, but she always did that. He had insisted that he was feeling much better. Nevertheless, a four-hour ride at his age wasn't normal, even if he'd decided to ride onto the U.S. Forest Service rangelands for which they held grazing permits. The forest land bordered their ranch, and they'd used the allotments for years.

She removed her hat, shook out her long brown hair, and leaned against the fence of the round corral she and her father had built for training horses. From there, she looked out over their nearby fields and thought about her father. She considered him the greatest man she'd ever known.

Noah Flemming was in his late seventies now and his health had been declining for the past few months. His wife had died of cancer when Lindsay was only six and his son, Dwight, was seventeen. Dwight had always had a rebellious streak and was constantly getting into trouble. Only a few months after the death of their mother, he'd left home for good. Noah and Lindsay hadn't heard from him for several years now. They didn't know whether he was dead or alive. Lindsay knew that Noah grieved the loss of his son as much as he did his wife.

Dwight had never been lazy, just misdirected. Maybe indifferent was a better word. He was brimming with energy, but he didn't care to use that energy on the ranch. It was his father's insistence that he do more to help that seemed to be the catalyst to his disappearance. After he was gone, Lindsay stepped up even at that young age and began to help Noah with the ranch.

Despite her slim build, by the time she was twelve, she could operate every piece of equipment her father owned. She loved animals, especially horses, and by age fifteen she not only worked the cattle with her father, but she could break and train horses with the best of them. After high school, she'd skipped college to stay on the ranch and continue to work with her father. Together they had developed a top herd of Hereford cattle and had some of the best Missouri Fox Trotter horses in the country. Not many people considered Fox Trotters good cow horses, but she knew better. She and her father had worked hard to get the very best ones they could.

She knew how much her father loved this ranch, although when she was in her late teens and early twenties, he'd offered several times to sell part of the ranch so she could go to college and then continue with her life elsewhere. He felt he could manage a small place by himself without having to hire help, he'd told her. But she had no desire to leave him here alone or to leave the ranch. She could hear his voice now. "How many times do I have to tell you? You're making a mistake. When are you going to accept one of these proposals and get yourself out of here?" But she'd steadfastly refused to be dragged away from the ranch or her father by anyone.

He'd finally deeded the ranch over to her a couple of years ago. "Your brother's never coming back," he had told her that Christmas morning when he revealed his decision to put the ranch in her name. "And even if by some miracle he did, you've earned it by the sacrifice you've made to help me run it all these years."

Lindsay smiled to herself as she thought about that. It had never been a sacrifice to her. She was doing what she loved to do, and she was with a man she loved as much as a daughter could love a father. Her life was good. But she knew that Noah felt bad that he couldn't do much to help with the daily work of the ranch these days. Basically, it was left to Lindsay. She didn't mind, although she had to work hard from sunup to sundown every day but Sunday, and even on the Sabbath there were some chores she had to do. As he got older and his health declined, Noah was forced to spend more of his time in the house in his big recliner, reading, watching TV, or simply sleeping.

When he did go out, it was to fuss with the mares and colts before taking his daily ride. And like clockwork, he was never gone for more than two hours. *It's far past a two-hour ride now,* she reflected. *He should have been back long ago.*

She squinted when she thought she saw a horse come out of the timber at the far end of their fields off to the southwest. She wasn't positive, but she was pretty sure it was a horse, although at this distance it was hard to see it clearly. She couldn't tell anything about the rider, or even if there was one. She stepped over to her red F250 truck and snatched her binoculars from the side pocket of one of the back doors. She soon located the animal in the glasses. A chill descended over her.

It was Shadow, the gelding her father had ridden out on before noon. Shadow was still saddled, but there was no rider. Panic engulfed her, and she tossed the glasses into the truck, grabbed her hat from the corral fence, and ran toward the horse barn. She whistled, and half a dozen mares, their colts, and one tall, elegant, chestnut-colored gelding lifted their heads from far out in the horse pasture. She whistled again as she grabbed a halter from the tack room. All thirteen horses began trotting toward the barn. Midnight, the champion black stallion, whinnied and circled his corral near the pasture in a perfect trot, his head high and his long mane and tail streaming. Lindsay was so worried that she barely glanced at him.

In five minutes she'd thrown a saddle on Rustler, her working mount, and was streaking toward her father's horse. Her cow dog, Prince, a black-and-white border collie, kept pace with her. When she drew near her father's horse, she noticed two things that compounded her worries. First, the bridle reins were dragging. That could mean her father had somehow fallen off the horse. If he did, considering his age, he could have been badly injured. Second, the rifle scabbard on the right side of the saddle was empty. Because of the recent threat of wolves, she and her father both carried .30-30 rifles when they rode out to check the cattle.

Lindsay didn't recall hearing any shots fired in the distance, but she'd been on a tractor until just fifteen minutes before she'd gotten worried about her father being so late. The noise of the big diesel engine would have covered the sound of shots, especially distant ones. So she most likely would have missed the shooting, had there been any. And there must have been some, or Noah would never have pulled his rifle from the scabbard.

She swung off Rustler's back and hurriedly pulled the bridle from her father's horse, tied it to the saddle horn, and then looked into his saddlebags. An empty sandwich bag was there, and his canteen was also hanging from the saddle horn. A quick shake of it told her that nearly half the water had been consumed.

She remounted Rustler. "Come on, Shadow, and follow us," she called to her dad's sturdy, dark gray gelding. "Let's go find him."

The horses fell into a smooth, mile-consuming foxtrot. Before long they'd crossed their land and entered the forest beyond.

It was her border collie that found Noah over an hour after they'd entered the forest. He was lying in a pool of blood near the mangled body of a big calf. They were both a few feet into a thick stand of timber halfway up a short ridge, about two miles south of the southern border of their ranch. Lindsay let out a strangled cry and leaped from the back of her horse.

2

Matt was near the county road that led to several ranches, including the one operated by Noah and Lindsay Flemming, when he got the call that Noah had been shot. The same terrible feeling he'd experienced when he'd found his wife and daughter in the crumpled van enveloped him. He wondered if the violence he'd hoped would never materialize had already begun. He talked to Lindsay on his cell phone as soon as he finished with the call from the dispatcher. Although her voice betrayed her emotions, she managed to give him clear directions on how to get within a couple miles of where her father had been shot by taking a forest-service road. She said she'd meet him on that road and take him back into the area where the crime had occurred.

It was about the wolves. He knew that because Lindsay had told him a dead wolf lay a short distance from where the calf had been ripped apart and where Noah had died. It was a horrible thing, and he told himself that he would turn over every rock in Montana if he had to in order to find and arrest whoever was responsible.

True to her word, Lindsay was waiting for Matt when he arrived. She was mounted on a beautiful chestnut horse and was holding the reins to a dark gray gelding. He assumed that the gray was the horse Noah had been riding that day, and a lump formed in his throat. Claw jumped out of the truck, and he and Lindsay's border collie began to get acquainted. He shut off his truck's engine, then grabbed his camera bag, evidence kit, portable radio, and a small satellite tracking device.

"Thanks for coming out here, Matt," Lindsay said in a strained voice. Her eyes were red from crying, and her hair was windblown where it hung beneath her felt hat. "I can't believe somebody would do this to Dad. He never hurt anybody in his life."

"I'm sorry, Lindsay," he said, feeling inadequate. No one knew better than Matt how it felt to lose a loved one, but he also knew that kind words actually helped numb the pain a bit. He knew she was suffering far more than she showed, and he admired her courage.

He put his gear into the saddlebags—all but the satellite tracking device. He worked with it for a minute, knowing he'd need it to give directions to those who would be following him. Then he shoved it into a saddlebag and turned, calling for Claw. "Sorry, old boy, but I think I'd better leave you here." He put the dog in the carrier he kept in the truck.

Then he accepted the reins to the gray horse from Lindsay. "You'll probably need to lengthen the stirrups. You've got longer legs than Dad," she said, her voice breaking as she spoke.

He worked quickly and soon was ready to ride.

"It's not far, but it's rugged between here and where D . . . Dad is," Lindsay said. "There's lots of downed timber and a couple of steep, rocky hillsides."

"Then I'm grateful to you for bringing the horse. I suppose I could have walked. That's what the others are going to have to do," he said.

"Others?" she asked numbly.

"Yeah, the sheriff and a couple more deputies are on the way, as well as some members from search-and-rescue and a wildlife officer."

"Search-and-rescue? But it's too late for Dad now," she said, sudden anger in her voice.

"They'll help us carry him out to the road. The mortuary is sending a car up too."

She nodded in understanding. "Who could do such a terrible thing?" she asked. Her anger quickly turned to sadness, and she began to cry again. "What am I going to do? What am I ever going to do?"

Matt could tell she was asking herself, not him. He simply said, "You lead. I'll follow."

He watched Lindsay from behind as the gray he was riding followed her chestnut gelding. His heart ached and anger began building within him. He wasn't sure exactly what he would find at the scene of the murder, but he knew that whoever had done this had to be brought to justice, no matter how hard Matt had to work to see that it was done.

Lindsay had not been kidding when she said it was rough terrain, but he was impressed with the way the two horses handled it. He'd heard that the Prescott Missouri Fox Trotters were some of the best of their breed in the country. Riding this gelding of Noah's convinced him that what he had heard was right. He'd never ridden a smoother horse. He was grateful that he didn't have to walk.

During the half-hour ride to the scene of the shooting, Matt and Lindsay engaged in minimal conversation. Matt knew that Lindsay was absorbed in her troubled thoughts, and he didn't want to disturb her. Besides that, it was hard to talk to someone riding directly in front of him. And at times they both had to pay close attention to where they were going, especially through the rough places. As soon as they arrived near the crime scene, Lindsay stopped and called back over her shoulder. "It's right up ahead," she said, pointing. "Just through those trees."

Matt rode up beside her. "I'll have to examine everything closely, so we need to try not to disturb any evidence we don't have to," he said.

"Oh, Matt, I was so upset when I found Dad. I hope I didn't touch anything I shouldn't have," she said. "I don't think I did, but I was so shocked that I'm not sure what I did for the first minute or two."

Matt had stopped beside her. He glanced down at her and, as she lifted her eyes to his, asked, "How long were you here before you called?"

"Not long," she replied. "Maybe ten minutes. But I couldn't get a signal on my cell phone here, so I had to ride to the top of that ridge over there." She pointed east as she spoke. "I stayed up there till I talked to you, then I rode straight out to the road to meet you. I had just ridden up when I heard you coming. Thanks for coming so quickly."

Without another word, they rode ahead, side by side through the trees. When Matt first saw the body of the man he'd known and respected for most of his life, he drew up short. He felt like he'd been kicked in the stomach. His breath came in ragged gasps. It thrust him back to that horrible moment when he'd recognized the face of his wife in the overturned van. And he remembered how difficult it had been to do anything at that accident scene. He wondered how Lindsay had coped. Having some idea of the sacrifice she'd made to stay with her father on the ranch instead of going out into the world and making a life of her own, he realized she must have loved him deeply.

"Matt, are you okay?" Lindsay asked.

He hadn't been aware of her riding over close to him. But he felt her hand on his arm, and he turned to face her. "I'm sorry," he said. "It's only been a year since . . ." He didn't need to finish.

"Since you found them sort of like this?" she asked, tears filling her reddened eyes once again.

He nodded.

"I'm sorry, Matt. This must be so hard for you. They should have sent one of the other deputies."

"No, I told the sheriff today I'd work any case involving wolves, and I intend to keep my word. Anyway, this isn't nearly as hard for me as it is for you," he said a little more forcefully than he intended. He was embarrassed that she seemed to be comforting him instead of the other way around. "Let's tie the horses over there." He pointed to their right, away from the body of her father.

She nodded at him, tears streaming down her face, and began to dismount.

Just then his portable radio came to life. "Matt, are you at the scene yet?"

It was the sheriff.

"Yes."

"We just pulled up behind your truck. Can you give us directions?"

"Just a minute and I can," he said.

He dismounted, tied Noah's horse next to where Lindsay was tying hers, and then opened the saddlebag to retrieve the tracking device. He pulled it out and began to work with it. A minute later, he gave the sheriff the coordinates he'd need to find them, told him to expect a hard walk, then put the unit back and got out his evidence kit and camera.

"What can I do to help?" Lindsay asked. "I want you to catch whoever did this."

His first impulse was to tell her just to stay back and let him work, but when he looked into her eyes and saw the pain there, he changed his mind. It would be good for her to stay busy. He knew that from personal experience.

"You could carry this," he said, holding out the bag.

"Sure," she responded as she took it from him.

"And you can watch for footprints. Did you notice any before?" he asked as he turned back toward the body of her father, which lay about fifty feet to the west of them.

"Honestly, no," she said. "All I saw was Dad, the calf he's lying beside, and a dead wolf right over there." She pointed, but he couldn't see the wolf from where they were standing.

"You could help by watching the ground and seeing if you can spot any tracks. I'll look, too, but two sets of eyes are better than one. But first, before we go any closer, I'd just like to stand here and look things over," he said. For two or three minutes, Matt scanned the area, trying to take in every detail of the scene. Finally, he said, "Okay, we can go closer now." As they moved forward, side by side, the first tracks he spotted were right near Noah's body. He pointed them out to Lindsay. "I'm assuming those are your tracks. I doubt that whoever did this was wearing cowboy boots."

"Yes, I got off my horse right there," she said, pointing again. "And then I ran over to Dad and knelt down beside him to see if I could help him."

"Was he dead already?" he asked.

"Yes," she said, and once more she began to sob quietly. In a muted voice she added, "He already felt cold and stiff to me."

For the next few minutes, Matt simply looked around and snapped photos. Lindsay watched him quietly. He looked up at her once, after taking several pictures of her father, and said, "If this is too hard for you, you can wait back by the horses."

"It's okay, Matt. It's hard, but I'll be okay. Thanks."

Noah's body was lying in blood, some of it his own, some of it from the calf the wolf had killed. His rifle was on the ground a few feet away, the barrel bent, the stock broken. "I didn't even notice that," Lindsay said as Matt took a picture of the rifle. "Did whoever shot Dad do that to his gun?"

"I would guess so," Matt answered. "It looks like they smashed it against this tree. My guess is that it was done in anger—in rage. You can see where the bark's been marred. I hope they left fingerprints on the stock. We'll check it when the other officers get here. But for the moment, we'll leave it right where it is."

"Are those his footprints?" Lindsay asked. She was looking at an impression in the soft dirt near the rifle. "It looks like some kind of walking shoe or boot made them."

"They're definitely not yours or your dad's. That's for sure," Matt agreed.

They found more tracks, and Matt studied each of them closely, taking more photographs. "It looks like there were three of them," he said. "At least, that's all the footprints we've seen so far."

The clearest prints were around the dead wolf. Matt photographed them carefully. "These people left plenty of prints behind. Of course, they may plan to get rid of their boots, in which case these prints won't do us any good. But I wonder where their vehicle was parked. They must have walked here from somewhere not too far away." Matt was speaking more to himself than to Lindsay as he tried to picture the events that had led up to the brutal murder.

Later, after the sheriff and the other officers arrived, Matt spent a couple of minutes bringing them up-to-date on what he had found. Then the newly arrived officers fanned out and began searching for anything that might be considered evidence.

"What are you all looking for?" Lindsay asked a moment later.

"We're looking for anything that seems like it doesn't belong here. No matter how careful we are—any of us—when we've been some-place, we always leave something behind, however tiny it might be, and we always take something away," he explained. "Criminals, even the best, aren't any different."

"What would they have taken away?" she asked. "Do you think they might have taken the money Dad had in his wallet?"

"That's possible, and we'll check all that out. But I was thinking of smaller, less obvious things, like specks of dirt, pieces of brush or trees, traces of blood, that sort of thing."

Lindsay nodded and said quietly, "I think I'll go back and wait with the horses now. This is really hard."

"Of course," Matt said. He watched as she walked away, her shoulders slumped and shaking, her head down. And he could hear her begin to sob. Watching her suffering once again revived memories he tried to keep dormant, and he had to work hard to shake the images that would reach out, grab him, and tear him apart if he let them. He had work to do. He couldn't afford to be distracted. Not now.

Noah Flemming had been shot twice at close range. From the size of the bullet holes in his chest, a small-caliber pistol appeared to have been used. It also seemed quite likely that one of the bullets was still in his body. That was one piece of evidence the killers had left behind.

Despite careful searching, the only other thing they found was a tiny blue thread that had snagged on the branch of a small spruce tree near Noah's body. "Well, they didn't leave much evidence," Sheriff Baker said as they wrapped up the investigation. "I'd be surprised if the shoe prints do us any good. And I'll bet they wiped Noah's rifle free of fingerprints. But the thread, that could be useful. That's the kind of thing people don't realize they left."

The sun was dropping low as they placed Noah's body in a body bag. They carried the body, strapped over the gray's saddle, back to the road. Matt, who was leading the horse, kept looking at Lindsay to make sure she was okay. He had a feeling her stone face was concealing most of the pain inside. He hoped she'd be okay alone that night at home.

"Would you like us to get a trailer and come get the horses, Miss Flemming?" Sheriff Baker asked when they were ready to leave.

"No, I think I'll ride home," she said. "Dad's horse will follow me."

"Sheriff, if one of these men would drive my truck around to Miss Flemming's place and leave it there, I'll ride back with Lindsay," Matt volunteered. It would be dark soon, and he hated to think of her riding all those miles alone in her present state of mind.

"Sure thing," the sheriff responded.

"Would that be okay with you, Lindsay?" he asked.

"You don't need to do that," she said. "Your sons need you."

"My boys will be fine," he said. "I'd like to ride back with you."

"That would be very kind," she finally agreed. "If you're sure you don't mind."

* * *

"Let's head out now. It's almost dark. The cops think we left hours ago," the young man said to his companions.

The others agreed and began to put on their backpacks. "Maybe now these ranchers will get the message. They can't just go around killing wolves like that old man did," the only woman among the three said angrily.

"Especially that wolf. We've been watching him and his pack for days now. He was hungry, and that calf would have made him and the others some darn good meals. He only did what nature intended for him to do. That old man got what he had coming," the third member of the trio said. Anger and hatred seethed from him like steam from Yellowstone's hot streams. "Kill and be killed," he added. "They'll learn."

* * *

Darkness settled in when Lindsay and Matt were still about a mile from the border of her ranch. They both had flashlights but used them only occasionally. Since the horses knew their way, the darkness wasn't a handicap. Prince romped in the forest as they rode, never straying too far away.

The moon rose only minutes after they reached the fence that outlined the Lazy F Ranch. It was full and round and dark orange as it cleared the mountains to the east. As it rose higher, its color faded, and it was soon almost white, lighting the terrain and making the ride easier.

Suddenly, the haunting call of a wolf drifted from the forest. Lindsay called to her dog. Prince stopped, his head tipped and his ears up. Lindsay moved her horse closer to Matt's and said softly, "I'll always remember Dad when I hear that sound. And I suppose I'll always feel as lonely as I do right now. Oh, Matt, I miss him so much already. I don't know what I'll ever do."

"You just learn to cope, Lindsay. That's all you can do."

"I'm sorry. I know you've suffered more pain than me," she said, her head turned toward him in the moonlight.

He thought of his wife and daughter and turned his head so Lindsay wouldn't see his tears. The hurt never went completely away.

But now his heart was also breaking for Lindsay. Choked up, he didn't attempt to speak again.

The silence was soothing as the two rode on. Then it was broken by the bawling of a calf and the lowing of its mother. Almost immediately, the howl of a wolf—the call of the wild—began again. After it stopped, Lindsay said, "That wolf sounds like it feels like I do. It's probably missing the one Dad shot. Doesn't it sound like it's crying?"

"I guess in a way it does," Matt agreed.

"You know, Matt, I don't hate the wolves the way some of the ranchers do. And Dad didn't either. I suppose in some ways they're reminders of who we are—westerners. They don't mean us any harm, but there are just too many of them now. It seems that the reintroduction program was too successful. The wolves need to be properly controlled and kept at the park where people can enjoy them and no one hurts them."

"That's the problem we face, all right," Matt agreed. "But there are people determined to stop the government from keeping things in balance."

"And I'm sure in their minds they think they're doing the right thing. But doing what they did to Dad, you can't justify that. I know it's only a small minority of them who would do such a horrible thing," she said sadly.

"You're right. Most of the activists aren't bad people. They just think differently than the ranchers and farmers do," Matt remarked. He knew their conversation was stiff and stilted, but he also knew that the longer he kept emotion out of the mix, the better it would be for both of them.

They rode quietly again. Lindsay was the first to break the silence. "The wolves are only doing what nature taught them to do. In fact, they're doing what we do. They're killing livestock to eat. We kill them for doing the same thing we do. I know Dad didn't enjoy killing the one he shot today. But he was only trying to protect what's he's spent his whole life building. Is that so wrong?"

Matt was thoughtful. "You're right. A lot of the people we see protesting aren't bad people, I'm sure. They just feel sorry for wild animals. And in a way, I agree with them, too. But the people who shot your father, they're different. They're evil."

"They had no reason to kill him." There was a noticeable catch in Lindsay's voice, and for a moment she let herself sob quietly. Matt respected her grief and rode on without speaking.

Finally, she continued. Like the nearby geysers, she couldn't stop the regular eruptions, but talking helped relieve the pressure. "You know, Matt, I suspect that if it wasn't the wolves that gave people like these a cause, it would be something else. Like I said, I don't hate wolves, but you just can't equate animal life with human life."

Matt knew that Lindsay wasn't expecting a response. He let nature reply. The sound of the horses' feet, the creaking of the leather saddles, an occasional hoot of an owl, the periodic lowing of the cattle, and the infrequent howling of the wolves were the only sounds they heard for the next ten minutes. Then Matt became aware of another sound, and he looked over at the young woman riding next to him. She was making no attempt to conceal her sobs now. He instinctively reached out and touched her arm. She looked at him and said, "Sorry."

"It's okay," he said. "You can't keep all the pain inside." And they rode on, soaking in the comforting sounds of the night.

When they approached Lindsay's yard, they let the horses move into their smooth foxtrot, and the distance to the big empty Flemming ranch house began to fade away. The other horses neighed a greeting, and the geldings answered as they neared the yard. Matt swung down from Shadow, opened the gate, waited while Lindsay rode through, then led his mount through and closed the gate.

He helped Lindsay unsaddle the horses in the barn and rub them down. Then they turned the horses into the pasture with the mares and colts and walked toward the house. Matt's truck was parked in front of the gate. After unlocking the truck, he turned to Lindsay. "I'll be in touch tomorrow. I'll let you know what we learn."

"Thanks, Matt," she said. "You've been a great help." She faced the house for a moment without moving. Then she turned back to Matt. "It's going to be so hard to go inside knowing Dad's not there."

"I could call and find someone in the Relief Society to come out and stay with you tonight," he suggested.

"I don't want to put anyone out," she said, but Matt could see from her expression that she didn't want to be alone.

"No one would be put out. I'll call the bishop. He'll want to come out himself and see you at some point. I'm sure most people don't know what's happened yet."

"Thanks," she said. "I would appreciate that. I really don't know how I'm going to cope."

Matt stood awkwardly and watched as she entered the house a moment later. Then he turned to leave, his heart heavy for her.

* * *

Lindsay shut the door, then stepped to her window and watched as Matt drove off. She'd never felt so empty in her life. Her father had been the only person she was close to in the years since her mother had died. And now he was gone, she was alone, and she honestly didn't know how she would ever handle it. She thought of her brother, Dwight, and wondered how she could let him know what had happened to their father so he could at least come to the funeral.

If he wanted to. And that was a big *if.* He'd always cared just for himself. Others' feelings had never mattered to Dwight. Proof of that lay in the fact that he'd been gone for such a long time and had made no attempt to contact them after the first few years. But he was her brother, and she felt a need for him now like she'd never felt before.

She thought about Dwight for a minute. She'd never understood what made him tick. He was a natural leader, but he let his abilities drag him in the wrong direction while urging others to follow his wild ways. Before he was old enough to drive, he'd been into drugs and alcohol, and several local boys had followed his lead. Lindsay's parents had spent many days in juvenile court with Dwight, but he never seemed to want to change.

Despite his illegal activities and wild partying, Dwight had always taken pride in his appearance. Although slight in build, he was admittedly handsome. His hair was always cut short and kept neat. Somewhat of a clotheshorse, he dressed in the latest fashions, spending more on his clothes than his parents could afford. And, of course, the girls had followed him around like lovesick puppies.

Lindsay dismissed her thoughts of the past and turned away from the window.

Several people visited over the next couple of hours, but she refused offers from the Relief Society to have someone spend the night with her. And she spent that interminably long night sleeping very little. Tender thoughts of her father were occasionally interrupted by warm, comforting thoughts of Matt Prescott. He had been an unexpected but welcome strength through those first hours after losing her father.

3

Detective Reese Bogart from Park County met Matt in Bozeman at nine that Tuesday morning. By then, Matt had met with the sheriff and three other deputies. The sheriff told him that he was to take the lead on the case but that they would do whatever they could to help. Matt wanted to ride back to the scene of the murder with Reese and try to follow the tracks of the killers. The sheriff assigned other deputies to begin processing the evidence that had been collected.

By nine thirty Matt and Reese had a couple of horses loaded in Matt's horse trailer, and they headed for the spot where Matt had left his truck the day before. During the drive he called Lindsay on her cell phone.

"Hi, Matt," she answered. "Learn anything yet?" She sounded very tired, and he expected she hadn't slept much the night before. Not that he had either.

"No, not yet, but we're working on it," he said. "Detective Bogart from Park County is with me. You'll remember that I mentioned him to you yesterday. We're on our way back up to the scene."

"What are you going to do there?" she asked. "I thought you'd finished everything yesterday."

"Reese has some experience in tracking. That's one of the reasons his sheriff gave him this assignment," Matt explained. "So we're going to try to follow the tracks those people left at the scene and see where they'd been before that and where they went afterwards."

"How are you going to do that?" she asked. "Do you need to borrow some horses?"

"Thanks, but no. I've got a couple of mine already loaded, and we'll use them, though I've got to admit I've never ridden a horse I like better than that one of your Dad's," he said.

"Yes, Shadow's great. Will you let me know what you learn?"

"Of course," he responded.

"Thanks. I appreciate it."

"How are you doing this morning?"

"I guess I'm okay, just numb. There have been people in and out all morning. And Sister Thompson just left a few minutes ago. Thanks for calling the bishop. His wife came to visit too. Anyway, I'm supposed to be at the mortuary this morning at eleven," she said. "That's going to be really hard."

"I understand," he said. "I'm sure sorry."

"Well, good luck, Matt. And thanks so much for all you're doing," she said. "Oh, looks like someone else is coming. People are so good at times like this. It makes me feel guilty for all the times I haven't gone to help others when I could have. The bishop and one of his counselors came just after the bishop's wife left this morning. The Relief Society president and both of her counselors came a little while ago. A couple of others brought food, as if I can eat it all. There's just me, and food is the last thing I need right now."

"I know, Lindsay. But people feel better if they do something. And you know that. I remember a cake you brought to the boys and me when—last year. By the way, my boys would love to come out and give you a hand when Keith gets off work. Jimmy isn't much help, but Keith will do whatever you need done. And he doesn't want a dime for it," Matt said. "And Jimmy is good at entertaining himself and staying out of the way."

"That would be nice, although it's not necessary. I mean, I could use a little help, but everyone else is busy too. Well, I'd better go. The doorbell's ringing," she said.

Matt was just turning onto the forest road when the sheriff called. "I just got an interesting piece of information," he said. "Bob Wooley, the wildlife officer who was up there yesterday, just finished examining the wolf Noah shot. He's quite certain it's had a collar on."

"A collar?" Matt asked, surprised. "There sure wasn't one there yesterday."

"No, but whoever shot Noah might have removed it," Sheriff Baker suggested. "We were just talking about it here at the office. Bob says there are a few wolves that the authorities at the park have put collars on. But he's not aware of any of them coming up this way. He wonders if maybe these activist people have tranquilized some wolves, put collars on them, and are keeping track of them on their own."

"Well, that could explain why they were close when Noah shot that one yesterday," Matt said. "Makes what Reese and I are doing today all the more important."

The two men rode as hard as they could into the rough country Matt had been in the day before. When they reached the scene of the murder, Matt took a minute to show Reese around. Then they began to follow the killers' tracks to the south. They passed a number of cattle as they went, and several of them had the Flemming brand on them, a slanted *F*.

The tracking wasn't easy, and whoever had left the tracks had wandered a lot, like they'd been following the wolf. A few times the officers spotted tracks that could have been made by a wolf. It was after one o'clock that afternoon before they rode up to what had been a campsite. It was in the middle of a large grove of pine and fir trees. "Looks like they didn't want the smoke from their fires to show up easily," Reese observed. "The tree branches are so thick that they would have dispersed the smoke quite well. That means only one thing. They didn't want people to know they were here. This tells us a lot. Honest people wouldn't care."

The detectives spent the next hour combing the campsite for evidence and taking pictures. There wasn't much there. The killers had been careful. Had Matt and Reese not expanded the search to a large circle around the campsite, they would have come up empty-handed. A hundred yards or so from where the fire pit had been, Reese discovered a spot where some garbage had been buried. An attempt had been made to conceal the spot, and Matt was sure he would have missed it had Reese not been with him. They dug up the trash and took several cans to be fingerprinted later, hoping the cans hadn't been wiped clean first. And they found some long hair hanging from a branch near the garbage site.

"There could have been a woman here," Reese said. But then he smiled and shook his head. "Or it could mean that a man with long blond hair was here as well. No way of knowing unless the DNA is processed."

"So the only thing we really know is that there were three people. Tracks show us that," Matt mused. "I don't suppose that whoever was here could have had anything to do with that e-mail your office was given."

"Well, *drastic measures* have been taken," Reese said. "Could be, I suppose."

After recording the exact location of the campsite and the garbage disposal site, they started on their way again. Their work became easier after that, because the suspects continued traveling in essentially a straight line.

"Probably going out to their vehicle," Matt observed at one point as they stopped on a sunny ridge, got off their horses, and stretched.

* * *

"There's two of them," the man said from a ridge far to the east, as he peered through his binoculars.

"What are they doing?"

"Wish I knew. But they're carrying both saddle rifles and hand-guns."

"Maybe the cowboys are figuring on waging a war against the wolves," the second one added.

"Or against those of us who are trying to protect them," the one with binoculars suggested. "I'm ready to fight these guys. So are some of the others. Well, they're on the move again. And they seem to be going pretty much straight west."

"Hey, I'm getting a signal again," the second man said with excitement. "I think our wolf is on the move. Forget those guys. He's not going toward them anyway. Let's see where this big fellow is headed now."

* * *

"They were parked right here. This road leads to the west. I don't think it ever connects with the road where we left the truck," Matt said as he again got out his GPS device and noted the coordinates in his notebook.

"What now?" Reese asked.

Matt looked at his watch. "I don't think there's much more we can do here. I suppose we should head back to the truck."

"Where exactly is it from here?"

"Well, let's use this handy little gadget and find out. Here, hold this map while I figure out the most direct route," Matt said.

Finally, he pointed to a spot on the map and said, "This is where we are on the map right now, and here's where the truck is."

"Looks like about four miles straight through," Reese observed. "But it also looks like there is some impassable country between here and there."

"Yeah, I suppose this would be the best route to take," Matt said as he drew a line with his finger. "Could be six miles or so. And it will take us back about the same way we came."

"Then let's get riding," Reese suggested.

* * *

"It's those same guys," the man with the binoculars said in disgust as he lowered his glasses. "And they're coming this way. Unless they turn north pretty soon, they'll be crossing our path."

"We need to make sure they don't see us," his partner said.

"But we're getting close to our wolf. We might get a glimpse of him soon. Or, I should say, of them. I'd say from the tracks and scat we saw back there that he's with several others."

His partner cautioned him again. "We'll keep track of him, but we don't want those guys seeing us. The less the cattlemen know about what's going on out here, the better it'll be."

* * *

It was after nine that evening, with the summer's daylight fading fast when Matt drove into his yard with the horses. Detective Bogart was already on his way back to Corwin Springs. Matt had talked to the sheriff an hour before and reported what they'd found. The sheriff in return had told him that they hadn't identified anyone from the fingerprints they found on Noah's broken rifle, but that they'd sent the DNA samples off for testing. He hoped they'd get something there.

After completing the call to the sheriff, Matt called his sons. They were at the Flemming ranch with half a dozen men from the ward, all trying to help Lindsay get ahead on some of her work.

They still weren't home when Matt finished unloading the horses and unhooking the horse trailer, so he called Keith's cell phone again. "We're still at the Lazy F," Keith told him. "Some sisters from the ward came out and brought more food. One of them is Grandma Prescott. And Grandpa's here, too. Sister Flemming has so much food now that she's insisting we all stay and eat with her. Just a second, Dad."

Matt guessed he'd put his hand over the phone during the ensuing silence. Then Keith came back on and said, "Sister Flemming and Grandma want you to come out and eat with us. We'll be finished here in a few minutes, and they'll have the food set out, she says. Can you come?"

"Sure, I'll come," he said. He needed to fill Lindsay in on what they'd done that day, even though he was really no closer to knowing who had killed her father than he had been the day before. "But don't let them hold everybody up on eating. It'll take me a while to get there."

By the time Matt pulled into the yard, the men from the ward had left. The only vehicles there that didn't belong to Lindsay were his son's old Ford pickup and parents' ten-year-old Chevy Lumina. He supposed his folks would drive that car until they died or the car died. If it was the former, he hoped that was a long way off.

"We saved you some," Lindsay said with a welcoming smile as she answered the door. "The others were ready to go, so we went ahead and fed them. I'm glad you could come out."

"You didn't need to save some for me," he said.

She smiled again, but it wasn't the smile he'd known before yesterday's tragedy. She was in pain, and it was only too apparent.

Matt started to tell Lindsay what had been done that day, but she interrupted him. "You eat first, Matt, and visit with your dad. Your mother and I will finish cleaning up here. Then we can talk."

He was almost finished eating when Keith came running into the house. "Dad, Claw and Prince are going crazy. They ran off, barking like mad. The cows are all bawling, too. Could it be wolves?"

Matt pushed back from the table with concern. "It seems unlikely, but I suppose it's possible. It could also be a skunk or a porcupine."

As he rose to his feet, he glanced at Lindsay, who was opening a window, her face stricken. "I can't hear much inside since we added the air-conditioning," she said.

They could hear now, and it was true that there was bedlam outside. "I'll get my rifle," Lindsay said. "And a spotlight."

"I have a rifle in the car," Matt's dad said.

"And mine's in the truck," Matt added as he hurried for the door. "You boys stay in here with Grandma. By the way, where's Jimmy?"

Lindsay and Matt's mother glanced meaningfully at each other. It was his mother who spoke. "We've been wanting to speak to you about him. He's in the basement watching cartoons. He's been silent most of the day. This thing with Noah has really affected him."

Matt groaned.

"I'm sorry, Matt," Lindsay said. "He's still pretty fragile, isn't he?"

"I'm afraid so. Just when I think he's about over his problems, they come back."

"Matt, you'd better go check on Lindsay's cattle," his mother said. "I'll sit with Jimmy until you get back."

"Thanks, Mom," Matt said, torn between the problems outside and the troubles inside.

As he started for the door, Keith said, "Dad, let me come. I can hold a light for one of you."

"Good idea," Matt agreed.

A minute later, the four of them started toward the corrals. Lindsay called Prince, and Matt and Keith both called Claw, but neither dog responded to the calls. A moment later the dogs rushed through the horse pasture and toward the cow pasture beyond. Lindsay and her father had more cows and calves than their range permit allowed, but they had pasture enough for the forty pairs that she had to keep home. It was these cattle that were upset. And it was from that field that the dogs suddenly broke into a fierce barking frenzy. Then the unmistakable sound of a fight reached their ears.

Lindsay shouted, "Wolves!" and began to run. Keith and Matt kept pace, but Matt's father fell behind. The fight raged. Finally, the spotlights they carried lit up the scene. The two dogs were outnumbered.

There were at least three wolves, perhaps more, in the pack. Lindsay fired her rifle into the air twice in rapid succession, and the wolves abandoned the fight and began to run. Matt dropped to one knee, and with Keith holding the light, he fired a shot at the retreating wolves. Lindsay also fired.

One of the wolves somersaulted through the air, crashed to the ground, and lay still. The others ran faster. Rifle shots filled the air again, but the wolves were beyond range. By then, Matt's father had caught up with them. "I think one of the dogs is down," he gasped.

They began running again. Keith was the first to reach the dogs. Claw was bleeding from several small cuts, but he appeared to be okay. Prince was not. He lay on his side, breathing hard. "Take my gun and light, Keith," Lindsay said as she thrust them toward the young man. "And shine the light on Prince for a minute."

Then she dropped to the ground beside her dog, tenderly speaking his name. "I left my phone in the house. Does anyone have one?" she asked without looking up.

Both Matt and Keith responded that they did. "Call the vet, please," she said, reciting his number from memory. Matt dialed, and while he told Lindsay's veterinarian what had happened, Lindsay picked Prince up and walked quickly toward the house holding him in her arms.

"Here, Dad, will you carry my gun?" Matt asked as he hurried toward Lindsay. "Your vet says he'll come out to your house," he said. "Every minute could count."

"I figured he would come. Dad and I give him a lot of business. I mean—well, you know—*gave* him a lot."

"You'll still give him a lot."

"If I can make it on my own," she said with a trace of bitterness. "It's going to be hard, maybe more than I can handle."

"You can do it, Lindsay. Here, let me help you."

"I can carry him. You'll get your shirt all bloody," she protested.

"That's okay," he said. "Let me take him."

As she handed him over, she said, "I sure hope the vet can save him. I'd be lost without Prince."

While the vet was working on Prince on a makeshift table in the barn, Matt tried to talk to Jimmy, but the young boy was silent and withdrawn, as he had been for days after the deaths of his mother and sister.

Matt's mother fussed worriedly and finally said, "Matt, you need to take him back to Dr. Lubek."

Matt nodded, wondering how he would ever do that with all that was going on right now. Dr. Lubek was up in Missoula—about a three-hour drive. "For now I just need to get him home," he said. "I'll call Dr. Lubek in the morning if he isn't better by then." He picked up his son and carried him out to his truck. He seemed so tiny and frail in his arms. By the time Matt reached the truck, Jimmy was fast asleep. As he fastened the seat belt around the sleeping boy, Lindsay approached.

"The vet says he thinks Prince will pull through. He's going to take him back to the clinic before he comes out of the anesthesia. He'll keep him there for a little while and see how he does." She choked back a sob and then asked, as Matt shut the truck door, "Is Jimmy any better?"

"No, I'm afraid not. I may need to call his psychiatrist tomorrow."

"I'm sorry, Matt," Lindsay said. "He was close to my father. He always sat by him in our Primary class. I'm afraid that . . ." She couldn't go on, as she began to tremble and cry. "A lot of people have been hurt by what those people did to Dad," she said after an awkward minute of silence. "Did you learn anything today?"

"Not much, I'm afraid," Matt said. Then he quickly told her what had happened that day. After he had finished, Keith approached the truck.

"Dad, I'll head home now if you want me to," his son said.

Matt shook his head. "Would you stay here with Jimmy for a few minutes? I think I better have a look at that wolf we shot and then bring him in so the wildlife officers can examine him."

"We can drive out to the field in my truck," Lindsay volunteered. "Then you won't have to disturb Jimmy."

But Keith said, "Dad, he's asleep. Why don't you let me take Jimmy home?"

Matt's folks arrived from the house at that moment. "We'll follow the boys," his father said. "And we'll wait at your place with them until you get home."

"Okay—if you don't mind."

"Of course we don't," his mother said.

The moon was up again, and it was bright as Matt and Lindsay drove into the field. "I think I missed," Lindsay said as they approached the place where the wolf had been shot. "I think you're the one who got him, poor thing. I wish we didn't have to shoot them. It's not their fault."

"It's a shame so many of them have been killed. I guess the real answer is finding a way to keep them where they belong," Matt said, glancing at her profile as he drove.

When they reached the spot where the dead wolf lay in the grass, they stopped and got out. They had barely glanced at the wolf when Lindsay said, "Matt, look, there's a light over there."

He looked up, but not quickly enough.

"It's gone now," Lindsay said before he had a chance to see anything.

"Where was it?" Matt asked.

She pointed and he said, "I don't know who's over there, but it does seem a little strange. Isn't that the edge of the forest?"

"Yes, it's right about there."

"I'd rather not risk your getting hurt or I'd head over there right now," Matt said. "Who knows, it could be the people who shot your dad yesterday," he said.

"I'll take the risk," Lindsay said with determination. "Let's go over."

"Only if you promise to stay in the truck," he said.

"Look, Matt. I've been taking care of myself for a long time now, even if Dad thought he was doing it," she answered. "And don't forget that I'm involved in this case now—Dad's death, the wolves, Prince, ranching by myself—this is all part of my life, and I need to help resolve it. So, yes, I'll be careful. But, no, I won't promise to stay in the truck." She looked at Matt momentarily and then added, "Who knows? You might need some help yourself."

Matt gunned the truck and bounced across the rough pasture as fast as it was safe to drive. He hadn't yet covered half the distance when he saw a sheet of flame near the edge of the trees where Lindsay had seen the light. He swerved at the same instant that he heard the bullet strike the side of the truck. He slammed on the brakes as he turned the truck sideways and came to a stop with Lindsay's side of the truck away from the gunman. "Jump out and stay out of sight beside the truck," he whispered urgently. "I'll need to come out your door too."

It appeared that whoever was shooting at them was using a pistol. Matt pulled his rifle out of the truck with him as he followed Lindsay, then he leaned up over the truck bed and fired a shot. He saw two figures jump up and start through the shadowy trees. One of them fired a wild round in his direction. A second later, Matt fired again. One of the shooters dropped to the ground but got right back up again and darted behind a tree. Matt jacked another round into his .30-30, waited, and watched. He saw occasional glimpses of the shadowy figures as they fled up a ridge and over it. Finally, he said to Lindsay, "You can get back in the truck now. They're gone, but I'm calling for help."

She climbed into the passenger side while he hurried around and got in the driver's side of the truck. He called the dispatcher and told her what had just happened. "Send me some backup. We might be able to catch them on horses or four-wheelers if we hurry."

It couldn't have been more than a minute before the sheriff came on the radio and spoke to Matt. "Don't go after them by yourself," he said. "Wait for some of us. They might try to set up an ambush."

"That's right, Matt. Please, let them go for now," Lindsay pleaded. "We don't need anyone else killed. Anyway, you need to get home and be with Jimmy."

Matt was torn. He was worried about his younger son, but he also didn't want whoever had just shot at him to get away. As he weighed his options, he knew he had no choice except to follow orders. The sheriff was right. It would be foolhardy to pursue armed individuals alone through the forest in the bright moonlight, especially when they had already shown no compunction about shooting at him. He could easily be ambushed.

He stopped at the edge of the field, climbed over the fence, and scoured the ground where the shooting had taken place. He found and collected one spent .38-caliber casing. Then he and Lindsay drove back to where the wolf's body lay.

As he examined it in the truck's headlights, he said, "Look, Lindsay. It has a collar on it. The wildlife officer that examined the wolf your dad shot says he thinks it had been wearing one, too, but that it had been taken off before the killers left the scene."

He also looked at the back door on the driver's side of the truck. The bullet had penetrated the metal, but stayed inside the door. He shook his head as he clicked his flashlight off.

"That was a close call, Matt. They could have killed you," Lindsay said with a tremor in her voice.

"Or you. I was crazy to let you ride with me while I was trying to get to them. I'm sorry. I should know better."

"I insisted," she reminded him. "But what's with these people? They're dangerous and desperate. It's like they're trying to start a war with the cattlemen."

"And with the law. In fact, I think they've started one," Matt said darkly. "And we're going to have no choice but to fight it out to the bitter end."

* * *

"How bad are you hurt?" one of the men asked his companion.

"He only nicked me. But he had a rifle. I guess we're going to have to get bigger guns," the other said. "I can't believe that guy's luck. He got the one wolf of that pack that had a collar. That makes me so mad. These guys will wish they'd never started this battle."

"You shouldn't have shot at that cowboy. Now they know we're here, and if they know we're here, they may be watching for the others. We're all going to have to get out of the area and let things cool down," the first man said.

"No, we're going to have to take the fight to them and do it soon," the other countered. "Avenger will understand. After all, they shot first, not us."

"But they shot a wolf."

"What difference does that make? Wolves can't shoot back. We have to do it for them."

4

Despite a full moon overhead and horses and four-wheelers for transportation, the sheriff and several of his deputies were unable to find the shooters that night. Follow-up after sunrise netted similar results. The activists had returned to a vehicle on a rarely-used forest road and escaped, just like Noah's killers had. They hadn't left so much as a cigarette butt behind.

Jimmy came out of his latest crisis after speaking with Dr. Lubek on the phone. She seemed to be able to help him when no one else, including Matt, could get a response from him. Dr. Lubek had wanted to see him in person, but when Matt explained what was going on in his life, she decided that a phone conversation with the boy might help. Matt was surprised when his son suddenly began to respond to the doctor on the phone. He wished she were closer so that he could have her spend more time with Jimmy.

Noah Flemming's funeral on Friday was a big one. Matt's heart felt heavy when he saw Lindsay walking behind the flag-draped casket, her head bowed, her eyes red, and her shoulders slumped. It brought back his own sorrow more intensely than he expected. He missed Carol and Sarah more that day than he had for some time. He left the funeral drained and depressed.

Matt and his parents drove to the cemetery, where he stood behind the large assembly of extended family and friends who had come to pay their respects to the grand old man they were putting in the grave that day. As he looked around he thought about the people. Many he knew, some he didn't. They were kind, supportive people who expressed their love to each other in dozens of different ways.

Matt remembered a fireside he had attended a few years before the Billings Montana Temple had been built. That fireside recounted the growth of the Church in Montana. He smiled in spite of himself as he recalled details about the missionary tour conducted in the 1890s by the First Council of the Seventy. Several general authorities had come to "hunt down" the "lost sheep" in Montana. Generally, the few members they had found were judged by the leaders to be a stiff-necked people, if not downright infidels, with a few good sheep mixed in. These were definitely the good sheep here today, he thought—some members, some nonmembers.

After the dedication of the grave, Matt started to walk back toward his car, but Lindsay caught his eye as he glanced back at her. He turned and walked back. "Lindsay, I am so sorry," he said brokenly.

She said, as she had before, that she didn't know how she was going to be able to cope without Noah's strength to keep her going.

"He raised you right," Matt said. "You'll make it. Time will help. Believe me, I know."

Her eyes grew moist again and she said, "If only Dwight had come."

"Have you heard from him?" Matt asked.

"No, and it makes me wonder if he's even still alive," she said. At that moment, an older relative walked up, and Matt excused himself.

As he walked to where his parents waited by the car, he thought of Dwight Flemming. The two of them were the same age and had gone to school together. Matt had never had much to do with Dwight. They simply ran in different circles, their interests rarely overlapping. Dwight had always been arrogant and selfish, not to mention rebellious—a small man with a big mouth. There was nothing but his physical stature that bore any resemblance to his father and sister.

"He could actually be in prison somewhere," Matt said, startled that he had spoken his thoughts aloud. He glanced around quickly and decided he had better keep his feelings to himself.

More emotions surfaced as Matt remembered Lindsay's despair. He was angry to think Dwight was so callous that he couldn't even take the time to contact his sister at such a time. He remembered Lindsay's comment that Dwight might be dead. Although he had no real basis for his assumption, Matt thought that was highly unlikely.

* * *

Reese and Matt worked long days all week, but they made no real progress toward identifying the killers. On the positive side, there were no further incidents as far as wolves were concerned in either of their counties or in any other counties in the region. One of the other Gallatin County deputies commented to Matt that the violent faction of activists must have given up and that maybe things would be okay now if they just backed off.

"I wish that were the case, but there's not a chance. They're just biding their time. And as far as leaving things alone, that's not an option. We have a murder here. And someone shot at me—and at Lindsay Flemming. This is personal now. I won't rest until we find these people and bring them to justice."

* * *

The phone rang in an apartment in Great Falls. A very tired Dwight Flemming groaned and reached for it. He'd had a late night, a busy night, and he was exhausted. "What do you want?" he asked when the receiver finally reached his ear.

"Hey man, have you seen the papers?" the voice on the other end asked.

"I don't have time for papers," Dwight said. "I'm a busy man."

"Maybe you should take the time," the caller advised him. "Didn't you say your father's name was Noah Flemming?"

"Yeah, what of it? I got nothing to do with him anymore."

The caller persisted. "Didn't you say he has a big spread down near Bozeman?"

"Yeah, but I got away from there a long time ago. All my father wanted me to do was be his slave on his ranch. Work, work, work. He could have hired plenty of people to work. Why are you suddenly so interested in my father?"

"Aren't you the oldest in your family? Seems like you told me that once."

"I have a little sister, and that's all. What's with all these questions, anyway?"

"I just thought you might want to know that your father croaked on Monday. Shouldn't you get that ranch now? And I thought maybe you could use a good ranch hand. I've got experience, you know."

Dwight struggled to sit up. He was really tired. "What did you say? My father's dead?" he asked.

"Don't you watch the TV or listen to the radio or anything?"

"I've been busy," Dwight said. "But tell me what you know. What happened to my father? Did he tip a tractor over or something?"

"No, but get this, Dwight. Your father shot a wolf, and it got him shot in return."

"Trust my dad to do something stupid like that," Dwight responded. "He's the kind that would get himself into a jam like that."

"Hey, some of them ranchers make good money. The wolf was probably in his livestock. He probably felt like he had to kill the wolf to save his ranch or at least his livestock. Can't say I blame him for that. Anyway, now that he's dead, you could say that someone did you a favor."

"My dad's affairs are nothing to me," Dwight said in irritation. "And I don't need any favors, but thanks for letting me know." Dwight wanted to get this guy off the phone. He was tired, but he also had things to do.

"Hey, Dwight, you could be one of them rich ranchers now, you know. Don't you think you better go claim your ranch? And when you do, give me a call. I'll help you out down there."

Dwight was out of bed now. "Yeah, I guess I better go take over," he said. "I wonder what my little sister will think when I show up and claim what's mine." He was just making small talk now, until he could free himself from the caller.

"She's a woman, Dwight," his friend said with disgust. "What would she want with a big ranch?"

"Probably nothing. I'm sure it will have to be sold."

"Unless you show up and take over."

"Yeah, unless that. Thanks again for the call. I owe you."

"And I won't let you forget it," the man said in closing. "I need a job."

Dwight's forehead was accordion-folded from the effort he had spent thinking the past few minutes. "I'll be in touch," he lied as he replaced the receiver. Dwight wanted his dad's ranch. He believed that he had every right to claim it. Thinking of what he could do with the money the place would bring him when he sold it brought him as close as he ever came to smiling.

* * *

Lindsay felt unready to teach her Primary class. She'd had no time to prepare adequately with all the events of the past week. She hurried with her chores, hoping to squeeze in a few more minutes to look over her lesson before she had to leave for church. Life as she'd known it would never be the same. So much had changed for her this past week it was staggering. She momentarily considered what the "new" normal would be like.

As she threw some hay to her prize stallion, she wondered whether Matt had remembered to help Jimmy get his talk ready for Primary today. He'd been so busy all week that she was afraid he might not have had time. And she knew that the boy would be embarrassed if he and his father had forgotten and he came unprepared. Maybe he would freeze up again the way he had earlier in the week when he'd learned that her father had been killed.

"I should have called and reminded them," she told her horse as she rubbed a hand across his flank. "But, honestly, I didn't even think about it myself until just this minute."

Lindsay finished what couldn't wait until later in the day and then ran to the house to get ready for church. She had just ten minutes to spare when she'd finished dressing. She sat down to quickly review the lesson, then she headed for church.

A nice, dark blue car she didn't remember seeing around the area passed her on the road just a mile from her house. She didn't get a good look at the driver but just got the impression that he seemed to be a smallish man—there appeared to be a considerable distance between the man's head and the top of the car. She thought nothing of it and turned her mind back to her lesson. Despite all the problems that had come into her life this past week, she couldn't let the children down.

The second counselor to the bishop was just approaching the pulpit when Lindsay walked in. Ordinarily, she and her father were early, and they generally sat in the same place each week. But that spot was filled now. She stood at the back door for a moment, looking for a place to sit. She spotted Jimmy waving at her and could see that there was a little room just beyond his brother in the center section. She smiled at Jimmy and hurried toward him. But as she started to make her way into the row, Keith moved, and the vacant spot was now between him and his father.

She felt certain the whole ward was staring at her, and she promised herself right then that she'd never be late again. Embarrassed, she sat down beside Matt. "Good morning," Matt said, leaning close to her ear. "I think Jimmy's going to be able to give that talk. Thank goodness he remembered, because I forgot until this morning."

"I'm glad," she whispered. "I was worried about him." Then she looked up to where the second counselor was speaking. "As a bishopric," he said, "we'd like to thank everyone who helped with Brother Flemming's funeral and the meal following it. And I know that his daughter has appreciated the response of the ward during this terrible tragedy."

As if on cue, the whole ward seemed to turn in unison to stare at Lindsay. She wished she could shrivel up and disappear. She didn't care for this kind of attention.

Jimmy did a fair job with his talk in Primary, although at one point he became a little flustered and a few tears appeared. Lindsay had noticed how his eyes sought out his father at the back of the room, and she could tell when he'd felt Matt's reassurance. He then went on without further problems. She loved all of her class members, but she couldn't deny that Jimmy Prescott was special. And she knew how her father had loved him. Suddenly, Lindsay was fighting with her own emotions as Jimmy finished his talk.

Lindsay ran into Matt as he and Jimmy waited at the door for Keith after the meetings. She stopped, stooped down, and spoke to Jimmy. "You did such a good job with your talk today. Thank you so much."

He grinned at her. "Dad helped me."

"That was nice of him. You've got a great dad, don't you?"

Jimmy nodded. "I miss your dad, Sister Flemming," he suddenly blurted, and tears rolled down his face.

"We both miss him, Jimmy. But we'll have to learn to get along without him, won't we?" Her voice was breaking as she spoke.

"I still miss Mom and Sarah," Jimmy said.

Lindsay clamped her jaws together firmly to keep from bawling. "I know you do," she said, and she straightened up. "I better get back to the ranch," she said to Matt.

"Yes, as soon as Keith comes, we need to get going as well."

"You will let me know anything you learn about . . ." Lindsay began, but again her emotions interfered.

"I'll keep you informed," Matt promised, and, as he watched her walk away, he thought of how hard life could be, and how unfair. Lindsay had done nothing to deserve what she was going through.

* * *

A dark blue sedan was parked in front of the house when Lindsay entered the yard. She remembered a vehicle that had looked like this one pass her on her way to church. She suddenly felt apprehensive. *Who could it be?* she wondered. There was no one in the car that she could see, but then the back windows were dark, and she couldn't see into the automobile. The car was an expensive one—a Lincoln. None of her relatives had driven a car like this at the funeral. She stopped the truck and stared at the car, her heart racing.

She stepped out of her truck and looked around her yard. She couldn't see anyone. It didn't make sense. Sweat began to pour off her face. She felt so alone, so vulnerable. She didn't even have her cell phone. It was in the house. But even if she had it, she would sound silly calling someone. She had no reason to believe that whoever had driven the car here was any danger to her.

She pulled herself together and started toward the car and her house beyond it. It was probably nothing, she told herself. But despite her self-talk, it didn't feel like nothing. Her mouth was dry and her knees weak as she forced herself to walk past the Lincoln. When she was even with the front door, she tried to look in the window without being too obvious. She saw no one. Where could the driver be? She turned and went back to her truck. Perhaps she should leave and wait out by the highway until the car left. She could borrow a phone at the nearest ranch house and call the sheriff's office if the unknown visitor didn't leave soon. The only problem was that she didn't know what she would tell the neighbor or the sheriff's office or anyone.

Lindsay hesitated at her truck and looked around her yard again. She couldn't see anyone. Of course, someone could be in the barn or behind the sheds. Again she tried to get a grip on herself. Surely she was overreacting; maybe someone was out back looking at her prize stallion. After all, she and Noah had him listed on a Web site. For that matter, it could be someone wanting to buy a colt. She knew that for many, Sunday was just another day. That seemed like a good explanation. Feeling better, she strode toward the barn and walked through it. But still she saw no one anywhere in the vicinity of the horses.

She again started toward the house, her apprehension stronger than ever. Twice more she nearly headed for her truck so she could leave, but she didn't allow herself to do it.

I don't know yet what normal is, but I do know I'm on my own now, Lindsay thought.

Finally, she got to the front door and took her key out of her purse. She put it in the lock and turned it. Her heart nearly failed her. *The door was already unlocked.*

She knew she'd locked it when she left for church. Now she was really frightened.

Just then, a voice from inside called her name. "Lindsay, is that you?"

The voice had a familiar ring to it.

"Come on in, Lindsay. It's just your long-lost brother."

5

Feeling foolish for being frightened, yet grateful that her brother had finally come home, Lindsay swung the door open and rushed inside, immediately brought to a halt by the odor of cigarettes. "Dwight, it's so good to see you," she said, choosing to ignore the smell and the cup that sat on the end table where he dropped the cigarette he was smoking.

He stood up from where he'd been sitting in Noah's favorite chair. His face looked much as it had the last time she'd seen him so many years ago—a little older, of course, but somehow different. Maybe he looked harder, she decided. His hair was graying and partially covered his ears, but it was clean and neatly combed. He wore a conservative, light blue sport shirt and gray slacks. He sported expensive-looking rings on two fingers. And the watch he wore had to be a Rolex. Other than the ring he wore in one ear, he looked like a successful businessman. For all she knew, he was. Maybe he'd changed. Dwight was still as handsome as she remembered him. They looked each other in the eye, and all she could see were coldness and emptiness. She felt a slight chill come over her.

But she was glad to see him, and she held out her arms to him. He stopped when he was still a couple of yards away. "Come on, Dwight, can't you give me a hug?" she asked. "I've missed you so much."

He moved forward awkwardly. Finally, he let her put her arms around him, but she felt no warmth in return. After a brief embrace, she stepped back and said, "Where have you been all these years? I've missed you more than you know, Dwight. I'm so happy that you're here."

"How was the funeral?" he asked, avoiding her questions. "If I'd heard about the old man's untimely death soon enough, I'd have been here for it. I came as soon as I could."

"It was really nice, Dwight," she said, cringing inwardly at the disrespectful way he referred to their father. "I believe every relative on both sides of our family was there. I'd forgotten how many cousins we had. But it was so nice to see them. They all asked about you."

"I'll bet they did," he growled.

"No, they really did, Dwight. We all wished you'd been there."

"Didn't know about it," he said.

"I'm sorry. I didn't know how to get ahold of you," Lindsay said. "I just hoped you'd hear about what happened since there was so much publicity about it."

"I'm a busy man," Dwight said. "My businesses keep me tied up. I don't have time for TV and newspapers and things like that."

"I want to hear all about what you've been doing, Dwight. I'll bet you're a good businessman. Just looking at you I can tell you're successful."

"I've done okay," he said.

"Well, I'm so glad you're here. I'm sorry you didn't hear about Dad in time for the funeral. It's been really hard this past week. I've been so alone. Having you here will really help. I miss Dad so much. I still can't believe he's really gone."

"Yeah, it's too bad," Dwight said.

The lack of feeling in his voice made her uncomfortable.

"It was awful the way he died. Why would anyone do something like that to Dad? He never hurt anyone in his life."

"Yeah, I suppose that's true. Good old Dad," he said mockingly.

Lindsay resented the tone of his voice, but she wasn't going to make Dwight feel unwelcome if she could help it. After all, he was her brother. And although she hadn't seen him for years and he'd been such a rebel before he left, she still loved him. With him here, she was no longer alone.

"Please sit down, Dwight. We need to get reacquainted. Can I get you a soda or something?" she asked.

"I've been sitting for over four hours," he said. "I wondered if you'd ever get back. I came as soon as I heard about Dad."

"I'm sorry," she said. "And by the way, how did you get in?"

He smiled then. "Dad was always predictable. The hidden key in the granary was right where he used to keep it."

"Of course," she said with a smile. "What about a drink?"

"I'll have a beer, if you insist," he said, his smile turning smug as he dropped his slight frame into her father's favorite chair.

"Sorry, I don't have any of that," she said, trying not to appear too shocked at his hurtful request. "I do have some soda pop."

"No thanks, I need something stronger," Dwight said. "After all, I just lost my father, and I haven't had time to get used to the idea."

"Are you hungry? I have lots of food in the house," she offered next, trying her best to play the part of the gracious hostess and not the grieving daughter or disappointed sister.

"Sure, that would be okay," he said. "I am hungry. All I've had today is a donut and a cup of coffee."

"Let's see what I have," she said.

Without taking time to change from her Sunday dress, Lindsay began to warm up a serving of casserole for him. When it was hot and arranged on a plate along with a slice of home-baked bread, some peas, and Jell-O salad, she placed it on the table.

"Sit down, Dwight. I'll grab you a glass of milk."

When she returned with the milk, she also had a large piece of chocolate cake.

"There you go, and I have plenty more. I'll hurry and change clothes while you eat. Then we can visit. It's just so good to see you, Dwight."

As she spoke, Dwight eyed the lunch she'd set out for him. To her surprise, he suddenly pushed back from the table and stood up. "You know what, Lindsay? I've been looking at that casserole and Jell-O, and I don't think I'm very hungry anymore. I still haven't gotten over all the casseroles and Jell-O salads we had to eat when Mom died. I guess that's the standard Mormon fix-all. Oh, yeah—along with pray, study the scriptures, and hold family home evening. How could I possibly forget those? Sure enough, they'll fix all your problems."

"Dwight," she said, feeling hurt and angry, "I'll open a can of stew if you'd like, or I'll fry some hamburger. In fact, I have some steaks in the freezer."

He raised a hand and said, "You don't need to go to the trouble. I need to get on my way anyway."

"Oh, Dwight, please don't leave," she cried. "I want to visit with you. I want to hear all about you. It's been so long."

"I've got to go. If I hadn't had to wait so long for you, we could have spent a little more time catching up."

"Sorry," she said. "I was at church."

"Of course you were," he said with a sneer. The look in his eyes suddenly scared her. "Still the good little Mormon girl, I see."

"Yes, I love the Church, Dwight. I'm teaching a Primary class."

"Oh, spare me. I don't care to hear about that, Lindsay. Not now. Not ever. And I really do have to go. I have business to attend to, but I'll be back," he said as he reached down and picked up the piece of chocolate cake. "This does look good. Just wish you had a beer to go with it. I really do need a beer, you know. A good cold beer would help me deal with Dad's death a lot better than any of your casseroles and milk and Jell-O." He immediately took a bite of the cake.

Lindsay was reeling. But she again reminded herself how much she'd missed her brother. She truly had. At one time, when she was a very young girl and he was not yet an arrogant and rebellious teenager, they'd been fairly close. "Please, Dwight. Can't you stay for just a few more minutes?" she pleaded.

"Not really. There are some things I've got to do. But like I said, I'll be back. Oh, and you're probably wondering why I came by," he said.

That statement puzzled Lindsay. "I assumed it was to see me," she said. "And to talk about Dad."

"No, not exactly. I had another reason," he said after chewing and swallowing his last large bite of cake.

Lindsay fought back the tears. She'd never been treated so cruelly in her life as she was being treated now, by her own brother. He was acting like a child, not an apparently successful forty-year-old man. "I'm sorry you didn't want to see me," she managed to choke out. "But I do wish you'd stay anyway."

"I'll take another piece of cake, sis. That's one thing those Mormon women can make that tastes good. And maybe that'll hold me 'til I get to Bozeman. But I'll be back," he said. "In the meantime, don't sell anything off this ranch. Since I'm the oldest, the ranch will be coming to me now that Dad's dead. And I expect to make a few changes with this place before I sell it. In the meantime, you can be figuring out where you'll be going and what you'll be doing. And remember, anything that doesn't belong to you personally will be staying here."

For just a moment, Lindsay was in shock. Then rage surged through her. She couldn't believe what she was hearing. "Dwight, I'm afraid you're in for a big disappointment if you came back just to get the ranch," she said, knowing her face was red with anger as she spoke. "This place isn't Dad's. It hasn't been for some time. It belongs to me. I have a deed to the entire place! Now if you'd act like a gentleman, I'd be willing to work with you on a few things, but you need to understand that you are standing on *my* property. Every cow, every horse, all the machinery, the trucks, the land and buildings—everything on this ranch is mine. For all Dad and I knew, you were dead! You didn't even have the decency to call or write him a letter and let him know you were okay. So he sold the place to me."

Dwight's mouth was hanging open. When she quit talking, his face darkened, and his eyes glowed with hate. "It's not that simple, Lindsay," he said ominously. "You can't just take what's mine. I'll have this place. It's my right as the oldest child."

"Dwight! You don't seem to understand. Dad sold it to me. I paid him in labor over the years as well as some of my own money. This ranch is not something that's being left to anyone. This ranch is mine. Now, if there are some of Dad's personal things you'd like, I'd be happy to discuss it with you."

"You rotten little thief," he snarled. "We'll see how long you keep this ranch! You'd better watch yourself. And don't you let anything leave this place. Not one thing!"

With that, he spun around and headed for the front door, his second piece of chocolate cake forgotten. He went out, slamming the door angrily behind him. Then he got in his fancy Lincoln and fishtailed for a hundred yards before finally slowing down for a curve in the lane. Lindsay was shaking as she watched him go. When he was out of sight, she sat down in her father's chair, the smell of the cup full of cigarette butts beside it almost making her nauseous. But she was too upset even to take time to empty it. As she sat, her tears flowed freely, and great wracking sobs shook her body.

For a quarter of an hour, she let the grief spill out. Finally, she forced herself to go into the bedroom and change clothes. Her appetite had left along with Dwight. After putting away the food she'd so recently gotten out for her brother, she emptied the cup he'd used as an ashtray, rinsed it out, and walked outside.

It was too early to do her chores, but she couldn't bear to sit in the house all afternoon, so she simply walked. She strolled slowly up the long lane that bordered her alfalfa fields, lost in thought. Before she knew it, she was over a mile from the house. She turned and started back for home.

Lindsay loved this land. Her father had loved this land. Even though her memories of her mother were distant, she knew she too had loved it. The only one in the family who didn't was Dwight. She steered off the lane, climbed through a fence, and before long found herself down by the river. Soothed by the pleasant sound of the rippling water, she sat on the bank and watched the stream as it passed.

As she sat there in the grass and gazed at the clear, rushing river, Lindsay thought for a long time about her father and the Flemmings before him. For four generations now, the Flemmings had lived in this fertile valley, called the Valley of Flowers by the Native Americans; raised cattle and horses on this ranch; and loved this land. Her great-grandfather Franklin Arthur Flemming and his family, survived the lean homesteading years before the First World War. They proved up their 320 acres and saved enough money to buy that and many more. Franklin's son Walter, who was Lindsay's grandfather, followed next. His family's trial was the Depression. By selling some of his livestock during those years and bartering what little he grew for what he most desperately needed, Walter was able to buy up other ranches that failed. When Franklin's son Noah took over the ranch, he was faced with the great drought in the West in the 1950s. But he now owned 19,000 acres of choice land and leased another 6,000 acres from the forest service for grazing.

She reflected on the good life her father had lived. He was one whose handshake and word had been his bond. And she consoled herself with the certain knowledge that her loss was her mother's gain. Lindsay knew the two of them were now happily together as they had been so many years ago. And she tried to be happy for them. But it was hard. Maybe it would have been easier for her if he had died naturally, but the violence surrounding his death had thrown a pall over her life.

Her thoughts turned to Dwight, and a sadness of a different kind passed over her. She thought back on how he'd looked when she saw him. He'd been clean and neat, the way she remembered him, except for the startling hardness of his face and the strange look in his eyes. But she had been able to overlook even that because of her joy at seeing him. Then she thought of how rude he'd been and how quickly he'd let her know that he had no brotherly feelings for her—no love, no desire to buoy her up during this time of grief, no sharing of hearts and hands, no working together on the land of their inheritance. It broke her heart. She let the tears flow again, as they had so much during the past week. But this was a new kind of grief.

* * *

Brooding as he ate his meal and sipped his second beer, Dwight wondered if Lindsay had lied to him about the ranch. Maybe it was just her way of trying to keep him from getting what was rightfully his. On the other hand, if she was telling the truth, he'd make her pay dearly for her treachery.

An idea began to form in his mind. He thought about it for several minutes. Dwight had spent years in real estate, and he'd done well, having discovered a few devious ways to get a little more than his share from clients' homes and farms. That had never particularly bothered him. But in all his years, he'd never had a big place like his father's to sell. He could make a lot of money off it. He smiled to himself. Yes, he'd get the ranch. Lindsay would wish she'd never even thought about keeping it for herself before he was through.

Of course, first he needed to make sure she wasn't lying to him, and a little call to the county recorder's office in the morning would tell him what he wanted to know. He didn't care if she found out he'd been asking about the Lazy F. It wasn't illegal to inquire concerning property titles.

He smiled to himself about what else he'd done that day, knowing she wouldn't do anything about it.

* * *

The afternoon had dwindled by the time Lindsay finally left the riverbank. She took her time with her evening chores, not anxious to go back into the house where the smell of Dwight's smoking undoubtedly still lingered. The last thing she did was gather the eggs, and then she went inside the house. She cleaned the eggs, put them in the refrigerator, shut off the air-conditioning, and opened all the windows, hoping the place would soon smell better. She berated herself for not doing that earlier.

With so much emotion expelled during the course of the afternoon, she was hungry now. She warmed up a few things and ate. When she finished and the dishes were done, she decided to go into her father's bedroom. She wasn't sure why. Maybe, she thought to herself, she'd feel closer to him in there.

She pushed the door open, stepped inside, then stopped and looked around. Something was terribly wrong. It took her a moment to figure out what the problem was. Many of her dad's personal belongings were missing.

She staggered backward out of the room. For a few minutes she was too stunned and hurt to do anything. Then her temper flared, and she reached for the phone. This was her house, and Dwight had no right to enter it without her permission. And he certainly had no authority to take anything. She dialed 911.

* * *

Keith answered the phone. "It's for you, Dad," he said. "It's the sheriff."

He and the boys had enjoyed a peaceful afternoon and early evening. All he needed now was to have that spoiled by more wolf problems, and that was almost certainly what the sheriff was calling about. He lifted the receiver to his ear. "Hello, Sheriff," he said. "Trouble?"

"I'm afraid so, Matt," Sheriff Baker said.

"Wolves again?" Matt asked.

"Not this time. It's a burglary, but the victim is Lindsay Flemming. Tom was going to go out, but he called me and asked if it would be better if you went, and I agreed that it would be. She's been through so much that we thought it would be easier for her if you handled it, since you've been working with her on her dad's murder anyway."

"Sure, I'd be glad to," Matt said, wondering who would have broken into Lindsay's place and why she had waited so many hours to report it.

Surely, if someone had broken into her place, she would have noticed it when she'd gotten home from church.

"Do you have to go, Dad?" Keith asked.

"I'm afraid so. Sister Flemming's house has been broken into. The sheriff wants me to handle it."

"Dad, that's terrible," Keith said. "How come these things keep happening to Sister Flemming? Will you be gone long?"

"I don't know, but will you please get Jimmy to bed for me?"

"Sure. I hope you're not too long."

"I hope not."

Matt made good time getting out to the Lazy F Ranch. Lindsay answered the door at his first knock. "Oh, Matt, I didn't mean for you to have to come. It's your day off, and the boys need you. Anyway, this has nothing to do with Dad's death."

"The sheriff asked me to come," he said. "And I was glad he did."

"I'm sorry to mess up your Sunday evening, but won't you come in?" she said.

After they were seated in Lindsay's living room, Matt said, "Okay, tell me exactly what's happened. I know you've had someone break into your house. But I'll need details."

"It wasn't just someone, Matt. It was Dwight."

"Dwight! He's been here? How do you know he was the one?"

Lindsay explained how Dwight had been waiting for her in the house when she'd returned from church. She told him how awful the visit had been and how it had upset her. "Anyway, I ate some dinner and then I decided to go into Dad's room. When I did, I knew right off that something was wrong."

"What did you see?" Matt asked as he followed her into Noah's room.

"Well, for starters, Dad kept a rifle on those hooks on the wall. Not the one he carried on his saddle, but one he had just for show. It was a gold-plated, lever-action rifle, an odd caliber that was given to him by the cattlemen's association about the time I was born. They'd had some kind of shooting contest that Dad won. He was a really good shot."

"Yes, I noticed that he hit that wolf right in the head. That's not easy to do. I suppose the missing rifle's worth a lot of money," Matt guessed.

"I suppose so, but it's worth more for sentimental value."

"What else is missing?" he asked.

"On that nightstand," she said, pointing, "there was a wooden carving. It was of a horse and rider. It was given to my parents as a wedding present by an old cowboy, a friend of my grandfather's."

"I see," he said.

Lindsay continued to scan the room. "I'm not sure what else is gone. I've been thinking, but I haven't really figured it out yet. I'm just afraid that's not all."

"When did you last see these things?" Matt asked, wanting to make sure he followed protocol and didn't allow himself to jump to conclusions he couldn't substantiate.

"Last Sunday," she said. "You'll remember Dad wasn't feeling well that day. I think I told you that, didn't I?"

Matt nodded. "He missed church. Jimmy missed him in Primary."

"Yeah, that's right," Lindsay agreed. "When I got home, I stepped in here to check on him. He said he was feeling better, and he was sitting in that chair beside his bed. He was reading the scriptures. When I came in, he laid them on the edge of the nightstand, right next to the carving. I know the carving was there then. And I think I remember seeing the rifle, too."

"Maybe you should check the closet and drawers," Matt suggested. "Did he keep anything valuable in any of them?"

"I hope Mom's wedding ring isn't gone," she said, her face growing dark as she stepped quickly across the room and opened the top drawer of a large dresser. She gasped. "Oh, no! It's gone," she said. "This makes me so mad! Dad always kept it right here. He used to come in here while I was still growing up and take it out and just look at it." She turned to Matt. "It was Dwight that took these things! I can't see how it could have been anyone else. He was here the whole time I was at church. He'd loaded this stuff in his big fancy car before I got home."

Matt nodded. "I suspect you're right."

"But I suppose those are the kinds of things that we would have to divide up, aren't they? He probably has as much right to them as I do," she said tearfully. "But you'd think he would have at least mentioned that he'd taken them."

"Do you really believe that?" Matt asked. "Judging from the way he treated you this afternoon, I would guess that he might have taken anything he wanted."

"That's right," she said, still angry.

"Lindsay, the house is yours, right?"

"Yes. The whole ranch is mine."

"So Dwight, even though he's your brother, had no right to come in here like he did," Matt said.

"But he knew where we kept the key," she countered.

"That's true, but that doesn't give him the right to use it. He's committed a felony here, Lindsay."

"But he's my brother," she said. "I can't send him to jail. I was mad when I dialed 911, but I don't want him to go to jail because of this."

"All the same, he did come into a house that wasn't his. And he took things he doesn't own. I will definitely have to do a report on this. Do you know if your dad by any chance kept a record of the serial number of that rifle somewhere?"

"Sure," she said. "He has a list of all his guns, including the serial numbers."

"Where's that list?" Matt asked.

"In the safe."

"Is there any chance Dwight knows how to get into it?"

"No, we've only had it a few years. Dwight was gone long before we got it. It's actually in the basement. He wouldn't have known about it."

Lindsay led the way into the basement. The list was in the safe, and Matt made a note of the serial number. Then he had Lindsay do a thorough search of the house. She discovered several more missing things, including her father's revolver and a hunting knife he'd used for years. None of the things that were taken, however, were things Dwight would have been able to identify as being Lindsay's personal property.

"He was thinking that anything he took of your father's was his if he wanted it," Matt said. "And I suppose, had the house not been deeded to you, he would have been right. That is, unless your dad had a will and he listed any of these items in it."

"He has a will. It's in our safety deposit box at the bank along with the deed to the ranch. But honestly, Matt, I don't want to have Dwight arrested over any of this. I don't want to be greedy," she said. "Like I said, I was angry when I called."

"Your choice," Matt told her.

When he left that night, Matt made sure all the windows and doors were locked. And he insisted Lindsay keep her pistol on her nightstand beside the bed. Her father had given it to her when she'd turned sixteen. That was one of the things Dwight hadn't taken, as it had been in Lindsay's bedroom on a shelf in the closet.

"I'll check with you first thing in the morning," he told her as she saw him to the door. "And call me if you need to. I don't care what time it is."

"Thanks, Matt," she said. "I hope I don't have to.

Ditto that, Matt thought as he left.

6

A trip into Yellowstone Park to meet with some key federal authorities was scheduled for Tuesday morning. Detective Bogart and wildlife officer Bob Wooley accompanied Matt to the meeting. An examination of the two recovered wolf collars showed just what Matt had anticipated. The collars were unlike anything that had been used on Yellowstone wildlife. And the conclusion reached by the federal officers mirrored that of the deputies. Someone was stealing wolves from the park, putting collars on them, and turning them loose on or near ranches. So far, the only ranch identified was the Lazy F, but they all agreed that it was only a matter of time until additional collars started showing up on wolves found on other ranches.

At the conclusion of the meeting, one of the federal officers said, "It looks like we're going to have to do something if someone's taking wolves out of Yellowstone. This is a big park. There are thousands and thousands of acres of back country. It won't be easy to put a stop to the thefts, if that's what's happening."

Matt spoke then. "I'm sure it would be worth the effort. Relations between the park and the ranchers are already strained. This kind of intentional thing will only make it worse. Together, we've got to solve the problem before things get out of hand."

The next several days were peaceful for Matt and Reese. Then Friday came. A fight broke out involving a group of activists who were protesting near a big ranch in Park County. Unfortunately, it was the teenage sons of some of the ranchers who started the fight. The ranchers weren't happy when their sons were arrested, and Sheriff Newton of Park County spent a couple of difficult hours trying to calm them down. They didn't want to hear that the protesters had the right to their own views and that as long as they were demonstrating peacefully, they were acting within the law.

On Saturday some sheep were killed by what appeared to be wolves in Park County, and another calf was found torn apart and mostly consumed just ten miles from Lindsay's ranch. It also came to the officers' attention that there had been more livestock killed in Sweetgrass County. The protestors became more vocal as the ranchers began to stir up the local and state authorities. Additional clashes seemed inevitable. The respective county sheriffs urged the ranchers to use restraint and promised that they would try to do more to protect their livestock. They also urged the protesters to be more understanding of the plight the ranchers found themselves in. Their livelihoods were threatened. Both sides promised to use restraint.

Matt called Lindsay several times that week to let her know what was happening, wishing he could report some progress on the investigation of her father's death. But he hadn't been able to learn anything more. Lindsay seemed to be doing fairly well, but upon pressing her a little, Matt discovered that she was falling behind on her work.

By Saturday she hadn't heard again from Dwight, although she knew he'd been busy. She had received a call from a friend who worked at the county recorder's office wondering why a man was in looking at the information they had on her land. From the description she gave her, Lindsay knew it had been Dwight. She supposed he was just making sure she was telling him the truth about the ownership of the Lazy F Ranch. She wondered if maybe now he'd be content with what he'd taken from the house and just leave her alone.

Matt and his sons spoke with Lindsay after church on Sunday. "The elders quorum president said that if you'd like, he would see if he could find someone to come help you get caught up with the work on the ranch. I know that with the funeral arrangements and family members visiting and Prince getting injured by the wolves, you haven't had much time lately," he told her.

"Dad," Keith said, "I have tomorrow off from the store. If it's okay with you, Jimmy and I could go out to the Lazy F then and help Lindsay for a few hours."

"Would that be okay with you?" he asked Lindsay.

"If Keith doesn't mind, I'd appreciate it. And I'll bet we can get caught up without having anyone else come out."

"I'll be there early," Keith said.

"That would be great. You could cut hay, and I could begin breaking a horse I haven't had time to touch. A rancher brought it in last week for me to start. But Keith, bring Claw. Prince has been back from the vet since Tuesday, and he's doing quite well. I think he'd enjoy the company."

"I'll do that. Jimmy wouldn't let me leave him home anyway."

"And, Matt, you would be welcome to come out after you get off work. Then you and the boys could have dinner with me."

"I hate to put you to the trouble," he said, although the idea appealed to him.

"It's no trouble. I'm still trying to use up the funeral food, if that's okay."

"Sure, as long as I don't get tied up on something. If I do, I guess the boys could eat with you anyway. But I'll try to make it," he finished.

* * *

Lindsay awoke on Monday morning before daybreak. She was grateful to Matt for letting his sons come that day. She knew Keith would be a great help. He was the kind of boy she wished her brother had been. He was a genuinely good kid. Just having the boys around would help ease her loneliness. The past couple of weeks had been very hard. Certainly, she had been alone at various times and at various places on the ranch over the years, but she'd never been alone like this before. And her dad was never far from her mind. Everything she did reminded her of him.

She knew she was being forward in inviting Matt and the boys to join her for dinner, but she felt that Matt was a good friend. She enjoyed being around him, and he wouldn't take offense.

She had most of her chores done before sunup, and she was soon busy moving water lines. With that finished, she hurried back to the barn. During the middle of the previous week, a neighbor had brought a horse for her to break. A lot of people scoffed when they heard she broke horses, but they didn't understand how it worked. She was gentle and took her time with them in the round corral. Before she ever put a saddle on a horse, she had the animal gentled and literally following her around the corral.

Very seldom did a horse buck when she got on. When on rare occasions it did, she was almost never thrown. She felt at one with every horse she rode. It was in her blood as it had been in Noah's. She loved breaking horses, and it paid well.

Since Keith was going to cut hay for her that morning, she would have the time she needed to begin working with the horse, one she knew was going to take extra time. The owner would have parted with the horse long ago if it weren't for its superb breeding.

By the time Lindsay was almost ready to begin working with the roan, Keith and Jimmy had arrived. She gave Keith his instructions, and he hurried to the machine shed. As soon as Keith was headed for one of the hayfields on her big John Deere windrower, Lindsay gave Jimmy the choice between playing in the barn and yard with the dogs while she worked with her neighbor's gelding or watching her work with the horse.

"But don't get too close to the fence while I'm working," she reminded him. "He's a pretty mean horse, and I don't want you to get hurt."

She let the roan into the round corral. It gave her a nasty look and kicked as it ran past her. The owner hadn't been kidding when he'd said it had a cranky disposition. Of course, that was part of the reason he'd brought it to her. Like Noah, Lindsay had established a reputation for taming horses. She had a feeling that this one was going to be particularly tough to break, but she had no doubt she could do it. She'd never failed with one yet, although she knew it could happen. Her father had met a couple during his lifetime that just wouldn't gentle down. But she had confidence with the roan. It was a beautiful quarter horse, and the owner very much wanted to be able to ride him. It just might take extra time.

She worked patiently with the big horse for over two hours before she was interrupted. A big, rough-looking fellow about her age, maybe a little older, came around the barn and approached the round corral. He reached the fence, put a hand on the top rail, and called out, "Are you Lindsay Flemming?"

"That's me," she called back.

"I need to talk to you about your place here," he said in a deep, slow drawl.

As much as she hated to, she left the roan standing in the middle of the round corral and walked over to the fence. She could see Jimmy watching from beside the barn. Both dogs were with him, and together they scampered out of sight, toward the front of the barn.

"What about the place?" she asked as she nervously looked the man over. He was dressed neatly in blue jeans, boots, and a brown western-cut shirt. He was clean shaven, but his jet-black hair was a little long and poked out from beneath a blue ball cap. His teeth were stained deep yellow, and he reeked of tobacco. He was tall, probably six foot three or four, and heavily built. His skin was dark, as were his narrow eyes. Lindsay hated the way they roamed over her body above his easy smile.

"I hear this ranch is for sale," he said smoothly. "Makes it just right for me, 'cause I'm lookin' to buy a place in the area."

Lindsay's stomach rolled. So much for Dwight not causing more trouble. He had to be mixed up in this, she thought bitterly. "You heard wrong," she said sharply. "I have no plans to sell. Sorry you got bad information."

"Funny thing," the big man said, still smiling and making no move to leave. "I didn't know it was yours. Your brother says it's his and that he's sellin' it."

Her suspicions confirmed, she said angrily, "My brother has nothing to do with this. The Lazy F is my ranch, not his. I don't intend to sell one acre of it."

"Yeah, I see. Well, Dwight warned me that you might not agree with him. Nonetheless, he says for me to take a look around, make an offer to him if I want. Says things aren't like you think they are."

"They're exactly like I think they are," Lindsay hissed. "You can leave right now, and when you see Dwight, tell him to get off my case. This is my ranch, and I intend to run it for the rest of my life."

"Easy, girl," the big fellow said. "My name's Lucas Mallory. I'm not here to cause trouble. I'm just lookin' for a ranch. Sounds like you and big brother need to talk. Anyway, I'm only here to look things over. I'll make my offer to Dwight if I like what I see. And frankly, *I like what I see*," he said salaciously as his eyes raked up and down her slim figure.

Lindsay felt her skin crawl, and she looked away from the stranger. Again she noticed Jimmy. He was peering around the side of the granary now, a frightened look on his face. He was close enough to hear what was being said, and he seemed to be scared. She needed to get this man out of here right now and make sure Jimmy knew there was no danger. She was well aware of how easily he regressed when things upset him. "Offer Dwight what you want," she said steadily, "but it won't buy you a thing. And as for looking around, the answer's no. This is my property, and I want you off it now."

"But Dwight said I could take a tour of the place, and that's what I aim to do. I can do it alone, or you can accompany me." He smiled at her again, but his eyes had narrowed. "I'd prefer that you show me around," he went on, his black eyes never leaving her face. "I'd like that."

"No, I said. You need to go now. This is my ranch, mine alone, and it is not for sale," she said, trying for Jimmy's sake to keep her voice down even as she felt rage building inside. "And you can tell Dwight that unless he wants me to press charges against him for theft and burglary, he'd better forget anything about my ranch. He's already tres- passed in my house and stolen from me. I wasn't going to have him charged, but my mind is changing rapidly. So, you either leave right now, or I'm calling the sheriff."

"Hey, hey, no need to get testy. I can come back another day, when it's more convenient," he said as he held both hands in front of him and stepped away from the fence. "But when I do, I won't be turned away again. Dwight says he can get a court order if he has to, that he doesn't aim to let some little gal steal what's rightfully his."

Lindsay opened her mouth to say more, then snapped it shut. There was nothing Dwight could do, she kept telling herself. And yet this dark stranger had sowed seeds of doubt. She watched him walk away, a decided swagger to his step. He seemed very sure of himself. *Not that it matters,* she told herself, *because I'm not selling.*

Jimmy and the dogs had disappeared. From the round corral there was no view of the house or the yard in front of it. The barn, machine shed, and granary blocked the view. She listened for a moment, hoping to hear the man's vehicle start up and leave. As soon as she heard the engine turn over, she turned back to the gelding, which was eyeing her in a way she hadn't seen from many horses. She experienced a momentary doubt about the big horse. *Maybe I've met my match,* she thought. *Of course, it didn't help that I was interrupted. I hate being interrupted when I'm trying to work with a new horse, especially a nasty one like this.* Lindsay realized that much of what she'd done the past two hours would have to be repeated. She waved her hands and yelled, "Get going, big boy." The horse began trotting around the corral.

He had made several circuits when Lindsay suddenly heard the dogs barking. Then one of them yelped as if it had been hurt. The other one continued to bark. She thought she could hear the engine of Mr. Mallory's vehicle still running, but she couldn't be sure. Certainly, he'd left when he first started the engine. The gelding was making just enough noise to make it hard for her to hear. Suddenly worried, Lindsay decided to go look. But as she climbed the fence, she forgot to watch the horse. Too late, she heard it running toward the fence. She was just swinging over when it struck. She felt a hoof graze her leg, and she leaped from the fence. She stumbled as she hit the ground and fell, her head striking the lowest bar of the corral enclosure. Then everything went black.

* * *

Keith looked at his watch. It was nearly noon, and he remembered that Lindsay had promised lunch right at twelve. He drove to the edge of the field, then shut off the windrower and jumped down. It took him several minutes to reach the house. When he knocked on the door, no one answered. He rang the doorbell. Still no answer. Finally, he pushed the door open and called into the house. "Lindsay," he said. "Are you in here?"

That's strange, he thought, *I know she said twelve, and it's almost that time now. I don't smell anything cooking, and the lights in the house are off. I guess she must still be working with that cantankerous gelding.*

Keith headed for the corrals, passing between the machine shed and the granary. It occurred to him that he hadn't heard anything from Jimmy or the dogs. He decided they must be in the barn.

All thoughts of Jimmy fled when he spotted Lindsay. She was sitting on the ground near the round corral moaning and holding her head. She was splattered with blood. His first thought was that the roan had kicked her. The gelding was standing at the far side of the corral, looking way too innocent, he thought. He rushed to her and knelt down. "Lindsay, are you okay?" he asked, knowing from looking at her that she wasn't.

"I . . . I fell," she stammered. "Must have hit my head on something. What time is it? How long was I out?"

"It's noon. Here, let me help you up," he said. The blood was coming from a gash on her forehead. "We need to get you in the house and wash your forehead. And you'll need a bandage."

"I'll be okay," she said. "Where's Jimmy?" As she asked, she looked stricken, and Keith caught his breath sharply. He felt like someone was performing an unnecessary Heimlich maneuver on him.

"I don't know. He must be in the barn," he said.

"We've got to find him, Keith!" There was a frightening urgency to her voice.

"Let's get you to the house first. Then I'll look for him. I'm sure he's okay," he said.

"Call the dogs," Lindsay suggested as he helped her to her feet. "They'll be with Jimmy."

"Claw! Prince!" he called. There was no response. He called them again as he began helping Lindsay walk. She was not only light-headed, but she was limping.

"Did you hurt your leg, too?"

"I think the horse must have kicked me as I was going over the fence. It's not too bad, though."

Keith steered Lindsay along the most direct route to her house. "Jimmy! Come help us, buddy," he called out loudly. "Lindsay's been hurt."

But like the dogs, Jimmy didn't respond. Something was wrong. Keith could feel it in his gut. "I'll be okay, Keith. I'm not quite so dizzy now. You go look for Jimmy and the dogs," Lindsay said. "I can get to the house on my own."

"Are you sure?"

"Yes, now go," she said in an uncharacteristically firm voice. She sounded frightened, and he wondered why. Jimmy couldn't be far, he told himself. But a cold fear swept over him, and he ran for the barn.

He turned on the lights when he got inside and began to call Jimmy's name. There was no response. He walked all through the barn, searching in every stall and corner as he went. He even checked the tack room, and he stopped and looked at the haystack, but there was no sign of his little brother. He went out the front door and then into the yard. He froze.

Prince was lying on his side in a pool of blood. Keith ran to him, knelt down, and examined him closely. It looked like he'd been run over. The area was saturated with blood.

"Oh, no, Prince. Who did this to you?" Keith cried out. Lindsay hadn't mentioned that anyone had been here. His father had told him about Dwight's visit, and his first thought was that he'd come back. He touched Prince. The dog was stiff.

Leaving the dog, he leaped to his feet, terrified now for his little brother. If Jimmy had seen someone run over the dog, it could put him right back into the condition he'd been in just last week. He could be hiding. He had done that before. "Jimmy!" he shouted at the top of his lungs. "Claw! Jim! Where are you?"

He darted into the machine shed. They weren't there. He headed toward the granary, continuously calling for his brother and the dog. But before he entered, Lindsay called him. "Keith, can't you find them?"

She was limping toward him, blood still caked on her forehead and smeared down her blouse and onto her jeans. "We've got to get help. We need to call your father. I'm afraid he—"

Keith cut her off. "Has Dwight been here again?" he asked urgently.

"No, but this has something to do with his friend, Lucas Mallory."

"Who?" Keith asked as he stuck his head in the granary and called Jimmy's name again.

"Some guy my brother sent," Lindsay answered. "He claims he was here to look at the ranch, that Dwight told him it was for sale. I told him to leave, and I thought he had, but just before I fell getting over the corral fence, the dogs started barking and one of them yelped. I was worried, and so I hurried too fast. I was careless and didn't watch that roan."

"Prince—" Keith began somberly.

"What about Prince?" Lindsay interrupted as she reached his side.

"He's over there," Keith said. "He's been run over. He's dead."

"Oh, Keith, no!" Lindsay cried. "Are you sure?"

"Yeah, I'm sure."

"What's happening? What is going on? I can't take anymore of this." Lindsay tried to control the trembling in her voice. "Could Jimmy be hiding somewhere? If he saw Prince get run over, it could have really affected him."

"That's what I'm afraid of. I need to call Dad. Do you have your phone?" he asked. "I forgot mine this morning."

"It's in the house. I'll go call your dad and get some help coming. You keep looking for Jimmy."

Despite her bruised leg and injured head, Lindsay ran toward the house.

* * *

Matt looked at his phone when it rang. Lindsay Flemming. He smiled to himself. He was looking forward to this evening.

"Hi, Lindsay."

"Matt! Jimmy's gone! We can't find him anywhere."

Matt felt like he'd been kicked in the stomach. "Did he go down to the river?"

"I don't know where he went. Hurry, Matt. You've got to come. Lucas ran over Prince and killed him. If Jimmy saw that, he could be upset and hiding or something. Claw's gone too."

"What!? Who?" Matt broke in urgently. Knowing how fragile his son's state of mind was, he was terribly frightened for him.

"A friend of Dwight's, or at least, someone Dwight sent to look at the ranch. Please, hurry!"

1

Matt, along with Reese, who was with Matt when he got the call from Lindsay, drove like there was no tomorrow toward the Lazy F Ranch. Matt felt as if his world would come to an end if he lost Jimmy too. He thought about the river that ran through the ranch. He was so afraid Jimmy might have gone there if he was disturbed. He suddenly whipped to the side of the road and stopped the truck. He turned to Reese. "You drive," he said. "I'm too upset."

While Reese took over, Matt silently prayed for his son. When they arrived at the ranch, Matt leaped from the truck. He spotted Lindsay. She was covered with blood, yet she hadn't said anything about getting hurt. He was now more worried than ever. She started toward him, limping badly. He ran to her and said, "What happened to you? Did this friend of Dwight's hurt you?"

"No. I'm so sorry, Matt. It's my fault. I should have kept a closer eye on Jimmy. Oh, Matt, my brother is so evil," she sobbed, holding her head in her hands.

Seeing Lindsay in this condition caused Matt to take control of himself. He couldn't let his emotions overpower him. "We'll find him," he said, trying to inject confidence into his voice.

Just then Keith came running up. "Dad, I've been down to the river, but I'm positive he didn't go there. I looked for tracks everywhere. There aren't any."

"That was the first thing I thought about," Matt said. "Let's let Reese have a look too. He's one of our best trackers."

"Point the way," Reese said, "and I'll get on it." He turned to Lindsay. "There will be more officers here shortly."

Keith and Reese headed toward the river, and Matt looked Lindsay in the eye. "Let's go sit down," he said. He was surprised at the control he now had over himself. "Then I want you to tell me everything. That's going to be our best bet for finding Jimmy."

They sat on some hay bales just inside the barn. "Okay now, first, tell me about this guy you called Lucas. What was he driving?"

"I don't know. I couldn't see his vehicle. I was in the round corral working with the roan gelding when he walked up. I talked to him there. After he left, I was trying to get over the fence to go check on Jimmy. That's when the roan came after me. He struck my leg, and I jumped from the fence. I guess I hit my head when I landed."

"You need to see a doctor," Matt said. "As soon as some of the other men get here, I'll have one of them run you into Bozeman."

"No, not until we find Jimmy. I'm fine, really. I just need to clean up," she insisted.

"We'll see. For now we'll let it go," Matt said to her. "Now, this Lucas guy. What did he look like?"

Lindsay described him while Matt wrote down the information. "He was clean-cut and dressed well. But he looked like someone who, well, someone who could be a friend of my brother, I suppose. If he's Dwight's friend, then he's probably lacking quite a bit in the good character department."

Matt shivered, but he shook it off and asked, "What did he come for? What did he want?"

"He said he'd come to look at the ranch, that he might want to buy it. When I told him it wasn't for sale, he said that Dwight said it was. Dwight wants this ranch, or at least he wants the money that it would bring if it were sold."

"Dwight won't get your ranch. Now, tell me what else happened," Matt pressed.

Lindsay had just finished her story when the sheriff roared into the yard and skidded to a stop. He was followed seconds later by a deputy. Matt ran out of the barn to meet them. "Matt, what's going on?" Sheriff Baker asked.

As briefly as he could, Matt related what had happened. Lindsay limped out to join them.

"You are going to see a doctor right now," the sheriff said to Lindsay. "You've been hurt."

"It's nothing," she insisted. "Forget about me. Let's worry about Jimmy."

No amount of argument would change her mind. Finally, she said, "I'll go in and clean up. I'll be fine. You guys work at finding Jimmy." She limped off toward the house.

Matt then told the others what had happened. "Whoever this guy is, he might have seen which way Jimmy and Claw headed. Do you think we could try to find him, Sheriff?"

"Absolutely. We'll get what we have on the air immediately," the sheriff said. "Why don't you men take another look around here? We can't be too thorough. That's a big barn. Start in there."

* * *

It was dark—very dark. Jimmy was having a hard time breathing. He didn't dare move. He lay silently, suffocating with fear. The big man had run over Prince. He'd seen it happen. He was afraid of him, afraid he'd die, just like his mother and sister had.

He could hear voices, but he shut them out by burying his head deeper into Claw's big neck. Both hands held tightly to Claw. He didn't want that scary man to hurt Claw like he'd hurt Prince. It was then that Jimmy had fled, taking Claw with him.

* * *

When Reese and Keith returned from the river, Reese said, "Keith was right. Nobody has been down there. I'll circle the yard here, make sure I don't see the little guy's tracks heading out anywhere."

While Reese and Keith were busy checking the yard, Matt went to the house to check on Lindsay. The other officer searched the places they'd already searched. Matt knocked on the door. When she didn't answer, he opened it and peeked in. She was at the sofa, kneeling. He entered silently and waited until she got to her feet. "Sorry," she said. "I knew it was you. I had to finish."

"Thanks, Lindsay."

She nodded. She looked better now. There wasn't a trace of blood on her, and a neat bandage covered the cut on her forehead. Her hair was loose, not in a ponytail. Except for her red eyes, she looked stunning. "We'll find Jimmy," he said with a confidence he wasn't sure he felt.

She nodded and came toward him. "It's my fault, Matt," she said again. "I should have kept him close while I was working with the horse. I should never have let Dwight's friend distract me."

"It's *not* your fault," Matt said. "I'm sure he's hiding. He's done that a few times since Carol's death."

The two of them went outside. Lindsay was still limping, but it wasn't as bad now. "I have a nasty bruise," she said when Matt glanced at her leg. "But that's all."

"I'm glad."

"Matt, you go back to looking for Jimmy. I can help now. I know this place better than anyone else."

"I hope so, because I don't know where else to look," he said. "I'm just so worried. I love that little guy." He couldn't say anything more. His heart could have been replaced with lead, as heavy as it felt.

Lindsay took his hand. "Come on, let's go search."

He looked at her upturned eyes and then nodded. "Let's start in the barn."

They had barely entered the big doors when the sheriff came running up. "An officer stopped Lucas Mallory. He was northbound from Bozeman. Lucas admitted that he ran over the little dog, and when he got out to see if he'd hurt it, the big dog came at him. So he jumped in the truck and left."

"Did he say if he saw Jimmy at all?" Matt asked.

"He says he saw him over at the barn, kind of hiding beside one of the big doors. But that was before he ran over Lindsay's dog. He said he'd have gone back and told Lindsay what had happened, but she'd been so angry at him for even being there that he decided to just leave."

Matt sank on a bale of hay. "Where do we look?" he asked, as an unrelenting pain pierced his chest.

Lindsay sat beside him, but Matt immediately stood and held his head in his hands. "Claw!" he shouted loudly, no longer able to conceal his frustration. Suddenly, from behind the haystack, a dog barked loudly.

"What's that?" Lindsay asked as she and Matt both turned to face the haystack.

"Claw, are you back there?" Matt shouted. The barking began again. "He's back there. I'll bet Jimmy's there too. But how did he get there?"

Matt began climbing up the stack of hay. When he reached the top he worked his way to the back and looked over. There, in a narrow space that separated the haystack from the wall of the barn, was the dog. His heart pounding, Matt peered deeper into the darkness and spotted a mound of loose hay. "Jimmy," he said softly.

A whimper answered him.

"He's back here!" Matt cried, and he jumped to the floor behind the haystack and began throwing loose hay aside.

"I'm coming to help you, Matt," the sheriff shouted.

Matt threw one last handful of hay back. There was his son, curled tightly in a ball, whimpering softly, and not moving. With a prayer of thanks, Matt tenderly picked up his son and checked him over. He must have fallen from the stack. Though the front, where Lindsay stood, was not hard to climb, the back side was a straight drop-off. Jimmy still hadn't said a word, but he threw his arms around his father's neck and clung tightly, his whimpering turning to sobs.

"It's okay, Jimmy. I'm here," Matt said. "I love you, son. You'll be fine."

He stood and held Jimmy. He'd been here all this time. Matt surmised that the dog had been right there with him, ignoring everyone else's call as he watched over his young master. Jimmy must have seen the car run over Prince. He prayed that his boy could talk about it in a little while, after he'd had time to calm down.

"Hand him up to me," Sheriff Baker said. He was leaning down from the top of the stack, his arms outstretched.

"Jimmy, we need to get out of this hiding spot of yours," Matt said as he hugged his son. "I'm going to hand you up to Sheriff Baker. Then I'll climb out and take you again."

But the boy only tightened his grip around his father's neck. "Son, you've got to let me hand you up to Sheriff Baker. I can't climb out of here and hold you too. The hay's too steep."

"Come on, Jimmy. I'll be really careful," the sheriff said.

But Jimmy wouldn't loosen his grip. Matt felt the boy's tears as they washed onto Matt's face and mixed with his own. "Please, son. I'll take you back as soon as I climb out of here."

But still he wouldn't budge. "Maybe he'll come to me," Lindsay said as she knelt beside the sheriff.

This time she stretched her arms down.

Matt said, "Sister Flemming's up there now, Jimmy. I'll hand you up to her."

Still he clung to his father. Then Lindsay said, "Come on, Jimmy. I love you too, you know. Please, let your daddy hand you to me."

Slowly, the tight grip eased, and Jimmy looked up. When he spotted Lindsay, he reached for her. Matt lifted him up, and she gently took him in her arms. She held him, his arms clinging tightly to her neck, while Matt, with the sheriff's help, scrambled out of the narrow hiding spot. Matt helped Claw out of the tight space, boosting him up and onto the stack. Then he said, "Okay, son, I can take you again."

The boy moved his head, saw his father, and reached for him. Once Matt had Jimmy securely in his arms again, he worked his way off the stack and back onto the barn floor. He looked at Lindsay, who was standing near them. Her eyes were full of tears, she had hay in her hair, and there was a little blood seeping from beneath the bandage on her head.

"Jimmy trusts you," he said in a choked voice. "Thanks."

"I love him," Lindsay said. "He's my little buddy."

The sheriff had left the barn when Keith came running in. "Where did you find Claw and Jimmy?" he cried.

"They were behind the haystack all this time."

Keith threw his arms around his father and his little brother. "Jimmy, I'm so glad you're okay. I love you, little guy. You scared us."

"He did that," Matt agreed. "And I love both you guys."

Then Keith asked, "How did they get back there? There's no room at either end for anything bigger than a cat."

"He climbed the front, and then he must have fallen or slipped back there."

"But that's a long fall. Is he hurt?"

"I don't think so. There was enough loose hay back there that it must have cushioned his fall. Then I guess Claw jumped down with him."

"I'm just so glad they're okay," Lindsay said. "I was so scared for Jimmy."

Matt's eyes caught Lindsay's as she spoke. And in that moment, she was more than just a good friend. He felt something tugging at his heart as he looked deeply into her eyes. He suddenly wanted to take her in his arms. "Jimmy, go to Keith," he said. "He'll take you to the house. Sister Flemming and I will be right in."

Jimmy, who still hadn't spoken a word, didn't resist going to his brother, and Keith carried him from the barn. Claw followed.

"I'm so glad he's okay. Matt, what is it?" Lindsay asked.

"Your prayers were answered," he said. "Thank you for being so concerned about Jimmy."

"I told you—I love him," she said with a tired smile.

"Thanks," he said, as he took a step closer to her. "I was so worried. I just hope he doesn't stay silent for long."

"He'll be okay. He knows how much his dad loves him."

Lindsay took a step toward him, and she winced as she did so. "Lindsay," he said. "We need to get you checked by a doctor."

"It's just a bruise, Matt. It's nothing really." She stepped closer. Unexpectedly, the two of them entwined their arms around one other. Neither said a word until they broke the embrace.

"Thanks for being such a good friend," Lindsay said as they looked into each other's eyes again. "Jimmy and Keith are lucky to have such a good dad. Let's go see how your boy's doing. Maybe he can shed some light on why he was hiding and why he was so frightened."

He stepped back from her. "Good idea. Let's see what he has to say."

But, as Matt feared, Jimmy had nothing to say.

8

Dwight Flemming shook his head in disgust Monday night as Lucas told him what had happened at the Lazy F. "You idiot, Lucas. You didn't need to run over her dog and get the cops after you."

"I didn't do anything. They just asked if I'd seen the boy when I left. I told them that he'd been standing by the barn. That was all that I knew. I don't know anything about the boy or the dog. And it wasn't my fault that crazy black mutt ran after the truck and got himself squashed."

"All you were supposed to do was tell Lindsay that you wanted to buy the ranch and ask to look the place over."

"And that's what I did," Lucas insisted. "That sister of yours is a feisty one. She's not just going to roll over and let you take the place."

"She wants a fight, does she? Then that's what she'll get," Dwight said with finality. "At the very least, one half of everything my dad had should be mine. And frankly, since I'm the oldest and I'm a son, it all should be. I expect that once she sees I mean business about collecting what my dad owed me and that I can offer her a few thousand when the ranch is sold, she'll take it to avoid a fight and be glad she got what she did."

Lucas shook his head. "I'm not so sure. She may be small and pretty, but she's tough as nails, Dwight. The horse she had in that pen was mean. Even I could see that, and I'm not much of a cowboy. She didn't have one bit of fear in her when it came to that animal."

"I'm not afraid of Lindsay, if that's what you're suggesting. I'll worry about her," Dwight said with a scowl.

"I'm not afraid of her either," Lucas shot back. "I'm just telling you she will fight you. I'm sure of it. So what do we do now?"

"You will be going back there, but when you do, I hope you can avoid further confrontations. I don't need any more ripples in my plans. And don't you forget it," Dwight said.

"When do I go back?" Lucas asked.

"Soon. Real soon," Dwight said thoughtfully. "But I may have someone go with you. I need to think about it. I'll give you a call. You can go now; I've got a lot to do."

* * *

The conversation still stung, and it had been twenty minutes since she'd hung up the phone. Lindsay had answered on the first ring, expecting a call from Matt reporting what the doctor had to say about Jimmy. It had been two full days since Jimmy had hidden behind the haystack, and he still hadn't said a single word. She and Matt were both worried sick. But it wasn't Matt on the phone, and she was slowly eating her lunch now while she waited for him to call.

Lindsay couldn't quit thinking about what she'd been told. She couldn't believe that Terrell Edinton had lost his confidence in her, and that she wasn't to touch his horse again. A friend of her father's for years, he'd never expressed anything but satisfaction concerning the horses Noah had broken for him. And in more recent years, he'd often told both her father and her that she was as good as Noah.

"I understand that the horse attacked you," he'd said. "You could have been killed. You seem to have lost your touch. Not once did my horses attack your dad."

She'd tried to explain about the distraction that had been caused by her brother's friend, Lucas, and the threat he'd posed, but he didn't want to listen. Finally, he'd said, "I'm sorry, Miss Flemming, but Grey Sadler will take over for you. I know his methods are a little different from yours, but this horse is going to need to be taught a lesson. Grey will be over to pick up the horse this afternoon."

She guessed it was Terrell's hiring of Grey to finish the job she really hadn't even had a fair chance to begin that hurt the worst. Grey was a nice guy in a lot of ways. She'd known him for years, having hung out with him occasionally at various horse shows, rodeos, and other horse events. She and Grey were about the same age, and they'd gone to school together. Like her, he'd never married.

A short, stocky, ruddy-faced man with bright red hair, piercing blue eyes, and a face that many women found quite handsome, Grey also had a bit of a temper. It wasn't so bad that it got him into trouble a lot, but she'd heard that it often flared when he was working with horses.

When they didn't do what he wanted at the exact time he wanted, he used force to get them to comply. She knew that many people worked with horses the way he did, but she didn't like it. He had a lot of work, and there were those who liked his style, but she almost hated to think what would happen when he and the roan gelding tangled. And it was sure to happen, because the roan needed extra patience, and Grey wouldn't have that. She sincerely hoped he didn't get hurt trying to ride the big horse.

The phone interrupted her thoughts. This time it was Matt. "Hi," she said, feeling a pleasant tingle at the sound of his voice. "How's Jimmy doing?"

Matt sounded tired and stressed. "He had a shock is all the doctor can tell me," Matt said. "She wasn't able to help him over the phone. I'll need to take him up to Missoula to see her."

"How long will it take for her to help him this time?" she asked as her heart began to feel even heavier than before.

"There's no way of knowing, Lindsay. She'll see him next week if he isn't speaking by then.

"The doctor also said that one of the best things we can do until we can get Jimmy up to Missoula is to give him a lot of love and take him places where he would have good memories," Matt added.

"That rules my place out," Lindsay said bitterly. "I've been nothing but bad luck for the little guy."

"Actually, I was thinking just the opposite," Matt countered. "He needs to see you. He adores you, Lindsay."

"I'd love to see him, but I don't think it should be here. Not until he's come out of this latest setback."

"Then why don't you come to our place for dinner tonight?" Matt suggested. "I'm not much of a cook, but I can buy some pizza and ice cream."

"That would be great," Lindsay said, surprised but pleased at the invitation. "What time would you like me to come?"

After settling on a time, Lindsay told Matt about the call from Terrell Edinton. "I'm going to need to stick close around the barn this afternoon until he comes, even though I've got a lot to do. That hay Keith cut for me is about ready to bale, and I still need to finish cutting the rest. But it can wait until tomorrow if it needs to."

"Maybe Keith can help again, Lindsay," he said. "You can talk to him about it tonight. I'm going to go to work this afternoon. My folks will watch Jimmy while Reese and I follow up on a few things."

After Matt hung up, Lindsay sat and stared at the phone. She wasn't seeing it, though—she was seeing Matt Prescott. Her feelings toward him were pleasant in a way she'd never known before. It was a bit unexpected, yet she was not afraid of what was happening. She found herself hoping that a relationship would develop between them.

Finally, she got up, grabbed her hat, and headed outside. She missed the sound of her father's voice as she left the house. Whenever he hadn't accompanied her, he'd always spoken to her as she left. She also missed the greeting of her dog when she went into the yard.

Lindsay busied herself cleaning horse stalls for the next hour. She avoided the one with the roan gelding, although it too needed to be cleaned and fresh sawdust spread on the floor. She looked out of the barn when she heard a truck and trailer pulling up. She suspected it was Grey Sadler. At least, it was someone almost as short as she was, and she didn't know who else would be coming to her place with a trailer who was as small as Grey. She knew he couldn't be over five foot five.

What Grey lacked in size, though, he made up in energy and sheer physical strength. He was muscular and athletic. When he exited the truck, it was with an energetic bounce. He had a smile that lit up his ruddy face like a spotlight. Lindsay had always enjoyed the time she spent with him. She'd even dated him a couple of times in high school. And those dates had been fun. She stepped out of the barn to meet him. "Hi ya, beautiful," he said cheerily. "Sorry about Noah. The world lost a great horseman and a good man when he was killed. Always admired your dad."

"Thanks," Lindsay said. She wondered how many other women he addressed the way he did her. The way he said it was not offensive.

It felt more like a compliment, and he'd spoken that way to her since they were teenagers.

"Sorry that horse kicked you," he said. "I hate to see pretty gals like you get hurt. But it must not have been too bad. Doesn't look to me like you're even limping now."

"I've got a bruise," she said. "But it's not bad. I was distracted by a guy who was here giving me a hard time. I was doing well with the roan before Lucas came by."

"Lucas? He have a last name?" Grey asked.

Lindsay smiled. "Everybody's got a last name."

Grey's face lit up again. "Of course they do," he said. "But did the jerk tell you what his was?"

"Mallory," Lindsay said.

"Lucas Mallory," Grey repeated, the smile fading from his face. "Tall guy, about a foot taller than me and a bit on the heavy side?"

"Yeah, that would be about right."

"Not a handsome chap like myself?" he asked, smiling again.

"That's right." Lindsay smiled too. She couldn't help but like Grey.

"His hair's a little darker than mine?"

Lindsay chuckled. "I'd say. It's very black. Sounds like you know him."

"Yes, but I don't know him well. I've met him in places you don't go and that I shouldn't," he said.

"Do you know him well enough to know if he'd be in a position to buy a ranch? One like mine?" she asked.

Again, Grey's face grew dark and brooding. "I doubt if he could even come up with a good down payment. He'd have to have at least one partner. Why do you ask that?"

"He said he wants to buy mine," Lindsay revealed. "He'd come to look at it."

"Buy yours! You're not going to sell this place, are you? Your daddy would roll over in his grave if he knew you were going to sell."

"I'm not, Grey. That's why I said he was harassing me. He claims that my brother wants to sell it to him."

"Your brother. You mean Dwight?"

"Of course. He's my only brother."

"Yeah, guess he is that. But he's been gone since you and I were just little kids. No offense, but he was always such a creep. I didn't know he was still around."

"No offense taken. I'm afraid Dwight isn't the kind of man my dad wanted him to be. Dad and I hadn't seen him or even heard from him in years. But he showed up the other day."

"Did your Dad leave a will? Not that it's any of my business. But surely he wouldn't have left stuff to a guy he hadn't seen in years and who had no interest in ranching."

"It's okay, Grey. Yeah, he left a will, but only for his personal stuff, and it's pretty much all mine," she began. "Dwight is mentioned, but only if he were to come back within a certain period of time after Dad's death. A year, I think, is what Dad put."

"What about the ranch? Did he leave it to you?"

"It's already mine. I have the deed."

"I'm glad to hear that," Grey said. "Always knew your dad was a shrewd guy. That means there's nothing even to probate in court. So what does your brother think he's doing offering to sell it?"

Lindsay shrugged. "That's the question I have. He can't do anything. I own this place free and clear. I don't have a mortgage on anything, not the cows, not the horses, not the property, not even the house. The only thing I owe on is my truck." She wasn't sure why she was telling Grey all this. But then she also couldn't see that it would hurt. He was, after all, a long-time friend.

Grey shook his head, but he still made no move to go looking for the roan gelding he'd come after. "Lindsay, if either one of those guys comes around here again bothering you, give me a call. I'd be glad to help you out."

"Thanks, Grey, but I'm sure I can handle them. They've got nothing to go on, no legal standing of any kind. And I don't think either one of them would try to hurt me physically."

"But you don't know that, do you?" Grey asked.

"Well, no, I guess not. But I don't think they would."

"Never underestimate to what extremes greed might drive a man. Don't take any chances with either of them. And I'd be glad to help, if you need it," he said sincerely. "Hey, don't you have a dog? I haven't seen one around. What's a ranch without a good cow dog?"

Lindsay's tone changed noticeably. "I had one, my border collie, Prince, until two days ago. Lucas—Lucas Mallory—not only harassed me, but he ran over Prince. Poor dog was killed on the spot. The thing that really tears me up is that Prince survived a wolf attack about two weeks ago and was healing well, and then . . ."

"Oh, Lindsay, I'm sorry to hear that. Wolves, you say? That's what got your father killed, wasn't it?"

"It was. He shot one that had killed a calf over in the forest, then someone shot him," she said, her eyes filling with tears as she spoke.

"That's scary, Lindsay," he said. "We can't be letting these wolf lovers do this to us. What's the sheriff doing about it?"

"Everything he can. He's assigned one deputy to work on practically nothing but wolf cases until they get the matter under control," she said, thinking fondly of Matt as she spoke and looking forward to the evening ahead.

"You've got a lot to deal with right now," he said.

"Apparently so," she responded.

"You be careful, Lindsay," Grey said. "Lucas can be mean."

"I will, believe me," she said.

"Could you use another dog?" he asked.

"I suppose so. I sure miss Prince. Actually, I've got to have one, but I haven't had time to deal with it yet."

"I've got some pups left from the litter my old dog had in early March. You could have one if you like," he offered.

"Really? What breed are they?" she asked.

"Border collie, same as yours was."

"Great. He was a super cow dog. I'd be willing to buy one," she said.

"No, for you they're free," he said.

"I can afford to buy one," Lindsay said seriously.

"Okay, then we'll work something out. But one's yours as soon as you want it. Now, let's have a look at this temperamental old pony. What's he going to be like to load?"

"Not easy, I'm afraid. He has a halter on, but hooking a lead rope onto it could be a trick. Terrell says he had three guys help load him to bring him down here," she said. "And it wasn't easy for them. In fact, they had to rope him."

"Well, that doesn't sound too bad. You and me, we might not be real big, but I think when it comes to horses, we're the equal of any four average cowboys around. Wouldn't you agree?" He was grinning, but she also knew he was quite serious. They might have different ways of handling horses, but there was one thing they had in common. Both of them had no fear of horses, only respect.

Grey backed the truck and trailer into the barn, and Lindsay shut the big door behind him. That way, even if the roan got away from them, he'd be trapped. Outside the other door, Lindsay had set things up so the roan would end up in the round corral if he stormed out of the barn.

It was soon apparent to both of them that if Grey was going to haul the gelding to his place that day, he'd have to be roped. And getting in the small stall with him to do that was out of the question. The roan wasn't about to share with anyone. So they let him into the round corral where he stomped and pranced for a couple of minutes before calming down. Grey shook out a lariat, making a large loop. Then he stood and studied the roan, who was eyeing him maliciously. Lindsay stood on the far side of the fence, watching them, her heart racing. She wanted so badly to be in there instead of Grey. She was still confident that she could handle this horse if given the time.

"I sure wish Terrell had let me have another go at him," Lindsay said, making her thoughts heard. "I still think I could have gentled him."

Grey turned and looked at her. "You're serious?" He walked back to the fence and grinned. "I'm in no hurry today. Maybe I could watch you work him for an hour or two. At least you could make it easier for me to put a loop around his neck. And who knows, I might even learn something."

"Grey, look out!" Lindsay shouted desperately as the roan suddenly started across the corral toward the cowboy.

9

The gelding thundered across the corral, charging toward Grey just as he'd done with Lindsay. His mouth was open with his lips drawn back, his nostrils flared, and his eyes shot fire. For the briefest moment, Lindsay was sure the horse was going to get Grey. But after the initial shock, Grey moved like a striking snake. Dropping his lariat, the young man leaped nimbly to the top of the fence and vaulted over just a fraction of a second before the horse reached him. The horse slammed into the sturdy steel poles of the corral with a thundering crash, but the fence, built for such incidents, held firm.

Lindsay watched Grey anxiously as his ruddy face grew purple, his eyes narrowed, and he slowly began to clench his gloved fists. He said a couple of offensive words and then added, "I guess that critter needs a lesson."

"Not on my place, Grey," Lindsay said firmly, stepping between the cowboy and the fence. "You were saying you'd like to see me work with him. I'd like to do that, but I don't want him stirred up any more. Terrell doesn't need to know. Anyway, maybe I can make this easier for both of us."

Grey shuffled his feet and looked past her at the horse. He was silent for a moment, but the anger began to leave his face. "I can teach him a thing or two," he grumbled.

"I'm sure you can. But I can too. Would you let me have another go at it?"

"I like you, Lindsay. You've always been a good friend. I don't want to see you get hurt, and that's exactly what that horse will do to you. How would I explain that to Terrell?"

"I know how to take care of myself. I'll be careful, and I'll watch him closely. Please. Give me a chance," she pleaded.

Grey took off his hat and ran his hand through his thick red hair. He looked genuinely worried. "Okay, I'll do it for you, beautiful," he finally said. "I wouldn't do it for anyone else. But you be careful. I'll be right here, and if that horse makes a move toward you, I'll have a loop on him so fast he won't know where it came from."

"Thanks, Grey. You're a dear," she said. "Let me get my whip, and I'll go to work."

"Whip?" Grey said, surprised. "I thought you didn't believe in striking a horse."

"It's not to hurt him with it, just give him an occasional sting. Just watch and you might learn something," she said. A couple of minutes later, Lindsay was in the corral, moving cautiously toward the gelding. She held the whip, which she cracked so loudly it sounded like a pistol shot. On cue the gelding whirled and started trotting around the edge of the corral.

For the next hour Lindsay didn't once allow her concentration to drift. She kept the horse moving steadily, faster and faster around the corral, while she stayed in the center, never allowing the horse to get behind her. She walked in a tight circle as it ran. From time to time, she'd turn the horse with a crack of the whip and send him running the other way.

She was so busy at her task, that she didn't notice when Grey moved away from the corral.

* * *

It was the sound of an engine and the crunch of tires on gravel that had drawn Grey's attention away from the corral. He was fascinated watching her. Seeds of doubt as to his own methods had been planted, and he wanted to watch every move she made. But he also didn't want to have her distracted by a visitor. He hurried around the barn to see who had come and what they wanted.

Grey recognized Lucas Mallory the moment the tall man stepped out of his old pickup. "Howdy, Lucas," he said, trying to appear friendly. "What brings you out this way?"

"Came to see Lindsay, Grey. Same could be asked of you. What are you doin' here?"

Grey forced a smile. "Nothing much. Just came to help my friend with a horse. But she seems to be doing fine on her own."

"Guess I'll give her a break from it," Lucas said. "I need to talk to her about the ranch here."

"What about the ranch?" Grey asked, trying hard to stay calm but determined not to allow anyone to interfere with Lindsay while she was working with the roan.

"I'm thinkin' about buying this place, but I need to know a little more about it. She knows what I want. I talked to her the other day. I told her I'd be back when I had a little more time to look around."

"I'm guessing there's nothing she can tell you that I can't. She already told me what her plans are. She isn't selling her ranch."

"Actually, it's not hers to sell, or to keep, for that matter. Her brother is older, and he's entitled to this place, you know, what with her old man meetin' an untimely death and all. She isn't goin' to have any choice. The ranch is going to be sold, and I'm interested. I'm here today to take a look at the place." Lucas started to step around Grey, but the smaller man moved quickly to block his path.

"She can't be disturbed right now," Grey said, his anger beginning to bubble up. "She's busy with a horse."

"I'm not interested in the horse," Lucas growled. "I came to see her, and I intend to do just that—now."

"I'm afraid not. I'm going to have to ask you to leave," Grey said.

"You ain't got no business askin' me to do anything," Lucas shot back. He stepped toward Grey, towering over him by a foot.

"You already got her hurt by that horse once," Grey accused. "You're not doing it again. Now get off this property."

Lucas looked at Grey with surprise. Then he started to laugh. "And who's goin' to make me go?" he asked. "A little guy like you? Don't make me laugh. I can make hamburger out of you in a minute flat."

"Listen, Lucas. I'm serious. Lindsay is a friend of mine. She doesn't want to be disturbed right now, and she isn't selling her ranch. So please leave."

"Why don't you leave instead?" Lucas asked.

"I will in time. My truck and trailer are in the barn. When I go, it will be with the horse I came to pick up, the one Lindsay's working with right now."

"Get out of my way, Grey," Lucas said menacingly. Like Grey, his temper was flaring. "I'm through foolin' around here." He started to go around Grey again, but Grey shuffled and blocked his path. "That's it," Lucas said as he brought his fists up.

Grey's anger had finally boiled over. Before Lucas could take a swing at him, Grey threw a punch to his solar plexus that bent the big man double. With his opponent's face down within his range, Grey threw a series of punches in such rapid succession that Lucas couldn't even begin to fight. The last one caught him squarely on the nose. Blood spurted out steadily. In almost the same instant, the big man toppled over.

"Get on your feet and get out of here," Grey ordered. "You've caused enough trouble around this place." The sudden violence had drained Grey of his anger. He stood over Lucas, watching him bleed and struggle to get up. He reached a hand down. "Here, let me help you up. Then you can get in your truck and leave. And I would suggest you not come back here."

Lucas was fighting to catch his breath as he wiped the blood from his face with the back of his hands. He tried to talk, but succeeded only in grunting. He ignored Grey's hand and finally got to his feet unsteadily. It took a minute before he tried to walk, but he was back to his truck before he was able to speak. Then, leaning against the door, he turned and said, "I oughta call the cops on you."

"You do that. And then you can try to explain to them how a man who is half your weight and a foot shorter was able to whip you like the cur you are."

The two men stared at each other for a moment. Lucas finally said, "We don't need cops, but you will want to watch your backside. I'll get you for this, Grey."

"Are you threatening me again? Look where that got you a minute ago," Grey said as he moved toward Lucas, who was fumbling with the door handle of his truck.

Lucas said nothing more as he finally managed to get in his truck, start the engine, and put it in gear. Then he rolled down his window.

"You knocked a tooth loose," he said as he spat a tooth from his mouth. "Your day's comin', boy. Count on it." He left in a hurry, scattering gravel as he accelerated.

* * *

Lindsay had allowed the horse to stop and was speaking quietly to him when she noticed that Grey was gone. Wondering what had happened to him, she decided he must have grown bored watching her. She again concentrated on the gelding. Her work from Monday had apparently done some good. The horse was doing exactly what she knew he eventually would. She just hadn't expected it to be so soon after the disastrous way things had ended that day.

The gelding was chewing furiously and his ears were turned toward her. Both were signs that he was accepting her as master. Lindsay clucked, stood in a less threatening position to the horse with her side to him, and waited patiently. Out of the corner of her eye, she saw Grey approaching. She hoped he wouldn't speak. He didn't. He stopped well short of the fence and stood very still. The big roan didn't even look his way. Soon he stepped toward Lindsay. Then he took another step. Remaining motionless, she kept making soothing sounds. Before long, he had come right up to her. She slowly lifted a hand and touched his face. He flinched only slightly and then let her begin to stroke him. After a few moments, she turned her back on him and began to walk away. He followed. She stopped and he stopped. She again began to gently rub him.

The worst was behind her. She'd gotten through his stubborn defenses. She stood there with him for several minutes. Then she gently shooed him away, and once again she had him moving in a steady circle around the pen. A half hour later she hooked a lead rope to his halter and led him over to the gate.

"He's ready for you now," she said to Grey, who was grinning from ear to ear. "Let's try to load him in a minute."

"I'm humbled," he said. Lindsay knew he was sincere. "I've never seen anything like it. Will you teach me how to do that? I've heard a lot about the method you and Noah use, but I always figured it was all blown out of proportion."

"You've just got to speak the horse's language," she said with a smile. "And you've got to be patient. I'd be glad to show you what I do, but I know that with your love of horses, it will come naturally to you once you begin," she said. As she was speaking to him, she noticed that he had blood on his shirt and hands. "Grey, what happened? You're all bloody. Did you get cut or something?"

"No, I'm fine. It's nothing," he said.

She decided to let it go for the moment. "Why don't you open the gate and come in. Let's see how he is with you."

Grey slowly approached the roan. After running his hands down his neck and along his back, he said, "I can't believe this is the same animal that attacked me only ninety minutes ago."

"Well, the rest is up to you," she said, wishing it were not true. She'd love to finish breaking this beautiful animal.

"No, I don't think so," Grey said. "I'll explain to Edinton. You deserve to finish breaking this horse yourself. But, in exchange for a pup, I'd like to watch you take the next few steps with him. Is that okay with you?"

"Really, Grey? That would be great," she said, "if Edinton agrees, of course."

"So, is this all you'd normally do in one day?" he asked.

"Sometimes, sometimes not," she said. "We can probably have a saddle on this horse shortly. If you still have some time, let's do it. Then you can tell me about the blood that's all over you."

"It's a deal," he said.

For the next thirty minutes, Lindsay worked with the gelding, rubbing him with a sack and working her whip all over, not striking with it but just touching him and then rubbing him underneath his belly, under his tail, on his head, neck, and back. Next, she introduced him to the saddle blanket and then the saddle. Fifteen minutes later, the horse was saddled and running around the corral with the saddle on his back. He had bucked when Lindsay first tightened the cinch, but not for long. "That was just for show," she told Grey with a grin.

"So, when will you ride him?" he asked.

"Actually, I think he's about ready for that. Give me a few more minutes here, and I'll get on," she said.

"Would you like me to?" he asked.

"I can do it, but after I do, if you'd like, you can ride for a little bit. But we won't take him out of this corral today," she said.

As always, when the time came to get on, Lindsay was slow and gentle. She started by simply putting a foot in a stirrup on the right side and then on the left. Next, she put her weight in the stirrup but didn't swing into the saddle. She did that on both sides for several minutes. When she finally mounted, she took her time. She lifted her leg across the saddle, waited for a few moments, and then slowly settled herself in. Next she pushed the toe of her right boot into the stirrup and just sat there.

She glanced over at Grey. He was grinning. "I've never seen anything like it, beautiful," he said. "You're an absolutely amazing woman."

Lindsay then dismounted and mounted the horse several times, alternating between his left and right sides. After that, she mounted and settled herself firmly in the saddle. "I'll see if he'll move now," she said. She soon had him walking around the corral, making no attempt to change his speed. After a few minutes, she dismounted, exhilarated as she always was at this point in the breaking of a new horse. Lindsay smiled and said to Grey, "Next time I'll run him. I don't like to push that. You ready for your turn?"

Grey had a short ride. "Rather uneventful," he told her, "by my standards. But amazing. This is actually fun."

After the roan was rubbed down, led back to his stall in the barn, and turned loose, Lindsay said, "Okay, Grey, now you can tell me about the blood."

"You had a visitor," he said. "I sent him away so he wouldn't distract you."

Instantly alarmed, she asked him who it was.

"Your old friend, Lucas Mallory," he said with a lopsided grin.

"Grey, what happened?" she asked. "I take it he fought you."

"Well, not exactly," he said. "I told him that it would be a good idea if he left, but he said he was going to talk to you. I explained that you were breaking a horse and that he shouldn't disturb you. He insisted and told me I couldn't stop him. He was wrong."

"You made him bleed," she said tentatively.

"Just his nose. Well, and his mouth too, I guess. I think he lost a tooth."

10

A secret meeting was held that night in Great Falls. The group called themselves the Wild Animal Protection Society. Their leader, a fiery man known to the group as Avenger, nursed a virulent hatred for the ranchers of Montana and Wyoming. He was esteemed by his followers as their leader in the movement to protect wolves and other wildlife. He had surrounded himself with activists of similar thinking. However, they were unlike the normal activists who protested, wrote letters to the editor, and frequented the state legislature. These activists were prone to whatever type of violence it took to impose their will on others. Some had come to their extreme views on their own; others had allowed themselves to be indoctrinated by Avenger.

Six men and three women made up the secret society, and each had been assigned a code name to use in their associations with each other. In the meeting that night, they addressed each other by those names as they plotted their next move against the ranchers.

Avenger spoke to the group at the beginning of the meeting. "A lot of people understand that the cause of the wolf and other wildlife is just. Without these people we wouldn't be able to create the stir we need to get politicians to listen to our view. The activists, with your quiet encouragement, are great at creating rallies, picketing sites, writing letters to the newspapers, and so forth. But none of them understands that more extreme measures must be taken if we are to succeed. That, of course, is why we keep most of our activities secret from them. At this point we can't afford to let anyone know exactly what we're doing to move our cause ahead. That's why we as a group can never mingle with them. Our interactions must be separate."

"They'd be surprised if they knew about us and how powerful we are," one of the members said with a grin. "We really have the law on the run. They don't have any idea what will happen next."

"Don't be so sure of yourself, Retaliator," Avenger warned. "We can't afford to underestimate the law. Our strength comes in our ability to operate in secret. And, of course, you know that's why we never refer to each other by our legal names. It's also why I've asked each of you to obtain identities separate from both your legal names and the names we know each other by in our group. Use your legal names or code names with each other. But when you mingle with activists and protestors, use assumed names. Remember, this is to protect each other."

Retaliator hung his head, momentarily rebuffed. One of the others, a man code-named Enforcer, nodded in agreement. "We always need to be vigilant," he said.

Avenger smiled appreciatively and said, "Thank you, Enforcer, and the rest of you. I appreciate your loyalty. Now, I'd like reports from each of you concerning your latest activities. Enforcer, let's begin with you."

Enforcer was enthusiastic about the work. He truly loved wolves. He also enjoyed mingling with the activists outside their clandestine group and stirring them up before quietly slipping away to let them receive the ranchers' wrath. He'd been successful in aggravating a number of people in one protest so that ultimately their actions provoked an attack from the sons of some local ranchers. He'd managed to slip away just before the violence began and long before the police arrived. No one knew that he had been the source of the provocation that had led to a big brawl and the arrest of several of the ranchers' sons.

Following his report, he was congratulated by the others.

Then Avenger said, "Defender, you'll be next."

But the activist known as Defender wanted to discuss some things with Avenger in private. "I'll talk to you about what happened after the meeting is over," he said.

"No, your work needs to be shared with the rest. Remember, the nine of us have no secrets from each other, only from those not of our group."

That wasn't entirely true, as both Avenger and Defender knew, but Defender knew better than to let others in the group know that. Avenger went on. "We have agreed to be open with one another in all of our activities. That's how we build unity. That's how we survive as a secret society. So, Defender, speak."

"Well," Defender said. "I did as Avenger asked." He went on to report only those of his latest activities that he knew Avenger wanted reported to the group. The other things he concealed. He reported about some scouting he'd done in Yellowstone Park. He'd located a large wolf pack and felt several could be removed with no one knowing the difference. He'd also packed in several pounds of prime beef that he'd spread around for them to eat. Avenger thought it might help to habituate the wolves to a beef diet. The remoteness of the area in the park that the pack ranged through was encouraging to the others. Very few people ever went there.

"Good," Avenger said after a short discussion. "We appreciate what you've done. Guardian, it's your turn."

The woman called Guardian was a particularly devoted and loyal follower of Avenger. She was also respected, and in some ways feared, by the others. She was large boned, nearly six feet in height, muscular, and not an ounce overweight. She wore her blonde hair long and straight, but kept it pulled back from her face. Her eyes, a very dark blue, revealed a combination of intelligence and passion. She was one of the more successful members of the group in quietly gathering public support without appearing to be a major player. She had recently been successful in getting a letter-writing campaign going and had filled her assignment so well that another woman had received the credit. They discussed her success for a moment before Avenger called on the young man known to the rest as Retaliator.

Retaliator was young, rash, and hot-headed. He was in the group partly because of his total lack of fear but also because of his hatred of authority. Following Retaliator's report about mingling with a small group of people in the northern part of the state, Avenger issued a reminder. "Don't let your temper jeopardize our success," he warned the young man sternly. That was a constant concern Avenger had with Retaliator.

Protector was next to report. The son of a rancher, he'd been kicked off the ranch by his family because of his laziness. He, like

Avenger, hated ranchers and was willing to do anything to hurt them. He reported on tidbits of conversations between ranch hands that he had overhead in some of the local bars, relating what was being said by them about the activists. Avenger was pleased. "Well done, Protector. That information has been most helpful."

The meeting continued with reports from Reactor, Keeper, and Harrier. Each report was discussed, and then suggestions were solicited for where to place wolves next. Since a couple of the ones in the vicinity of the Lazy F Ranch had been shot, Protector suggested that more be loosed there. Harrier and Keeper, the other women in the group, suggested a ranch in Park County called the Running R. Following some discussion, they finally decided that the Lazy F should be targeted next, followed by the Running R.

Avenger suggested that they still needed one more ranch to target. "I know a guy who is part owner of a ranch that's called the S/S," Defender commented. "His older brother is the other partner. I over-heard him in a restaurant telling some other cowboys that he'd kill every wolf in the park if he got the chance," he added.

"What's his name?" Avenger asked.

"Grey. I think the last name's Sadler, but I'm not sure. I know it starts with an *S*. That's where the S/S brand comes from."

"It's Sadler, all right," Guardian said. "I've heard of him. He breaks horses some. Has a bit of a temper, too. He's a small, red-headed guy who thinks he's tough. If he's badmouthing the wolves, then I agree with Defender that his ranch would be a good choice. Like Lindsay Flemming's Lazy F, it borders the forest."

"Do you know where that ranch is located?" Avenger asked.

"Not exactly. Do you, Defender?" Guardian asked.

"Yeah, I know about where it is," Defender responded. "It's in Sweet Grass County. I'll find out exactly where it is. Then I can show you when we have wolves ready to turn loose there."

Avenger nodded. "Good," he said. "We'll place the S/S ahead of the Running R on our list. It's time someone teaches people like Grey Sadler a lesson."

The list of ranches to be targeted complete, the group began to discuss the capture of some of the wolves Defender had located. If Avenger and his people were caught tranquilizing and removing wolves from the park, they could end up in federal prison. That wasn't on any of their lists of places to go.

* * *

The last member of the society had finally left. With a sigh, Avenger pushed himself back from the table at the front of the room. This cloak-and-dagger business was taxing. He reached into the large drawer under the tabletop and pulled out a Transformer—a child's toy. He quickly shuffled it from hand to hand, transforming the figure and watching it intently.

"They're all just like you, Transformer," he said. "I've given each one a fancy name—Defender, Protector, Keeper, Retaliator—and special assignments, a little authority. Now they think they've gone from common to exceptional, and they're prepared to save the wolves of the world. What they don't know is that they're just my little plastic men and women. My plan, the big plan, isn't theirs—never was. But you can bet your life they'll help carry it out, and they won't have a clue that they're doing it. Let them use their two-bit code names and strut around behind closed doors convincing each other that they're the Knights of the Round Table. But we know the truth, Transformer. They're really my pawns."

* * *

It had been a comfortable, pleasant evening, but it was getting late. Keith had gone to his room to read a good mystery. He loved to read, and since that kept him from watching too much TV, like many of his friends did, Matt encouraged his reading. He just made sure that what he read was decent.

Jimmy was finally asleep, dreaming whatever it was that the boy dreamed about during his recent troubled nights. It had been difficult getting him to bed that night. He seemed frightened of something. Matt was sure that if his son would talk, he'd tell him what was bothering him.

It was Lindsay who'd finally succeeded in getting Jimmy to bed, but it had required over thirty minutes in a rocking chair. The boy had let her take him in her arms and sing to her. She held him tightly, went through a dozen Primary songs, and finally smoothed his hair with her hand for several minutes before he drifted off. Matt had sat and watched the two of them, relishing the sweet sound of Lindsay's voice and grateful for the obvious affection she had for his son.

Once Jimmy was asleep, Lindsay and Matt had gone out onto the deck in the front of his house and sat talking for longer than either of them realized. Finally, Matt looked at his watch. "Oh, my," he said. "When did it get so late? I'm sorry you have to drive home alone at such an hour. I wish I could go with you, but I don't dare leave Jimmy alone with Keith too long. He doesn't sleep well, and when he starts screaming, which he does two or three times every night, I need to be where I can get right to him and calm him down."

"Oh, Matt, he's got to get better soon," Lindsay said earnestly. "It breaks my heart."

"Dr. Lubek says that violence and frights will continue to affect him this way for some time. But this is a particularly bad episode, and she doesn't know why. Seeing Prince run over must be part of it, but I keep wondering if there's something more. If he would just come out of it again and talk, we could probably get to the root of this latest problem and solve it for him."

"I'll keep praying for him," Lindsay said.

"Thanks. That's the most important thing any of us can do for him."

"Yes, I agree. And I'd better head for the ranch. I have a lot to do tomorrow. I promised Terrell Edinton that I'd work with his gelding every day for the next few days, and I've also got the haying to do. It will help a lot that Keith is coming out again. He's a good worker."

"I'm glad Terrell changed his mind about letting you break his horse," Matt said.

"Thanks to Grey Sadler. He called Terrell after he left my place, and Terrell called me. Grey had it all worked out, so I didn't have to say anything except agree to keep working with him. Terrell was really nice about it. It was almost like he hadn't called me before and told me I'd lost my touch," she said.

"I hope Grey learned something, Lindsay. I've heard that he isn't particularly gentle with horses. He breaks them the old western cowboy way. Your method is a lot better."

"Honestly, I think he was impressed. He'll be back at ten in the morning to watch me work with the roan again. He says he wants to try my method. I hope he will."

Lindsay stood up, and Matt did the same. He took her hand in his and together they walked to her pickup. Then she turned to face him. "Matt, thanks for such a lovely evening."

"You're welcome, but you're the one that made it nice," Matt said as he opened the door for her. She hesitated, looking up into his face, smiling. Neither said a word. But as if on cue, Lindsay stretched upward and Matt bent down. Their lips came together briefly at first, then with an urgency neither of them had realized they felt. Their arms encircled each other, and even after the unexpected kiss ended, they continued to embrace.

Matt spoke first. "Where did that come from?" he asked with a grin.

"I don't know, but I liked it," she said. Then she gently pulled away from him. "Call me tomorrow. Let me know how Jimmy is."

"I will," he said as he helped her into the truck. "If you'll call me when you get home."

She smiled. "I'll be fine," she said. "You don't have to worry about me."

"Please. I'll still be up," he said.

"Okay," she said affectionately. "If you'd like me to."

Long after Lindsay left, Matt stayed outside. He wandered around his yard, walked through his barn, which wasn't even one-third the size of Lindsay's, and then sat on his porch. The ranch was comfortable, although a little on the small side.

Matt knew that before his father, Joseph, had begun teaching at Montana State University, he had made some big plans for his land. He had decided to experiment with new rangeland conservation techniques on the ranch. Because of a deal Joseph had worked out with his older brother, Thomas, he would increase the size of the ranch to 4,500 acres. Joseph knew he could increase productivity in his hay fields and put the grazing lands to better use. It was the old idea of minimizing expenses and maximizing profits, but on an agricultural scale.

The details had never been spelled out precisely for Matt, but he knew that somehow Thomas's son-in-law and daughter obtained inside information about a huge resort area to be developed between Bozeman and West Yellowstone. Two days before Thomas was to sign over his land to Joseph, he instead made a land swap with someone else—someone lacking the inside information he possessed. The land he received in exchange for his ranch later became part of Big Sky Resort, Montana's premier winter and summer resort, complete with condos, lodges, restaurants, hiking, biking, golf, fly fishing, white-water rafting, incredible scenery, wildlife, acres of skiing and snowboarding terrain. Thomas made millions and built himself a mansion. Joseph, on the other hand, could not afford to be a full-time rancher on his small spread. He finished a PhD and taught others the principles of land management that he knew would save many Montana farms and ranches.

Eventually, he and Matt's mother, Ellen, moved into town and sold the ranch to Matt. Sometimes Matt would start to contemplate the "what ifs," but tonight he simply petted Claw. Tonight he had real worries. "I wish you could talk," he said to the big dog. "I know there's something you could tell me that would help me know how to help Jimmy."

Not until he figured Lindsay should be just about home did he go back inside. Then he checked on his sons. Jimmy was still sleeping peacefully. Matt told himself it was because of the soothing effect Lindsay had on him. He softly shut the door to his son's bedroom and then checked beneath the door of Keith's room. He could see that the light was out. He must have finished reading and gone to sleep.

Matt wandered back into the kitchen, fixed a slice of toast, poured a glass of cold buttermilk, and sat down at his table. He kept looking at his watch, thinking that surely Lindsay should be home by now. He began to worry, and as he worried, he thought about Carol and Sarah. He hadn't worried too much about them that tragic night. He knew that Carol had always been a careful driver. She never continued to drive if she got too sleepy. And she didn't usually drive too fast. He'd been on duty that night, and he'd been busy. He'd just assumed that they would all be home when he got off his shift. Carol and the kids had made the Bozeman–Jackson Hole trip so many times over the years that it wasn't something to fret about.

As he thought about that night, a heavy sadness engulfed him. It had been over a year, and yet as he thought about Carol, he could almost hear her calling him to come to bed like she used to do when he sat up too late reading. He felt weighed down with loneliness. He thought about the wreck that night, and he got up from the table and began to pace, his toast half-eaten, his buttermilk barely touched.

It had never made sense that Carol had lost control on a straight stretch of highway and rolled the van the way she did, even though it was a stormy night. Jimmy had been unable to tell him much of anything. All he seemed to remember was that Claw had found him and had cried with him. It seemed like history was repeating itself with Jimmy again. There was something he knew about that day out at the Lazy F that had given him a terrible fright, but he was unable to verbalize it. That night the previous year, he'd been able to talk, but he simply couldn't remember anything. The silence that time came a day or two later. Deep down, Matt was almost certain that if Jimmy could remember, he would shed light on what had happened. And when he did, Matt felt he would learn that the wreck had not been due to carelessness on Carol's part.

He stopped pacing and looked at his watch again. He wished Lindsay would call. He just needed to hear her voice, to be assured that she was okay, that nothing bad had happened to her as it had to his wife and daughter.

At that moment it occurred to Matt that feeling a strong affection for another woman had made him vulnerable. He wondered if he could handle the worry that came with a relationship. It had been easy with Carol, but things were different now. He'd learned that bad things could happen, even terrible things, to those he cared about.

As he waited impatiently for Lindsay to call and assure him that nothing bad had happened to her, he began to doubt himself. He hadn't really thought too much about where this relationship might lead. As he thought about it now, however, he realized that it could end up in marriage. And he wasn't sure that would be such a good idea. He wondered if marrying Lindsay would make him so vulnerable to worry and stress that he would make both their lives miserable. He wondered if he should end this relationship now, while it was still new, before it followed a course that would make things worse for both of them.

The more he wondered, the stronger the doubts became. The fact that Lindsay hadn't called when he knew she should have been home some time ago only added to his concern. Maybe she didn't understand what caring for someone else was all about, making it hard for her to remember something as simple as a phone call. She couldn't know how worried he was because she'd never had to worry in this way.

The longer Matt paced and waited for the phone call that he was now sure wasn't going to occur—the call she'd simply forgotten to make—the more determined he became to put this relationship aside before it became too serious. He enjoyed being with her. There was no doubt about that. And his boys liked her. In fact, Jimmy adored her. But he was becoming more convinced that allowing it to develop would eventually cause them both a lot of pain. It was almost a relief when he heard Jimmy cry out. He hurried to the boy's room, lifted him from his bed, and held him close, soothing him, comforting him, expressing his love for him.

After a while, Jimmy settled down, but Matt continued to hold him, no longer expecting the call he'd been hoping for. In fact, he now hoped she wouldn't call. He wasn't sure what he'd say. He needed time to think before he shared his doubts with Lindsay and ended the relationship. It would probably be best to just be friends, the way they had been before. That was safer.

* * *

Lindsay trudged through the pasture, far beyond her house, shining her light this way and that. From the moment she'd driven into her yard and heard the howl of a wolf and the frightened, distant bawling of her cows and calves, she suspected that wolves were again into her cattle. If this kept up, she would be forced to give up the ranch. She couldn't afford to lose many more calves and still pay the never-ending bills.

She missed Prince. She now had a vet bill for him, adding to her expenses, and she'd lost him anyway. Life seemed to be that way. Nothing ever went perfectly smoothly for anyone. Her dad had told her that many times, and he'd been right. Of course, she would have paid to help Prince when he was injured, even if she'd known that in the end he would die.

She thought about Grey. He said he'd bring his pups tomorrow, and then she could choose one of them. She needed a dog, both for company and for help on the ranch.

With Prince along, she would have found where the wolf had attacked by now. And she would be less nervous than she was all alone. She clutched her rifle tighter, shined her light around again, and then shut it off. She looked beyond the pasture at the shadowy trees far to the south. Her stomach tightened as she remembered how she and Matt had been shot at just a few nights ago. *What if those same people are out there again?* she asked herself. She was probably foolish for walking out here in the darkness alone, looking for another dead or injured calf.

She couldn't see any lights like there had been the other night. But why would there be? It was just an unlucky coincidence that some of the activists had been on her place when a wolf struck.

Or was it? She felt chills run up her spine as that disturbing thought lingered. Maybe she should head back, she told herself. She was fairly sure there was one. She hoped it was only one, not more. She wished she'd driven out here in the truck like she and Matt had the other evening. But she'd chosen to walk because she didn't want anyone to see her truck and shoot at it.

She wished Matt was with her right now. And even as she wished it she remembered that she'd promised to call him when she got home. But the cry of the wolf had sent her urgently into her fields, and she'd completely forgotten. She wanted to call him right then, despite how late it was, but she couldn't. Her cell phone was in her purse, and her purse was still in her truck. She knew she would feel foolish calling so late. Surely he knew she was okay. She'd explain tomorrow when she called him about another wolf attack. He'd understand.

Lindsay felt the need to finish up and get back to the house. She began to run toward where she'd heard the frightened bawling of the cattle, shining her light ahead of her. But it was difficult to see, and she stumbled and fell hard. Her rifle and flashlight flew from her hands when she tried to catch herself. For a moment she lay in the darkness and cried in frustration before realizing that the light was no longer shining. She wasn't hurt, just overwhelmed, but she needed her light to continue her search. She felt around and soon recovered the rifle. Then she found the flashlight. No light. The bulb must have broken when she'd dropped it.

Drying her tears, she got to her feet and began to make her way back home with only the light of a few stars to direct her. By the time she reached her truck, retrieved her purse, and headed for the house, it was well after one in the morning. She felt foolish calling Matt this late, but she'd promised, so she dialed his number.

She counted as it rang. She was up to seven and about to hang up when Matt finally answered. "What took you so long?" he asked.

He sounded angry and she was taken aback. "I'm sorry. I forgot to call when I got here," she said.

"Are you okay?" he asked.

"Yes, I'm fine," she said, fighting back another outburst of tears. "I'm sorry if I woke you."

"You didn't. I haven't been to bed yet. I've been up with Jimmy, and I've been worrying about you. What woke you? Surely you've been asleep after all this time," he said.

"No, I haven't slept either." She thought about telling him why she'd forgotten to call, but she decided against it. She didn't want to worry him about the wolves right now with all he had to worry about with his son.

"Well, we both better try to get some sleep now," Matt said. "I'll call you tomorrow. You and I need to talk."

Lindsay was stung. Unless she misheard or misunderstood what he'd just said, Matt was having second thoughts about their relationship. Did her not calling like she'd promised make him that angry? *What have I done? For the first time in my life, I actually care for someone. Is it over already?*

11

After hanging up his phone, Matt felt like kicking himself. The very sound of Lindsay's voice had reminded him of what a wonderful person she was. And he remembered how fresh the loss of her father still was. He'd been thoughtless, and he felt terrible about it. To add to his guilt, she'd sounded sincerely sorry for not calling earlier. She must have been feeling really bad about it or she wouldn't have called him that late when she finally remembered.

He not only felt guilty, he felt selfish. He felt like a heel.

What if he did have to worry some? Wasn't she worth it?

Matt dialed Lindsay's number, but before it began to ring, he hung up. How often would this happen if he let this budding relationship develop? And how miserable would he make her over the years? She was the one he was thinking about, he told himself. It wasn't fair to make her life miserable. She deserved happiness with a man who didn't bring so much extra baggage into the relationship.

He'd never watched over Carol's shoulder, and it wouldn't be fair to watch over Lindsay's. Yet he was so afraid that he would. And he was sure that such a thing would be hard on her. After all, she had practically run the ranch by herself for years and had gained an independence that would be hard to overcome. Once he fell into justification mode, Matt convinced himself that another reason not to let this thing develop was his boys. Lindsay was so young and had so much life—so much enthusiasm—in her. It seemed unfair to burden her with an instant family. It would be especially unfair to give her the weight of caring for an emotionally scarred boy like Jimmy.

No, he couldn't allow their friendship to continue to move in the direction it had so unexpectedly taken. By the time he finally fell asleep,

Matt had persuaded himself that he was doing the right thing for Lindsay by quelling their relationship. He would cover all the reasons with her tomorrow, and he convinced himself that she would agree with him when she looked at every issue in the bright light of day.

* * *

It was a beautiful morning—a gorgeous blue sky enveloped Montana's Big Sky Country as far as the eye could see. The sun was shining brightly and birds were singing songs of celebration in the tall trees surrounding Lindsay's yard. Her horses neighed a greeting when the door to the house slammed shut behind her—they knew she was coming. The roses alongside the house were as beautiful as she'd ever seen them, and they smelled intoxicating. A rooster crowed, and she could hear her hens cackling. Her big tom cat came up and rubbed his yellow fur against her leg, begging her to pet him. Yes, it was a beautiful morning.

Lindsay felt miserable.

During the few hours she'd been in bed, she'd tossed and turned and worried. It wasn't the wolves or the loss of her calves that had disturbed her rest. It wasn't the threat to the ranch that her seditious brother was making. It wasn't even the still-fresh sorrow over the death of her father. No, it was the words Matt had uttered in their short phone conversation.

We need to talk.

Those four words sounded so ominous. There was more to that sentence than one might see on the surface, she was certain of that. She'd betrayed his trust by not calling as she'd promised. She had been so foolish to forget something that apparently was so important to him. But it was done now. She couldn't imagine the hurt she must have caused him by her thoughtlessness. She prayed it wasn't too late to salvage their relationship, but she had the sinking feeling that it might be. She suddenly began to miss her father more than ever. This was something she could have talked to him about. And he would have given her wise counsel. She felt fresh tears come. Oh, how she needed her father right now.

But he was gone. In the barn, she fell to her knees beside a bale of hay. Her Heavenly Father wasn't gone. She poured out her heart to

Him. Although she had already prayed that morning, it had not been with the same intensity. When she finally got up and brushed the dirt off her jeans, Lindsay felt a little better. This would take time, she decided, and she would simply need to be patient.

She forced herself to do her chores. Then she went to the field and moved her water lines. She baled hay until it was time to work with the roan gelding. By the time she got back to the barn, Grey was already there, and it was five minutes after ten. He grinned and said, "Good morning, beautiful. Are you ready to teach?"

"I'll just do what I usually do," she said glumly. "And you'll need to watch, that's all."

The ready smile dropped from Grey's face. "Hey, Lindsay, what's wrong? You seem rather blue today. That's not like you."

She couldn't tell Grey about her troubles with Matt. That was a personal matter. So she said, "Wolves again—in the night. I haven't even searched this morning to see what damage they did. I looked last night, but I didn't find anything."

"Hey, we can go have a look in a minute. I'll help you," he said soothingly. "But first, come look at these pups. They're in the truck."

Lindsay had been so wrapped up in her worries that morning that she'd forgotten all about the puppy Grey had promised to bring. She followed him to his pickup. He had brought three for her to choose from. They were tied in the bed of his truck so they couldn't jump out. After he let them loose and placed them on the ground, the smallest of the three, one with more white on it than the others, ran straight to Lindsay. The two larger ones began to scamper around her yard.

She picked up the little one, checked and found that it was a female, and said, "I'd like this little girl."

"But you haven't even looked closely at the others," he protested. "They're both males and bigger than her."

She smiled. "That's okay. This little princess chose me. She's the one I want."

"What will you call her?" he asked, grinning. "I haven't given any of them names."

"Princess, of course. My Prince has been replaced by Princess."

"Well, that was easy. I hope you'll like her."

"She's already cheered up my day," Lindsay said, stroking her new puppy affectionately.

"So I see. How about if we let the pups come with us while we go check your cattle?"

They put the two male pups in the back of the truck where Grey tied them again. Then he and Lindsay drove his truck to the pasture, Princess riding in the front on Lindsay's lap. The wolves had made their kill over a mile from the house. There wasn't much left but bones and hide. "There was more than one here," Grey said coldly. "We've got to do something about these wolves. That must have been a beautiful calf."

"It was. Dad knew how to breed cattle. We have good ones. But the wolves are making short work of them."

"I'm sorry. We've got to stop them, Lindsay. If they'd stay in the park, it would be okay, but we shouldn't have to tolerate them here on our ranches." Grey had never been good at hiding his anger.

Lindsay nodded in agreement. "The wolves have friends," she reminded him as they threw the remains of the big calf into the truck. "People friends, I mean."

"Yeah, I know," he said. "Violent friends. But they've got to be stopped, no matter what it takes. We better call the sheriff. And if I were you, I'd go check the cows you have in the forest. You might be missing more calves."

"I'm expecting a call from a deputy today, Grey. The sheriff has assigned Sergeant Matt Prescott to investigate any wolf-related problems. He's also investigating my father's death. I'll tell him when he calls."

"All right," Grey agreed. "Matt's a good man from what I hear. I hope he can catch them. But in the meantime, we've also got to get the wildlife folks to do something. These wolves that have left the park need to be found and destroyed. For that matter, I think they need to thin down the numbers in the park so they won't be forced to migrate."

Lindsay nodded, although she didn't fully agree. She hated the thought of the wholesale slaughter of any animals, even wolves. It went against her nature. And yet she knew that, generally speaking, Grey was right. The cattle and sheep ranchers couldn't afford the damage that increasing numbers of wolves would cause.

On the drive back, she told Grey about the collars that had been found on the wolves they'd killed.

"What does that mean?" Grey asked apprehensively.

"I'm not sure, but Detective Prescott and the sheriff think that someone might be bringing wolves here."

"And turning them loose on you?" Grey thundered.

"It's possible, I suppose, but I'm sure I'm not the only one being affected. They've alerted the park authorities. They're going to watch for anyone who might be somehow sneaking wolves from Yellowstone. I know it sounds far-fetched, but the two with collars weren't isolated accidents. Wolves don't put collars on each other. And these collars hadn't been on them all that long."

"Don't some of the wolves in the park already have collars?" Grey asked. "I thought the federal wildlife officials keep track of some of the wildlife that way."

"They do," she agreed. "But these collars aren't like any they've used."

"This worries me," Grey said, rubbing his face. "It sounds serious— and suspicious."

Matt hadn't called by the time they returned to the ranch. Lindsay left her phone in the barn while she worked with the roan gelding. When she finished, there were no missed calls. Her heart felt heavy again. It seemed that Matt was paying her back for her thoughtlessness last night. *I guess it serves me right.*

"Hey, beautiful, I'm hungry. How about if we run into town? I'll buy you some lunch. You've earned it, and I wouldn't mind one bit eating with someone so pretty," he said as he exaggerated his grin. "Then I'll head for home. I can't wait to start another horse using the Lindsay Method. I think I can do it now."

Lindsay knew she didn't have time, but his invitation was tempting. "Sure, if we aren't too long. But there's still more to teach you before you give it a try. You've got to be patient, you know."

"I'll look forward to it. I don't mind spending more time with the beautiful Lindsay. We'll take my truck to town. Do you mind if I leave the pups here with yours?" he asked. "We could shut them up in the barn while we're gone."

"Sure, that would be great," she agreed, even as she wondered why Matt still hadn't called. The more she waited, the more she dreaded the call. He must really be angry with her. She didn't want him to be angry with her—not now, not ever.

* * *

Matt was tired. He hadn't made it into the office until after ten that morning. Keith was at work at the grocery store, and Jimmy was with Matt's mother now, but the little guy had a hard night. Matt wasn't sure how he could wait until the next week to take him to Missoula. Jimmy desperately needed help. The silence and sadness that had again become Jimmy's world was tearing at Matt.

So was his impending talk with Lindsay. He kept putting off calling her. It was going to be so hard. And once he called, he knew he had to go out to the ranch and tell her face-to-face how he felt and why it was important that they be nothing more than friends.

At twelve thirty, the sheriff came into his office. "How about joining me for lunch, Matt?" he said. "You look like you could use a break."

Matt looked up from the paperwork in front of him. "I need a break from life," he said gloomily.

"Hey, your boy will get better. Just hang in there. And be glad you've got Miss Flemming to support you. She's a great young woman, Matt." Matt was too tired and worried to hide his feelings well.

"Is something wrong?" the sheriff asked. "I've seen the way she looks at you. Maybe I'm wrong, but I thought there might be something happening between the two of you."

"It's not a good idea, Sheriff," Matt said as he shoved his chair back from his desk and got to his feet. "I've got too much baggage for her or any other woman to deal with."

"I'm sorry to hear that."

"Yeah, well, that's life, I guess."

They stopped at a popular café in the center of town. The place was busy, and it wasn't until Matt and the sheriff had found a table that Matt noticed Lindsay sitting in a booth across the room. He recognized Grey Sadler in the booth with her, and he remembered that he had promised to bring her a puppy today and to watch her work with Terrell Edinton's horse. Despite himself, he felt a slight twinge of jealousy. He knew it was foolish—and selfish. After all, he'd pretty much written her off, and she had the right to be with whomever she chose. But the jealousy wouldn't go away.

He wished they hadn't come here. He also hoped she wouldn't notice him. Matt intentionally chose a seat with his back to Lindsay to make it less likely that she'd spot him. Unfortunately, that put Sheriff Baker facing Lindsay's direction. It wasn't until after they placed their order that the sheriff said, "Say, there's the Flemming girl now. Looks like she's with Grey Sadler. Is he part of the problem?" He raised an eyebrow in suspicion. "He's a handsome guy."

"I don't think so," Matt said. "I mean, I don't think he's part of the problem. He and Lindsay are breaking a horse together."

"Really? That doesn't sound right," the sheriff said. "She's got a reputation like her father had. They say she's as gentle as a kitten with every horse she breaks. Grey, on the other hand, is pretty heavy with the whip."

"I guess he realizes that," Matt said. "Apparently, he's hoping to change his reputation. He's trying to learn some of Lindsay's methods."

"Well, I'll be. Hope it works. He's not a bad sort of kid, and she's someone he'd probably enjoy learning from."

The officers ate silently for a while. Then the sheriff asked, "Have there been any more wolf complaints the past few days?"

"No. Maybe the two that have been killed will make a difference."

"Unless your theory is right, Matt. If someone's bringing some in on purpose, then it won't stop."

"That's the worry," Matt agreed.

He noticed the sheriff look up from his plate a minute later and smile. "Hello, Miss Flemming," he said. Matt's lunch went flat. "And how's Grey Sadler doing these days?"

"I'm doing just fine," Grey said. Matt forced himself to turn. Grey was grinning broadly. Lindsay was not.

"Hi, Grey," he said. "How's the horse breaking going?"

"Better, I think. At least, it will be after Lindsay gets through changing some of my bad habits."

Matt stood up and pushed his chair in. "Good afternoon, Lindsay," he said stiffly.

"Hi, Matt. How's Jimmy this morning?" She didn't meet his eye as she spoke, and he felt terrible.

"He's about the same. He had a rough night."

"I'm sorry," she said. "So did I."

Matt knew exactly what she meant, and he wished he could reach out and take her in his arms, but that would be the wrong direction to go in now. He should never have let himself kiss her last night.

Grey spoke up. "Yeah, she had a bad night all right. Sheriff, we've got to do something about the wolves. Lindsay spent an hour or two last night stumbling around up in her pasture trying to find another calf. She heard wolves again. We found the calf this morning, and there wasn't much left. Nice big calf, too. There had to have been more than one wolf."

"Oh, Lindsay, I'm sorry," Matt said, hoping she knew his apology was for being so sharp with her last night. Now he knew why she hadn't called. It was wolves again. It seemed like the wild creatures were targeting her ranch.

Lindsay knew what he meant, but the sheriff and Grey didn't.

"Yes, I'm sorry about your calves," Sheriff Baker said. "As bad as things are getting now, I hate to think what it will be like in the winter when wild game is harder for the wolves to find."

"We need to hunt some of those wolves while watching out for those crazy wolf lovers who killed Lindsay's father," Grey added bitterly.

"I understand your feelings, Grey. Really, I do. But hunting them might not be wise," the sheriff said. "It will only agitate the more peaceful activists. I would prefer that you and the other ranchers leave the problem to us. Matt's working hard on it. In fact, Matt, maybe you better run back out to the Lazy F and have another look."

"Yeah, I'll do that," he said.

"I'll run Lindsay home right now," Grey offered, saying nothing more about his wolf hunt idea.

But Lindsay turned to him. "Why don't you go on, Grey?" she said. "If Sergeant Prescott will give me a ride, we could talk while we're traveling."

Another double meaning. Her eye caught Matt's, and he flinched at the pain he saw there. "Yes, that would be fine," he said. "We do need to talk."

It was her turn to flinch. But he held her eye. "My truck's at the office."

"We'll give you a lift over there, Miss Flemming," the sheriff said.

"Great." She turned to her lunch partner. "Thanks Grey. Will I see you tomorrow then?"

"Sure thing, teacher," he said. "I'll just stop by and get my pups on my way home. I'll leave Princess in the barn for you."

"Thanks, Grey. You don't know how much that little dog means to me. I get so lonely now that my dad and my dog are gone. I'll probably even let Princess live in the house. And that will be a first for me," she said.

Matt was still standing when Grey left. It hurt him to hear Lindsay admit how lonely she was. "Should we go then?" he asked.

She forced a smile. "You guys need to finish eating first. I'll sit here with you."

The sheriff finished quickly, but Matt just pushed his plate back. He couldn't take another bite. He hadn't been this miserable since those first weeks after losing Carol and Sarah.

After taking care of their checks, the three of them headed for the sheriff's car. Lindsay rode in the back and didn't utter a word. Matt felt awkward. It almost seemed as if the evening before at his home, when the two of them had had such a good time, occurred ages ago, or not at all. So much had changed in so little time.

In his truck a few minutes later, Matt tried to make conversation, but it was almost as hard as training a cat to fetch a stick. Finally, he asked her about her new dog. "So you're calling her Princess? That sounds nice."

"Yes, to take the place of Prince. Silly, huh?" she said without looking his way.

"That was nice of Grey to bring her to you. I'm sure you'll enjoy her a lot," he said. For some reason he couldn't get the stiffness out of the conversation. "And I'll bet she'll be good company. What time did the wolves get your calf?" He hadn't intended to bring up anything that would lead to discussing their relationship—but the question slipped out before he realized it.

"Matt," Lindsay said suddenly, ignoring his question, "I'm so sorry I upset you last night. It was so thoughtless of me to forget to call you."

"Was it because of the wolves?" he asked.

"I guess they could be my excuse, because I heard them howling and the cows were bawling like crazy way off in the pasture when I drove into the yard. But I should have called before I ran off into the pasture."

"You shouldn't have run off like that at all, Lindsay. Remember what happened when you and I did that the last time?"

"Of course I remember," she said. "How could I ever forget?"

"Yeah, well, it could have happened again. It's not the wolves I'm so worried about. It's these people who are making the wolves their cause that worry me," he told her.

"I know that," she said. Then before he could say something else, she went on. "Matt, you said we needed to talk. Is it because I forgot to call you? I feel terrible about that. I'm sorry that I made you so angry. I didn't mean to."

"I'm not angry. I wasn't angry last night," he said.

"You sounded angry."

"I'm sorry. I'm not now, and I wasn't then. It's something more complicated than that, I'm afraid. I'll explain as well as I can as soon as we get to your ranch," he said. "I'd rather not do it while I'm driving."

"Why not right now, Matt? You can talk and drive. This is tearing me up. Say what you have to say now, please."

"Are you sure?" he asked.

"Yes, I'm sure."

"All right, Lindsay. But hear me out, please. Then we can talk about it if there's anything left to talk about after that." He hated doing this. He looked over at her. She was watching him now, and once again he was struck by how enticing she was. No, not just enticing as in desirable, but as in gentle and kind and sweet and beautiful . . .

Whoa, man, he thought. *You're going the wrong way here.* But he knew he had to push ahead. It was more for her sake than his, he reminded himself, that they not let this friendship develop into something more.

"Lindsay, I let myself get carried away last night. I shouldn't have done that. We are good friends, and I don't want that to change. I mean, I always want us to be friends. But to let our relationship be more than that would be a mistake. There are several reasons and, believe me, they're important ones. I'll explain them the best I can. But I'm afraid it—us—we—just can't work."

"Didn't you mean what I felt from you when you held me and kissed me last night?" she asked.

"That's just the problem," he said. "I did mean it, but it just can't be that way. There will be way too many problems for both of us if we don't stop what is happening."

"Matt, I have strong feelings for you," she said, her voice almost breaking. "Isn't that enough to build on, to make things work in our future?"

"I don't think so. This is much too complicated. We've just got to agree that it won't work."

"I enjoy being with you, Matt. I can't see what the problem is," she said.

"Let me explain. Then maybe you'll realize that I'm right. Believe me, there's no future for the two of us, but it's because of me, not you."

12

Five members of the Wild Animal Protection Society entered Yellowstone Park in two vans early that Thursday afternoon. The vans were custom-altered to make them perfect for hauling a tranquilized wolf out of the park. A space beneath the backseats and a pile of camping gear held a hollow, wolf-size compartment. Vehicles were never inspected as they entered or exited the park, but in the unlikely event that someone looked into those vans, there would be nothing remarkable to attract attention.

Avenger was adamant about the appearance of propriety. When his followers were in the park to remove wolves, they were to have nothing on the vans, in the vans, or on their persons to suggest they were anything but ordinary tourists. Outside the park, they mingled with other protesters, and even helped organize events. In the park, they had other work to do that required no attention-drawing behavior.

They planned to hunt that night in the area Defender had located. But that would have to be after dark. Then they could exit the park the next day and deliver their wolves, if they were successful in getting a couple of them, to their destination the following night. If it took them an extra day or two to get the wolves, that was acceptable. The most important part of their assignment was to work slowly and care-fully. They could not afford to be seen by others in the park while they were hunting. In fact, they couldn't openly carry guns in the park, not even tranquilizer guns. But Avenger had found a way around that. Now his followers carried a tent when they went into the park's back country. Two of the tent poles were actually tranquilizer guns—quite effective ones.

They had to hike some distance to get their quarry, and depending on when and where they were successful, they might have to carry the wolves out of the park, beyond the boundaries, and bring the vans around to pick them up miles to the north. It was hard work, but the results had been good so far.

They now had a couple of small, active wolf packs working in two counties. The two newly tracked wolves were to be the first of several they planned to place in the forest bordering the Sadler brothers' ranch.

Despite the urge and sometimes the need to communicate, Avenger strictly prohibited the use of cell phones or radios. He was adamant. In fact, he seemed paranoid about having a signal overheard. As a result, his members were on their own on this hunt, as they were on every mission they carried out in the name of the cause. He would not know how they fared until they finished and returned to report to him.

The leader of today's hunt was Enforcer. Guardian was usually in charge, but Avenger had another assignment for her, one that only a woman could do.

* * *

Dwight Flemming was determined to get his hands on the Lazy F. He'd had words with Lucas when his friend reported back about the fight with Grey Sadler on his second visit to the ranch. Dwight wasn't convinced that Lucas's version of the events was accurate. He had a tendency to tell his stories in a light most favorable to himself.

Regardless of what had actually happened, Dwight felt confident that he was weakening his sister's resolve to keep the ranch. He figured that the time might be approaching for him to make another visit to Lindsay.

He decided he'd probably go in the next few days. His attorney had promised to begin a suit against Lindsay for the property. Dwight was hoping that she would be served with the complaint before he visited her again. He also hoped they didn't end up in court, not because he didn't think he could win, but because it could take months or even years for the court to act. He didn't have that kind of time, nor did he want to spend that kind of money on an attorney. He wanted the money that the sale of the ranch would bring him—and he wanted it now, not in five years.

Depending on how his visit went, Dwight would decide on what course of action to take next. Most likely, he'd send Lucas back again, but not alone. Another friend, a woman by the name of Kendra Norse, had already agreed to accompany Lucas. Kendra would pose as Lucas's fiancée, and Dwight would see that they had money to flash in front of Lindsay, a tactic he hoped would elicit a more favorable response from his sister. He also planned to have them take a series of digital pictures during that next visit.

So what if Lucas and Kendra did not really have the money to buy the ranch? That wasn't his point in sending them. Their only purpose was to continue softening up his sister. Dwight had already located a development company that was interested in the property. If all worked out as planned, the company would simply make a better offer than Dwight's friends' bogus one. The pictures he needed Lucas and Kendra to take would be for that company. He had no doubt that the pictures would seal the deal. They would want to look at the property firsthand, of course, but it was such a beautiful ranch with such tremendous potential for development that he knew they would want it. The sale would follow shortly—a very lucrative sale.

* * *

Lindsay had listened without interrupting as Matt enumerated his reasons for discontinuing their newfound relationship. She had to admit that he appeared to be thinking mostly of her, and she was touched by that. When they reached the ranch, she said, "Would now be a good time for me to talk? I've heard every word you said, and I appreciate the concern you have over my future. But will you listen to me now?"

"Of course, but I think you can see that I'm right," he said.

"Don't answer right now, Matt, but I want you to think about something for a few minutes. Then I'll give you my reaction to what you've told me," she said. "Matt, do you want to be right? Is that what you actually want?"

He started to say something, but she interrupted. "Not now, Matt. Just think about that for a little while. Then you can answer. Right now, I want you to meet my new dog."

They got out of the truck and walked toward the barn. Princess came running out and began jumping around Lindsay's feet the moment she opened the door. "She loves you already," Matt said, smiling for the first time that day.

"I'm really grateful to Grey for bringing her," she said. "I just need to keep anyone or anything from hurting her now that I have her."

As they spoke, a couple of trucks came roaring up the lane and into the yard. "I wonder who that is," Lindsay said. She didn't want to be interrupted. She wanted the chance to plead her case to Matt. Then, if he rejected her, despite the pain it would inflict, she'd accept his decision. But she wanted a chance to let him know the new but wondrous depth of her feelings for him and his boys before he made that decision.

The trucks came to a halt in a cloud of dust. Two men jumped from each. One of them approached Matt and Lindsay. "Grey Sadler sent us. You must be Lindsay Flemming."

"That's right. I'm Lindsay," she said.

"Grey said you were behind on your haying."

"I am, but I can get it."

"So can we. We work for the S/S, and we finished getting the hay up this morning. Grey told us to get on down here as soon as we were done."

"Funny, he didn't mention that to me," she said.

"He wouldn't. Good men, the Sadlers. My name's Drake. We know what to do. If you'll just show us around a little, we'll get to work."

"Really, this isn't necessary."

"Grey called me a bit ago. He said you'd be out here with a Sergeant Prescott." He nodded a greeting at Matt. The two men knew each other fairly well. He went on. "Grey thought maybe the two of you would be riding out to look for more wolf damage. Said he'd come back and help us a little later."

Lindsay looked at Matt. They hadn't considered doing that, but it sounded like a good idea. It would be easier to talk to Matt if they were riding. They were both more relaxed on horses. It seemed to put them more in touch with the land and with the Lord. Lindsay remembered her father's favorite quote, attributed to the Montana artist, Charles M. Russell: "You can see what *man* made from the seat of an automobile, but the best way to see what *God* made is from the back of a horse."

She'd love to have a few hours alone with him again. If this did happen to be the last time, at least she'd have this ride to keep in her memory. She hoped it wouldn't be the last. She recognized that her feelings for him were like nothing she'd experienced before. The word *love* came to mind, but she shoved it aside, fearing that such a thing might never come to pass. But she could hope.

Matt nodded. "That might be a good idea," he said.

"Great. We'll do it. Drake, I'll pay you, men. Let Grey know that. Matt, would you mind catching Shadow and Rustler? I'll show these guys what to do. I'll pack a couple of sandwiches in case it takes us very long, and then we can be on our way."

By the time she'd finished with the men and sandwiches, Matt had the horses saddled and two canteens filled with water. "Let's throw a couple of flashlights in the saddlebags," he said. "And I think I'll take a camera, just in case we come across another dead calf."

Lindsay put her rifle on the saddle and Matt also got his. Within minutes they were riding northwest across the ranch. With the horses moving into a mile-eating trot, they soon came to the end of ranch property and entered the forest. There, as the terrain became rougher, they slowed to a walk.

Lindsay rode up beside Matt. "Okay," she said. "It's my turn to talk. But before I do, are you ready to answer my question now?"

"Let's see, you wondered if I wanted to be right about what I told you."

"Yes, and be honest with me, Matt. I can handle it."

"Well, guys never want to admit they're wrong. And I pretty much follow the pack there. But I really do think I'm right. Honestly, Lindsay, I'd bring too many problems into a relationship with you. It's just not fair to you."

She smiled at him. The forest smelled fresh and clean. She loved it out here. And more than ever, she realized how much she loved to be with Matt. It had come as a surprise the past few days, but it was the truth. She took a deep breath and said, "You haven't answered my question yet."

"Okay, Lindsay. Of course I don't want to be right, but the fact is, I am."

"Maybe, but I hope not. Now hear me out," she said. Then she carefully explained that she had avoided relationships in the past, afraid that encouraging one might necessitate her leaving her father alone at the ranch. But since he'd been taken from her, she'd done a lot of thinking.

"I don't want to be alone anymore, Matt," she said with a lump in her throat. "I miss Dad so much that I ache every hour of the day. But even before his death, I was getting lonely in a different way. I felt like something was missing from my life. I knew he couldn't live forever, and I'd thought a lot about what I'd do after he was gone. Of course, I figured it would be a few years, but I was thinking about it, and so was he. We talked about it too. In fact, just a few weeks ago he told me that I should start dating. I argued with him, and yet deep down I knew he was right."

"And he is right," Matt said. "But there are a lot of guys out there with a lot less baggage than me."

"Maybe I wouldn't mind the 'baggage,' as you call it. We could at least date and see how things go. I'd like that, and I think you would too."

"But maybe you should date some other guys and see what happens," he suggested, not looking at her as he spoke.

"I could do that, if someone asked me, I suppose. But I like being with you, Matt. I really do."

"And I like being with you," he admitted. "But it just wouldn't be fair."

They rode around a thick stand of half-grown pines before Lindsay spoke again. "You say that you would worry about me whenever I went anywhere if we got really serious. You're worried that it would bother me with you watching over my shoulder all the time or calling me to make sure I was all right. It's true that I have developed a certain amount of independence. Okay, maybe a lot of independence. But I also had my dad for my whole life. Don't you think he fussed over me and worried? He about went crazy when I insisted on breaking horses with him. Believe me, having someone like you fuss over me again would be nice. I don't want anyone to rule my life, but to have someone be worried about me would never upset me. It would only make me feel, well, secure, I guess." In a softer voice, she added, "Or maybe treasured."

"Really?" he asked, sounding genuinely surprised.

"Yes, really," she answered firmly. He said nothing, and she went on talking. She poured out her heart to him, surprised at how bold and frank she was being. "Matt," she finally said, "I've never had this kind of friendship before. It's new to me, but I like how it feels. You've been loved, and that's great. But please, don't throw away what we could have because of how you think it might affect me. I want to give us a chance, regardless of whatever so-called baggage comes with you. So, if you want to call off our relationship, don't do it for my sake. Do it for yours. If you don't think you can handle it, then I'll accept that. I won't like it, but I won't whine. If you're concerned that there would be too much stress in your life with me in it, then so be it. I'll just go on being lonely, but I'll cope. But please, Matt, please accept the fact that I'm willing to try, no matter what."

They rode in silence to the top of a long ridge. Suddenly, Matt pulled Shadow to a stop and swung off. Not sure what he was up to, she did the same. Her heart beat erratically. She hoped he wasn't about to end her hopes right here in this beautiful spot.

She led her horse over near him, but suddenly he said, "Get back in the trees." Then he began leading his own horse out of sight.

"What is it?" she asked as they tied the horses to a couple small trees.

"Hikers," he said. "Get down. We'll crawl to the top of the ridge. It may be nothing, but I don't want whoever's there to see us."

Lindsay nodded nervously and followed him. They were less than a mile from where her father had been murdered. Horrendous things could happen in this beautiful forest—she didn't need to be reminded of that. She trembled as she crawled. Up ahead a few feet was a small patch of scrub oak.

"In there," Matt whispered, pointing.

Side by side, they entered the wild shrubbery. "In there we can see but not be seen," Matt said. "I wish they were closer. There are definitely three of them. One's big, one's somewhat shorter, and the other one's shorter still." The resemblance to a child's story hit Matt suddenly and he added, "And I don't think they're the three bears, even if Goldilocks is here."

Lindsay giggled softly, then she whispered, "I can't tell if they're men or women."

"Neither can I," Matt agreed. "But the middle-sized one is carrying something over his shoulder. Could be a rifle."

"Oh, Matt," Lindsay asked nervously. "Could they be the people who killed my father?"

"It's possible. Of course, they could also be some perfectly innocent hikers, although hikers don't usually carry guns. That smaller one could be a kid."

"Do you think they'll come any closer so we can get a better look?" Lindsay asked.

"I wish they would."

As soon as he said that, the three hikers passed out of sight behind a rocky knoll. When they emerged again a couple minutes later, they turned and headed straight toward the ridge where Lindsay and Matt were hidden.

The hikers continued toward them for three or four minutes, but before they were close enough for Matt and Lindsay to make out their features, they turned and headed off at an angle. "Stay here," Matt suddenly said.

"You're not going to approach them are you? I'm pretty sure now that the middle one is carrying a rifle."

"No, I won't do that. If it is the killers, they wouldn't hesitate to shoot me. I won't take that chance, but I do want to get my camera from the saddlebag. If they turn again and come closer, I'd like to get some pictures."

Lindsay was relieved. "Okay, but hurry."

Matt crawled back beside Lindsay in the scrub oak three or four minutes later. "They aren't much closer, are they?" he whispered.

Lindsay shook her head, and Matt snapped a few pictures. "Waste of time at this distance," he mumbled. "Wish they'd come toward us again."

A short time later, the three hikers descended into a tree-covered valley about four hundred yards away. Lindsay and Matt continued to keep watch down the hillside. Lindsay, though tense and worried, was grateful she wasn't alone. *They may be three perfectly innocent people,* she thought, *but again, they could be the very people who murdered Dad.* The thought made her shiver.

Suddenly, from the valley below them, a voice drifted their way. It was definitely a woman's voice, and it sounded excited. "Look, Enforcer," Lindsay thought she heard her say. Then her words were unintelligible. A moment later she thought the woman said, "Their tracks," but she couldn't be sure.

She glanced at Matt. He too was straining to hear. "Might be looking for deer," he whispered very softly. "Could be poachers."

Lindsay nodded. Then she heard a voice again. It was difficult to tell if it was a man's voice or a woman's. It carried up the hill from the heavily timbered ravine below them better than the other voice had. The words were unmistakable. "They've come this way after eating that calf back there."

Lindsay's stomach lurched. They were following wolves. *They* were *her enemies!* Matt's hand found hers, and his touch calmed her.

"They're heading east," the high-pitched voice said. Then, momentarily, the smaller person came into view. Whoever it was had been close enough that Lindsay could see something, possibly a pistol, strapped to his or her right hip.

A deeper voice reached them, but its owner must have been much lower in the ravine. His words were unintelligible. Neither could they make out a single word when the female spoke again. But the small person's voice was still fairly clear when he or she said, "We should get some pictures of them if we get close enough. That would make Avenger happy. Especially if there really are three of them. It's just too bad those creeps killed the ones with collars on."

Lindsay and Matt exchanged glances. Matt confirmed her own feelings when he whispered, "Dangerous wolf lovers, that's for sure."

The deeper voice spoke again a moment later, still unintelligible. Then the small person said, "Okay, okay. I'll be quiet. I don't want to scare the wolves, either."

Nothing more was said after that. And none of the three came into view. But Lindsay thought she could hear their footsteps on the gravelly slope far below them. Slowly, the sound faded away. Ten minutes later the three figures emerged from the trees, their backs to

Lindsay and Matt. They seemed to be moving more quickly now and directly away from the ridge concealing Matt and Lindsay.

Lindsay and Matt didn't move from their hiding spot until the three activists had disappeared into the distant trees. Finally, Matt said, "Whoever they are, they were using code names. The e-mail sent to Reese used four names—Avenger, Guardian, Enforcer, and Protector. Avenger must be the leader. Enforcer is the large man we saw. At this point we don't know about the others."

Matt glanced at her after they'd reached their horses, and Lindsay said, "Matt, I still wonder if they're the ones who killed Dad."

"That's possible," Matt agreed. "I just wish we could have gotten a closer look at them."

"I'm sure the woman said something about a calf. Let's ride the way those three came from. Maybe we'll see it," Lindsay suggested. "I probably have another dead calf."

"My thoughts exactly," Matt agreed as he swung onto Shadow. "If there is one, we'll find it. I'd also like to take some pictures of the tracks those three have left. It'll give us something to compare with what we found at the scene where your father was killed. And who knows, maybe they'll leave some other telltale signs behind."

An hour later, after passing a number of Lazy F cattle, they had taken pictures of the hikers' tracks and another dead calf, one carrying the Lazy F brand. The tracks did not seem to be quite like the ones Matt had seen earlier. After half an hour of poking around the dead calf's carcass and the surrounding area, they still had found nothing. Matt said, "Let's head back, but we'll veer to the west. I don't want to run into them, and it'll give us a chance to look for more evidence of what the wolves have been up to. And maybe we'll spot more of your cattle."

They did find more cows and calves. To Lindsay's dismay, two of the cows had no calves with them. Their udders were swollen and they kept bawling for their calves. "Dad and I didn't bring any cows up here without calves," she said. "I think I'm losing quite a few."

An hour later, as they rode through a large stand of timber, Lindsay said, "Matt, I never did find out what you're feeling. You've been awfully quiet. Are you still determined to call off what we've been experiencing?"

He stopped his horse in a small clearing surrounded by tall, thick timber. "I've been thinking, Lindsay. I don't talk a lot when I'm thinking. Let's take a break here. I'm just about ready for one of those sandwiches you made." She followed his example, dismounting and tying up her horse as he tied his.

She began opening a saddlebag, but he said, "Not yet, Lindsay. We haven't finished talking. Let's get that done. Then we'll eat a sandwich."

If I can eat after I hear what you have to say, she thought grimly. She began to tremble, and her stomach was rolling. Silently, she prayed that he wasn't about to end something she felt could be so good, something she honestly hadn't expected, but now yearned for. They walked a few feet from the horses. He turned to her. "How sure are you about what you told me?" he asked, his face very somber.

"I meant every word, Matt. I want to give us a chance, to see if there's something there. But if you feel like it would be too much of a burden on you, I guess I'll just have to understand," she said, unable to keep her voice from shaking.

He reached out and took one of her hands in his. "Lindsay, I'd worry about you all the time," he said. "I wouldn't be able to help myself."

"Is that such a bad thing?" she asked.

He smiled, and she tried to read his smile, but she couldn't.

"It could be," he said.

She nodded, feeling a heavy sense of dread come over her.

"Lindsay," he said. "I've been thinking a lot while we were riding. I guess I'm going to need your help deciding what to do. I can't do it on my own."

"What can I do?" she asked. "I'm willing to help if I can."

"Then will you forgive me for being so selfish?" he asked.

"You weren't being selfish," she answered. "You were thinking of me."

"No, I was thinking of me," he admitted. "But if it's okay with you, I'd like to give it another try. I'd like to ask you out on real dates and just, well, you know, spend time together, get to know each other better. You could also continue to go out with other guys if you'd like."

"Like who?" Lindsay asked.

"I'll bet Grey would like to take you out again."

"Again?"

"Yes, you know, like your lunch date."

Lindsay frowned. "That wasn't a date. We were just both hungry."

Matt started to chuckle. "I'm just kidding. But the two of you do look good together."

"He's not my type," Lindsay said firmly.

"Maybe I'm not either, but I'm willing to work at finding out. Would that be okay?"

Lindsay smiled at the way he was shifting from foot to foot as he spoke. He was really uncomfortable. It was like junior high again. She knew his mentioning Grey was an attempt to put himself at ease. It hadn't worked.

"I'd like that a lot, Matt," she said as she boldly stepped close to him.

13

Jimmy remained in his withdrawn, silent world. He went to Primary class with Lindsay and sat with her during sharing time, but he was in a shell that seemed impenetrable. After church, Lindsay invited Matt and the boys for dinner. They spent the afternoon and evening at the Lazy F. It was the first time Jimmy had been back since the day he'd fallen behind the haystack in the barn. Matt worried about him, but even though he remained silent, he did play on the lawn with the dogs.

Matt was tense until well into the evening. It seemed that whenever they went to Lindsay's ranch, they had trouble of some kind. But this Sabbath day turned out to be different, and by the time he and the boys were ready to go home, he was relaxed and as happy as he'd been since before the accident. He was even beginning to think that there just might be a future for him and Lindsay. The idea appealed to him, even though he knew he'd worry about her.

It was hard to go back to work on Monday, but Matt knew that he and Reese had a lot to do. After comparing the tracks he and Lindsay had found with the ones at the murder scene, Matt suspected that at least one or two of the people they had watched from the ridge had been there when Noah died. The tracks were not a 100 percent match, but that could mean the people wore different shoes the day Lindsay's father was killed. Matt felt that he was closer now to solving the crime than at any time before.

Since that day in the mountains when Lindsay and Matt had seen the three hikers, nothing more had happened. Of course, wolves could be killing cattle out in the forest, Matt told himself, and the calves might not have been discovered yet. He suspected that Lindsay and others were losing stock on a regular basis.

Grey and a few other concerned ranchers had decided to fight back. They announced that they were going on a wolf hunt Tuesday. They were scheduled to start early in the morning, and their purpose was to shoot as many wolves as they could find. Matt had tried to convince them not to go, as had the sheriff, explaining that their hunt might inflame more of the protesters, the ones who were law-abiding people. But the ranchers were angry, and they were determined. Matt hoped that no one got hurt and that things didn't get worse as a result of the hunt.

* * *

Thanks to the help of Grey's ranch hands, Lindsay's hay was in the stack. She had time today to take the roan gelding for a longer ride, and she looked forward to it. Grey had been amazed with the big horse. All signs of meanness were gone, and he was breaking nicely. Grey himself had ridden him for a couple of miles on Saturday, and he'd had a good ride. But today, Lindsay was going to ride for about ten miles. She intended to ride a little distance into the forest bordering her ranch. Her main objective was not to look for more carcasses of her valuable Hereford calves but to work the horse in some rough country. Of course, she would still keep her eyes peeled for any sign that the wolves were still at work on her herd.

She finished her chores and moved her wheel lines before saddling the horse. She planned to be gone for only a few hours, but she packed a lunch and took plenty of water just in case. She had barely finished saddling the roan when she heard a vehicle pull into her yard. Her stomach knotted up. She was not expecting any visitors today, and, lately, several of them had brought nothing but trouble.

But it was Matt who'd stopped by. "Looks like you're going for a ride," he said. "I'm sure impressed with what you've done with that horse."

"He just needed a little tender care," she said with a grin.

"So, are you planning on riding very far?" he asked.

She hoped he wouldn't ask that question. She knew he would worry at the thought of her riding beyond the boundaries of the ranch. But their relationship had become such that the last thing she would ever do now was try to mislead him. She told him her plans. As she expected, he frowned.

"Could you use some company?" he asked after a tense moment of silence. "Or would that mess up your training?"

"Having another horse along would be good for this one. But I know you have more important things to do. It's really not necessary. I'll be careful," she said.

"Actually, I'd like to have another look around up there. I could look while you work with the horse."

Lindsay had to admit that she was pleased, so she told him she would fix him a lunch while he saddled Shadow. But before they were through the first pasture gate, Lindsay recognized the truck of Lucas Mallory. It was flying up the lane in a cloud of dust. "Oh, no," she muttered.

"Do you recognize that outfit?" Matt asked.

"Lucas Mallory."

They turned and rode back. "Looks like he's got someone with him," Matt said.

"It's a woman," Lindsay said. "I guess we'll see what they want. Not that I don't have a pretty good idea."

She rode right up to the truck as Lucas and the woman got out. Lucas was dressed neatly in a pair of new jeans, a dark gray western shirt, a tan cowboy hat, and a pair of black boots. He wasn't a bad-looking man, but his face still showed the effects of the beating Grey had given him. One eye was puffy and dark, and he was missing an upper front tooth.

The woman was also dressed in western clothing. Like Lindsay, her hair was in a ponytail. She smiled as Lindsay came to a stop on her horse.

Lindsay was unable to smile back. "Hello," she greeted them, struggling to sound civil. "As you can see, I'm busy again today, Lucas."

"That's okay," Lucas said. "We won't need a tour guide. We'll find our way around. Dwight told us where the boundaries are."

"This ranch is still not for sale," Lindsay said hotly. "Dwight can't give you permission to go on my property. You'll have to leave."

"That's not what your big brother says," the tall woman said. She smiled, but the smile fell short of her eyes.

"It's not his to say," Lindsay told her. "What's your name, anyway? And what's your business here?"

"I'm Kendra Norse, Lucas's fiancée," she said. "We're interested in buying this ranch and settling down here after we get married."

Matt leaned forward on his horse. "Folks," he said, "maybe you didn't hear Miss Flemming. The ranch is not for sale, not to anyone. And nobody is going to be looking it over. Now you two need to look elsewhere for a place to buy if you're serious about ranching."

"And who might you be?" Lucas asked, not trying to hide his contempt.

"This is a friend of mine, Sergeant Matt Prescott of the Gallatin County Sheriff's Department," Lindsay said quickly. "He's leading the investigation into my father's murder."

She immediately noticed the peculiar look that came over Lucas's face. Apparently, he had no desire to tangle with a cop. "Well, I guess we could come back another day," he stammered. "I can see that you're busy, and we sure don't want any hard feelings. Say, isn't that the horse you were trying to tame when I was here the other day? He sure seems gentle enough now." He was clearly trying to alter his previous belligerent image.

"He's doing well," Lindsay agreed. She noticed during the short exchange that the woman's face was dark with anger. The glance she threw Lucas could have frozen flames. In an animal it would have been called a snarl.

"We'll finish what we came for, Lucas," Kendra said. "Dwight says this place is supposed to be his and soon will be and that if we want it and can meet his price, we can have it. So we'll just have a look around like we planned."

Matt began to slowly shake his head. "Get back in your truck and leave," he said. "If you don't, I'll arrest you both for trespassing."

"Hah, that would be good. Dwight's lawyer would have us out before you even got back to Bozeman with us," she sneered. "And then we'd have him sue you for false arrest."

Lindsay became anxious as Matt got off his horse. "You've got thirty seconds to get back in that truck," he said as he pulled his cell phone from his pocket and punched in a number.

The woman didn't budge, but Lucas stepped backward. Matt held the phone to his ear. "You have fifteen seconds left." Then he spoke into the phone. "Sheriff Baker, Sergeant Prescott. It looks like we have a little problem out here at the Lazy F Ranch. There are a couple of trespassers that are refusing to leave. Could you send a car out this way to haul them back to jail? I'm arresting them for trespassing."

Finally, to Lindsay's relief, Kendra stepped to the truck. "You'll be hearing from Dwight's attorney." She spat out the words. "This isn't over. We're legitimate buyers, and we have the money for a down payment and the credit to come up with the rest. Dwight knows that."

"Then Dwight can help you find another ranch," Lindsay said. "I'm not selling this one."

The two hesitated as if they had more to say. Then they both looked at Matt's stony face and the phone he still held to his ear. A moment later Lucas and Kendra drove away in the truck. Matt told the sheriff what was going on. "I think these two friends of Dwight's could be trouble," he concluded. "But for now, they got smart and left."

Lindsay laughed as she watched Lucas's truck retreating down her lane. "I'll bet Lucas is getting an earful right about now. His fiancée didn't look too happy."

Matt didn't even smile. "If they're associated with Dwight, and it appears they are, then we need to consider her a bad one. I need to find out more about her. In the meantime, you watch out for both of them. If either of them comes around again, call me. Now, let's ride."

Lindsay nodded. She had to admit that those two scared her, even if Lucas did appear to be afraid of cops. That didn't mean he couldn't be a threat to her.

* * *

"What do you mean, Lindsay's getting cozy with a cop?" Dwight asked. He was so angry that the veins stood out on his head, and the pressure inside his skull felt like his head could explode.

"That's what it looked like," Kendra told him. "She said he was a friend and that he was leading the investigation of your father's death. From the way they looked at each other, though, I'd guess they're more than just friends."

Dwight stormed around for a minute. Then he stopped and faced the other two.

"He's probably just after the ranch."

"I have to agree," Kendra said, and Lucas nodded in agreement.

"Did they tell you his name?" Dwight asked.

"Sergeant Matt Prescott."

Dwight slammed his fist against the wall. He had to shake his hand afterward, it was stinging so badly. "Prescott!" he thundered. "I went to school with him. That worthless, greedy skunk. He probably is after the ranch for himself. That spread he has isn't big enough to support a family of field mice. I'm telling you, no cop is going to step in and get that place. It's mine!"

"I told him we'd be back with papers from your attorney," Kendra said.

"Actually, I'm going to have them served on her before I see her again." Dwight had settled down after smashing his hand. "I've been thinking that it's about time I make another visit to my dear little sister. I'll call my attorney first thing in the morning and tell him to get her served as soon as he can. She's not going to cheat me out of my property."

* * *

Grey and one of his hired hands rode over a ridge and started back toward the ranch. Although the men had been riding since sunup, they had seen no sign of wolves. They spread out in pairs and covered as much forest as they could, keeping in touch with each other on powerful two-way radios.

They had heard a shot fired about eight that morning and estimated that it came from two or three miles beyond where they were riding. It had not been followed by any others, and they soon forgot about it.

The cows they came across were all doing well, as were the calves. They worked their way north, and for the first time, Grey found something to worry about when he spotted one of his cows without a calf. She was bawling loudly, her udder painfully swollen. He called the others and told them that he and his partner were going to take a closer look around. After spending a couple of hours, they still found no sign of the missing calf.

They finally gave up and rode on. Shortly before noon the entire group turned and started back toward the ranch. It was Grey who spotted the wolves—feeding on a dead calf.

He pulled out his rifle and leaped from the horse in one swift movement, his hired man only seconds behind him. The wolves fled from the calf, but not before Grey put a bullet in the lead one. It turned a somersault and hit the ground. Then, after struggling to its feet, it ran on. The other man got a shot off but missed the other wolf.

Grey swung onto his horse and headed up the rough hillside after the wounded wolf. He could see that it was bleeding badly and expected to find it down at any moment. But it kept going for more than a mile before finally collapsing. When Grey approached it, the animal arose and started to move again. He shot it again from the back of his horse. Then he got off and walked toward it.

He recalled hearing that two of the wolves found on or near the Lazy F Ranch had worn collars. This one had a collar as well. He bent down and unfastened it, then started back toward his horse, the collar in his hand.

Grey didn't hear the bullet that struck him in the back. He just felt the powerful impact and went down face first. It took him a moment to realize that he'd been shot. But he had no time to worry. He passed out after the first agonizing minute.

* * *

A panicked 911 call came in shortly after two o'clock on Tuesday afternoon. Matt was in his office when another deputy came running in. "There's been another shooting!" he shouted. "Sheriff wants me to ride with you."

Matt got that sick feeling that always accompanied such an announcement. "Where?" he asked.

"In the forest. The victim is still alive, but barely."

"Where on the forest?" Matt asked as he started for the door. He wondered if Lindsay had ridden up there again today. They had experienced an uneventful ride the day before, but she had mentioned wanting to ride the roan again that morning before his owner came and tried him out that evening. "Was it near any of the ranches in the county?"

The other deputy was running to keep up. "It happened in the forest above the S/S Ranch somewhere," he said as they reached the outer door of the sheriff's department.

The announcement left Matt feeling both relief and alarm. He worried about Grey and the others who'd decided to hunt for wolves in the forest near their ranches. They already knew what these still unidentified persons were capable of doing if anyone shot a wolf and they were around to witness it. Noah Flemming's murder was proof of how deadly that small group of activists was. "Do we know who was shot?" he asked.

"It was Grey Sadler. They've got a helicopter going in. He's pretty bad, I guess. He was shot in the back and lost a lot of blood. He was just a few miles from his ranch when it happened."

Matt knew he had a long afternoon and night ahead of him. And he had to get Jimmy to Missoula by two the next afternoon to see Dr. Lubek. Nothing would stop him from keeping that appointment. His son still hadn't spoken a word since the day Matt had found him behind the haystack, and Matt worried about him constantly.

Five other men met Matt at the forest. He'd ridden one of their horses over a mile to get to where Grey had been shot. The hired hand and some other ranchers who had been riding only a few hundred yards from Grey had heard a shot and assumed that Grey had finished off the wolf. Then, just three or four minutes later, they heard another shot. Again, they assumed Grey had had to shoot the wolf once more. But when they tried to call him on their radios, he didn't answer.

They'd found Grey lying between the wolf and his horse, unconscious and bleeding. The wolf had two bullet holes; Grey had one. He had been shot in the back and left to die.

The big surprise on the mountain that day was a discovery they made about the dead calf the wolves had been eating. The wolves hadn't killed it. *A bullet had!* And that could mean only one thing. The wolves were being taught to eat fresh beef. The activists were not only trying to protect wolves, they were encouraging them to kill the ranchers' stock. That was puzzling. Most of the people in favor of letting wolves roam freely did not want them eating cattle. Matt was now quite certain that there was something different about the violent group that had shot two men and also cattle. He didn't think of them so much now as activists. He wondered what their real motivations were, how they differed from the mostly harmless, well-intentioned people who set up their pickets and wrote letters to local newspapers.

Matt didn't leave the mountain until nearly midnight. As with Noah Flemming's killing, there was not a lot of evidence left at the scene of Grey's shooting. Matt found a couple of footprints, but they had been partially obscured by someone sweeping over them with a pine bough. He had broken a few small branches from some bushes near where Grey had been lying. He couldn't see anything on them, but he hoped that a good lab could turn up some small fibers of clothing that might have brushed up against them. The bullet that had hit Grey in the back was still in him. Matt hoped it could be removed and compared with the one that had been taken from Noah's body.

He and the other deputies had searched for a bullet in the calf but had no luck there. He was anxious to find some kind of evidence linking Noah's killers and the person who'd shot Grey. The urgency of making a case and arresting whoever was behind the rash of lethal violence was pushing at Matt. It had been over four weeks since Noah's death.

* * *

Grey was in intensive care at Bozeman Deaconess Hospital when Matt arrived there early Wednesday morning. It was clear Matt wouldn't be talking to the rancher anytime soon, if at all. He left feeling angry, sad, worried, and pressured. Those responsible for the terrible crimes that had occurred in the forest had to be stopped, and soon, before someone else was hurt or killed.

14

It was oppressively hot in the doctor's waiting area as Matt paced nervously around the room. Jimmy had been with Dr. Lubek for nearly thirty minutes. Even though he felt assurances as he prayed for his son, he still wondered if the doctor might tell him that this time the boy would never talk again. It haunted his dreams at night, and it haunted him now.

He spent the first few minutes with Dr. Lubek, filling her in with more details of what had happened to trigger this latest episode. Then she'd told him to wait while she spent some time alone with the boy. He couldn't imagine what was taking so long, because he figured that any conversation that occurred would be one-sided, that the doctor would be the only one talking.

The door opened and a receptionist said, "Mr. Prescott, you can come back now. The doctor would like to speak to you for a moment." The minute he stepped into the office, Jimmy scurried across the room and into his arms. Matt hugged him tightly before turning to Dr. Lubek.

She smiled reassuringly at him. Matt had been surprised upon first meeting her a year ago. He had expected a much older woman, one with a stern demeanor and gray hair secured in a bun. He'd been wrong. She was in her mid-thirties, was attractive physically and intellectually, had long black hair, and smiled with her eyes as well as her mouth. That smile now made him feel better, as it had before. She was very competent.

"Jimmy is a special boy, aren't you, Jimmy?" she said.

Jimmy nodded soberly. Matt's gut wrenched when there was still no verbal communication from him. Not that he'd actually expected that result this quickly. It wasn't like he hadn't been through this before.

Dr. Lubek went on. "Jimmy's had a very bad fright," she said. "As we visited, it became quite apparent that there is someone or something he fears a great deal. There could be more that happened than just his witnessing a dog getting run over. Whatever it was, it has brought back a lot of the suppressed memories we dealt with earlier. It does happen. I think I warned you of that months ago."

"You did, but this is worse than it's been since the accident."

"This is why I say that something brought back memories of that accident. The death of the dog could be the entire problem, but it might not be." Dr. Lubek paused thoughtfully. Matt sat holding his son, wishing she could tell him something more hopeful. "Jimmy's is not an isolated case, Mr. Prescott. Nor will he be one who will never speak again. This is just another setback, that's all. We'll have him talking normally before long. Won't we, Jimmy?" she said as she again looked directly at the little boy and smiled.

Jimmy showed no reaction. Dr. Lubek then asked him to wait with the receptionist while she and Matt talked. It took a moment to convince the child that he'd be safe before he and the young woman stepped out.

As soon as they were gone, Dr. Lubek went on to explain that she'd questioned Jimmy thoroughly, and that he'd answered quite well with nods or shakes of his head. Then she'd asked him to draw some pictures for her in response to specific questions she asked him. She showed the crude pencil drawings to Matt. He just shook his head as he looked at what he decided was meant to be an ugly face attached to a long stick body. The most clearly-drawn feature was the mouth, and it was evidently frowning.

The second picture Matt looked at was Jimmy's attempt at drawing a car of some type. He knew after studying the drawing for only a moment that Jimmy had been trying to draw the wreck that had killed his mother and sister. The roughly sketched wheels were sticking up in the air. The third picture was of some kind of animal. He couldn't be sure, but he wondered if it might be Claw that his son had tried to represent in the picture.

The doctor gave Matt time to look the pictures over thoroughly before she spoke again. When he finally looked up, she said, "Mr. Prescott, this is why I think that what happened took your son back to the horrors of the accident that killed your wife and daughter. I know this may sound strange, but I get the feeling that it's more than the great loss he suffered that day that's causing his present condition. There is something else."

"Like what?" Matt asked.

"I'm not sure. But let me ask you something. Was the dog, the one you found behind the hay with Jimmy that day, at the accident too?"

"Oh, yes, that was the first time I'd ever seen Claw."

"He's not a real wolf, is he?" she asked. "I remember your mentioning before that he looks like a wolf."

"We think he may have some wolf blood in him because he has a howl very similar to that of the ones that come from Yellowstone. And he has some physical characteristics that are also similar to those of the wolves I've seen," Matt explained. "But according to my vet, he's more dog than wolf."

"Did this dog you call Claw just show up at the accident?" she asked as she pointed to one of the pictures Jimmy had sketched.

"He was with my son when we found him that night. Jimmy had left the accident, and we were searching for him. As I said, I'd never seen him before then. But he and Jimmy have been practically inseparable ever since then."

Dr. Lubek smiled again. "That's what I gathered from Jimmy. The question I have is this: Where did he come from?"

"I've wondered the same thing for months," Matt said. "And I have no idea. But what does the dog have to do with Jimmy's condition now?"

"I was coming to that," the doctor said thoughtfully. In a moment she continued. "I know it's a stretch, but the fact that the dog was present at both of your boy's traumatic experiences may mean something. And again, it may not. What do you know about the man who ran over the other dog that day?"

"Not much, but I'm learning a few things. It seems that he's somehow connected with Miss Flemming's brother." He went on to tell Dr. Lubek about Dwight and how he wanted the ranch and seemed bent on doing whatever he could to take it from Lindsay.

"I see," Dr. Lubek said. "There is probably no connection, but I wonder if there was something about him that is making Jimmy's problem worse. As a precaution, I would suggest that you be careful about letting Jimmy be around any strangers if you or another adult that he trusts implicitly cannot be right with him."

"We've been doing that," Matt said.

"Good. I'd like to see him again in a week. In the meantime, if anything of significance happens with Jimmy, any improvement or any further fear or regression, call me as soon as you can. But be assured, your little boy will get better."

"So is it going to take longer this time?" Matt asked, discouraged.

"It could. But don't let it get you down. And always be positive with Jimmy," she said as she walked with Matt to the door of her office.

On the long drive back to Bozeman, Jimmy seemed less withdrawn, looking with interest out the truck windows. Whenever Matt spoke to him, he always turned and looked at him. He almost smiled when Matt said, "I'll bet old Claw will be glad to see you when we get home." But the boy remained silent.

* * *

The yapping of her new puppy, Princess, caused Lindsay to hurry to the door of the barn. She was silently praying that none of Dwight's friends had come to harass her again. She'd been cleaning stables since about one that afternoon. She was tired, but the hard work helped keep her mind off her worries and her continuing heartache over the death of her father. Everything she did reminded her of Noah, keeping the pain of his loss achingly present much of the time.

She was also very worried about Jimmy's well-being. She kept hoping Matt would call, but she knew he might not want to do that while Jimmy was with him. He'd warned her earlier that he might not be able to say anything meaningful about the visit to the psychiatrist with the boy listening. She knew she just had to be patient and wait.

Lindsay felt a stir of nervousness as a deputy pulled into her yard and got out of the car. He was an older fellow that she'd seen around a few times, but she didn't really know him. He had some papers in his hand. He walked over to her and said, "I'm sorry to do this, Miss Flemming, but I have to serve this on you."

She reached for the papers he was holding out. "What is it?" she asked as she took the pages from his hand.

"You're being sued," he said flatly. "Don't ignore this or you could have a judgment entered against you."

As he spoke, she unfolded the papers. It took only a moment to realize what it was all about. Dwight was serious about taking the ranch from her. He was suing her for the property, which the papers stated was rightfully his. Although she knew he had no legal claim on the ranch, the suit worried her anyway. She also knew that right didn't always prevail in the courts. So who could guess what might happen? At the very least, it would cost her a lot of money to fight her brother in court—money she needed for other things.

It made her angry. She wished that Dwight had remained lost to her. It would have been better that way. All he was doing now was causing her more pain and trouble. At first she'd felt like trying to find a way to share with him, but now, as she scanned through the papers, she had no such charitable thoughts.

The old deputy was waiting while she looked the papers over. When she finally looked up, she was embarrassed. "Thank you," she said.

"I'm sorry, Miss Flemming," he said.

"It's okay. It will all work out," she said, hoping she was right.

Lindsay's first thought after the deputy left was to call Matt and tell him about the complaint Dwight had filed against her, but after thinking it over, she realized she didn't want to burden him further right then. She knew how worried he was about his son. She went to her house and sat down on the front porch. Then she opened the bundle of folded pages again and began to read carefully from the beginning.

The tone of the complaint made her so irate she could hardly sit still as she read. Basically, Dwight and his attorney were accusing her of attempting to steal the ranch from Dwight. It spoke of *devious actions* and *undue influence,* along with other phrases that were intended to show how she had secretly plotted to take the land for herself upon the death of her father. It even went so far as to allege that Noah had not been of sound mind in his later years, and that she had taken advantage of his disability in her attempt to enrich herself

while depriving her brother. Finally, it asked the court to declare her
deed to the Lazy F Ranch null and void, having been obtained
through deceit and fraud, and to award the entire ranch to Dwight.

It was vile and malicious from the first word to the last, and her
hope of negotiating a peaceful settlement with Dwight was now
totally out of the question. She had to secure an attorney right away.
She thought of the man whom Noah had hired to draw up the papers
when he decided to turn the ranch over to her in the first place.
Nearing retirement, Morris Kincaid might not have the time to help
her, she feared. But she also knew that he would be angry at the very
suggestion that her father's mind had been slipping. Morris had
known Noah well, and she hoped he would be willing to fight to
preserve what her father had desired concerning her and the ranch.

If he didn't want to help her or didn't have the time, maybe he
could suggest another lawyer who could represent her. She was more
determined by the minute to stop Dwight from getting anything else.

All right, Dwight, you've taken enough. I ignored that before, she
thought, *but I'll do whatever it takes to stop you from stealing what is
legally mine.*

Lindsay went into the house and got out her phone book. In a minute
she had Morris's secretary on the line. She explained that she needed to
retain Mr. Kincaid to defend her in a lawsuit, and she described what the
suit was about.

The secretary put her on hold for a short time and then came
back on the line. "Could you come into town this afternoon?" she
asked. "Mr. Kincaid would like to see you as soon as possible."

"I'll need to clean up first," Lindsay said, relieved that she hadn't
been put off.

"Can you be here by four thirty?"

Lindsay glanced at her watch. "I'll be there," she said. "Thank you
so much." She rushed to get showered and changed.

* * *

By the time Matt got home, Keith had completed his shift at the
grocery store. Leaving Jimmy with his big brother, Matt hurried into
town alone. He wanted to stop at the hospital to see how Grey Sadler

was doing. If the young cowboy had regained consciousness, Matt hoped he could give him some information about who shot him. He also dialed Lindsay's cell phone as he drove. He was surprised that she didn't answer right away. She'd asked him to call when he could and let her know what the doctor said about Jimmy. He hadn't wanted to talk to her about Jimmy in the boy's presence, but he wanted to talk to her now. He let the phone ring and ring before finally giving up.

He began to think about all the things that might have gone wrong, reasons she might not be answering her phone. Worry began to gnaw at him. He tried her home phone, but she didn't answer it either. He left a short message on both phones, asking her to call when she could.

When he arrived at the hospital, he hurried in, trying to shift his thoughts from Lindsay to Grey and finding out who had shot the young rancher and left him to die. He was surprised to find that Grey was no longer in intensive care. Upon entering the room to which Grey had been transferred, he found the young cowboy awake and coherent, although lying on his side because of the bullet wound in his back.

As Grey and Matt talked, Grey's face grew dark. "You've got to find who did this to me. When you do, I think you'll also have the person who killed Lindsay Flemming's father."

"Did you get a look at the individual who did this before you were shot?" Matt asked.

"I was shot in the back. Didn't even know anyone was around," he said bitterly. "I guess I was careless. Should've known better. You will find him, or them, won't you, Sergeant?"

"Yes, I will, Grey," Matt said with determination. "I won't quit looking until I have them in jail."

Grey seemed to relax a little then, and he spoke wanly. "You better get them before I get well enough to go after them myself. I might not be as kind as you. They might not get to go to jail."

Matt didn't think Grey was serious, but he said, "Leave it to me and the other officers, Grey. You just concentrate on getting well."

Matt was visibly disappointed that he had failed to get more information from Grey, but it was clear that the cowboy had been taken by surprise, ambushed just like Noah Flemming had been. This was the third time that murder had been attempted, counting the shots that had been fired at him and Lindsay. Even though there was little evidence to connect the three incidents, it seemed likely that the same people were behind all of them.

Whoever they are, they're cold-blooded killers. Matt shivered at the thought.

After leaving the hospital, he again called Lindsay's cell phone. This time she answered. "Matt," she said. "I'm sorry I missed you earlier. I left my phone in the truck when I went in to meet with Morris Kincaid. I was just listening to your message."

"Morris Kincaid?" Matt said in surprise. "What did you need to see him about? Surely *you* don't need a lawyer."

"I'm afraid I do, Matt. It's my brother again," she said. "He's suing me over the ranch. Are you in town?"

"Just left the hospital," he said.

"Oh, good. I'm in town, too. Can I meet you somewhere? Then you can tell me about Jimmy's appointment today, and I can tell you what Dwight's trying to pull on me," she said.

Five minutes later, Lindsay was climbing into Matt's truck with him in the parking lot of the sheriff's office. "How's Jimmy? Did the doctor do him any good?"

Matt gave her a brief rundown of the visit with Dr. Lubek. "I hope he's going to come out of this sooner than the doctor thinks. But now, Lindsay, tell me what you were doing at Morris Kincaid's office. What is Dwight suing you about?"

Lindsay opened her purse and pulled out a copy of the papers she'd been given earlier. She'd left the originals with Morris. "He's suing me for the ranch," she said as she handed the papers to Matt.

He read in silence for a while. He couldn't believe what he was reading. "This is ludicrous," he said when he was about halfway through the complaint.

"Keep going; it gets worse," Lindsay said.

When he finished, Matt handed the papers back. "He doesn't stand a chance," he said. "That ranch is yours and has been for some time now."

"That's what Mr. Kincaid said."

"He's a top-notch attorney, Lindsay. He'll take care of this. Dwight doesn't have a snowman's chance in Hades of winning."

"I hope you're right," she said. "Oh, he makes me so angry."

"Don't worry. Now, why don't you come into the office with me for a minute? I just need to check on a few things. Then you can come out to my place and see Jimmy. It would be good for him."

"I'd love to," she said. "By the way, how's Grey? Is he going to make it?"

"He's a tough one, Lindsay," Matt said. "He's already doing amazingly well."

* * *

Avenger wasted no time getting to the point of the meeting of his secret society. "Take those two wolves above the Lazy F Ranch," he instructed his followers concerning the animals they had most recently captured. "And don't put a collar on either one of them. We can't afford to have more collars falling into the hands of the law."

"What's next, Avenger?" Enforcer asked. "After we get these wolves turned loose, what do you want us to do?"

"Nothing," Avenger said. "Just lay low. I think we should back off for a few days and let the wolves do their thing."

"There's a group that's planning a protest in Yellowstone Park this weekend," Retaliator said. "Maybe some of us could go up and hang out with them."

"No, don't show up there or at any other gathering. Let others make the noise now. We have a lot to lose. They don't. I don't want the law looking down any of your necks for any reason, even a peaceful protest. I'll call you when I have something more for you to do. In the meantime, do nothing after those wolves are turned loose," he said.

More than one member of the group of activists disagreed with their leader as they left the meeting that night. They didn't want to just sit around; they enjoyed stirring up trouble. But when a couple of them began to grumble on the way to their cars, Guardian took charge. "Don't any of you get any ideas about going off on your own," she said darkly. "Avenger is in charge, and we do what he says."

"And if we don't?" Harrier asked flippantly.

Guardian spun around, landing a fist squarely on the other woman's mouth. As Harrier wiped the blood away, Guardian said quietly, "Then you'll get that and more."

15

Although the Lazy F and the S/S Ranches had suffered the heaviest losses, other ranches nearby were also losing calves and sheep as the wolves continued to rampage through those areas. Ranchers now carried rifles whenever they were out with their animals in their pastures or on the forest rangelands. The murder of Noah Flemming and attempted murder of Grey Sadler had given rise to widespread apprehension. The damage to the livestock was of great concern, but not nearly as worrisome as the danger to ranchers and their families from the radicals who seemed to have made it their mission to protect the straying predators with lethal force.

As publicity over the havoc that was being done to the herds escalated and outrage over the out-of-control wolf population stirred up ranchers and many businessmen who depended on the ranchers for their livelihood, the activists became more visible and protests increased. Matt and other law enforcement officials brooded about an increase in violence. They particularly worried that more of the peaceful protesters might get stirred up and become violent. Despite long hours of hard work, little progress was made in identifying the most radical activists, those who had committed murder in the name of their cause.

Matt and Reese showed up at several of the protests that were staged in their respective counties over the weekend. They singled out several individuals and questioned them, but they got nowhere. It was almost as if those who were involved in the violence mingled very little with the loudmouths who attended the demonstrations. The men and women they talked to seemed as angry about the violence as anyone else. One young man summed up the situation. "Murder only hurts our cause. We'll do whatever we can to help you catch these people."

"We appreciate that," Matt had responded. "If you see or hear anything that seems suspicious to you, we'd like to know about it."

"You have my word," the fellow, who gave his name as Dave Adamson, said. Others chimed in with their willingness to watch and listen as well.

While law enforcement moved ahead with a discouraging lack of success, Matt still had to deal with his own problems. Jimmy's progress toward recovery was abysmally slow, and Matt worried about him constantly. At the same time, he could see how severely the pending lawsuit was affecting Lindsay. She grew increasingly fearful of losing the ranch, despite firm assurances from Morris Kincaid and Matt himself that she had nothing to worry about.

June wore itself out, and in the first week of July, Morris announced to Lindsay that he had succeeded in getting the judge who had been assigned to her case to conduct a hearing on his motion to dismiss the lawsuit. So, on the following Monday, she appeared in court with Morris and Matt. Dwight walked into the courtroom in company with his attorney, both with decided swaggers. Dwight was dressed sharply in a dark blue suit, white shirt, and tie. He stepped over to Lindsay and said, "Why don't you just give it up? You can't win."

On the advice of her attorney, Lindsay didn't speak to Dwight. However, she had received no instruction about nonverbal communication, and she gave her brother the full effect of an angry glare. Matt also restrained himself from saying what he was thinking to the arrogant man. Dwight laughed at them, then strutted over and sat down beside his attorney at the plaintiff's table. Less than an hour later, as Dwight and his attorney left the courtroom, the swagger was gone. Both were angry, and Dwight flashed Lindsay a look of raw hatred. She shuddered and clung tightly to Matt's arm.

"Well, so much for that," Matt said with a sigh. "You won."

She had indeed. After listening to the arguments of both attorneys, the judge had then summarily dismissed the suit, stating that it was frivolous, that there was no merit at all to Dwight's claim. "I told you not to worry," Morris Kincaid said with a grin as the three of them stood up to leave. "There was nothing else the judge could do. Your brother has no basis to make any claim on the ranch."

So it was over. Dwight had been defeated in his effort to steal the ranch from her. But somehow, Matt had the sinking feeling that Lindsay hadn't heard the last from her brother. An angry and selfish man, he was also determined. Matt worried about him, but he kept his worries to himself and let Lindsay celebrate her victory.

He left Lindsay at the courthouse where she was still discussing things with her attorney and went back to the sheriff's office. The work was piling up. The pressure to find the killers mounted daily. Criticism of both him and the sheriff for failing to solve the cases was being poured out on them by both the local press and a number of ranchers. Matt couldn't blame them for their censure. Five weeks into the case and it still seemed like he was miles away from making an arrest.

The relief at the dismissal of Dwight's lawsuit that morning did little to cheer him. His heart was so heavy with the worry associated with his son that it outweighed everything else in his life. Sitting at his desk a few minutes later, he saw three young people being ushered in to see him. He immediately recognized Dave Adamson, the protester who had offered to help. Two young ladies were with him.

Matt stood and shook their hands. "How can I help you?" he asked.

"We might have a little information," Dave said. "We don't know if it will help, but we'll let you decide that."

"That's great. I appreciate your coming in. What can you tell me?"

"Well, like I said, it might not be much, but I've noticed that two or three people we see quite often at our gatherings have not shown up lately. It just seems strange. When they are there, they are quite vocal, but they always leave before the rest of us do."

"Do you have names?" Matt asked.

"That's another thing that's been bothering us. We only know the names of one of them, and she's a friend of Sue's. Most of us know each other quite well. They've always seemed, well, a little different from the rest of us, even Sue's friend."

"Who's Sue?" he asked.

"I am," one of the girls said. "We aren't really tight friends, but we used to hang out with each other quite a bit. Her name's Sally Simpson. I met her at school a couple of years ago. She's from Helena."

"Good, what more can you tell me about her?" Matt asked.

"This is what really got to us," Dave said. "I overheard her talking to one of the other activists one day, and he called her Jill."

"But I know her name's Sally," Sue broke in. "When Johnny mentioned her and called her Jill, it made us suspicious. But there's more."

"Let's hear it," Matt encouraged.

"Well, it was just a couple of days ago that I was sitting in my apartment in Great Falls when someone knocked on the door," Sue said. "It was Sally. I was really surprised to see her because she hadn't come around for several months, and she'd become quite standoffish at our gatherings. But she had been to my place before. Anyway, I invited her in and we talked for a few minutes. She seemed worried about something. After a bit she asked if it would be possible for her to spend the night. She said she wouldn't be any bother. So of course I told her she could.

"My roommate is spending time with her family for a few weeks, so I told Sally she could use her room. I offered to fix something to eat, and she told me she'd like that. I didn't have much in the apartment, but I told her she could just relax while I went out and got a few groceries. Anyway, I left. Then, after I got to my car, I realized I hadn't fed my dog. I went behind the duplex to feed her. I wanted to do it then so I wouldn't have to when I got back."

Johnny broke in then. "This is where it gets really weird," he said.

"Yeah, really weird," Sue agreed. "And scary. The window to my roommate's bedroom was open, and I could hear Sally's voice. It wasn't like I wanted to eavesdrop or anything, but I just sort of stood there. I guessed she must be using my roommate's phone, and I wondered if it was long distance. She seemed agitated over something, and she was talking quite loudly. She said something about *Avenger*. This doesn't make sense, I know, but it was like she was using someone's name. A minute later, she said, 'I don't think people should be getting killed, that's all.' Again, this is weird, but she called whoever she was talking to *Keeper*. Does this make any sense to you, Sergeant Prescott?"

"Actually, it does. Do you remember anything else she said?" Matt asked.

"Yeah, she said she was mad that Avenger wasn't letting any of them do anything. She said something about Avenger being the one who'd named her *Harrier,* and that she wasn't happy not being busy. She said, and I remember this exactly, 'If I'm Harrier, then I should be harrying, but I won't kill anyone, and that's where he seems to be heading with our society.' Then she said something about being willing to do anything else, but she wouldn't kill people. That shook me up. I don't remember exactly what she said after that, but she did use some other weird name."

"Did she say anything else?" Matt asked.

"She said something about wanting to quit, but she was afraid to. That's as much as I remember."

"I appreciate what you've told me," Matt said. "Now, you say Sally's from Helena?"

"Yes, and I have her address there if that would help."

"It would be great," Matt said.

He wrote down the address and descriptions of Sally and the two other people they were suspicious about. He sat thinking about what he'd learned for several minutes after the trio left. Then he placed a call to a detective in Helena whom he'd assisted with a case. Locating and speaking with Sally Simpson was suddenly a high priority.

* * *

The Wild Animal Protection Society met that hot July night in Great Falls. The only one absent was Harrier, and she said she was ill when the meeting was called. Avenger excused her with instructions to contact him as soon as she was well again. He was impatient and brooding as he called the meeting of his band of renegade activists to order. He told them it was time to stir up more trouble, that their recent days of restless inactivity were over. He had business for his group to conduct.

His instructions that night were brief but to the point. The law was proving helpless in its efforts to find them or to even identify them. "They have no idea that we even exist as a group," he said. "So we're safe." He went on to explain, "Further violence is not only justified but necessary. We need to apply more pressure to get the ranchers to leave the wolves alone."

Avenger emphasized that the ranchers needed to be taught lessons they could no longer ignore. The members of the secret wildlife society

were to act discreetly but quickly in order to turn things even more in
their favor.

When the meeting broke up, they left in small, excited groups to
carry out their assignments. Only the man known as Defender walked
out alone that night, deep in thought about what he'd been instructed to
do. He was still thinking about it as he got into his truck and drove
away. He had never seen Avenger as intense as he'd been that night. This
society he had joined had started out as an organization created for the
purpose of focusing attention on the plight of wolves and other wild
creatures. He was sympathetic to that cause, but it had lately turned into
something more sinister. That night, Avenger had essentially declared
war on the Montana ranchers and those who supported them. Defender
was afraid of Avenger. He went back to ask him a question after he left
the house, but had never gone in. He'd been shocked by a short conversation he overhead between Avenger and Enforcer.

"Harrier should have been here tonight." Avenger said. "I excused
her because she said she was sick. I don't believe her. She's become
dispensable. And then there's Defender. I didn't like the way he was
acting tonight. He seemed less than enthusiastic about his assignment.
If he doesn't carry it out, he'll be dispensable too."

"I'll do whatever I need to," Enforcer replied. "You just give me
the word if it becomes necessary."

Defender turned and cautiously left after that. What had he
gotten himself into? He and Harrier could both end up dead if they
weren't careful. In fact, he wondered if it was already too late for her.

Engrossed in thoughts about the assignment Avenger had given
him, he headed south for Bozeman. What he was about to do was
probably the most dangerous thing he'd ever done in his life. Not
only dangerous, but downright stupid. The problem was, he was
committed, and he feared that there was no turning back. He had
sworn his allegiance to the secret society. And fear for his life now
forced his loyalty.

* * *

Matt and Jimmy returned from their latest trip to Missoula. Despite Dr.
Lubek's continued encouragement, Matt was discouraged. He ached to

talk with Lindsay. Just hearing her voice was soothing. He wished he had time to date her the way he wanted to, but he was far too preoccupied. Despite that, his feelings for the attractive rancher were deepening. She was becoming immeasurably important to him.

Because Keith was working an evening shift that day, Matt decided to take Jimmy and see Lindsay out at her ranch after work. He dialed her home number but got no answer. Then he tried her cell phone. She didn't answer that either, so he left her a message. Then he remembered her mentioning that she had a new horse coming in that day that she hoped to begin breaking that afternoon. He suspected she was still working with the horse and that her cell phone was in the barn. She never had it on her when working in the corral with an unbroken horse.

"As soon as we get our chores done, we'll drive out and surprise Sister Flemming," he said to his silent little son. Thirty minutes later, he loaded Claw in the back of the truck, buckled Jimmy into his seat, and headed out to the Lazy F Ranch.

Although Jimmy still wasn't speaking, he did squeal with delight when Lindsay's little border collie met him in her yard. It wasn't much, but it was progress, Matt thought hopefully as he watched Jimmy, Claw, and Princess play beside the truck for a minute.

Lindsay's pickup was parked inside her garage. He looked around and then decided she must still be out at the round corral. "Come on, Jim. You and the dogs can help me find Lindsay. She's probably on the other side of the barn."

As he walked around the barn, the dogs scampered ahead and Jimmy took hold of his hand, skipping beside him. The boy seemed happy, and Matt conceded to himself that Dr. Lubek was doing more good than he'd given her credit for.

There was a pretty sorrel filly in the round corral. It had on a halter, but no lead rope. A saddle blanket and Lindsay's saddle were on the top rail of the fence. A bridle hung from the saddle horn. As he got closer, Matt could see that a lead rope and her whip lay in the dirt almost directly below the saddle.

But Lindsay wasn't there. That seemed strange. She normally didn't leave a horse she was working with until she'd finished the day's routine.

Maybe she walked up to the house to grab something to eat, Matt thought. *There's plenty of daylight left. She might have planned to work with the horse some more but got hungry and took a break.*

He took Jimmy by the hand again. "Okay, sport," he said. "She must be in the house. Let's go surprise her."

After ringing the doorbell twice but getting no answer, an old familiar chill began to run up Matt's spine. He opened the door and hollered inside. "Lindsay, are you home?"

The house was silent. He walked in, still holding Jimmy's hand firmly. The kitchen looked like maid service had just been there. If she'd eaten recently, she'd cleaned up already. He shouted for her again, but there was still no answer. He opened her dishwasher. The dishes in it were clean, dry, and cool. It had been several hours since they were washed. There were no dirty dishes anywhere. It was apparent she hadn't eaten dinner yet.

Okay, Lindsay, what are you doing? he wondered as the chill became a sick feeling in the pit of his stomach.

He took Jimmy back outside where they looked around for a few minutes. Matt couldn't see Lindsay anywhere in the fields. All the tractors were in the shed with the rest of her equipment. Matt was vexed.

Darn it all, Lindsay, where are you? he thought. Then he became worried. But he tried not to share that worry with Jimmy. His son didn't need anything more to be frightened about.

He shouted her name several times. Then he looked directly at Jimmy. "Gee, son, maybe she isn't home." He tried to keep his voice steady, even nonchalant, while inside he was panicking.

Matt hadn't checked the barn, although if she were in there she would have heard him shouting for her. He moved toward the barn and entered, wiping the sweat from his face once he was inside. Outside it was very dry and hot, a typical Montana summer's eve. But inside the barn it was much cooler. A couple of horses neighed, and another one stamped. He checked their feed boxes. Empty. Lindsay hadn't done her chores yet that evening. To keep his own worry at bay, Matt quickly fed and watered the horses. One stall gate was hanging open. He guessed that the young sorrel filly in the round corral was supposed to spend the night in that stall. He put hay in there and filled the water trough, so that when Lindsay came back from wherever she was, she wouldn't have to do it.

If she came back.

That awful thought, unbidden, hit him like a ninety-mile-an-hour fastball. He had to bend over for a moment to ease the pain. Jimmy stayed right beside him. Matt pulled his cell phone from his pocket and dialed Lindsay's cell phone number again. *Maybe she'll answer it now,* he thought hopefully. But he jumped when he heard the familiar ring of her phone. It came from inside the open door of her tack room. He hurried over and looked inside. The light was on, and her purse was sitting on a chair just inside the door. The ringing was coming from inside the purse.

Matt closed his phone, and the ringing in the purse stopped. He wiped a bandana across his face again. Although it was fairly cool in the barn, he was dripping with sweat. He opened his phone again and called the sheriff at home.

It took only a moment to explain to Sheriff Baker that Lindsay wasn't at home and why he thought she should be. "I'll be right out," the sheriff promised after listening to Matt's description of what he'd found at the ranch and how inconsistent it was with Lindsay's normal behavior.

While he was waiting for the sheriff, Matt put the new filly in its stall in the barn and, with Jimmy's help, finished the rest of Lindsay's evening chores. The last thing they did was gather the eggs, one of Jimmy's favorite chores at home and at the Lazy F. They carried the eggs into the house, cleaned them, and put them in Lindsay's refrigerator. When they stepped outside again, the sheriff was just pulling into the yard.

Trying to stay upbeat for Jimmy's sake, Matt again explained why Lindsay's absence didn't make sense. And then he explained why it might make sense.

Dwight.

* * *

Dwight.

He had to be responsible for what was happening to her. Nothing else made sense. Lindsay was sitting in total darkness, her hands and feet bound with duct tape. She struggled again, but it was no use. She was at the mercy of her captor, or captors, as she preferred to think. It was simply not logical that Lucas was doing these horrible things to her all on his own. He wasn't gutsy enough.

As she lay there helplessly in the darkness, she tried to remember what she could of that day, assuming it was still *that day*. For all she knew, it could be the next day by now.

Lucas acted differently when he'd come to the corral that afternoon while she was beginning to break the sorrel filly. She panicked when she first saw him. But he said, "Hey, I'm not here to cause you any more trouble. I'm sorry that I won't be able to buy your ranch, but I see now that you're serious about not selling it. Dwight had me convinced that it was really his, not yours. The court sided with you, it seems. Dwight was lying to me about the whole thing, and for that I'm sorry. Kendra and I should have done our homework. We shouldn't have listened to him."

He seemed genuinely sincere. Then he said, "I'd like to talk to you about your dog, and make it up to you for his loss." Lindsay honestly believed he meant it. "Please believe me. I didn't mean to hurt it. When it ran in front of the truck, I tried to avoid hitting it, but I couldn't. I wanted to tell you what I'd done, but I didn't think you'd understand, so I just got out of there. I can see now that I shouldn't have done that."

Lindsay had climbed out of the round corral then, dropping her whip and lead rope below her saddle. Then she faced him and said, "What's done is done. It's funny, though. He was never one to chase cars."

"I don't know how it happened or why, but believe me, I'm sorry," he said with a drawl. "If it hadn't been for your brother, I wouldn't have been here and your dog would still be alive. I can see now that it was all a big hoax. Your brother seemed so sincere about his right to your ranch and how you were being so awful in stealing it from him. All Kendra and I wanted was an honest chance to buy it. Anyway, I came to tell you I'm sorry. I want to pay you back for the loss of your dog. I know how valuable a good cow dog is on a ranch. I have some money in the truck."

Lindsay shook her head. "I don't care about the money, Lucas. I just wish they could find whoever it was that killed my father. He should still be here, helping me with this ranch. He had some good years left in him."

"Yeah, I'm sure sorry about him. It doesn't make any sense at all that someone would commit murder over a wolf. I wish there was some way I could help find whoever did it, but I wouldn't even know where to start looking," he said.

"Thanks," she said. "Now, I really must get back to the horse I'm working with."

"Please, before you do, I want to give you some money. I'd feel better about what has happened if you'd just accept that," he pleaded.

He looked so sincere that Lindsay gave in. She walked through the barn with him and over to his truck. He opened the door, looked inside, and said, "Doggone it. I must have dropped my wallet. All I need now is for someone to find it and clean me out."

Lucas's concern seemed genuine, and that was understandable. Identity theft was a real worry to many people. She said, "Hey, don't worry about it on my account. I just appreciate the thought."

Lucas nodded. "Oh, there is one more thing, while I'm thinking of it."

"What's that, Lucas?" she asked him.

"That little boy who was here that day—I hope that seeing me run over your dog didn't scare him too bad."

"Something did. I don't know if it was that or not," she said. "But he hasn't spoken a word since."

"That's terrible. I'm so sorry. I sure didn't mean to cause him any harm. Is he going to be okay?"

"I hope so," she said.

"I hope so too," he responded earnestly.

She started toward the barn then. She heard Lucas open his truck, and, assuming he was getting in, she didn't look back. A moment later, she felt something prick her back. As she started to turn toward Lucas, her legs gave way. That was all she remembered.

She regained consciousness only an hour or so ago in this dark, filthy place. It took her several minutes to recall what had happened earlier. She was still feeling dizzy and slightly disoriented, but her memory was clear. Lucas was the one who had pulled a hoax on her. He must have tranquilized her and then kidnapped her. And he'd done it all for Dwight. She couldn't believe her brother was so vile. He wanted the ranch, and apparently he was willing to go to any length to get it.

Lindsay's biggest fear now was that she might die in this forsaken place in the middle of nowhere. And since she had no will, she feared that Dwight, as her closest kin, would end up with the ranch.

Dwight and his insidious plan, she thought as tears began to flow.

16

Matt tried to think of who might have had anything to do with Lindsay's disappearance. Lucas Mallory had to be considered a suspect, as did his fiancée, Kendra Norse. But one person stood out in Matt's mind as the prime suspect: Dwight Flemming. The only motive he could imagine that would cause Dwight to do such a thing was his greedy desire for the Lazy F Ranch, or at least for what the ranch was worth to the right buyer. But that was a serious motive. The idea that Dwight would harm Lindsay to get his hands on the ranch was appalling, but Matt realized it was not only possible, but plausible.

He didn't think Dwight would personally harm Lindsay. He would leave that kind of dirty work to someone lower in his pecking order. That way, if she permanently disappeared or turned up dead, and Dwight could prove that he had nothing to do with it, he very well might end up with the ranch. After all, he was her closest relative. Matt shuddered at the thought. Could that be what it was all about? Although distraught, he forced himself to focus. Lindsay was alive. He was convinced of that. She could well be in serious danger, but she was alive. He had to find her before it was too late. And he wanted to bring her worthless brother and his cronies to justice.

Watching Matt a little later, the sheriff suggested that perhaps someone else should take the lead on the investigation into her disappearance.

"Not on your life, Ethan," Matt said. "No one else will work as hard as I will to see that we find Lindsay."

"But you have so many things to worry about right now," the sheriff said. "There's your younger boy, for one thing. And then there's the murder of Noah Flemming and the attempted killing of Grey Sadler. You could keep working on those cases."

"All these cases are important to me, Ethan. Please, you've got to let me continue to at least oversee them. I'll take all the help you can give me. But please, leave me in charge of the investigations, especially Lindsay's disappearance."

The sheriff nodded his head slowly. "Okay, we'll give it a try for a week or so. I'll shift some deputies to aid you, but if it gets to be too much, nobody will think less of you if you step down and let someone else lead out."

"I know that. And thanks. Now, the first thing we've got to do is find that good-for-nothing brother of Lindsay's."

That proved, over the next few hours, to be impossible. Even with the cooperation of several police agencies, they found not even a trace of Dwight. Matt began to wonder if he used more names than Dwight Flemming. There was a current driver's license in his name, but the address in Cutbank, just south of the Canadian border, was a home owned by someone else. And no property was registered to him. It was also strange that there were no vehicles in Montana or any of the surrounding states registered under the name Dwight Flemming. If only he had a picture of Dwight that could be circulated. Surely someone had seen Dwight besides Lindsay and those who were in court with him the day the judge had thrown out his lawsuit. Contact with Dwight's lawyer proved as fruitless as everything else. The attorney, citing client-attorney privilege, clammed up.

Even though Matt didn't have Lindsay's consent, he went to the prosecutor's office the morning following her disappearance and presented the facts related to Dwight's burglary of Lindsay's home and the thefts that had occurred. By noon, charges were in place and a felony warrant was issued. Matt was satisfied that if and when Dwight surfaced, he'd be arrested. Then he would have a chance to grill him on Lindsay's whereabouts.

A hunt was also on for Lucas Mallory and Kendra Norse, but they still hadn't been found anywhere in Montana or the surrounding states. The fact that all three of them seemed to have disappeared simultaneously only served to increase Matt's conviction that they were involved.

Matt had just hung up the phone early that afternoon when Grey Sadler came into his office. "What are you doing out of bed?" Matt asked as he rose to greet the young cowboy.

"I've come to help find Lindsay." Grey grimaced.

"But you're hurt too badly," Matt argued. "We're doing everything we can to find her. You've got to take care of yourself."

"I'm a whole lot better now," Grey said, although his pale face and pain-filled eyes related a different story. "That snake I pounded on at Lindsay's ranch that day has to be part of this. I feel it in my gut."

"Lucas Mallory," Matt said bitterly. "I'm sure you're right. But we can't find him. We won't quit trying, though. Here, sit down." The young man was getting paler by the second.

"That's because he's got Lindsay somewhere, and he's staying out of sight while he holds her. Do you know where he lives?" Grey asked after painfully seating himself.

"Yes, and I've had officers go to his place. He rents a house just outside Great Falls, but there's no sign of life there. And his truck hasn't been seen for a couple of days by any of the neighbors. If he shows up there, we'll nab him. I've got officers keeping an eye on the place. I've also issued a bulletin on him in the Dakotas, Wyoming, and Idaho."

"Good, glad to hear it. But what about Lindsay's brother?" Grey asked.

"We're working at finding him," Matt said, and he explained that there was now a warrant out for Dwight for burglary and theft. He also told Grey of his suspicion that Dwight might be using a number of aliases.

"What about the woman who claims to be Lucas's fiancée?" he asked.

"Her name is Kendra Norse, according to what she told Lindsay. Of course, that might not be her name at all. Like the others, we can't find a criminal record on anyone by that name. And we can't locate her either."

Grey shook his head. "So it's like none of them even exist?"

"Yeah, it's like that, I'm afraid."

Matt was thoughtful for a moment. Then he said, "I think I'll take a run out to the Lazy F. My son went out and did Lindsay's chores earlier, but I'd just like to have a look around and see what I can find.

It might be a waste of time, but I'm going to drive out to see if I've missed a clue somewhere."

"I'd like to ride out there with you," Grey said as he painfully rose to his feet. "If you don't mind, that is. Or I can take my truck."

"You can ride with me," Matt said, and he too got out of his chair. "I'll get you back to your truck when we're finished."

Matt had no idea what he was looking for; he just had a feeling that he needed to drive out and look around. His feelings suddenly took shape when he left the county road and started up the lane toward Lindsay's ranch. A van was charging toward him. Matt hugged his side of the road as the van thundered past.

"Hey! That's Kendra Norse!" Matt yelled as the van passed.

"Any idea who was with her?" Grey asked as Matt jammed on the brakes and slid to a stop.

"No idea," Matt said as he turned his truck around.

"Young guy," Grey said, sounding very weak. "I got a good look at his face as they passed. He looked sullen. You know, like a child that's been scolded."

"Are you okay, Grey?" Matt asked as he glanced over at the rancher.

"I'll be all right," Grey said with a grimace. "Go get 'em."

Matt got on the radio, called in his location, and told the dispatcher he was in pursuit of a couple of possible suspects. "I'll send backup," the dispatcher told him.

At first it looked like Kendra was going to make a run for it. She was going well over the speed limit when Matt overtook her van. And she either couldn't see or ignored his lights when he turned them on. Of course, that didn't surprise him. They were mounted behind his grill and not as easy to see as bar lights. But when he pulled up beside her on the state highway where she'd headed west and signaled her over with his hand, she stopped almost immediately.

"Stay here," Matt said to Grey as he got out. "But if that young guy tries something, shout at me."

"You got it," Grey said.

Matt approached the vehicle slowly, his hand on the sidearm that was tucked in its holster inside his pants. "Stay right where you are!" he shouted when Kendra began to get out of the van. "And tell your friend to stay put as well."

She obeyed, but peevishly. A moment later he was at the window. The young passenger spoke first. "Got a problem, Officer?" he sneered.

Matt ignored him and addressed Kendra. "Could I have a look at your driver's license and registration?" He tried to play the role of the polite law enforcement officer but wished he could pound the truth out of both of them.

The woman wasn't nearly as polite as Matt. "You got no business stopping me," she said. "You were speeding."

"That so? Then give me a ticket and let me get on my way. I've got stuff to do."

Matt waited while she dug in her purse for her driver's license. He was anxious to see it, since the state of Montana didn't have her on record. A moment later she handed it to him.

He glanced at it while she dug in her jockey box for the registration. It was a Georgia license with a Georgia address. The name was Kendra Norse, and the picture looked right. She seemed to be having trouble coming up with the registration. While he waited, Matt glanced around inside the front of the van. He couldn't see into the back. A black curtain was drawn across the full width of the vehicle behind the front seats. Matt had every intention of taking them both into the office for questioning, and when he did, he'd find out what, if anything, was behind that curtain. What he spotted in her glove compartment as she retrieved the registration gave him a reason for detaining them.

Before she could shut the door of the glove compartment, he said, "Those look like eagle feathers, Kendra. Would you hand them to me?"

She looked up sharply and slammed the little door shut. "Those are turkey feathers," she said. "And you can't have them."

The headstrong young man beside her spoke up. "Ain't anything illegal about a turkey feather, copper boy. So why don't you mind your own business and leave us alone."

It would be easy to dislike that young man, Matt decided. But he kept his voice even. "I know eagle feathers when I see them. And I would guess the two of you do as well. I'll take that registration now. Then you can get those feathers for me."

"You'll have to have a warrant," she said as she handed over the registration.

He glanced at it, then glanced again when he realized it was not registered in her name. It was registered to a Carlton Shuler, with an address in Great Falls. Surely he hadn't just stumbled on an alias of Dwight Flemming's, he thought. "Who is Carlton Shuler?"

"A friend of mine," she answered.

"And I suppose he gave you permission to drive his van today."

"Yeah, he did," she said. "Like I just said, he's a friend."

"I'll have to verify that. In the meantime, I'm going to have to take you both in."

"For speeding?" she asked indignantly. "I already said give me the ticket. That's all you can do."

"Actually, I can arrest you. Issuing a ticket is my option. But there's also the matter of the eagle feathers," he said. "I can't issue a ticket for that. And, of course, there is the further matter of the ownership of the van. It's not yours. So I'm going to have to locate the owner and make sure you have permission to be driving it. Then I'll discuss the eagle feathers with him as well."

Matt was aware of two things occurring as he spoke. Grey was getting out of the truck, and Kendra's young passenger was reaching inside a bag on the floor between the two suspects' seats.

Matt took half a step back, pulled his pistol, and aimed it past Kendra. "Mister, don't you move."

The young man looked at him with hate plastered across his face. Kendra had the same expression on hers. "Now, pull your hand out slowly, and it better be empty," Matt said. "And don't you make any move at all, Kendra, while he does that."

Their expressions darkened, but the young man did as he was told. "Now, keep both of your hands in sight. In fact, why don't you just put them on the dash and keep them there until I tell you otherwise."

The young man reached forward and placed his hands on the dash.

"What's your name?" Matt asked.

"Jude," the kid said.

"Jude who?"

"Just Jude."

"No last name?"

"That's right. I ain't got one."

"You, Kendra, get out of the van. Keep your hands in sight. I'll open the door, and then with your hands on the back of your head, step out onto the pavement." As he spoke, he put his pistol away. He wanted both hands free when she got out.

Cars were occasionally passing them, but there was plenty of room for Kendra to exit the van safely. Instead she said, "It isn't safe to get out here. Somebody runs over me, I'll sue you for everything you've got."

Matt ignored her and swung the door open. When he did, he was aware of the far door opening as well. Jude jumped out. Matt grinned at the surprise on his face as he turned, started to run, and bumped into Grey Sadler, who wrapped his arms around the young man and held him tight.

Matt didn't see what happened next on the other side of the van. He saw Kendra's leg swing at him. He dodged, and her foot glanced off his thigh. Woman or not, she was still a criminal, and Matt shoved her hard, more out of reflex than anything else. She flew back against the van. Matt grabbed her by the arm, spun her around, and slammed her against the side of the van again. A moment later he snapped a set of handcuffs on her wrists.

Not until then was he able to figure out what was going on with Jude and Grey, although he had a feeling Grey could take care of himself despite his injuries. Grimacing in pain, Grey held both of Jude's hands securely behind his back. At that moment, the backup he'd been promised arrived. Trooper Mike Standler of the Montana Highway Patrol took a quick glance at the situation. "Looks like you two have things under control," he said.

After both suspects were secured in the back of Trooper Standler's patrol car, Matt went back to the van. The bag the young man had put his hand in lay open between the seats. He could see a pistol inside. He retrieved it and found it fully loaded and ready to fire. He was pretty certain that Jude would have used it if he'd had the chance. A moment later Matt also retrieved the eagle feathers he'd seen. He now had plenty of charges to hold the two of them.

Another deputy arrived, and Matt had him stay with the van until a wrecker came to pick it up. "We'll do an inventory of it in a little while," Matt said. "In the meantime, don't let it out of your sight. Follow the wrecker in and stay with it in our impound yard until I can come look it over. I'm going to follow Trooper Standler into Bozeman. He's going to haul those two in for me."

Grey was back in the truck waiting for Matt. "Are you all right?" he asked. "The last thing you needed was to have to fight that kid."

"I'll live," Grey said. "But you're right. I really shouldn't be wrestling thugs like that in my condition."

Matt pulled onto the roadway behind the Montana Highway Patrol unit. Grey, obviously in a lot of pain, said, "By the way, I wonder what those two were doing out at the Lazy F."

"That's what I've been wondering. We've got to find out if we can," Matt said. "And the sooner the better." He picked up his radio and called the dispatcher. "Do you have any other units in our vicinity?" he asked.

"I'm nearly to your location," the sheriff broke in.

"Great. Would you mind following Trooper Standler into the jail while I run out to the Lazy F and see if I can figure out why these suspects were out there?" he asked.

The sheriff agreed and showed up a few minutes later. They all pulled to the side of the road. "Grey, maybe you better go with Sheriff Baker," Matt said. "You look like you're hurting. You may want to run into the hospital and have them check you out."

"I'll be okay, Matt. I want to go out to the Flemming place with you." Matt looked dubiously at him, but Grey just smiled. "You never know. You might need my help again."

Matt couldn't argue with that. If it hadn't been for Grey's help, they'd probably still be chasing the flighty Jude, whose Georgia ID identified him as Jude Norse, if it hadn't been for Grey's help. He suspected that the young man and Kendra were brother and sister.

Matt and Grey pulled into Lindsay's yard a few minutes later. "You can stay in the truck, Grey, and take it easy while I take a quick look around," Matt said.

"Actually, I'll feel better moving around. Anyway, a second set of eyes can't hurt. If you'll just tell me what to look for, I'll see if I can help."

"I don't know exactly what I'm looking for, Grey. I was hoping that maybe they left a note for us. The connection between them and Lucas is too strong to ignore," he said. "And who knows, maybe by some stretch of luck they brought Lindsay back."

That was wishful thinking. Matt wasn't surprised when they found that Lindsay wasn't home. And there also wasn't a note that they could find anywhere. There was, however, some damage to Lindsay's property. A window in the house had been broken, and it appeared that someone had been inside. The front door hung open. "More charges for our two smart friends," Matt said to Grey. "Let's go inside and see if they've done any more damage. And maybe there's something missing. If there is, we'll find it in the van later. But we'd better not touch anything. I'd like to look for fingerprints here when I get a minute."

In the barn they found further vandalism. Someone had taken a knife to a couple of saddles, severely damaging them. And several sacks of grain had been cut open and the grain scattered on the floor. The young filly that Lindsay had been hired to break had been turned loose from her stall, as had a couple of other horses. Fortunately, they'd gone into the corrals in the back, and it took Grey and Matt only a few minutes to return them to their stalls. Had the horses gone out the front door of the barn, which had been standing wide open, they could have scattered anywhere.

"So I wonder why all the damage?" Matt mused after putting the horses away.

"Somebody got mad. It's that simple," Grey said.

"But if that's the case, what made them lose their tempers?" Matt asked.

"His temper," Grey corrected him. "I'd be willing to bet that the kid was the one who got mad and did all this, but I don't have a clue as to why."

Nor did Matt, but he was more afraid than ever for the young woman he was falling in love with.

* * *

A door opened somewhere beyond the room she was being held captive in. Lindsay supposed it was Lucas again. He'd come late the night before, given her some food, let her use the bathroom, then tied her up again and left her for the night. The next time he'd returned had been in the late morning hours. He'd repeated the previous night's routine and then left again. He didn't say ten words to her either time. She tried to talk to him, but other than asking her if she was okay, he generally ignored her questions and comments.

She assumed that she was about to get more of the same silent treatment now. This time she was surprised. "I'll take the tape off and leave it off for a while if you promise not to try to get away."

"Why would I promise that?" Lindsay asked stubbornly.

"It would just be a lot easier on you if you did."

"Well, maybe you could explain what you and Dwight think you'll achieve by kidnapping me."

"All I can tell you is that it's for your own good."

"Oh yeah, and how's that? My livestock are going untended. The wolves have a free hand with my calves while I'm gone. Others are worried about me. I could go on, but I won't. Gee, Lucas, I'm sorry if I can't see how this is for my own good."

"Trust me. It is."

"Trust you? Are you serious? You stick a needle in me with some kind of tranquilizer in it, kidnap me, stash me in this dark, filthy room with only a bucket, and you expect me to trust you?"

"Yeah, that's right, trust me. I know what I'm talkin' about. Just cooperate with me, and you may get to live. Doesn't that mean anything to you?"

It meant a lot to her. She just couldn't figure out what this man and her brother had in mind. "Listen, Lucas, I'm sure this is all because of my ranch. Well, no matter what happens, Dwight will never have it. If he'd been decent when he finally showed up, I'd have figured out a way to share with him. But there's no way now. He doesn't deserve anything my father had. What I can't figure out is why, after all these years, Dwight shows up and wants something he wasn't willing to put any effort into."

"His dad drove him away," Lucas said.

"He told you that?"

"Yes, he told me that. He says that all your dad ever wanted from him was work, work, and more work."

"That's not true. Dwight was always out causing trouble. Despite that, my father treated him fairly. He treated everyone well. He was a fair and gentle man. Dwight was just selfish, that's all. He always had other things he was doing, but he never lifted a finger to help with the chores or with the haying or the cattle or anything else on the ranch. All my dad ever did was ask him to quit running around and help out some. So what did he do? He ran off. And did he even have the courtesy to let Dad and me know what had happened to him? No, he didn't."

Lindsay paused for a breath before she continued. "Well, actually, he called home twice the first couple of years after he left, but all he wanted was money. Dad sent him some the first time, but when he asked the second time, Dad told him that if he would come home, they'd talk about it. Dwight said he'd make his own money then. We never heard from him after that. Until after my father was murdered, that is."

Lucas flinched. "I'm sorry about your father," he said. "I'm just tryin' to help you avoid the same fate."

"Well, thank you for that, Lucas." She spit out each word angrily, emphasizing them one by one.

"You're welcome," he said as he backed toward the door to the little prison room. "I gotta go pretty soon. You'll be locked in here for a while. If you'll promise to behave, I'll take the tape off you. Then you can move around more freely."

"What else can I do but behave?" she asked. "I'm your prisoner—yours and Dwight's, that is."

Once again, Lucas flinched. "I'll take that as a promise," he said. He removed the tape from her hands and feet. "I'll be back. And please, when I come, don't try somethin' stupid. I don't want to see you get hurt. I know you don't believe me, but it's true."

A moment later, Lucas was gone. Lindsay tried the door, but she was not going anywhere. All she could do now was think. She had plenty of time for that.

17

The interviews Matt had hoped to conduct did not occur. On the advice of the same attorney that had brought Dwight's lawsuit against Lindsay, both Kendra and Jude Norse simply refused to talk. Both were immediately bailed out of jail by that same attorney and their van returned from impoundment.

The failure of either suspect to talk left Matt with no clues as to Lindsay's whereabouts. It was especially discouraging since he strongly suspected that the pair was somehow involved in Lindsay's disappearance. With them free on bail, Matt found himself hoping that some kind of ransom demand would show up. At least he would then have more hope that Lindsay was still alive.

He found it increasingly hard to focus both at work and at home. Jimmy required a lot of attention, but much of the burden of caring for him was of necessity shifted to Matt's parents and Keith. Grey had definitely suffered a setback after wrestling with Jude Norse and was ordered to stay in bed for a few days. Nevertheless, he was making sure things were taken care of at the Lazy F Ranch. He and his older brother sent some of their own ranch hands over each day to work on Lindsay's place. Matt drove out there whenever he could just to keep an eye on things. He'd taken her little dog, Princess, home with him.

Leads came into the sheriff's office quite regularly as the week passed, and Matt and several other officers diligently followed up on each one, but none of them bore fruit. Matt had hoped that the officers in Helena could find Sally Simpson and that she might be able to shed some light on Noah Flemming's murder. However, her parents said they hadn't heard from her for several weeks. Continued efforts to locate Dwight and Lucas were also futile. Matt didn't give up, but he kept working until he felt like he would collapse.

* * *

The room where Lindsay was being held captive was dark. Earlier, she had discovered that the solid log walls were windowless and that the ceiling sloped upward to a rough board ceiling. It was apparent to her that she was in some type of cabin. She was now standing beside the heavy plank door that separated her cell from the rest of the cabin, trying to identify the activity in the room beyond.

On the far side of that room, an argument was escalating. She made out very few of the words being bandied back and forth, but she was almost certain that two or three other people had come in shortly after Lucas brought her a cold sandwich and a can of pop and emptied her latrine bucket. She heard two different vehicles arrive at the cabin a few minutes apart. Although she had been unconscious when Lucas had brought her to this place, she was quite certain it was in the rural countryside, away from any main roads. The only times she remembered hearing vehicles were when Lucas came and went.

She recognized one of the angry voices. It was Kendra Norse, the woman who had appeared at the ranch with Lucas, claiming to be his fiancée and saying they wanted to buy the place. Kendra's was the only female voice she could hear. She knew Lucas's voice, although he seemed to have less to say than the others. The other men—she thought there must be two of them—she couldn't identify. The argument suddenly stopped, and someone approached the door through which she was listening. Her blood froze when she heard an unfamiliar male voice. "She's supposed to be dead. See that it happens."

There was a muffled response from across the room. Then came an angry outburst from Kendra. The only words she could decipher were "your job" and "better be soon."

Someone else crossed the room toward the door where Lindsay stood listening, a man, she thought. That guess proved to be correct a moment later when the man said, "I'll help if you want."

A male voice said, "The boss gave his orders. We follow them. And that's that."

But more discussion ensued. Again, it was on the far side of the room, and Lindsay couldn't follow the conversation. She could tell, however, that there was a lot of anger in the room. Judging from the intensity pervading the discussion, for the first time, Lindsay feared for her life. And her brother was behind it. Surely he was the one who had been referred to as "the boss." She wondered what kinds of things he had done since he'd left home so many years ago. Whatever it was, it involved criminal activity, she was quite certain. And it sounded like it could be organized crime. She didn't like to admit it, but she found that she despised Dwight, maybe even hated him. He was a selfish, evil, devilish man.

Even though Lindsay's room was almost pitch black, she knew it was still daylight. When Lucas had opened the door to give her some food earlier, she had looked at her watch in the light that had shone in from the doorway. The fact that she couldn't find any light switches or electrical outlets in the room convinced her that there was no electricity in this cabin, and thus reinforced her conviction that it was in a remote location.

It had been a little after five PM then. She judged it to be closer to six now.

More conversation was taking place across the room, but even though it was just a blurred humming sound, it didn't seem like the angry bickering that had occurred just moments earlier. Whatever the men and woman were talking about, they were doing it calmly now. Another minute or two passed, and she heard a door slam. After that it was quiet in the cabin. Lindsay was alone again.

She knew, however, that it would be only be a matter of time before someone returned, probably Lucas. She heard the words repeated again and again in her mind: *She's supposed to be dead. See that it happens.*

She dropped to her knees and began to pray. She'd done a lot of that since Lucas had brought her here four days before. At least, she thought it had been that long. Her praying now took on a new urgency. She felt that unless a miracle occurred, her days, maybe even her hours, were numbered.

After praying, Lindsay sat thinking about what she had heard from the room beyond her door. Kendra Norse and Lucas Mallory were just two of the people who took orders from her brother. They had been at her ranch at the behest of Dwight. She was sure she'd never seen the others, but they must be just as treacherous.

Isn't there anything good left in Dwight? she asked herself. What had made him so hateful and evil? She'd never been able to understand his rebellious teenage years or his anger when he'd left home. It was obvious now that he'd discarded the teachings and values of his parents.

It made her angry to think that Dwight would so brazenly order someone to kill her. He wanted her dead so that he could have the ranch for himself. But he didn't even want the ranch—just the money from the sale of it. That thought fueled her anger. She wished that she'd let Matt bring charges against him for stealing her father's belongings. If she'd had any idea how much worse he'd become, she'd have asked to have him arrested. Not that it would have helped—he had people who would do his bidding at the drop of a hat. And even if he'd been in jail, he could have ordered her murder.

As Lindsay's anger continued to build, she found her courage beginning to grow as well. And that courage was a direct answer to her prayer. She was determined that she wasn't going to die without a fight. She thought about the small room she was in, trying to picture anything she might use as a weapon the next time Lucas opened the door. She'd had enough light when he was in there with her that she knew essentially where everything was. But she didn't remember seeing anything that would make a good weapon . . . unless . . .

Her nasty latrine bucket was still standing empty beside the door where Lucas had left it earlier. It had a handle, and although it was plastic, she could swing it. It might break when it hit Lucas, but it might also give her the short time she needed to race out the door and escape. It was the only thing she could think of.

All she could do now was wait until Lucas came back. But while she was waiting, she knew she had to stay awake. She didn't dare fall asleep, because the next time Lucas came in would probably be the last.

Then she had a terrible thought. *What if Kendra or one of the others comes with Lucas when he returns?* There was no way she could fight two at once with nothing but the bucket as a weapon. But it was all she had. There was no other option. She just hoped that Lucas would be alone when he came.

By the time Lindsay finally heard a vehicle pull up in front of the cabin, several hours had passed. She was wide awake now, but she'd been fighting sleep for the past several hours, and it had been difficult. She believed it was likely the middle of the night. *It's now or never,* she thought as a tremor passed through her body.

A light suddenly shined beneath her door. Whoever was in the other room had turned on a lantern. Although she could hear someone moving around, she heard no voices. She grabbed the bucket and listened carefully. She was certain there was only one set of footsteps crossing the room toward her. Apparently, Lucas, if that's who it was, had come back alone. She silently prayed and tightened her grip on the bucket's handle.

The doorknob moved slightly. She waited for it to open, scarcely daring to breathe. She held the bucket back as far as she could reach, ready to swing it forward with every bit of strength she could muster the moment Lucas came into the room. But the door didn't open. Lucas, or whoever was on the other side, was apparently just standing there. She couldn't imagine what he was waiting for. She wanted to get this over with. She was ready to make her stand against her enemy.

Why had the killer come in the middle of the night if not to carry out Dwight's order? And why had he started to open the door and then not carried through with it? It made no sense. Maybe he was just checking to see that the door was still locked. Which it obviously was. No one had been there to unlock it since the four of them left earlier.

The seconds ticked by. Suddenly the footsteps receded, and the light was extinguished. The outside door opened and closed. A vehicle started up and then drove away. Bitter tears of disappointment stung Lindsay's eyes. She had been mentally prepared to fight for her life. She didn't know if she could stay awake all night, worrying about when her killer might choose to come back. And if he did, and she was asleep, she would have no chance of defending herself. In absolute despair, Lindsay grabbed the doorknob.

It turned!

She pushed gently and the door swung open. She could hardly believe what was happening. Whoever had been here just minutes ago had been unbelievably careless. Or was he waiting outside to kill her when she exited the house? Had the car gone only a short distance and then stopped? Was the driver sneaking back at this very moment? Or was there more than one killer waiting for her to come out the door?

Lindsay's heart pounded in her chest. Sweat rolled off her face, and her hands were moist and slick. She carried the bucket, still her only weapon. She hesitated at the front door, then tried the doorknob. It too was unlocked. Freedom was only a few feet away.

Or was it death that awaited her in the chilly darkness outside this lonely cabin?

Lindsay hesitated. Then she stepped back from the door, uncertain what to do next. She wished she could turn on a light and try to find a more effective weapon than her bucket. But there were no lights, and even if there had been, she would have been afraid to use them. She could see a window in one wall of the room, but something heavy covered it, and only a few glimmers of light seeped around the edges. She turned and felt her way around the room. She wanted to be away from this place, to step outside the door and make a dash for freedom. But fear restrained her.

She moved more quickly away from the door, the door that led to freedom or death, and walked through an interior door and into an adjoining room. Just enough light came through a window there, one with no blinds or curtains covering it, so she could tell she was in a small, crude kitchen. There didn't appear to be any taps over the sink, and there was no refrigerator, but a woodburning cookstove stood against one wall. Cupboards and drawers lined another wall, and a table with four wooden chairs sat in the center of the room.

Lindsay dropped her bucket on the floor and began yanking open drawers. *There they are,* she exalted. *Kitchen knives.* She picked out two of them—a small paring knife and a butcher knife. She tucked the paring knife into her pants, but she held the large one in her hand. It had weight to it, and it was sharp. She summoned up the courage to go out the front door.

Before leaving, she checked the cupboards, hoping to find food she could carry with her. The cupboards were closer to empty than to full, but she found a couple of flat cans that felt like they might contain sardines or kippers. She shoved them in a pocket and felt around some more. Finding nothing else and anxious to leave, she made her way to the outside door again. She hesitated, listening carefully for sounds of someone waiting outside for her.

She heard nothing. Tightening her grip on the steel-bladed courage she held in her hand, Lindsay opened the door a few inches and peeked out. It was a clear night, with stars shining brightly above the pine trees that surrounded the cabin. The thin sliver of moon offered minimal but helpful light. She looked back and forth for a moment and saw no one lurking nearby. After taking a deep breath and offering a short prayer, she stepped through the doorway and onto the small porch. Once more she looked around her. Then she darted swiftly across the driveway and into the trees beyond. Suddenly, she possessed hope.

Because the area she had entered was not densely forested and the ground was flat, Lindsay kept running once she left the clearing in front of the cabin. But she also moved carefully for fear of stumbling.

Finally, when her lungs were burning and her legs felt like they were ready to fold beneath her, she stopped. For a long time she just sat on the needles below a tall, gnarled pine, taking in great gulps of cool air. Gradually, her heart rate slowed, her breathing became normal, and strength returned to her legs.

Lindsay had no idea where she was except that it was somewhere high in the mountains. For all she knew, she might not even be in Montana. Right now, it didn't matter. All she knew was that she was free and alive. She had every intention of moving on until she found someone who would give her aid, someone who would help her get in touch with Matt.

Before getting to her feet, Lindsay offered a prayer of thanks to the Lord for the miracle of her escape. And she prayed that she would be able to find safety somewhere ahead. Then she got to her feet and began to move again. With the aid of the stars, she tried to travel in a straight path. She shuddered as she considered the consequences of walking in a circle, as lost people often did, and finding herself back at the cabin.

She judged from the position of the moon and stars that she was going in a southerly direction. Although she didn't know where that would take her, she was determined to keep walking in the same direction. She would either find safety or some impassable obstacle such as a river too deep or swift to cross or a mountain too steep to climb. If the latter happened, she'd revise her plan then.

By the time the eastern sky began to take on the early gray stages of approaching day, Lindsay was totally exhausted. The terrain had become rough, and her chosen direction had her constantly climbing. She was tired and thirsty, her legs were sore, and her cowboy boot–clad feet were blistered and swollen. She wasn't sure whether she'd be able to get her boots on again if she took them off. So, when she selected a resting place beneath a rock outcropping, she left them on in spite of the pain.

Soon the sky was blazing with morning colors, and eventually the sun emerged over a high mountain peak far to the east. The way Lindsay was feeling, she doubted whether she could keep going without some sleep. Looking over the area, she decided it was secluded and well hidden. With that assurance, and praying that her captors wouldn't discover she was gone and come searching for her, she sank onto her side on the ground and allowed herself the luxury of sleep, her right hand still clutching the butcher knife.

When Lindsay awoke, she felt the warmth of the sun as it beat down on her from almost directly overhead. She was stiff and sore, and the butcher knife had slipped from her hand. She lay there for another couple of minutes, her eyes closed, enjoying the warmth and dreading the pain that moving would cause. A branch snapped nearby, and her eyes popped open.

She found herself staring at a dark gray wolf. Its eyes bored into hers, and its teeth were bared. Even as fright began to overtake her, her mind cleared itself and she began calculating. She judged the wolf to be about ten feet away, too close for any type of heroics. She didn't dare look away from the animal, fearing it would lunge at her. She began to move her right hand very slowly, searching for the knife she'd dropped in her sleep, but it eluded her. The wolf took a step closer.

Lindsay couldn't believe what was happening. After escaping death at the hands of her captors, wolves would now finish the job? she thought. A shiver shook her body despite the warmth of the sun. And a prayer formed in her heart.

18

The anger on Junior's face was frightening. Lucas knew that this man was a lot like Dwight and that both men could turn violent with only a little provocation. He just hoped that he hadn't provoked Junior too much already. "Why did you bring Dwight's sister up here in the first place?" the man demanded. "You should have just taken care of her right there on her ranch. That's what Dwight wanted you to do."

"He didn't say he wanted it done there, and anyway, they were probably watchin' the ranch," Lucas said. "I was lucky to find her and get her out of there at all."

"Then why didn't you finish her off as soon as you got her here?" Kendra demanded.

"I decided to poison her, and I needed somethin' to do it with," he said.

"Whatever. You should have done it there and then got rid of her body so no one could find it," Junior shouted. "And what's the story with that door latch?"

"It was workin' fine," Lucas said. "I'm not sure how this happened. See, the lock is busted inside." He held it in his hand and offered it to the other man.

"Yeah, I can see that," Junior growled.

"She got lucky, that's all. She must have been messin' with it when it broke. How was I to know it would do that? It was fine when I put her in there, and it was still okay the last time I checked it."

"Well, it's not too late to fix the problem," Junior said as he pulled a pistol from his waistband and checked the clip. The threat didn't escape Lucas.

"What do we do now?" Lucas asked, trying to ignore the gun in Junior's hand.

Junior put it back and then looked at Lucas, his steely gray eyes burning with disgust and anger. "You track her, Lucas. You know how to do that. You go after her, you find her, and you do what you should have done in the first place."

"Then I better get goin'," Lucas said quickly, trying to cover his obvious relief. "Just give me a few minutes to fill my canteen, pack some food, and change out of these boots."

"Not so fast. I think maybe we'll send someone with you," Junior said. "Just in case you need some help." He turned to the young man standing next to him. "Jude, you go with Lucas. And don't either of you come back until the job's done. Is that clear?"

"I'll take a rifle," Jude said eagerly. "We'll get her."

"And you better both make sure there isn't so much as a trace of her that will ever be found," Junior added.

"Don't worry. She'll never be seen again. That cop friend of hers will regret that he ever messed with me and my sister."

"That cop friend of Lindsay's better never know what happened to her or who did it. Is that clear?"

"I didn't mean it literally," Jude said defensively. "I just mean it will serve him right. He even took my eagle feathers."

* * *

The wolf was still standing there. It hadn't come any closer, but neither had it backed away. Lindsay didn't know how long she could lie immobile, but she knew she didn't dare move. If she could just grasp the knife, she would at least have some defense if the wolf should attack. The knife had to be somewhere within inches of her. She was certain that she'd barely moved as she slept. Finally, out of sheer desperation, she began to feel around again for the knife.

The wolf immediately noticed the slight movements of her hand and arm. Its head swayed back and forth for a moment. Then it stepped back. With newly found courage, Lindsay shouted at the wolf and waved her arms. To her relief, it spun around and ran into the trees. "I should have tried that earlier," she said to herself. She sat up, spotted the knife lying a good two feet away, and moved to get it, surprised that it was so far from where she had awakened. She must not have slept as motionless as she'd thought.

Every muscle in her body hurt. She felt like she'd been tromped by a horse and then dragged through a rock pile. When she finally got to her feet, Lindsay was hit with an even more excruciating experience. She wasn't used to walking for miles in boots and, to make matters worse, with socks that hadn't been changed for days. She was sure her feet were a solid mass of blisters.

Also hungry and thirsty, Lindsay decided to open one of the tins she'd shoved in her pocket at the cabin. Then she would look for water. She was in the mountains, and she knew there would be water. At least she wouldn't die of thirst.

Lindsay shoved the butcher knife between her belt and her jeans, then pulled out the only food she had. Both tins were identical: sardines. Lindsay's list of her top one hundred foods didn't include the oily, salty little fish. However, under the current circumstances, she couldn't be particular. She put one of the tins back into her pocket and opened the other. She slowly ate the first fish, swallowing hard to get it down and keep it there. Then she started to walk. The pain was unlike anything she'd ever experienced before, but she had no choice. She had to keep going if she wanted to live. For all she knew, Lucas could have returned to the cabin, found her missing, and started after her hours ago. She would eat as she walked. Her greatest ally was putting the distance between her and the cabin.

The forest ahead of her was thick, but the terrain now took her downhill. Gratitude was hardly descriptive of how she felt at that moment. She just didn't have enough energy for further climbing. Each step was difficult, but walking became easier the longer she continued. Moving actually aided her aching muscles, although her sore feet were rebelling. After a few minutes she stopped and leaned against the huge trunk of a fallen tree. She took a moment to finish the sardines. *Who would have ever thought I'd eat a whole can of sardines and then lick out the tin?* she thought as she shoved the can back into her pocket. "Leave no trace," her father had taught her. "If you pack it in, then you pack it out." Lindsay realized that while she might not be leaving any obvious traces, she was probably leaving enough unintentional ones.

She was ready to start walking again when she had the eerie feeling that she was being watched. The hair on the back of her neck bristled. She looked around, saw nothing, and finally worked her way around the tree and continued down the hillside, but the feeling persisted. She kept checking behind her. Nothing but trees, rocks, and shrubs. She thought about the wolf, wondering if it was back there somewhere, following her, patiently waiting for her to fall or to sleep again.

She grabbed the handle of her large knife, thinking that she'd keep it in her hand as she had done during the night. But she changed her mind. She needed her hands free now. In her weakened state, it would be all too easy to stumble. If she did, she would need both hands to help break her fall.

For an hour she kept up a steady pace, continuing essentially downhill. Her thirst was now so intense that her tongue was almost double its normal size. Water was constantly on her mind. She thought she heard the sound of running water, but this was not the first time. Mother Nature had deceived her several other times. But this sound was like a stream or a waterfall, and it was ahead of her somewhere. Encouraged, she hurried on. Fifteen minutes later, the sound was much louder.

When Lindsay came to some ledges that she couldn't get down, she veered to her left. Then she saw the wolf again, but not for more than a couple of seconds. It was definitely following her. She saw it twice more before finally working her way around the ledges. The wolf was getting braver, following her more closely, its presence nerve-wracking. It was almost as if the animal had a sixth sense that dinner was being prepared, that it only had to be patient.

Lindsay angrily shoved the thought from her mind and concentrated on reaching the water that now sounded very near. She forced her way through a thicket of young trees and spotted the stream. It was running fast but was not more than a hundred yards away. It took her another five pain-filled minutes to reach it. Then she drank deeply and gratefully from the clear, fresh, mountain stream. For several minutes she stayed beside the water, drinking frequently.

Finally, Lindsay knew it was time to move on. She wanted to go south, and south meant crossing the stream. It was neither deep nor wide, but it was rapid. She didn't want to soak her leather boots if she didn't have to, knowing that would only make walking more difficult. So she moved downstream, staying as close to the bank as the terrain and vegetation would allow.

A little later, when she found a fallen tree that spanned the entire stream, she used it as a bridge. She barely had time to congratulate herself on making a dry crossing when she groaned. Now she had to climb a mountainside. A steep one. *Okay, thirty seconds for self-pity,* she thought, *then I'm tackling the climb.*

Looking back after a couple of minutes, Lindsay gasped. A wolf was standing on the far bank of the stream, near where she had climbed onto the trunk of the fallen tree. The wolf was not alone! A second one was approaching the first one from the trees. And then to her shock, a third wolf emerged from the timber a few seconds later and joined the other two. She watched, scarcely breathing, to see if more would come. None did.

Small comfort, she thought. *I didn't have much of a chance against one with just my knife. Against three, I'm probably wolf food.*

She started to climb the mountainside again, glancing back frequently. She'd begun to hope that the wolves wouldn't attempt to cross the stream. Her hopes were dashed when all three of them plunged into the stream and lunged across. The cold water, with its strong current, was no deterrent. Once out of the stream, they stopped only long enough to shake the water from their coats. Then, effortlessly, they began trotting up the hill toward her. They no longer attempted to stay out of Lindsay's sight. It seemed as if they had decided that not only was she of no danger to them, but that given time she would be easy prey.

Her options now seriously limited, Lindsay did the only thing she could. She continued on. She wasn't sure what she would do when sheer fatigue made her rest again. In the meantime, she would cling stubbornly to a statement she had heard years earlier when the wolf reintroduction program was initiated: *Wolves will generally not attack humans unless they're provoked.* She decided it was to her advantage to disregard some of the other reasons for wolf attacks, such as rabies, extreme hunger, and aggressive disposition.

* * *

"We're gaining on her," Jude Norse said gleefully. "We'll have her in our sights soon."

"Don't underestimate the woman," Lucas warned darkly. "You never know what she might be capable of."

"Hah!" Jude scoffed. "She don't even have a gun. Anyway, ain't no woman who can hurt this man."

Lucas laughed. "Not even your big sister?"

Jude took a moment to answer, but then he said, "In case you ain't noticed, Lucas, my sister's more like a man than a woman. She's husky and tough as nails."

"Yeah, I've noticed all right," Lucas said. "That's why I asked you the question."

Jude puffed out his skinny chest and said, "No woman can hurt this man. And that means my sister, too. Not that she'd ever try. Hey, where'd those tracks go?"

"That's what I'm tryin' to figure out." Lucas was moving in a large circle, his eyes searching the ground beneath and around him. "Looks like we've lost 'em."

"*You* seem to have lost them. You're the one who's supposed to be the great tracker. You better find them quick. We ain't got time to lose. I aim to see that woman dead before the sun sets."

Lucas searched the ground. He fanned back and forth, going farther and farther to the west. Jude followed for a while, and then said, "I don't think she came this way. She was going south, always going south. Let's move back that way until we come across her tracks again." He pointed to the east and began heading in that direction.

"Hope you're right," Lucas said.

A few minutes later, Jude let out a whoop. "Here they are. Like I said, she's heading south. If she keeps going this way long enough, she'll lead us right into the park."

Lucas acknowledged that the young man had indeed found Lindsay's tracks again. "I'll take the lead now."

"Maybe I should," Jude said. "You seem to have lost your touch." And without waiting for a protest, the headstrong young man led out.

They made good time. Before long, Jude announced, "Hey, man, look. I think she laid down here. Probably slept. I'll bet we're getting close. She went this way when she left, still south."

It was Lucas who spotted the tracks of the small pack of wolves. It appeared to him that they were following Lindsay. Jude was so excited about following the tracks of the small cowboy boots that he hadn't noticed the animal tracks. Lucas didn't bother to mention them to the conceited young man. *We'll see where your high and mighty attitude gets you*, Lucas thought.

* * *

From the top of the ridge she'd been climbing for what seemed like hours, Lindsay was finally able to get a good look at the surrounding mountains. She was relieved when she discovered that she wasn't all that far from home. She knew those distant mountain peaks, and they gave her comfort. She studied the area for several minutes before making the decision to turn to the northwest. She didn't think there would be much chance, if any, of running into her pursuers. But if she kept going south, she'd end up having to trudge through acres and acres of tundra, and she wasn't up to that. Besides, she was headed toward Yellowstone Park, and there was a lot of hiking ahead, very rugged hiking, if she kept going that direction.

Her decision made, Lindsay turned west. After dropping off the ridge, she looked back. The wolves were still following her. But they showed no signs of closing in on her and attacking. She continued to plod along, heading northwest now, trying to ignore, as much as she could, her pain and her pursuers.

* * *

"We're getting closer to her," Jude crowed. "She thought she was being so smart by changing directions on us. But she didn't fool me for a second."

"I think she figured out where she was and where she'd end up if she kept going south," Lucas said. "Seems to me that she did what any of us would have done. Change direction. It would be pretty stupid to head into the tundra and try to cross it."

"Whatever. We'll soon have her. And we can leave her body here where no one will ever find it," Jude said with relish.

Lucas looked at his companion. He again reminded him, "You shouldn't underestimate Lindsay, Jude. She's a smart woman."

"Just because you let her get away from you doesn't mean she can escape from me. You just follow and watch. I'll do what you couldn't, and maybe you'll learn something."

His young companion's arrogance was grating on Lucas. He was a hard young man to like. For the life of him, Lucas couldn't understand why Dwight thought so much of the kid. Anyway, Lucas was not the fool Jude thought him to be. He had his own plan. Jude wasn't going to get a lot of glory at his expense. But for now, he was content to let the young man enjoy himself.

* * *

Although darkness was closing in, the wolves were not. Neither were they falling back. They didn't seem interested in hunting for prey, and this confused Lindsay. She knew it could mean that they had recently enjoyed a kill. On the other hand, maybe they considered her to be their next meal. And when they were hungry enough or she was weak enough, they'd move in on her. That was a terrifying thought.

Thinking of their hunger reminded Lindsay of her own growling stomach. But it was more than hunger that seemed to be bothering her now. She was beginning to feel a little sick, not that it was particularly surprising to her after all she'd been through. But when, after a few minutes, she realized she was getting worse, she began to worry. Then it struck her. She'd been drinking water from mountain streams, and those clear, fresh streams that looked so inviting could very well be contaminated with giardia. Of course, it could be something else too. Whatever it was, she hoped she suffered only mildly. She knew that if her diarrhea got a lot worse, she would quickly become weak and make easy prey for the wolves.

When an hour later, she was not feeling worse, Lindsay began to worry less about giardia and more about where she could safely spend the night. Darkness couldn't be more than thirty or forty minutes away. Perhaps in answer to her ongoing prayers, she spotted a huge fir tree that had an unusual tangle of heavy branches about fifteen feet above the ground. Although she would have liked to have continued walking until it was fully dark, she realized it would not be wise. She stopped beneath the tree.

She looked up, studying the few branches between her and what she thought might make a tolerably safe place to spend the night. As tired and sore as she was, she knew it would be a challenge to climb the tree. On the other hand, she realized that the probability of finding a ladder was represented by a minus number. The only way she was going to be able to rest this night, and probably the only way she could survive it, was to climb. After making sure both knives were secure, Lindsay started up the tree. As she climbed, the small pack of wolves inched closer. Twice, she slipped and nearly fell, but with strength she didn't know she possessed, she was able to grab a branch and save herself. After ten minutes of mind-numbing pain, she reached her goal.

It was even better than she thought it would be. Several sturdy branches had intertwined themselves and created what looked like a giant bird's nest. Needles from farther up in the tree had fallen over the years and been trapped in the nest. She scrambled in, amazed at how comfortable it was and how secure. The needles were so deep that she was able to squirm down into them and place some of them over her as a covering. She had not only found a place where she could rest out of reach of the wolves, she had also found a warm shelter for the long and chilly night ahead.

The pain in her gut eased as she let her body relax. She couldn't see the wolves now unless she sat up and peered over the edge of her nest, as she had come to think of it. But she could hear them prowling below. She was safe for now. She tried not to worry about what morning might bring. She prayed that by then they would have tired of the sport and gone in search of more conventional game.

She didn't know what time she fell asleep, but it was very dark when she awoke. Even though she'd burrowed deeply into the soft bed of needles, she was beginning to feel chilly. A stiff breeze was blowing. As she looked up, Lindsay could see the sliver of moon that had risen sometime since she had climbed into her place of security. Clouds raced below the moon, driven by an ever-increasing wind. There was a feeling of impending storm in the air. That was something she didn't need.

She thought about the wolves as she closed her eyes, trying to fall asleep again. She hoped they'd moved on by now.

As if the wild creatures could read her mind, a wolf suddenly began to howl, a long and mournful sound that sent chills racing through Lindsay's body. It was not coming from directly below her, but it was nearby. A second wolf joined in, then a third. For several minutes they kept up their wild call. Then, as abruptly as they'd begun, they ceased. Other than the wind that whistled through the trees, the night again became peaceful.

* * *

"Hear that, Lucas? There's wolves close by," Jude said.

When it became too dark to see Lindsay's tracks, the two men had been forced to camp for the night. They had only a small fire, but it was comfortable. As they chewed on jerky and trail mix, Lucas realized how tired and sore he was from the long day of walking. He welcomed the chance to get off his feet and rest.

"Did you hear them?" Jude asked again. "They aren't very far away, I'd say."

"How could I help but hear them?" Lucas answered irritably.

He was not impressed with the intelligence of the young man. His sister had brains. She must have received the family's allotment, he thought sourly. And he wished the kid would just shut up so he could eat his jerky in peace.

"This is great, tracking a woman. I can't wait to see her face when I get her in my sights. I'll bet she starts begging just before she dies. I hope she does. I wanna hear her beg."

Lucas offered no response. It wasn't worth the effort. Jude was such a loser. But he did think about Lindsay Flemming. She must know they were coming after her. She must also be terrified. This was no strategic war game downloaded onto a handheld PC being played out in these high mountains of southern Montana, despite what Jude thought. This was serious business they were involved in.

The wolves howled again. "I wonder if our victim can hear them?" Jude said with a chuckle in his voice. "I'm sure she can. I'll bet she's shaking in her britches. Too bad she doesn't know how close we are."

Once again Lucas didn't bother to respond. But he suspected that the younger man was right. Lindsay was probably somewhere nearby.

And those wolves knew exactly how close she was. They'd been following her all afternoon. Jude still hadn't figured that out, and Lucas wasn't about to tell him, at least not yet. But that Lindsay was afraid was almost certain.

Lucas lay on his side and pulled the thin blanket he'd brought with him over his shoulders. He needed sleep. Tomorrow could be a hard day. Especially if it stormed, and it felt very much like it was going to. It would be hard for him, but it would be even harder for the woman they were tracking.

And it would be hard for Jude. The kid was just too stupid to realize it.

* * *

Despite her exhaustion, sleep was stubborn in coming. Lindsay lay with her eyes open, staring up at the sky through the branches above her. The clouds were getting thicker and blacker as the minutes dragged on. She wished she knew what time it was. Her watch was old and didn't light up anymore, and it was too dark now to see it. *Not that it matters,* she thought sadly. *Even if I knew the time, there's nothing I could do that would be different from what I'm doing now.*

The hours passed. Lindsay managed to sleep for short periods of time, but she woke up often, shivering with cold. The wind had picked up and now carried with it a hint of moisture. It was the kind of wind that used to send her mother running inside, breathing heavily and coughing. *Now, why did I think of that?* she wondered. But thinking about her mother comforted her.

Lindsay's mother, Constance Duncan, was born in Nebraska during the Great Depression. Unfortunately, her birth coincided with the Dust Bowl. After years of drought, strong, hot winds blew in from the West, plucked up the dry soil from farmlands and rangelands, ranches and pastures, and carried it eastward. Fine sediment filled fence rows, stream channels, road ditches, and farmsteads. Dirt and sand coated the insides as well as the outsides of buildings. Crops failed, animals suffocated or starved, and lives were forever changed.

For Constance, there was still more. The thick, airborne dust impaired her breathing and caused a respiratory disease. She became weak and frail. In desperation, the Duncans sold half of their remaining farm and, in 1940, took their five-year-old daughter to Primary Children's Hospital in Salt Lake City.

Her illness turned out to be a cloud with a silver lining. At the hospital the family met Walter and Elizabeth Flemming, ranchers from south central Montana whose daughter had been caught in a stampede. One knee had been crushed, the other leg broken, and part of one hand severed.

A deep friendship developed between the two families as the girl's health improved. Having little to return to in Nebraska, the Duncans moved to Montana, where they were converted to the Church, in large measure because of the Flemmings' influence. This set the stage for the 1957 marriage of Constance to the Flemmings' son Noah.

Lindsay loved that story as much as she loved her parents. Her mother never experienced robust health, but neither did she give up. She gave birth to two stillborn children during her first five years of marriage. Six years after her second stillbirth, Dwight was born. And eleven years later, when Constance was forty-four, Lindsay completed the family.

Perhaps it was because of the recent death of her father, but Lindsay felt a sudden and overwhelming closeness to her mother. She had spent such a short time with her mother before cancer had claimed her. Now Lindsay felt her presence again. *Oh, Mom, I won't give up either,* she cried.

Lindsay awoke later to the crash of thunder. Then lightning sliced jagged patterns through the sky. She sneaked a peek at her watch during one of the long moments of brightness. It was almost four in the morning. Daylight was not far off. She nestled deeper into her bed of soft fir needles, rolling herself into a ball to keep warm.

19

A whimper from Jimmy's room between the distant cracks of thunder caused Matt to jump out of bed and flip on his light. He hurried to the boy's bed and sat down beside him. "What's the matter, little buddy?" he asked as he put his hand tenderly on the boy's head. "Did the thunder wake you up?"

Jimmy looked up in the dim light that entered the room from the hallway. As usual, he didn't make a sound. Matt sat beside him for several minutes, stroking his hair, holding his hand, and speaking soothingly to him. Within a few minutes, the thunder ceased and Jimmy was asleep again. Matt wanted, more than anything in the world, for Jimmy to get better, to emerge from his sad world of silence.

He leaned down and kissed his son's cheek, tucked his covers around him, and left his room, leaving the door ajar so that he'd be sure to hear any further cries. Matt didn't return to his bedroom. Instead, he wandered into the living room and sat down on the sofa, deep in thought. Next to his concern for his youngest child was his worry over the woman he'd grown so fond of. He wondered where she was at that moment and what she was going through. It had been almost a week now since she'd disappeared. He found himself trembling with emotion and fear for her.

He recalled his reluctance about allowing the relationship to develop. Initially, he hadn't wanted to worry about her as he had for his family. He'd been mostly concerned about how he would feel when she was gone somewhere and he was waiting for her to return. Not in his worst imaginations had he expected anything this terrible to happen. But as he sat and thought about her, he didn't regret his decision to continue their tenuous relationship. Right now he longed to be with her, to put his arms around her, and to draw her head against his chest while stroking her long brown hair.

Yes, he missed her, and he was tormented worrying about her, but he wasn't sorry that he could worry, that he'd allowed himself to . . . to . . . to love her. He had to admit that he loved her. It couldn't be anything else that he was feeling. He didn't know exactly when it had happened, but he now loved her and he always would. He just wanted her back. He needed her back. Jimmy and Keith needed her back. He couldn't even think the most horrible thought. He had to believe she was alive. Slowly, he slid from the sofa and onto his knees. As he prayed, he was surrounded with the comforting feeling that Lindsay was indeed still alive but in grave danger. He pleaded with the Lord to spare her and to comfort her and to return her to him and his boys. Again he prayed for Jimmy. All he wanted, he realized as he ended his prayer, was a duo of miracles.

* * *

The thunder and lightning passed with only a few drops of rain falling. The sky above her was still black with star-smothering clouds. And the slender moon offered little light. But so far Lindsay had been spared a cold soaking.

She thought about Matt and his sons. How she wanted to see them again. She knew how Matt must be suffering. It was bad enough that he had to worry about Jimmy's health. But to have him subjected to worries over her was more than he should have to bear. She remembered, as she had so often the past days, how difficult it had been for Matt to let their relationship continue to develop.

And she recalled that what had held him back was the fear of having to worry over her. She'd assured him that she could take care of herself, that she would be fine. But she wasn't fine. She wasn't even close to fine. And now he must be worrying himself sick on her behalf.

Or was he?

That unsolicited thought caught her by surprise. Surely he hadn't decided she wasn't worth the worry she was causing. Surely, he couldn't just put thoughts of her aside. *That couldn't happen.* She closed her eyes and tried to imagine his face, the face she'd come to adore, to love. She knew she honestly loved him. What she saw in her mind was very clear. She saw a man on his knees, his head bowed low, his arms folded. She even thought he was shaking, perhaps crying.

Surprisingly, even more than his face, that sacred image gave her comfort. *Matt was praying for her.* That knowledge came to her with undeniable certainty. He cared deeply for her, perhaps even loved her. Doubts about his devotion took flight and hope for her survival became ever more urgent. He was praying for her to come back. He wanted her to come back. And more than anything in this world, she wanted to make it back to him, to feel his strong arms around her. The soreness of her muscles and the pain of her blistered feet didn't matter. She wouldn't give up. She could make it. For the sake of the man she loved, she had to make it.

Over the next half hour, as she huddled for warmth in the cold night, the sky slowly showed signs of light. The clouds that had been so thick were thinning now. She was anxious to get out of her makeshift nest and be on her way again. After a few minutes, it was almost fully light, and she knew it was time to descend, as painful as that would be. Her growling stomach reminded her of the tin of sardines she still had left. She was tempted to eat them before she left the tree. Then she decided that, despite her hunger, she would be wise to save them a little longer. She could wait and then eat in a few hours. She knew that later she'd be even hungrier than she was now. She stirred and began to sit up when she heard something that froze the blood in her veins.

It wasn't the wolves. *It was the voice of a man. No,* she realized after listening intently for a moment, *it was the voices of two men.* They were too far away for her to understand their words, but they were also too close to risk climbing down from the tree.

They weren't talking loudly, but they were conversing. And they were coming steadily in her direction. She wondered about the wolves. Would the presence of these men frighten the wolves off, if they hadn't already left? she wondered.

Not that it mattered much. If they were friends or employees of Dwight's, they would present more of a danger to her than the wolves did. She continued to lie still, hoping they would pass on by. Then, with a jolt, she realized that wasn't likely if they were following her tracks. Her tracks would lead to this tree and not beyond. They'd be a dead giveaway. She shuddered at the unintended pun.

Now she found herself wishing that it had rained, and she hoped it still would. Unfortunately, the clouds were not thick enough or low enough. She lay still and listened, moving only enough to wrap her hand around the handle of the butcher knife, although she knew it was practically useless against gun power.

Maybe the thick bed of needles beneath her tree wouldn't show her tracks, she thought as she tried to make hope her ally. Then she remembered that the tree was surrounded by grass and that her tracks wouldn't show up well in the grass either. Maybe they'd think they'd lost her trail and leave, searching for it elsewhere and giving her a chance to escape.

The men's voices were intermittent, but they continued to approach. Soon she was able to hear what was being said and to identify who was speaking. It was Lucas and a young man whom Lucas called Jude. She listened in growing fear to what they were saying.

* * *

Lucas stopped at the edge of a grassy clearing. Lindsay's tracks led there but then disappeared. His annoying companion, studying the ground intently, said, "She's pretty consistent about the direction she travels. I know we won't see any tracks in the grass, but they'll show up again after we cross this clearing."

"I'm sure they will," Lucas agreed, "if we just don't lose them in the rocks over there. If she was being careful when she reached that area, she could have stepped from rock to rock and we wouldn't have any idea which direction she went. Not exactly anyway."

"She hasn't been careful so far, so why would she start now? I doubt she'd do it just because there's a long, rocky patch ahead," Jude scoffed. "Probably never occur to the stupid woman."

"Hey, what's that?" Lucas asked suddenly.

"What's what?"

"I heard something behind us."

"Like what? You don't think the woman's going to sneak up and take our guns away, do you?" Jude mocked.

"Hey, Jude, you better start payin' attention. I'm tellin' you, Lindsay Flemming is no dumbbell. Yeah, I suppose it could be her," Lucas agreed. "Let's get out of these trees and across the clearin'." He began to walk. "But more likely, it's the wolves we heard in the night that are behind us."

Jude laughed out loud. "Are you scared of wolves, too?" he asked. "First the woman terrifies you, and now it's the wolves. Oh, no, I'm sooo scared."

Lucas shook his head. That was probably better than clobbering the immature idiot. "No, I'm not afraid of the wolves, but we are in their territory."

"Then let's run," Jude said, pretending to shake with fear.

Lucas wanted to punch him, but it wasn't worth the effort. He just walked on. He stopped as he passed beneath a huge, gnarled fir tree that stood near the center of the clearing.

Jude stopped beside him. "What are you stopping for?" the younger man asked. "You don't really believe the wolves are going to get us, do you? We are their friends, remember? That's why we call you Defender." The boy laughed. "Some defender you are. Now me, I'm Retaliator, and when we catch that woman, you'll see that Avenger gave me the right name. I have it all figured out. I'll retaliate for the way that Flemming dame is treating Avenger. So let's get moving. If we keep going, we'll catch her in a few minutes. She can't be far ahead of us now. When we do, I'll kill her. I'm a good shot. I won't miss."

"Nobody said you weren't a good shot, Jude."

"Call me Retaliator. We're on the job now, Defender."

"That doesn't make any difference out here, Jude. Anyway, Dwight can't hear us. So just shut up and listen for a minute. You're actin' like a fool. Never underestimate your enemies," Lucas said, "even when you think you have the advantage. Now, listen for a minute. I'm sure we're being followed."

"Call me a fool one more time, and I'll leave you here dead!" Jude exploded.

"Okay, okay," Lucas said impatiently. "I'm just tryin' to help you realize that we need to be careful."

"That woman scares you out of your wits, doesn't she? You think she's going to ambush us. And what will she use for a weapon? Her puny hands? What a scary thought."

"In case you forgot, there are knives in the cabin. I'd be surprised if she didn't take one when she left there," Lucas said.

"You're a fool," Jude retorted. "What if she does have a knife? That's nothing. We have guns. Let's get going. We have an enemy of the wolves to get rid of. And I'm tired of waiting for you. I want to get it done."

"Okay, let's move on," Lucas agreed, wanting more than ever to slap his cocky companion.

The two of them moved from beneath the huge, misshapen fir tree and soon approached the sparse timber and large rocky slope that lay just ahead. Lucas stopped again and looked back. There was definitely something or someone following them, although not closely. He glanced to the right and then to the left. Jude kept going, but Lucas didn't worry about him. He wanted to know what was back there. He watched intently for a couple of minutes. He thought he saw movement in the trees to the left, fifty feet or so to the south of the lone fir tree.

He squinted, attempting to get a closer look. He knew what it was. He'd hunted enough wolves to recognize one when he saw it, even with only a passing glance. But this one was behaving differently from others he'd seen slipping through the timber. He felt his stomach churn uncomfortably, and he pulled the pistol from its holster.

"Hey, you coming?" Jude called back.

Even as Jude spoke, Lucas saw another wolf. Then a third. They were visible for only a few seconds before they vanished. "What are you watching?" Jude demanded. "Do you see the woman?"

"It's wolves. They're over there." Lucas pointed.

Jude hurried back toward him and looked to the south. "I don't see anything," he said. "You're seeing things."

"That's right. I'm seein' wolves," Lucas said angrily.

"So what? We ain't after wolves today. Anyway, they'll hear us and avoid us if there really are any."

"There are wolves behind us," Lucas said ominously. "But they aren't tryin' to avoid us. They're stalkin' us."

Jude snorted. "You're crazy. There ain't any wolves out there and if there were, they wouldn't be after us. Come on, we got a woman to take out."

Lucas moved on—nervously. The wolves were acting abnormally, not like the ones he'd captured in the park. Something was wrong.

* * *

Lindsay still didn't dare sit up. Her mind was whirling and her body ice-cold after what she'd just learned from the men who had been beneath her tree. Lucas and Jude weren't just Dwight's friends or employees; they were part of some secret society, something like the Gadianton robbers. And Dwight wasn't just Dwight; he was Gadianton himself. He was also called Avenger, the leader of the violent group of people Matt had mentioned. He'd told her about an intercepted e-mail that had been written by someone who called himself Avenger. Avenger and Dwight were one and the same!

What had made the revelation even worse was that Matt and the other officers believed her father's killers were part of the mysterious group. If that was true, then she couldn't escape the hideous conclusion that Dwight might have orchestrated her father's murder even as he'd ordered hers. Somehow she had to let Matt know what she'd learned.

At the moment, that was impossible—she had dangerous human enemies close by. Both Jude and Lucas were after her. If her pursuers found her now, she knew she would die. And she also knew that her wild enemies were nearby. But she hoped that the wolves would follow Lucas and Jude so she could change directions and escape from both the men and wolves.

For now she'd have to wait. Shifting her body just enough to ease the aching a little but not enough to attract attention, she listened for Lucas Mallory and his friend. But they were too far away.

Suddenly, a loud shout pierced the morning air, followed by a rifle shot. Seconds later came a shrill scream. If she'd ever heard a scream of terror, that was it. The ghastly sound brought her out of her bed of fir needles and sent her scrambling to the edge of the nest. Working in tandem, two wolves were attacking Jude. He swung his rifle at them as he kicked and tried to get away. Finally, he knocked one of the wolves down and broke free from the other one. He took off running up a rocky slope to the west.

At that moment, she heard a pistol shot, then another. She could only assume it was Lucas fighting the third wolf, but she couldn't see him. She turned her head back toward Jude again. The pursuing wolf latched onto him and pulled him down. As he struggled, he dropped his rifle but managed to get on his feet again, break free, hurl a rock at the wolf, and run once more. The second wolf, the one he'd clubbed with his rifle, wasn't badly hurt, and it joined the pursuit. Lindsay turned away. She could watch no longer.

Moments later she heard footsteps passing rapidly beneath her tree. She turned to the other side of the nest and peered over the edge. Lucas was racing through the clearing, his pants torn and one arm bleeding. He looked back several times, but he didn't stop running. He stumbled, and as he lurched forward, something fell to the grass. He didn't bother to pick it up, and a moment later he disappeared into the timber. She listened for a moment as the crashing noises continued. It sounded like he stumbled several more times, but he must have picked himself up quickly. Each time, after a pause, she heard the sound of breaking branches and pounding feet.

Lindsay finally turned back to the far side of the nest. There were still only two wolves at the spot where Jude had died. She could only hope that the third was either dead or badly injured. She reasoned that otherwise it would either have been pursuing Lucas or joining the others by now.

It was time for her to go. She put her large knife back between her belt and her jeans and climbed carefully over the branches to the trunk of the tree. She lowered herself slowly to the ground. She was tempted to jump down the last five or six feet, but fear of turning an ankle or wrenching a knee made her cautious. Finally, she was standing below the tree, shaking from the strain of the descent and wondering which way she should start walking.

A steep mountainside lay in her path directly to the north. It was much too steep to climb. To the south the ground also sloped steeply, and somewhere far below, she knew there was a raging river. That narrowed her choices. She had to go in the same direction as Lucas for a few hundred yards before she could turn north, where the slope was no longer too steep for her to handle. At that point she could gradually work her way back to the northwest again.

The pain in her feet was intense, and it took several awkward steps before the stiffness left her legs. She followed the path on which Lucas had fled only minutes before. At the edge of the grassy clearing, she spotted what he had dropped.

Lindsay couldn't believe her luck. It was his pistol. She picked it up and then entered the forest. There she popped the clip out, discovered that there were still several bullets left, and rammed it back in place. Feeling vastly more secure, she started on again.

Lindsay hadn't gone more than a couple hundred feet when she remembered the rifle that Jude had dropped. It wasn't that she feared his using it. There was no doubt that he was dead. But she did consider the possibility that Lucas would come back looking for it. He was probably unarmed now, and it was in her best interest to see that he stayed that way.

With the pistol firmly in her hand, she plodded back toward where the rifle lay. Lindsay was a good shot with both a pistol and a rifle. Her father had taught her well. Had she not been confident in her ability, she probably wouldn't have had the courage to turn back. If the wolves attacked, she was sure she could shoot them before they got to her.

The rifle lay in some rocks about a hundred yards from where the two wolves were circling around and nudging Jude's body. She worked her way toward it, using what few trees there were for cover. It was fifty feet from the nearest tree. When Lindsay passed that tree, she was without concealment. But the wolves seemed uninterested in her approach. The breeze was blowing from them to her, and she walked as unobtrusively as she could.

She reached the rifle, picked it up, and started backing up in the direction she'd just come. She didn't take her eyes away from the wolves for more than a second or two at a time. At one point they both looked at her but immediately lost interest. When Lindsay made it back to the last tree she'd passed, she leaned against it, willing her heart to stop pounding so wildly and her lungs to breathe again.

She considered killing the wolves. She knew they would be easy targets from where she stood. But reason got the best of her. Shots would alert Lucas. She couldn't risk that; she didn't want him to know she was armed.

Lindsay veered slightly to the south where the timber was thicker and where she had heard Lucas fire two shots from the pistol. She'd gone only a few steps when she spotted a small backpack. It was torn open and much of the contents had spilled out. She snatched it up and looked inside. Jerky, a couple of candy bars, and three MREs—meals-ready-to-eat. She stuffed the goods tightly into her pockets. A small canteen lay on the ground, along with several other items. But only one interested her. A bottle of little pills used to decontaminate water. Her stomach was still unsettled.

Before leaving the area, Lindsay picked up one last item—a book of matches. A few moments later she discovered where Lucas had shot the third wolf. She got close enough to it to make sure it was dead, and not suffering, and then she headed for the clearing. She crossed it and continued the same way Lucas had fled earlier.

It took all her willpower to continue on. Her feet felt like they were being branded and her muscles had tied themselves into huge knots. But stopping was not an option. Lucas could be anywhere, and even though she now had the guns, she couldn't discount the possibility that he might have another pistol. She knew he'd been injured by the wolf, but he was still, in all likelihood, in a lot better shape than she was. And it went without saying that he was larger and stronger than she was. If he surprised her, he could easily overpower her.

Before too long, Lindsay was able to veer to the north and began to make her way up the mountainside. She tried to stay hidden in the timber as much as possible. She paused occasionally to catch her breath and to listen. About twenty minutes after starting up the slope, she heard something moving along the mountainside below her and to the east. She lowered herself into some scrub oak and watched. Lucas slowly came into view below her. He was headed back toward where the wolves had attacked. He seemed much calmer now, more determined. He passed close enough below her that Lindsay could see the empty holster. He carried a knife in one hand.

Thank goodness, she thought. *So he doesn't have another pistol.*

Although his pants were ragged and she could see that his leg had been bleeding, it didn't look too serious. His arm was still bloody, but he swung it easily back and forth as he walked.

Lindsay held her breath and waited quietly while he passed by. When she could no longer hear him, she knew it was time to leave.

20

Lucas gazed only momentarily at what remained of Retaliator. He hadn't liked the young man from the first time they'd met. He found it hard to feel bad about what had happened to him. He actually felt worse about having to kill a wolf. At heart, Lucas truly admired wolves. It was only because he cared about them that he'd become part of the society Avenger had formed. Lucas was drawn to the idea of protecting them and helping them spread beyond the park. At that time he hadn't realized that Dwight had other objectives. But he'd finally figured it out.

The entire group shared his passion for the beautiful creatures, including Jude. That wasn't what he had against the young man. It was his brashness, his cockiness, and his superior attitude that had grated on Lucas. He was not like his sister. She may have been cold and hard, but she wasn't cocky.

Lucas turned away, thinking about the wolves. He'd learned this morning that there was another side to the wolves he had never seen before. It was a rare but dark side that now had him wondering how smart it really was to spread them intentionally into the ranching areas the way they'd been doing. He looked around again, just to make sure the two surviving wolves that had so viciously attacked Jude weren't still in the area. Unless they were carefully hiding, he decided, they must have moved on.

The only reason he'd come back was to get the guns. He couldn't find either of them. It didn't take him long to figure out what had happened. He'd first noticed Lindsay's tracks about a half mile before reaching the clearing. He could tell that they were coming from the same direction he'd been heading. He'd known she was close by, and he could only conclude that she'd found the guns and was now armed to the teeth.

He was pretty sure she would be weak from hunger and possibly sick from drinking untreated water. And there was no way her feet didn't hurt. She had been wearing cowboy boots. It was a wonder she could still walk. Tracking her wouldn't be a problem now, Lucas concluded confidently. He could catch up with her, but that was where it could get tricky. Armed as she was, she would be watching for him. And here he was, carrying only a knife. How quickly the tide had turned.

He did one more quick search of the area, hoping that he might get lucky and find a gun, but what he found made him even more nervous. Lindsay had taken a few items from Jude's pack. She had food now and could provide herself with safe drinking water. She could regain some of her spent strength. It was more urgent than ever that he catch up with her soon and stop her before she could use the guns on him.

Lucas headed straight for the point where he'd come across her tracks earlier. He didn't think he needed to worry about an ambush yet. He was certain she'd be pushing on right now. And perhaps she wouldn't even consider an ambush. But once he was closer to her, he knew it would be wise to be careful. She had every reason to shoot him down cold if she saw him.

He could see that Lindsay wasn't trying to hide her tracks. It looked like she was trying to get out of the mountains—to get help. He had to find a way to stop her.

* * *

Jude's food helped immensely. So did a deep drink of safe water. Strength began to flow back into Lindsay's pain-racked body. Her muscles were getting accustomed to the strain, but it was her raw, tender feet that slowed her flight. Boots had never been intended for hiking long distances—they were for riding.

The rifle Lindsay carried was both a comfort and a burden to her as she pushed desperately onward. It gave her an advantage over

Lucas, but its weight also made her arms ache. She was a small woman, and it was a large rifle. It was slowing her down. She knew it, and yet she hated to part with it. Lucas would be coming.

She didn't like to think about that. He had to be stopped or she would die. It was his life or hers. That thought, combined with her love for Matt, helped her pick up the pace. Their future depended on her.

Although her body was in pain, her mind was clear. Lindsay was thinking and planning ahead as she trudged through the forest. For another hour she maintained a straight and steady course. But after that, her main tactic would be to mislead Lucas, if she could. If that failed, maybe she'd be able to surprise him.

Ambush would have been the proper word, but she found it repulsive. She just wanted to gain the advantage and stop him from pursuing her. She tried several tactics over the next few hours. First, she was more careful about where she walked, trying to make it more difficult for him to see her tracks. That meant passing over rocky areas instead of going around them. It also meant doubling back frequently and then changing directions.

Finally, it meant stopping often to watch and listen. Although she knew it would slow her down, she also realized it might save her life and make reaching safety possible.

* * *

Lucas was no fool. But, as he had told Jude so many times, neither was Lindsay Flemming. She was smart, and she was determined, and she was making this much harder for him. So be it, he thought. Lucas was in his element now. He was a hunter, experienced at hunting wild game, including wolves and bear. And wild game was cunning. Granted, the past few years he hadn't hunted to kill, but rather to photograph and to capture. But in doing that, he'd been forced to learn from the animals how to be wily himself. It was time to put that experience and knowledge to work now.

He was not about to let a woman outsmart him. He could see what she was trying to do, and he knew how to turn it in his favor. Just like so many wild animals had done over the years. Just like the three wolves had done to Jude and him that morning.

* * *

The day was wearing on. The thought of having to spend another night in this wild country brought tears to Lindsay's eyes. All her attempts to spot Lucas had failed. She knew he was not far behind her. She'd spotted the familiar print of his shoes twice when she was doubling back. This dangerous game with her deadly enemy was slowing her down. It meant she wouldn't be reaching safety today.

Lindsay looked at her watch and then studied the area around her. There was less than an hour before darkness set in. As much as she wanted to stop and rest, she had to go on, hoping that she might be able to lose Lucas during the night. She finally decided on a compromise. For five minutes, she sat beside a large rock, partially obscured by bushes. Not only did she rest, but she looked down the mountain, watching for the slightest movement. When she saw nothing to alarm her, she moved on again.

Long ago she had stuffed the pistol in her waistband, but she still carried the rifle. Its weight was becoming unbearable. She shifted it from arm to arm as she walked. Half an hour passed. It was already dusk and would soon be dark. Then the game of hide-and-seek would end. She'd simply flee for her life under the protection of darkness, something she should have done the night before but hadn't because of the wolves. In retrospect, it was a wise decision.

She topped a small ridge, caught her breath, shifted the rifle, changed directions, and then started down again on the same side she'd climbed. This would have to be the last time she doubled back before full darkness smothered the forest in its blessed blackness.

The ridge was steep here. She slowed down but stumbled anyway, not the first time that day. This time she fell hard on her stomach, and her head struck a large branch on the ground. She dropped the rifle and lay stunned for a moment, face down. A minute or two passed before she was able to reach for the rifle.

"Not so fast." The words came at the same moment that a large shoe with a torn, bloody pant leg hanging over it stepped squarely on the rifle. Fear shot through her with the intensity of a bullet, and she tried to pull the pistol from her belt. She couldn't lose now. Not after all she'd been through.

Lucas grabbed her by her shirt and hoisted her to her feet with one hand. A long, deadly knife gleamed in the other. *Oh, Matt*, she cried to herself, *I'm so sorry.*

* * *

"Do you mean to tell me that Retaliator and Defender aren't back yet?" Avenger shouted as his two most trusted members of the Wild Animal Protection Society stood silently in front of him.

"I'm afraid not," Enforcer said.

"What could possibly be taking them so long?" he demanded. "The two of you should have gone after her."

"We thought about that," Guardian said. "But Lucas had the assignment from you. And he's the best tracker of the whole group."

"I know that. It's not Lucas who worries me. It's your brother, Guardian. Sometimes he's a foolish and immature kid, and that can be a risky flaw. And Lindsay, as much as I hate admitting it, may be smarter than I thought." Avenger paced for a moment. Then he stopped and faced them again. "If Defender and Retaliator haven't returned by noon tomorrow, you two go after them. My sister must not be allowed to return to the ranch—ever. Is that clear?"

Enforcer and Guardian both nodded.

"And if you have to kill them, then do it. When that happens, I'll have no use for Defender and Retaliator. I don't want to see them ever again. And you know what that means."

"But Retaliator's my brother," Guardian protested.

"And Lindsay Flemming is my sister! That doesn't mean she can live. Do what I say, Guardian. I won't allow weakness in our group. We have a mission. Remember that."

After they left, Dwight paced silently, his head bent, his arms folded tightly across his stomach. Then he went outside, locking the door behind him. He opened the garage and backed a vehicle out, one he'd obtained just that day. It was an older model Ford pickup, an F-100, dark green with a few dents and scratches. Although his preferences ran to much fancier vehicles, it ran well, and no one would be looking for him in it. Not even members of his secret society would expect to see him in an old truck. That was important because he didn't want them to know everything he did. He trusted only one man completely. Himself.

* * *

Jimmy awoke in the middle of the night, and Matt held him for several minutes, soothing him, stroking his hair, and rocking him. After he succeeded in getting the boy back to sleep, he walked to the front window. The county road was usually empty this time of night, with only an occasional car passing by. He gazed outside, thinking about the woman he'd come to love. She had been gone too long now. If her abduction was for ransom, there should have been a note before this. Oh, how he wished there was a note. At least then he'd be reasonably certain Lindsay was still alive.

The idea that Dwight Flemming was involved was seated deeply in his mind, but Dwight had vanished. He was after something that didn't belong to him, and his sister stood in the way of his obtaining it. He was behind her disappearance. That was, in Matt's mind, a solid fact. If she was never found or if she was found dead, Dwight stood to inherit the Lazy F Ranch. That recurring thought was what frightened Matt the most. Dwight wanted the ranch. He didn't need a ransom. He only needed his sister to be out of the way so he could claim it.

Lights came from the direction of the highway. An older pickup passed by, traveling slowly. The house was set back too far from the road for Matt to see more than that. His thoughts turned to what mattered most: the well-being of those he loved. He watched until the lights disappeared. Then he turned and went back to bed, where he tossed restlessly, worried sick about Lindsay and Jimmy.

* * *

Dwight drove several miles before turning back. When he reached the little ranch he was interested in, he slowed down again and cruised by one more time. There had been a light on somewhere in the house when he'd passed earlier, but it was dark now. He kept going. He was certain this was the correct address. Had Sergeant Prescott stayed out of the picture, he wouldn't have had to take such drastic measures to obtain the ranch. *But Prescott had meddled.*

Back on the highway, he turned north, heading for Great Falls. He'd found what he was looking for. He just wasn't sure what action he should take next. Lindsay wasn't coming back. That he was sure of. If Defender and Retaliator had somehow failed, he was fully confident that Enforcer and Guardian would finish the job for them.

Well, almost total confidence. The only thing that worried him was the fact that Guardian seemed to have a greater attachment to her brother than he'd thought. But if she failed in her assignment because of her immature brother, if she disappointed him, she knew the consequences. Perhaps it wasn't a worry after all.

Dwight sped up, pleased with the old green truck he was driving. It would do for a while. Then he would have to make another trade. He thought about Prescott, the man Lindsay had become far too friendly with. He was a worry to Dwight. It was apparent that the man was determined and more capable than he'd thought at first. He would continue to be a thorn in his side if he were allowed to pursue the investigation into Lindsay's disappearance.

He drove for a little longer, thinking about the problems Prescott presented. There really was only one answer: the man had to be eliminated, but it must look like an accident. Dwight was good at that.

As he drove, Dwight realized that in the case of the cop, he would not only have to come up with a plan, but he would have to execute it himself. "And that's the right word, *execute.*" He chuckled. There were some things that he didn't want any of the other members of the Wild Animal Protection Society to know about. This would be one of them. No one would ever suspect that what happened to Matt Prescott and his boys was anything but another tragic accident in that unlucky family.

* * *

So far so good, Lucas thought as he drove east, away from Bozeman, away from Gallatin County, and through Park County. He was staying off the main roads. The last thing he needed right now was to be stopped in the van he was driving, the one with the hidden compartment the society had used to transport tranquilized wolves over the past few months. His face was grim, his mind on the future. This was a dangerous business he had become involved in. But he was a determined and committed man. He would see this thing through to the bitter end.

He hoped he'd been careful enough. He was fairly confident that he had been. Every move he'd made the past few hours had been planned with the idea of concealing his tracks, of making sure that no one, not even his own colleagues, found any trace of Lindsay. He knew what he had to do now, but he also knew the value of caution.

He allowed himself to think about the pretty young rancher. She'd put up a fight. She'd displayed a type of courage he had never witnessed before. And she'd also, after his superior strength had overtaken her on that hillside, displayed something he had little experience with. She'd left him musing over the power of love and what someone was willing to go through for the one who was loved. He'd never loved anyone and had never been loved. He had been stunned when she'd expressed the love she had for the cop and his sons.

He wondered what it would be like to have someone in his life who felt so strongly about him, who would be willing to do for him what she had been willing to try to do for Matt Prescott. He'd come to admire her, strange as that seemed. He drove a little faster, trying now to look forward to what he was determined to do, and not back at what he'd already done.

* * *

The van was gone from the cabin in the mountains when Kendra Norse and Junior Welker arrived. And the cabin was empty. There was no sign that anyone had been in it recently. But the tire tracks from the van led down the winding, rough road away from the cabin. Where were Jude and Lucas? Had someone stumbled onto the cabin and stolen the van? That was possible, they supposed.

"Junior, what if it was Lindsay who took the van?" Kendra asked.

"Impossible. Lucas would have taken the keys with him. She couldn't have started it without the keys," Junior reasoned. "And I don't see any tracks around where it was parked."

"Think about this," Kendra said. "What if she somehow outsmarted Jude and Lucas? What if they're the ones lying dead somewhere in these mountains and she drove the van away?"

"But the keys?" he reminded her.

"If she killed them, she could have taken the keys from Lucas."

Junior's face went dark. He moved into action, looking for the young woman's tracks. There were none. Finally, he conceded, "You might be right. We may have greatly underestimated that woman."

"So what do we do now?" Kendra asked.

"We don't have a choice. We have to find where they all went," he said as he began to assemble a pack from the van they were driving. "But we better hurry. If we're right, we'll still have to find her and get rid of her or Dwight will have our heads."

Five minutes later they were on their way. In ten minutes they'd found Lindsay's faded tracks, with those of Lucas and Jude following. But the going was slow. Neither of them could track the way Lucas could, and the tracks were now several days old.

21

Matt walked out to get his mail before taking Jimmy to his grandparents' house and then going to the office. He felt empty, deflated, depressed. Dwight and his accomplices were winning. He needed a break on this case—a big one. It was the most important case he'd ever worked, and, judging by the way he was feeling now, it would probably be his last. He just didn't have what it took anymore; he was afraid. It might be better to spend the rest of his life in some other line of work. He wondered momentarily what life would have been like had his ranch been large enough for him to be a full-time rancher. *Don't go there now,* he silently warned himself.

He opened the box and pulled out a handful of letters. He began to thumb through them as he walked back to the house. Mostly bills. It was always mostly bills. Law enforcement wasn't exactly a lucrative vocation. He glanced at the last envelope, the one that had been on the bottom of the stack. His mind began to reel. His name and address were written in pencil on the front of the envelope, but there was no return address. The envelope was postmarked the day before and had been mailed from Bozeman.

He rushed into the house and threw the rest of the mail on the kitchen table just as Keith came into the room. "Anything good?" the teenager asked somberly. The troubles that surrounded Matt had taken a huge toll on Keith. He was not the same carefree, cheerful kid he'd always been. Matt was worried about him as well as his little brother.

Keith stepped beside his dad. Matt was carelessly ripping open the envelope. Both father and son gasped as they read the handwritten note inside. Written in pencil, the note said: *Nobody knows where she's at but me. Here's what you need to do. I'll need fifty grand. Start getting the money together. You'll hear later where to take it. And Sgt. Prescott, you make sure you handle this as a personal matter, not a police matter. Don't say a word to your boss or any of the other cops. Do as I say or you'll wish you had.*

There was nothing else. "Dad, does this mean Lindsay's alive?"

"I don't know. I honestly think that she is. It might not mean that, I'm afraid, but I've got to treat it as if she is. We've got to hope that she is."

"Does that mean you won't tell Sheriff Baker about this?"

"That's what it says, son. I need to think about this for a while, though. And other than you, I don't want anyone else to know anything about this letter, at least right now."

"What about the money, Dad? We don't have that kind of money."

"I'll find a way to get it, Keith. At least it's a small amount."

Keith gasped. "A small amount? Fifty thousand dollars is a small amount?"

"For this kind of thing, it is. And that's what worries me the most. If Lindsay is still alive, I'd think this guy would be asking for a lot more than that, something like a million dollars." Matt began to shake, and his son put a comforting arm around him. Just then Jimmy walked into the room. "We'll talk more later, Keith," he said as he nodded toward his younger son.

"Sure, Dad," Keith said, an understanding look in his intelligent blue eyes.

"I'll see what I can figure out."

* * *

Dwight had seen a propane tank just outside the fence at Prescott's house. That meant his house was heated with gas. That became the foundation for Dwight's twisted plan. An explosion because of a propane leak. All three of the family members inside the house. The middle of the night. A perfect plan. Of course, it meant a discreet trip there during the day when no one was home.

Dwight had worked for a gas company back in his early twenties, and so he was familiar with gas lines and appliances, not to mention gas problems. This would be an easy fix, but he had to make sure his intended victims were home when they needed to be for his plan to succeed. And, of course, he couldn't afford to be recognized by anyone. That would mean using some type of disguise and several different vehicles.

He soon had the entire plan laid out in his head. No one would ever be able to tie him to the *accident.*

* * *

After spending the night in a hastily fashioned campsite, Junior and Kendra were several hours into their work for the day. They'd left at sunup, as soon as they'd been able to see tracks. They were just approaching a gorge. It appeared that Lindsay, who'd been traveling in a fairly consistent southerly direction, had changed her mind and not continued on toward Yellowstone. They figured it out before going as far as she had, the same way Lucas had apparently figured it out earlier.

Lindsay's tracks had gone downhill a ways and then back up and across her original path, then she'd begun to walk toward the northwest. They both noticed the wolf tracks and wondered about them. "They can't be some of the ones we brought out of the park," Kendra said. "They must have come on their own. That's good."

"I think there were three of them," Junior observed.

Around noon, they arrived at the edge of a large grassy clearing. In the center was a lone gnarled fir tree with a nest of thick, intertwining branches about fifteen feet above the ground. Tracks near the clearing were thick. Junior spoke. "There are a lot of tracks here. The only ones that I don't see going in more than one direction are your brother's. It seems to me like somebody left going the way they came."

Kendra had noticed the same thing, and she felt a nervous rolling in her stomach. "Let's look on the far side before we head back to the east," she said. "Maybe there's something more over there."

Kendra had always considered herself a tough, unemotional person. But what she spotted up the nearby rocky slope dropped her to her knees. There was no mistaking what had happened to her brother. "I don't know how she did it, but she killed him," Kendra said darkly, wiping away tears and getting back on her feet. "And then the wolves came. I want to find her alive, Junior. I want to make her pay for what she did to my brother. And then I want to feed her body to the wolves, piece by piece."

Junior said, "I understand. I'll be there to help when you need me."

"I know you will," she said. "I've got to bury him. It's the least I can do."

"We don't have a shovel."

"I'll cover him with rocks."

"Okay, I'll help then."

"No, this is my job," Kendra said sharply. "I want to be alone with him while I do this. You go ahead and look around some more. I don't see his pack. I suppose she took it, but would you look around and make sure it isn't here somewhere?"

"Of course. And Kendra, I'm sorry about Jude," Junior said.

She nodded her head. "So am I."

"I'll give you a few minutes," he told her as he turned away. "Let me know when you've finished."

"I will," she said, her teeth clenched firmly. "I bet his carelessness got him killed, but he was still my brother, and I intend to find out why Lucas let it happen."

Junior was glad he wasn't Lucas. Dwight would want him dead when he learned how he'd botched things. And now Kendra was enraged at him. He had a feeling that life would not be easy for the big man when they found him again. *If they found him*. He wasn't at all sure that they wouldn't find his body just like they'd found Jude's.

He soon spotted the torn pack, gathered up what was left of it and its contents, and took it all back to Kendra. She acknowledged with a nod of her head, and he moved away again. It was only a couple of minutes later when he found the body of a wolf. There was very little left of it either. Forest scavengers had moved in quickly to take advantage of the easy feast.

After carefully examining what was left of the wolf, Junior concluded that it had been shot. When Kendra joined him a few minutes later, and he pointed the wolf out to her, she was angrier than ever. "That woman got his rifle from him and killed my brother, and then she had the gall to shoot a wolf," she said, seething. "Oh, I hope she's still alive. I want my turn with her."

Tracking Lindsay away from the scene of the carnage had been easier because the tracks were more recent. And they discovered that Lucas had been behind her, stalking her. After a while, Junior said, "She knew Lucas was following her. Look how she's doubled back here."

Kendra acknowledged his comment with a grunt. Her anger was palpable, and it hadn't faded as the hours passed. He was glad that her anger wasn't directed at him. She could be downright dangerous in her current mood. They made slower progress after that. Each time they had to double back, Kendra cursed softly. For his part, Junior was forced to grudgingly admit to himself that Lindsay was being incredibly smart. He fully expected to find Lucas's dead body at any time. But when he didn't, he began to realize that Lucas—tall, lanky, sometimes clumsy Lucas—had figured out what she was up to and had been playing it smart himself.

Eventually, Kendra also figured out what had been happening. "They're both smart, Junior. But I'm pretty sure Dwight's sister is the smartest. We'll soon be finding Lucas, or at least what's left of him."

"I don't think so," Junior said. "He knows what she's been trying to do."

Kendra looked surprised. "But we already know she's the one that gets out of here alive," she said.

"We do?"

"Yes. The van was gone. And there were no tracks around it. Seems to me like somebody erased them. Why would Lucas go to the trouble?"

She had a point. "You're probably right," he admitted. "Although the ground there is rather hard. I suppose we might have just missed them." But he didn't believe that. He wasn't as sharp at tracking as Lucas, but he wasn't bad at it either.

It was getting late when Junior found where the two of them had come together. It was clear that some kind of struggle had occurred on that steep hillside. And someone had lost some blood, which they found mixed in with the dirt. "We were wrong," he said. "Lindsay lost the fight here. There's only one set of tracks leaving this place. And those were made by Lucas."

Kendra nodded her head and said darkly, "I wish I'd been here then."

"And he was carrying her," Junior said. "See how deep his tracks are here and how he's slipping going up this slope?"

"Yeah, and there are drops of blood. We should find where he left her body pretty soon," Kendra said. "And when we do, I will make sure it's not hidden."

"Why would you do that?"

"So that our friends the wolves can mangle her body like they did my brother's," she said coldly. "It's the least I can do for Jude."

An hour later, as it was getting darker, they came to a huge rock-slide. Lucas's tracks ended there. "He's dumped her here somewhere, but it could take us hours to find her body," Junior said. "You know how these areas are. There are holes big enough to hide a buffalo in. Anyway, that was what Avenger wanted. He's gotten even with her now. I think we better get back to our van. It'll be getting dark soon, and I don't want to have to spend too much time walking after dark if we don't have to."

Kendra reluctantly agreed, although she wanted to find the woman's body and see that it was wolf-ravaged. She finally said, "When we see Lucas, I'm going to have him show me where he put her. It can wait, but I've got to even the score for my brother. Then I'll deal with Lucas."

As they walked back toward the cabin, Junior asked the question that had been bothering him. "So why did Defender go to the trouble of hiding his tracks and then drive off in the van?"

Kendra had been puzzling over the same thing. "Perhaps he's afraid of what Dwight will say when he finds out he let the woman kill my brother," she suggested. "He doesn't call himself Avenger for no reason."

"That's all true, but it still doesn't make sense," he said. "He took the van."

"Maybe someone else came along and hot-wired it," Kendra suggested. "I know you can do that, and so can Dwight. I suppose there are plenty of people who can besides the two of you."

"Okay, but if that's what happened, then where's Defender?" he asked.

"Maybe he hadn't had time to get back to the cabin yet when we were there this morning. Maybe he's waiting there for us now, wondering like we are, who took the van."

"That seems more likely, except that it's still a real stretch that someone would steal the van. People are seldom up in this part of the forest. If there were some, what are the odds they'd steal the van?"

"Maybe it was taken by backpackers," she said. "They might have had someone who was injured or ill and our van provided them with a quick way to get to help."

"I don't know, it seems pretty far-fetched, but consider this," he said. "Maybe we were wrong about who killed whom. Maybe she killed him."

"But it was his shoes that made the tracks, not her boots," Kendra argued.

"She might have put his shoes on her feet."

"Maybe, but they'd have been awfully big for her. Anyway, there's no way a little woman like her could have carried a big man like Lucas."

Junior nodded in acknowledgment. He didn't know any more than he had when he'd initiated the conversation. Neither of them did.

* * *

Matt had left work early that day, using the excuse that he wasn't feeling well. And that part was true. He felt like he was going to come apart at the seams at any moment. He wanted to be with his sons. Anyway, he was not accomplishing much at work. The only thing he'd done that meant anything was something he couldn't tell anyone about.

He'd quietly compared the handwriting from the ransom note with the signature he'd photocopied from one of the court documents Dwight Flemming's attorney had prepared in the failed lawsuit against Lindsay. Dwight's signature on the court papers was not remotely similar to the writing on the ransom note. He concluded that someone else, most likely one of Dwight's minions, must have written it. But he had no way of knowing who that might have been.

He picked up Jimmy at his folks' house at noon and accepted his mother's invitation to have lunch with them. His mother and father both appeared to be as concerned for him as he was for Jimmy and Lindsay. He tried to assure them that he was okay, that he was coping with the pressure, but he knew he hadn't convinced them. Heck, he couldn't even convince himself. He left for home about one that afternoon.

When he was just a few hundred yards from his driveway, a small blue car pulled onto the road. He couldn't tell if it was coming from his yard or not, but it could have been. Or it could have been parked beside his mailbox. He stiffened until it passed him. It was a Nissan. The driver, a young woman, waved cheerily at him. He didn't recognize her, but then he hadn't gotten a good look at her face. He did notice that she had long black hair and appeared to be a little larger than Lindsay.

It frustrated him that seeing another woman made him think of Lindsay. But he knew that was only to be expected, since she was almost always on his mind. He stopped at the mailbox, although he knew that there would be no mail because it came first thing each morning. And that morning was when he'd found the note someone had anonymously mailed to him. But he stopped just in case there was another note, one just stuffed in there, not sent through the mail. As he opened the mailbox, but before he looked in, the thought struck him that if there was one, it might have been the girl in the blue Nissan who'd left it.

But the mailbox was empty.

He spent the rest of the afternoon with Jimmy. They played with the dogs for close to an hour, spent some time with the horses, and checked their small herd of cattle. Then he took Jimmy inside and read to him. He'd fallen asleep with Jimmy in his arms a little after three and hadn't awakened until Keith got back from the store at about five thirty. He and Jimmy both had a good nap.

Now he was paying for it—it was nearly two o'clock in the morning and he was wide awake. He walked past Jimmy's door and listened. Then he silently opened it just a crack and peeked in. Jimmy's nightlight gave just enough illumination that he could see the handsome, sleeping face of his son. The nap didn't seem to have had the same effect on Jimmy that it had on him. He shut the door quietly.

He checked and found that Keith was also asleep. The two of them had sat up late talking. Both of them could think of little else but when and how the next communication would arrive from the person or persons who had taken Lindsay. It could come in the mail, like the first one, or it could be delivered a number of other ways. They even checked their e-mails, just in case it was sent electronically, but neither of them had new communications.

Keith had finally gone to bed around midnight. Matt never had. He was so wired that he felt like he could explode. He paced about the house in the darkness for a long time, and finally, a few minutes ago, he'd come outside. He sat on a chair on the deck at the front of the house, staring into the darkness, brooding.

For the second night in a row, he saw car lights up the road. Soon a vehicle passed slowly by. It wasn't a pickup, though, like the night before. It was a sedan, but that was all he could tell. He wondered for a tense moment if it was going to stop at the mailbox. It went right on by and then sped up.

Sitting there a few minutes later, Matt was still wide awake. He wanted to go inside and go to bed, but he wasn't looking forward to that. He knew he wouldn't sleep. He stood up, stepped off the front porch, and walked across his lawn, going nowhere in particular. Suddenly, Claw began to bark. A moment later the big dog came running from the barn, where he spent most of his nights, and streaked past Matt and into the trees that bordered the county road, just beyond the mailbox.

Matt ran into the trees himself just in time to see a shadowy figure running hard from near his propane tank, Claw only a few jumps behind him. Whoever it was leaped into the car that was parked there just before Claw reached him. It took only a moment before the engine came to life and the car peeled onto the highway, its lights off, and sped away. The lights didn't come on until the car was several hundred yards down the road.

Matt thought about running to his county truck and going after the vehicle, but he repressed the thought almost as quickly as it had come. There was no way he was leaving his boys here alone. He could call into dispatch, but that was a useless idea. He couldn't even give a description of the car because it was such a dark night. Even if he could, he had no proof that any criminal activity had occurred.

He and Claw walked back onto the lawn, wondering what someone had been doing there. Why he'd seen him running to his car was no mystery. Matt would do the same if someone's dog came at him the way Claw had done. He wondered what there was about the situation that had alerted Claw. Claw and Princess had been in the barn while Matt sat on the porch. Claw didn't run from the barn every time a car came by. It was strange.

He knelt on the grass and petted both dogs. He was aware that the door to his house opened and closed. As he turned, he saw Keith and Jimmy coming toward him, hand in hand. Claw left his side and bounded toward them.

Before going to them himself, he decided to check his mailbox, just in case.

22

"What was Claw all ballistic about?" Keith asked when Matt met them partway back to the house.

"A car was stopped on the road out there through the trees," Matt said, turning and pointing. "I got into the trees in time to see someone running to a car that was parked there. He was just past the propane tank when I first saw him. Claw almost got a piece of him."

"Do you know who it was?" Keith asked.

"Not a clue," he said.

"So did they put something in the mailbox?" the boy asked next, a tremor in his voice. "I saw you look in it."

"No, it was empty. But the guy was closer to the tank than the mailbox."

"That's weird."

"It's probably nothing. Maybe someone needed a restroom break, and our little bunch of trees might have looked like a private spot."

"Yeah, that's probably it," Keith agreed. "You've got to be tired, Dad. Have you even been to bed yet?"

"No, and if I went now, I don't think I could sleep."

"I'm wide awake now, too, and so is Jimmy. Maybe we should go for a ride and see if we can make ourselves tired," Keith suggested. He looked down at his little brother. "You'd like that, wouldn't you, Jimmy?"

Jimmy nodded silently.

When both boys had been toddlers, a ride in the car could generally put them to sleep faster than anything else—rocking, soft music, or even a drink of milk.

"Sounds like a deal to me," Matt said. "Maybe we could go to town and get a treat or something."

They walked around the house, and Matt opened the garage. "We'll go in our truck, not the county's," Matt said. "You guys get in. I'm going to run and grab my cell phone."

A minute later he slipped his cell phone into his shirt pocket. Then he reached onto the top shelf of his closet where he kept his pistols. He loaded the small .38-caliber revolver he used as an off-duty weapon, holstered it, and placed it inside his pants. He hated to go anywhere without a weapon the way things had gone lately.

As he backed his Chevy truck from the garage, Matt noticed Claw and Princess as they ran again through the open barn door. He stopped, got out, and told Claw to get back in the barn. Princess obediently followed Claw, and after they were both inside, he gave the door a shove and returned to the truck. It didn't sound like the door latched, but it didn't matter. If Claw pushed on it and got out, he wouldn't go anywhere. He was good about staying in or near the yard and corrals. And he knew Princess wouldn't leave Claw.

They hadn't yet made it into Bozeman when Matt noticed that Jimmy was asleep.

"I guess he wasn't as wide awake as I thought," Keith said as he too noticed the younger boy. "So where are we going?"

"Are you in a big hurry to get back to bed?" Matt asked.

"No, I'm wide awake, Dad."

"Then let's stop at a convenience store, grab some snacks and drinks, and then maybe run out to the Lazy F. I haven't been out there for a couple of days, and I'd like to, you know, just kind of check on things. Maybe we'll be ready to sleep after that."

A few minutes later, they were munching on nuts and chips and sipping bottles of juice as they drove out to Lindsay's ranch. Despite everything he knew to the contrary, Matt couldn't help but hope that by some miracle he would find Lindsay home. He knew it wouldn't be, but he could dream, and he could hope, and he would continue to pray.

* * *

As the old rusty sedan drove slowly past the Prescott farm again, the driver noticed that the lights were out now. *They've finally all gone to bed,* he thought. He drove on past, then turned and drove back, stopping at the edge of the county road, just out of sight of the house. He shut off his lights and engine and sat there thinking for several minutes.

What he planned to do wasn't going to be easy, and it certainly was not going to be pleasant, but it was necessary. He'd already put it off far too long. That big dog certainly wasn't any help; in fact, it was a downright nuisance.

He was surprised that the dog hadn't come out again now like he had when he stopped earlier. Maybe the cop had locked him in the barn, he thought. Maybe Prescott was tired of waking up every time a car passed on the road. Not that it happened much. He'd noticed that at this time of night the road was basically deserted.

Even as he thought that, he saw lights approaching from the direction of the state highway. He debated about what he should do. After a moment, as the headlights came nearer, he started his car, pulled onto the roadway, and drove toward the other vehicle. It was then that he made up his mind and committed himself to a firm plan of action. He'd come back—very soon—and do what needed to be done. It couldn't wait another day. It had to be tonight.

He passed the other vehicle on the narrow road but didn't get a good look at the driver. Then he watched in his mirror for a moment, slowing down as he did so. The other car passed the Prescott farm. Before long its taillights were nearly out of sight. There was some traffic besides him on the road at night, he concluded. But not as much as on the road that passed the Lazy F. He'd seen at least three other cars after leaving the ranch before reaching the county road just after midnight.

He had known it was risky going there. But no one had bothered him. He'd feared that each of the three cars might be a deputy's vehicle and that an officer might attempt to stop him, but each time the vehicle had simply gone on its way.

He turned and drove back up the road. He left his car where he'd parked earlier and started toward the house, sufficiently armed to stop the dog if he had to. He took a long way around, wanting to make sure Prescott's little barn was not open. When he could finally see it, even though it was dark, it looked like the door facing the yard was closed. He assumed that the door on the other side of the building was closed too, so he headed for the house.

As he passed the garage and started up the back walk, a light suddenly illuminated the yard. For a moment, he panicked, searching for a hiding place. The closest cover was the garage. He darted toward it and rushed around to the side. He stopped and held his breath, listening for the slightest sound from the house.

There was none, and he finally looked back around the corner of the garage. It was then he realized that he had activated a motion-sensitive light. He waited for a few more seconds, and the light shut itself off. No lights had gone on inside. Everyone must still be asleep. He took a deep breath, looked around, and once again started for the house. The light came on again, but this time he didn't hesitate. He hurried toward the back porch. The dogs were barking in the barn, but the walls muffled the noise. Once he reached the porch, he unscrewed the bulb about a half turn, plunging the yard into darkness.

Then he did what he'd come to do.

He'd barely stepped from the porch after he'd finished when he heard a loud slam from the vicinity of the barn. *The barn door!* he thought, even as he spotted a shadowy figure tearing toward him. He knew it had to be the big dog. He whipped his arm up, waited until the dog was almost on him, and fired. The dog made several more feeble leaps before collapsing at his feet.

That was close, he thought as he tore around the house and back to his waiting car. But before he drove off, he sneaked a look back. No lights in the house. No doors opening. His heart hammering, he started the car. His night's work was finished. Now he needed some sleep.

As he drove away, a set of headlights appeared in the distance behind him. He sped up. When he reached the highway, the lights were no longer back there. He couldn't imagine where they'd gone, maybe to one of Prescott's neighbors up the road a ways. *Doesn't matter,* he told himself.

* * *

Matt pulled the truck into the yard of the Lazy F and parked near Lindsay's huge barn. The barn doors were closed, and everything was quiet around the yard. He almost felt silly now. There really wasn't anything he could do here except look around. Jimmy woke up as

Matt was getting out of the car. Keith reached for him, and the three of them walked into the barn, turned on the lights, and strolled through the doors.

Thirty minutes later, they had walked all around the corrals and even into the closest pastures, lighting their way with flashlights. Matt couldn't think of anything else to check except the house. He found the key Lindsay kept hidden. He checked to made sure the refrigerator and freezer were running. He also looked carefully throughout the house to see if everything was as he remembered it from the last time he'd been there with Lindsay.

He hesitated before going into her bedroom. Then he told himself that as long as he was checking things out, he might as well be thorough, even if it made him feel like an intruder. He froze when he opened the door and flipped on the light. Someone had been in this room!

"Dad, what is it?" Keith asked from over his shoulder.

Matt turned and looked at his son. "Where's Jimmy?" he asked.

"I laid him on Lindsay's sofa. He's asleep again. What do you see, Dad?" he insisted.

"I'm not sure," Matt said. "Something doesn't seem right."

He stood very still in the doorway and let his eyes wander at random around the room. Keith, who had squeezed in beside him, stood and silently studied the bedroom.

Finally, Keith broke the silence. "I don't see anything wrong."

"I realize now what caught my eye. You don't know Lindsay like I do," Matt said. "She always keeps things neat. Have you ever seen a cupboard door left open in her kitchen or things not neat and clean and orderly throughout the house?"

"Well, now that you mention it, no. But she's been gone for several days," Keith said.

"Exactly. I know that when she left this room the morning she disappeared, she'd have left everything in perfect order. That's just the way she . . . is." He'd almost said *was*. He was not ready for that. He had to keep both faith and hope.

"It looks pretty good to me," Keith said, puzzled.

"Her closet door; it's hanging about a quarter of the way open," Matt pointed out.

"Oh, yeah. I see that now."

"And look at the chest of drawers. The top drawer isn't shut all the way."

"Yeah, now that you mention it, I can see that, too."

"And the door to her bathroom is open. She never leaves a bathroom door open."

"What are you saying, Dad?" Keith asked with a tremor in his voice.

"I'm saying that someone has been in this room, someone other than Lindsay."

"Is anything missing?"

"I don't know, but I'm going to look closer. Not that I can necessarily tell, but it's worth a try."

He wasn't sure if anything had been taken, even after he'd examined the room more closely. After leaving Lindsay's bedroom, he thoroughly searched the other areas of the house. He finally decided maybe he was wrong. Perhaps Lindsay had been in a hurry that morning. Or maybe she'd planned to come back in from wherever she'd gone after getting dressed. Did it really matter? What mattered was that Lindsay was missing and he wanted her back.

After locking the house, Matt carried Jimmy to the truck. "I guess we'd better get home," he said. "We might as well try to get some sleep before morning."

Matt and Keith talked most of the way home. It was one way to ensure that Matt didn't fall asleep at the wheel. As they pulled into the yard and turned to enter the garage, the headlights splashed across the front of the barn. The door he'd swung shut earlier was hanging open.

"Didn't you shut that door when we left?" Keith asked, alarm in his voice.

"Well, I gave it a shove, but I'm not sure it latched. Claw must have decided he wanted to come out," he said. "I'm sure that's all it is."

But as he pulled the truck into the garage, he felt uneasy. He remembered the car that had stopped near the mailbox earlier and the way Claw had reacted. And now, although it was clear that the dogs were free to come and go from the barn, he couldn't see Claw anywhere. Ordinarily, he would have come bounding out to greet the truck with Princess trailing behind.

He got out of the pickup. "Carry Jimmy in to bed, would you, Keith? I'm going to have a look around."

The garage had been built several years after Matt's farmhouse, and it sat back about thirty feet from the house. As he and the boys left the garage, Princess came running to greet them. "Here's Princess," Keith said. "I wonder where Claw is."

"I'll look in the barn and around the corrals while you take Jimmy in. Then if you want to come back out, that would be fine," Matt said.

Keith headed up the walk for the house as Matt started toward the barn. Suddenly, Keith shouted, "Dad! Come here!"

There was such alarm in his voice that Matt whipped around and began running toward his sons, his heart pounding. He found Keith kneeling beside Claw, who was stretched out on the sidewalk just a couple of feet from the porch steps.

"Dad, somebody's killed our dog," the boy said softly, a catch in his voice. He laid his little brother on the grass as Matt knelt beside them.

Matt touched the dog. He was still warm. He put his face down against Claw's black muzzle and was fairly sure he felt breath coming from the dog's nose. He straightened up and put his hand on Claw's side, feeling for the slightest movement from behind his front leg that would indicate he was still alive and breathing.

He was aware of Jimmy waking and sitting up and Keith placing his hand on the dog's head. "He's alive," he said. "We need light. Why didn't the porch light come on? I know it was working when we left."

Matt got to his feet and stepped onto the porch. He reached up and checked the switch on the light with his fingers. It was in the automatic position like he always kept it. He touched the light bulb and could tell that it was loose. He gave it a half turn, tightening it. The light came on immediately. "That's funny. It was loose," he said as he stepped back off the porch.

"Claw," a little voice said.

Matt nearly choked. That was the first word he'd heard from Jimmy in weeks. He stood, almost paralyzed, and watched Jimmy as he stood up and stepped over beside his brother. He looked down at his beloved dog.

With one motion, Matt bent down and swept his little boy into his arms. A miracle had just occurred.

Keith leaped to his feet and was staring in wonder at Jimmy. "Dad, he can talk again," he said. "Jimmy, you can talk. Say something else."

But suddenly Jimmy's eyes grew wide, and he gasped as he stared into the darkness beyond the light. Then he threw his arms around Matt's neck and clung tightly to him. "It's okay, Jimmy," Matt said. "You're safe. We're all safe. Claw will be fine."

Jimmy didn't respond. "Jimmy, are you okay?" he asked.

Not a word. As quickly as he'd recovered his ability to speak, he'd lost it again. Matt wished he knew what was going on in his little mind. What had he seen as he looked into the darkness a moment ago?

Claw stirred, then struggled to get up. "Dad, Claw's trying to get up," Keith said. "What was the matter with him?"

Matt thought he knew, and it was frightening. It made him wonder if there really was someone out there that Jimmy either saw or thought he saw. "I think he's been tranquilized," he said darkly. "Leave him, Keith. Let's get in the house, now!"

Matt was reaching for the door when he realized he was staring at a piece of paper that had been taped there. He tore it off and began to read. Then he read again.

"Dad, someone's been here," Keith said, stating the obvious. "Maybe they still are. Do we dare go inside?"

"Let's get back in the truck. We're leaving," Matt said softly, as if someone were there in the darkness listening to them. "And let's take the dogs with us."

"I'll bring Claw," Keith said, and he scooped the big dog up in his strong arms and followed Matt and Jimmy to the garage. "Should I just put him in the back, Dad? Or will he jump out when he wakes up?"

"Put him in the dog carrier."

"But it's in your sheriff's truck."

"Then we'll take it instead. Just put Claw in the carrier. Lindsay's puppy can ride in the front with us."

In a few minutes they were back on the road and headed toward Bozeman. "Where are we going? To the sheriff's office?" Keith asked.

"No, I can't tell anyone about this," he said, touching his shirt pocket where he'd put the note that had been attached to the back door of their house. "We're going back out to Lindsay's."

23

Matt and the boys didn't enter the house when they returned to the Lazy F Ranch. Instead, they went to the barn and stretched out on the hay. Matt knew they could have gone to his folks' place, but he didn't want to wake them and cause them more worry. And for some reason he was drawn here, even though the woman whose vibrancy had given life to the ranch had vanished.

It was a warm night, and with only a light blanket from his truck to cover them, they actually slept a little. They were doing Lindsay's chores that morning when Grey Sadler and a couple of his men drove into the yard. "Don't tell them what's going on," Matt cautioned Keith when he spotted the truck. "We've got to keep everything quiet for now."

Keith nodded his head in understanding. Jimmy was quiet as usual. It was almost as if he hadn't spoken that solitary word during the night. He played with the dogs while the others worked.

"What are you guys doing here?" Grey asked cheerfully after getting out of his truck. "We can take care of things."

"Just thought we'd help out a little," Matt said. "You must be feeling better again. Don't overdo it, Grey. Let yourself heal."

"I am," Grey replied. "The doctor says I need to stay in bed, but I've had about all of that nonsense I can stand. I'll heal faster if I'm busy."

They talked for a few minutes, then Matt said, "I appreciate what you fellows are doing. I wish I could do more myself. But the boys and I need to get back."

"You just catch whoever's behind all this and find Lindsay," Grey said. "We'll make sure her place doesn't go to pot while you do that."

"Thanks. It looks like you have things under control," Matt said. "I hope you're not neglecting your own place. That's an awfully big ranch you have, and I know it takes a lot of work."

"I have plenty of good help. We'll be fine, Matt. By the way, we lost another calf a night or two ago. Those pesky wolves are still wreaking havoc."

"I suppose Lindsay's losing some, too. But we'll just have to wait and see. There are more pressing matters to take care of now." As Matt spoke, he was thinking about one of those matters, and it involved the note he'd found on the back door of his house a few hours ago.

"What are you going to do now?" Keith asked as they were driving into Bozeman a few minutes later.

"First, we'll go home and check things out there. Then, since you don't have to be to work until this afternoon, we'll get you and Jimmy safely to your grandparents' place. After that, I guess I'll need to beg some time off from the sheriff, without telling any outright lies, and then go to the bank."

"What will you do there? We don't have enough money to pay what the guy says he wants," Keith reminded his father.

"I realize that, son. I'll have to borrow it, but that should be easy enough. I have my ranch equity account. All I'll have to do is draw the money out in cash against that. Then we'll see what happens tonight when I follow through on the directions."

The latest message had simply listed a time, a phone number, and where Matt should be driving when he made the call. Although it hadn't mentioned the money, Matt assumed he'd need it tonight. He wasn't about to take a chance on not having it if he did need it.

* * *

Dwight didn't know if he had succeeded or not. His first inspection of the house had been disappointing. He'd discovered that Prescott no longer relied entirely on propane. He had an electric stove, an electric water heater, and an electric dryer. That left only the heat, and he had installed a few electric baseboard heaters throughout the house. There was still a furnace in place that Dwight had decided must be used only for supplemental heat on the coldest winter days. The pilot light was out, and the gas had been turned off outside the house. He'd originally planned to use a functioning pilot light as the means of triggering an explosion.

But after a lot of thought, he had decided that under the circumstances an explosion wasn't necessarily the best option. Another idea had come to him, and it wasn't too bad. He thought it could really work. He had just needed to make sure there was a way for the gas to leak out of the furnace. Then, when the family was asleep, he would have simply sneaked up to the outside tank, turned on the gas, and let it do its deadly work. The house would have filled with propane, and the three of them would have died in their sleep. And no one would ever know that the pilot light hadn't malfunctioned. A quiet but lethal accident, he told himself with satisfaction.

If all had gone well, Prescott and his boys would be dead by now. It was the waiting that was hard. Obviously, he couldn't just call and ask. As soon as he heard back from Enforcer and Guardian that his sister was dead, any possible barriers to his obtaining the ranch would be removed. He was about to become a much richer man.

* * *

The moment Matt opened the door he knew there was a problem. He shouted for Keith and Jimmy to run to the barn. The smell of propane was almost overpowering. The smallest spark would blow his house into the millennium and beyond. But this was crazy. Weeks ago he had turned off the propane. Someone had meddled and meant it to be lethal.

He left the back door hanging open and rushed to the propane tank. As he'd suspected, the valve had been turned back on. Whoever it was must have been in the house sometime to make sure that when he turned the valve it would fill the house with the lethal gas. Had he and the boys been sleeping inside, they would all be dead now. He offered a silent prayer of gratitude that they'd been inspired to spend the last few hours of the night in Lindsay's barn. Someone wanted him and his sons dead, and that someone had nearly succeeded.

It took only a moment to shut off the valve and cut the flow of propane to the house. Then he began to carefully open windows and doors, allowing the remaining trapped gas to dissipate. As he worked, he thought about what had been done during the night. The intruder had tranquilized Claw, left a note on the door, and tried to kill him and his family with propane gas. But something just didn't fit. Why would someone ask for fifty thousand dollars and at the same time try to murder him? He could come up with only one answer that seemed logical. *Two different people had been at his home during the night, acting independently of each other.*

That didn't make sense either. He was certain Dwight was behind it all. Surely he wouldn't work against himself. He wondered what critical clue he was overlooking. Did he have other enemies he didn't even know about?

When Matt arrived at the sheriff's office late that morning, he went straight to the private office of Sheriff Ethan Baker. He couldn't risk mentioning the ransom demand at this point, but the matter of someone trying to kill him and his sons was another issue altogether. He wanted the entire department to be aware of that.

Sheriff Baker invited Matt to sit down. "Matt, you don't look so good. Have you been able to get any sleep at all lately?" he asked.

"Very little. And last night was no exception."

"All right, what happened that I need to know about?"

"Well, someone shot my big dog with a tranquilizer. He's going to be okay. But after that happened, my boys and I decided to spend the night at Lindsay's ranch. What little sleep we got was in her barn."

The sheriff looked puzzled. "Why would someone tranquilize your dog?"

"So he or she or they could go about their other business," Matt answered.

"Which was?"

"Attempting to kill us," Matt answered soberly. "And if we hadn't found the dog and decided not to go in the house, they would have succeeded."

After finishing the account of the propane incident, Matt and Sheriff Baker and a couple other deputies drove out to Matt's ranch. A representative of the propane company met them there. "Your pilot light went out," the representative said after carefully inspecting the furnace.

"I shut off the pilot light in May," Matt said. "It was working fine then. And as a precaution, I also shut the flow of gas to the house off at the tank. I do that every spring."

"Well, it's not off now. And it's been tampered with so that plenty of propane would leak out."

Sheriff Baker said darkly, "Meaning that someone has been in your house. You're right, Matt. They meant to kill you and your boys."

The sheriff and his officers discussed the attempt against Matt's life in depth that afternoon. They all concluded, as had Matt, that somehow the criminal events of the past six weeks were tied together.

"Okay, guys, it's urgent—no, I'll rephrase that. It's imperative that we find these people," Sheriff Baker said, pounding his fist on the conference table in frustration. "We've got to put every available officer on it. With the exception of you, Matt. I hate to do this, but your safety and that of your boys must come first. You need to take some time off. Take the boys where they won't be hurt and get some rest. You look like you're about to explode."

Matt couldn't deny that. But before he left the office, he shared *almost* everything he knew about the case. He kept only the existence of a certain hand-written ransom demand to himself.

As a law officer, he knew he would go by the books and insist that anyone in his position—the recipient of a ransom note—cooperate with the police and not try to go it alone. But as a man who had received a ransom note for the woman he loved, he felt the great burden of involving anyone else. He knew only too well how someone's well-meaning actions could result in disaster, even death. No, this time he had to trust himself alone.

Matt had a little time on his hands with nothing to do. He didn't want to raise questions at the bank in town about why he needed fifty thousand dollars in cash. So he picked up Jimmy and Keith, made a call to Keith's boss to get him excused from work, and drove north, stopping by his home only long enough to park his sheriff's truck in the garage and get his personal vehicle.

Later that afternoon in Great Falls, he received the cash from a bank, using his ranch equity line, which he had just recently brought down to a zero balance. Then he took the boys to dinner. After returning from the city, he stopped at his place long enough to tend to his animals. Then he took the boys into town and left them with his parents who, after Matt explained the danger they were in, agreed to take them to a motel in West Yellowstone until he told them it was safe to return.

After delivering one final word of caution to his loved ones, he again read the latest note and headed east from Bozeman. At exactly nine o'clock that night, as he was driving, he made a phone call to the number that had been included on that same note. A muffled voice answered.

Matt said, "I'm ready. What do I do next?"

The indistinct voice gave him instructions, very puzzling instructions. "Mess up, Prescott, and you'll never see your little honey again," the voice said darkly.

"Let me talk to her. I just need to hear her voice," Matt pleaded.

"Sorry, but she's not with me right now."

"How can I know she's okay if I can't talk to her?"

"You'll just have to trust me, I guess. But you can't talk to her now. Do exactly as you're told. You'll get more instructions when I see that you're willing to follow directions. Be there at midnight sharp. And don't be late." He didn't mention the fifty thousand dollars.

He had been told to drive to a rural area several miles south of the town of Bridger, over on State Highway 310. Matt was quite sure he had plenty of time, but he didn't waste any either since he had no way of knowing how long it might take to find the meeting place.

* * *

Dwight was in a dark, volatile mood. The news his two most trusted associates had just delivered had only added fuel to the anger already festering in him from having learned that somehow Prescott and his boys had made it out of their house alive. He was also angry that Prescott's dog had nearly bitten him.

Now he had to arrange another accident, and it needed to be soon. It also meant that even an exceptionally well-planned accident might be viewed with suspicion by Prescott's fellow cops. That was not something he needed right now.

Then to be told that Jude had messed up and died as a result and that Lucas had not been heard from made him absolutely livid. "Now let me get this straight," he stormed at Kendra and Junior. "You're quite certain that Lucas finished his job and killed my sister. Is that what you're saying?"

"Yes," they answered in unison.

"But you didn't find any sign of her body?"

"That's right." It was Junior who was speaking now. "But it has to be in the huge slide area that Lucas's tracks led us to. And there was blood."

"But you didn't make sure he left her body in that area?" Dwight asked, his face purple with rage.

Junior shook his head. "It was almost dark, and it might have taken us hours. You have to understand what a large area that is."

"I don't have to understand anything!" Dwight barked dangerously. "I just need to know that no one stands in the way of my getting that ranch. And both of you need to know that too."

Junior and Kendra glanced briefly at each other. They had expected that Dwight would be upset, but he was far more than upset now. He was in a deadly mood.

"Sorry if we were wrong," Junior said contritely, hoping to calm Dwight. "Anyway, we made the decision to get back to the van and try to find Lucas. He knows exactly where he hid her body. But we can't find him, and he hasn't made contact with us. We were hoping you'd heard from him."

Dwight turned away for a moment, trying to keep from exploding. Finally, he turned back to them. "Find Lucas, you incompetents! And when you do, bring him to me—alive. I have to know with absolute certainty that lovely little Lindsay is out of the picture. Then the two of you can take care of Lucas. He's outlived his usefulness."

Kendra and Junior both nodded their heads.

"If you haven't found Lucas by tomorrow night, go back to that rockslide area and search until you find Lindsay's body. Bring me proof that she's no longer going to stand between me and what is rightfully mine," Dwight said darkly. "You have forty-eight hours. Now get out of here. I have places I need to be tonight and things I need to do."

* * *

As they drove away from the meeting place, Kendra said, "I can't believe he's so angry. He didn't even seem to care that my brother was dead or that a wolf had been killed. There's something more that's eating on him."

"Do you think the ranch has become too important to him?" Junior asked.

"I think so. We could use the money from its sale for our work, but we've done okay without it," Kendra observed. "It's not like Dwight doesn't have a lot of money."

"I wonder where he needs to be tonight, or is that just a figure of speech," Junior mused.

"I wondered the same thing. I suppose if we needed to know, he'd have told us."

* * *

The place the person with the muffled voice had described had proven more difficult to locate than Matt had expected. And it was five minutes after midnight when he pulled up beside an old corral and cabin. The place clearly hadn't been used in decades. The cabin, which he had been instructed to enter, was nothing but four rotting walls. The roof had long since caved in and the doorway was missing its door.

He got out of his truck, bringing a flashlight with him. He wondered if he was being watched from somewhere out in the darkness, or even from within the crumbling cabin. His palms started to sweat and he felt light-headed and faint. He was short on sleep and long on tension. If, after what he was doing now, he learned that Lindsay was dead, he wasn't sure how he could ever cope. He'd barely made it through the loss of Carol and Sarah. He didn't know if he could go through such a thing again. And yet he had to remember it was possible that he'd find her alive. The man with the muffled voice might only be after money.

Matt approached the ancient cabin slowly, realizing he might be walking into an ambush. A sheet of flame could erupt from a gun in the old cabin at any moment, and his sons would be left without a parent.

He stepped through the open doorway, and dust puffed up beneath his feet. He stood for a moment, slowly shining his light around. He had no idea what he was looking for. He'd simply been told that he would know it when he saw it. He stepped farther into the cabin, carefully stepping around a portion of the collapsed roof. When he did, his light struck something that stopped him cold.

Draped over a broken, rotting roof beam was Lindsay's light blue western-cut blouse. It was torn and caked with dried blood. Matt stepped over and picked it up, his heart beating like a steel drum and his hands shaking uncontrollably. He hurriedly carried it back to his truck, wondering what it meant. Why, if the person who was demanding money wanted him to believe she was alive, would he leave something like this for him to find? Was it some kind of cruel joke?

When he held the blouse in front of the headlights, something fell from one of the pockets and fluttered to the ground. He reached down and picked it up. It was a tiny piece of paper that had been folded once. Inside he saw a message, printed in now-familiar handwriting: *Be at the Lazy F at two o'clock AM, and don't be late. Come alone. And don't bring a gun.*

24

A nondescript gray car followed at a safe distance with its lights off as the truck being driven by Matt Prescott turned off the county road and onto the lane that led to the Lazy F Ranch. Kendra Norse and Junior Welker didn't know what Sergeant Prescott was up to, but they intended to find out as they parked down the road and got out to make their way to the darkness of the machine shed.

* * *

A glance at his dashboard clock told Matt he was a couple of minutes early. He parked in front of Lindsay's garage and sat there with the motor running, his lights off. He didn't know what to do next. The note had been pretty sparse on details. He looked around and couldn't see any other vehicles parked in the yard. He knew there wasn't room for one in the garage. When he'd last looked, it had been filled with Lindsay's truck and her father's large black Ford F-250 that hadn't been driven since his death. Of course, there was always the barn. There was room to park several trucks in there.

He pulled his pistol from his waistband and shoved it beneath the seat next to the box containing fifty thousand dollars in hundred-dollar bills. He'd been told not to bring a weapon so that when he got out of the truck, he'd be unarmed. As for the money, he figured he could come back for it when he needed it, and when he did, the hidden gun might come in handy.

Suddenly, the porch light came on, stayed lit for three or four seconds, and then went off again. Matt's heart leaped into his throat, and he felt as if he would suffocate. Possibilities of what the flashing light might signal raced through his mind. He finally decided it was a signal for him to come to the house. It was the thought of what might await him there that worried him.

The light came on a second time and then went off again. He wiped his hand across his forehead, offered a quick prayer, shut off the engine, and got out of the truck, steeling himself for whatever came next.

He began to walk toward the house, his mind suddenly calm. He was as prepared as he would ever be for what lay ahead. He opened the small gate, stepped through, and continued up the sidewalk. When he had stepped onto the porch and reached the door, he hesitated. He wasn't exactly familiar with the protocol for such a situation. Should he ring the bell, knock, or just wait for some signal from within?

Again the porch light came on, and Matt could hear footsteps inside. He stood where he was, waiting and wondering what was about to happen. Suddenly, the phone in his pocket began to vibrate. He jumped, startled at the unexpected happening. He pulled out the phone, opened it, and looked at the number displayed there. It was Lindsay's home number. He was being called from the phone inside the house.

"This is Prescott," he said into his phone.

"Good. Now, don't try anythin' stupid. Just open the door, step inside, and close it behind you. Don't make any quick moves, and don't do anythin' else 'til I tell you to." A muffled voice, identical to the one he'd talked to hours earlier, issued instructions.

Matt reached out and tried the doorknob. It opened easily. He pushed slowly on the door as he walked forward. He stepped inside the house and then shut the door behind him. He faced a dark room. Suddenly, a blinding light struck him in the eyes, forcing him to use his hand as a shield. The same voice he'd heard only moments before spoke from the far side of the room.

"Listen to me, Prescott, and keep your hands where I can see them. You'll get to see Miss Flemming again if you do exactly what I say. First, I need answers to some questions. And every word you say will be recorded."

The voice was deep, similar to what he remembered from the few words Lucas Mallory had spoken when he was with Kendra Norse at

Lindsay's ranch. He began to wonder if he was the one in the room. Whoever it was, he just wished he'd turn off the spotlight. He could see nothing but the light. "Where is Lindsay?" he asked.

"That's jumpin' ahead. I'll get to that in time. Which reminds me, Prescott, we are not alone. I brought a witness."

"Who's your witness?" Matt asked, not expecting an answer but feeling the need to ask.

"I'm not sayin' who it is," was the muffled response. "Do you think I'm stupid?"

No, just evil, depraved, and rotten to the core, Matt thought. He wished the man across the room would get rid of whatever he was holding over his mouth so he could hear him more clearly. "Okay, so what do you want to know?" Matt asked impatiently.

"Have you got the money?"

"It's in the truck," Matt said.

"And your gun? Where's that?"

Matt hesitated. But he decided to be honest. "It's in the truck, too."

"I meant for you to leave it home."

"I wasn't home when I read your note. But I can't get to my gun anyway, at least not from here," Matt said.

"Of course not. Well, I guess that'll have to do then. You don't have another one on you, do you?"

"No. I'm unarmed."

"You better not be lyin' to me. Now, let's get down to business."

"I've answered your questions. I've followed your instructions. I've died a thousand deaths the past week trying to find her. Now you tell me where Lindsay is."

"Not so fast, Prescott. There are some things I need to talk to you about first. Some assurances I'd like you to make to me and my witness here. And that's why I'm recordin' this. I wanna make a deal with you."

"What kind of deal?" Matt asked. He was getting tired of the runaround, and the bright light shining in his eyes was driving him wild. And he wished the idiot with the light would prove to him that Lindsay was okay, that she was alive. That was what he wanted more than anything.

"I know who killed Noah Flemming," the muffled voice announced.

"I'm sure you do. Would you care to tell me now?" Matt asked. "I have reason to believe it was Lucas Mallory."

The room was silent for a moment, and Matt hoped he hadn't said too much. But a moment later the voice began again, and this time it was clear, no longer muffled. "I can assure you that it was not Lucas Mallory. I'm Lucas, and I didn't do it, but I know who did."

"Give Lindsay back to me and tell me who killed her father. If you do that, you have my word that I'll do whatever I can for you, Lucas. I just want Lindsay back. And I do have the money. You can have it. Just take me to her." He knew his voice betrayed his emotions.

"There's a light switch right behind you. Flip it on," Lucas said.

Matt switched the light on, and the man claiming to be Lucas flipped off his bright light and placed it on the sofa beside him. Then he picked up a pistol from his lap and motioned with it. "Sit right over there. Then we can talk."

It was Lucas. In the present location, and without his female sidekick, Mallory could easily be mistaken for a model for the Sportsmen's Big and Tall Shop in Bozeman. He had medium-length dark hair that Matt remembered and, thanks to Grey Sadler's handiwork, was still lacking one front tooth.

As Matt moved to the large recliner Lucas indicated, he glanced around the room. He saw no one but Lucas. However, the door to Noah's bedroom, which was slightly to the left of and behind Mallory, was open. Matt distinctly remembered leaving it closed when he and the boys had been there the previous night. Matt guessed that the other person Lucas claimed was with him was hidden in that room. He suspected that whoever it was also had a gun. He didn't see a tape recorder, but that didn't mean there wasn't one. He sat down and faced Lucas.

"I'm listening, Lucas. Lay out your terms."

"First, I want to be able to walk free after you arrest the ones who killed Noah Flemming."

"I can work on that, but I can't guarantee anything. I mean, this is kidnapping, Lucas. Why don't you just take me to Lindsay, take your money, and then go wherever you want to after you tell me who I'm looking for. I won't come after you," Matt promised.

"That's not good enough."

"Not good enough? You go free. What more could you want?"

"I want to live, that's what I want," Lucas said with a strange look on his face.

Could it be fear? Matt wondered.

"That's what I'm offering," Matt said impatiently.

"No, you don't understand at all!" Lucas said. "Dwight Flemming will have me killed."

"For betraying him?"

"That's pretty much it. I want you to take me to jail, but I want to be able to get out when the others are caught, includin' Dwight."

"And who are the others? I take it Dwight had something to do with his own father's death?" His eyes darted to the open doorway behind Lucas as he spoke. He thought he heard something, almost like someone trying to quietly clear their throat. He wasn't at all sure that Lucas was being straight with him, that even greater danger didn't dwell in the darkness of that room.

"Do I have your word?" Lucas asked. "Remember, I have a witness."

"Yes, you have my word. I'll do everything in my power to help you if you can give me enough information to make the arrests and to get convictions. And, of course, if I get Lindsay back alive."

"That's fair, I guess. Okay, you can come out now," Lucas called over his shoulder toward Noah's room.

Matt stiffened as a shadow moved from the far end of the adjoining room. Then his eyes popped open, and he sprang to his feet, his heart beating like a jackhammer.

* * *

"At least we know they're both in there, though I can't imagine what the cop and Lucas have to talk about. And with the van that's parked in the barn, we know it's got to be Lucas," Junior said quietly as he peeked around the edge of the equipment shed and watched the house.

"I suppose he's going to kill him like he did the Flemming woman, but I'm not sure why he'd do it here," Kendra said. "He was supposed to kill her here and didn't. It makes no sense."

"Maybe he figured the cop would come here if he could make him think the Flemming woman was alive. But I'd think he'd know that Dwight wouldn't like that. By the way, that was a good idea you had of following Prescott when we spotted him."

Kendra was strangely silent. Junior looked back toward her in the darkness. "Are you okay?" he asked.

"Just thinking. I know I said I wouldn't do this, but hear me out anyway," she said. "What if Dwight's somehow in on this with Lucas? I think he'd like to be rid of Prescott. It would only make sense because he could cause trouble over the ranch."

It took Junior a moment to reply. "Dwight could be in there," he said. "He might have already heard from Lucas before we met him. They might have set this all up. And if so, we shouldn't be here. They probably plan to take Prescott out and get rid of him."

"And then we would find Lucas, and Dwight would be rid of both of them," she said softly. "Maybe we should just get out of here."

"No, we're here now, so let's watch. At least we can see who comes out. If it's just Lucas and the cop, we can do what we need to do. If Dwight's with them, then we'll wait. Our car's hidden well enough," Junior suggested. "And by the way, don't think I don't trust Dwight."

"Me either," Kendra answered. "He has the right to do what he feels is necessary. And we'll follow his orders."

* * *

Matt was bound tightly. And at that moment he didn't care if he ever got loose. The last person in the world he would have expected to come walking out of that bedroom was the one who held him bound. Her arms were so tight around his neck that he could barely breathe.

Lindsay was alive! She was right here in her own house! She was the one Lucas had been referring to when he'd said he wasn't alone. It made no sense at all, but after the two of them could let go of each other, he intended to get to the bottom of it. For right now, though, he was so overwhelmed with joy that all he wanted was to hold her, and she seemed to want the same.

Lucas was the one who finally broke up the celebration. "You need names, and I'm ready to talk. Lindsay says I can trust you. I just needed to see how I felt after havin' a chance to see and talk to you. That's why I insisted that we pull this little ruse. But frankly, I'd rather talk at the jail. I don't feel safe here," Lucas said.

"But certainly we're safe here," Lindsay protested. "None of Dwight's other people would ever think you would bring me here. I think the way we faked my death was quite convincing. If they found where we came onto that rockslide area, they'd think my body could have been dumped anywhere in there. It would have taken hours before they could be sure it wasn't."

"Don't underestimate your brother," Lucas said. "He'll want proof. I've told you that." He turned to Matt. "Really, I want to get out of here now. And here, take my gun. I don't need it anymore."

Matt shoved the pistol into his waistband. "Let's go, then."

"I'm coming too," Lindsay said. "I don't want to be alone."

"Of course," Matt answered. "I wouldn't think of leaving you here until your brother and his henchmen are in custody."

When they reached the door, Matt turned off the living room lights and then the porch light.

"Matt, it's dark out there. Why did you shut off the porch light?" Lindsay asked.

"I just feel safer in the darkness right now," he said. "Lucas wasn't the only one who made a middle-of-the-night visit to my place when he left the note on my door."

"Oh, Matt! What else happened? Are the boys all right?"

"Yes, well, not any worse than they were. I'll tell you all about it when we're on our way to town," he said, and he opened the door. "Lucas, you go first and stay in front of us." Despite what Lindsay had told him, he wasn't about to let the big man get behind him.

* * *

"There they come. I wish there was more light. But there are three of them. I can tell that much," Junior whispered.

"Lucas is the tall one in front. Dwight must be the short one behind him," Kendra said softly. "I wonder if he'll tell us about this later, or if he'll just say nothing."

"If he wanted us to know, he'd have said so. Come on. Let's get out of sight. They'll need to come past us to get to the van in the barn," Junior said.

They both crept toward the back of the machine shed and knelt down in the weeds and grass there. They waited, expecting to hear the door to the barn open at any moment. Instead, they heard the doors closing on Matt's pickup. "Hey, why would they take his truck?" Kendra asked urgently. "They wouldn't want the van to be found here."

"I guess they'll come back after it." Junior suddenly sprang to his feet, raced along the side of the shed, and looked around the corner. The light in Prescott's truck was on. The three of them were just getting their seat belts on.

Kendra slipped to his side. "That's not Dwight. It's Lindsay!" she said urgently. "She's alive, and Lucas has turned her over to her lover boy. That traitor!"

Junior had already made those deductions for himself. He knelt on the ground and took aim with his pistol. "We can't let them get away. Start shooting," he said as he pulled the trigger.

25

Matt saw the flame from the corner of his eye and jammed on the accelerator at the same moment. A bullet struck the body of the truck somewhere near the front. "Duck!" he shouted as he began to fishtail. Another shot, followed by a third, rang out. He'd barely managed to turn the truck toward the lane when he felt a front tire blow, jerking the steering wheel out of his hands. A second later another bullet shattered both the rear window and the windshield. Lucas and Lindsay were bent over low, and the bullet appeared to have gone right over them.

Matt tried to accelerate again, but the engine only coughed and then died. Steam exploded from beneath the hood. He grabbed his pistol. "We're sitting ducks here. We'll get out on my side, but stay down. I'll return fire."

"I'll help," Lucas shouted as the truck bounced to a stop, the passenger side facing the assailants' positions. "If you'll let me take my gun."

Matt hesitated. "No. Lindsay can use it." He handed the pistol to Lindsay, who took it with trembling hands. He held his own pistol firmly in his right hand. "I'll have to go first, then Lindsay. Stay down when you get there."

Matt let go of the steering wheel and dived out the door. A second later Lindsay followed and then Lucas. Bullets kept coming from beside the machine shed. Matt fired back when another sheet of flame gave away the position of a second assailant. He had no idea how many there were. Lindsay fired a split second later, and then it was silent.

When another shot rang out and gravel sprayed the three of them, Matt and Lindsay fired again in almost perfect unison. Then once more it was quiet. Matt listened for what seemed like an eternity.

"They must be down," Lucas said, his voice low and tight.

"Or circling around us," Matt countered as he dug out his cell phone. "Keep your eyes peeled while I dial 911."

A few moments later they heard a horse snorting followed by the furious pounding of hooves and a desperate scream. "Someone's in the stallion's corral," Lindsay said as Matt completed his call and shut the phone. "I think my stallion may have tromped one of them," she whispered.

"Let's hope so," Matt replied angrily. "You two slip into the grass at the side of the lane there," he said, pointing to the heavy growth that bordered a hay field to the north.

"Where are you going?" Lindsay asked. "I can't go without you."

"Don't worry, I'm going to follow you," Matt said. "Now go! Stay low and keep the truck between you and the yard. I'll send Lucas and then I'll come."

"You two go," Lucas said in a barely discernible whisper. "I don't think I can make it. I've been hit."

Matt turned to Lucas. "Where were you hit?" he asked.

"It's my leg—I can't walk."

"Then I guess I'll carry you."

"No, this is all my fault. I can't put you in more danger. You two go."

"You're coming with us," Lindsay said fiercely. "You saved my life—carrying me all that way. The others would have killed me if it hadn't been for you. I can't leave you here for them to kill. You did so much to keep me alive."

"I think the bone's shattered," Lucas protested. "Leave me. And if you give me a gun, I can defend myself if I have to."

Matt had no idea of everything Lucas had done for Lindsay, but he could see that she felt strongly about leaving him. He said, "Lindsay, you'll still have to go first. Take my phone. Keep an eye open and shoot if anyone comes while I'm bringing him across."

"You can't—" Lucas began.

"I can't leave you here," Matt said. "You're my prisoner. Hurry, Lindsay. Go now!"

As soon as Lindsay was into the tall grass, Matt lifted the big man into his arms and, bent over, hurried toward the field as fast as he could. Matt sighed with relief when they were finally hidden in the tall grass and no more shots had been fired at them.

"If we stay low, we should be safe now," Matt said.

"Where are we going?" Lindsay asked in a strained whisper.

"We'll make our way through your tall hay and around to the back of the garage. If help doesn't get here soon, we'll take your truck and make a run for it, but I don't think that'll be necessary. Help will be here. You keep the phone, but don't take it off silent. We don't need it ringing and giving away our position if the sheriff tries to get in touch with us. Lindsay, you take the lead. Swing well out into the hay and then back to the garage. I'll help Lucas, and we'll be right behind you. They shouldn't be able to spot us even if they use a light."

Despite his injury, Lucas was able to help himself quite a bit. They were only halfway to the garage, taking a roundabout path deep into the field, when he said, "I'm done in. Leave me here. You can come back for me later. No one will ever find me out in this hayfield."

"We can rest here for a few minutes," Matt said. "I'm sure someone will be here soon."

A minute later, sirens pierced the air. Matt turned to Lindsay. "I'll go meet the other cops. You stay here with Lucas. I'll use one of their phones to call you when it's clear."

"No, Matt, you take the phone so you can talk to the sheriff or whoever's coming. I don't want them to mistake you for one of those guys," she said. "You can just shout to us when it's safe. Someone will have to come get Lucas anyway."

"I'll call for an ambulance," Matt said as he took the phone, gave Lindsay a quick, hard kiss, and then started through the hay on his hands and knees.

* * *

Lindsay lay thinking about all that had happened. It had been so hard for her to stay in her father's bedroom and keep her presence secret while Matt and Lucas talked in the living room. She had wanted to run out and throw her arms around Matt to relieve him of the worry. The words he said to Lucas still rang in her ears. He had told Lucas that he loved her. She couldn't have heard anything sweeter. But she restrained herself from leaving the room because she'd promised Lucas, and she owed him. As strange as it seemed even now, Lucas had done so much for her. Despite all the terrible things he might have done in his life, he had saved her life. She couldn't comprehend why he'd done it.

She listened as the police cars came closer. And she thought back to when Lucas had surprised her on that steep hillside. She'd thought she was about to die, and she had fought hard. He had cut her, but not seriously, in the struggle. She was still amazed as she recalled what he'd told her after getting her under his control. "I don't wanna hurt you," he'd said. "I'm tryin' to protect you from Guardian and Enforcer."

"Who are they?" she'd asked.

"Kendra Norse and Junior Welker. They're part of your brother's secret band of killers. And they'll kill you if they find you. If they catch up with us and see that I haven't already killed you, we'll both die."

"But you're one of them," she'd protested.

"Not anymore," he'd replied. "How do you think that door in the cabin happened to be unlocked? I did it so you could get away, then I busted the inside of it and told them that I couldn't imagine how it happened. And after that, I did everything I could to keep that rotten Retaliator—that's Kendra's brother, Jude—from catching up with you. If I wasn't on your side, I could have told him you were in that gnarled old fir tree."

"You knew that?" she'd asked.

"I suspected it. It looked like a likely place for you to go. It's what I would have done with wolves trailing me."

Lindsay had finally decided to trust him. After that he had carried her for hours. It hadn't been easy for him. Then, when they'd reached the van, he'd helped her get in and hide—in the same hidden compartment where Dwight's people had concealed tranquilized wolves as they brought them from the park and relocated them on and near her ranch and others. He had her ride in there so that if any of the group happened to see him, she would be concealed. But no one had met them, and he had taken her safely out of the mountains. He'd helped her sneak into her house in the middle of the night so that she could get clean clothes and some loose fitting shoes that would give her feet relief. He'd even helped her cut the boots off her feet and then doctored them for her.

Lindsay had trusted him fully after that, and when he told her of his plan to get Matt on his side, she reluctantly went along with him.

She stayed hidden where he told her to while he'd set his plan to get Matt to come to them in motion. And now she knew that she would do whatever she could to help him. She only hoped that with his help in return, they could stop Dwight from succeeding.

The police cars roared into the yard. She looked up from the tall hay where they were hidden. Lights came on and officers rushed about. Matt appeared from the far side of her garage. Then she sank back on the ground. "Are you doing okay?" she asked Lucas.

"I'll live," he said. "And, Lindsay, that guy of yours is a good man. He doesn't trust me like you do, and I don't blame him, but he's a good man."

* * *

Junior was dead of a gunshot wound. He'd died beside the machine shop, his pistol in one hand. Kendra was still alive, but barely. She had stumbled into the stallion's corral and startled him. Although she managed to get under the bottom rail as he pounded her with his hooves, she passed out there. She had numerous broken bones and had lost a lot of blood.

Lucas was hauled to the hospital in the same ambulance as his former partner. A pair of officers was sent to meet him there and to keep a close guard on his hospital room until Dwight was found and arrested.

With the exception of one member of the secret society, a man they had called Protector, whose real name was Johnny Redding, the rest of the secret society was not likely to cause anymore immediate problems. At least that was Lucas's assessment. The most violent ones had been Kendra, Junior, Jude, and Johnny.

It had been Jude Norse who had shot and killed Noah Flemming. He had already paid for his crime. However, Johnny and Kendra had been with him, and Lucas understood that the law would pursue Protector until he too was brought to justice. Kendra, besides being at the scene when Noah was murdered, had been the one who had shot Grey Sadler. If she lived, she would stand trial and most likely spend the rest of her life in prison.

Lindsay and Matt visited the hospital that afternoon. She still limped painfully because of the damage her feet had sustained in the mountains. But they were healing, and her spirits were high. Matt spoke briefly with the deputy standing guard outside the door before they entered Lucas's room. They talked briefly, and then Lucas's face went grim. "Matt, don't let her out of your sight," he said, glancing at Lindsay. "Dwight hates her. You've both got to be really careful. He'll get both of you if he can. You also need to watch out for Johnny. He'll definitely help Dwight."

"We'll be careful," Matt promised. "I'm grateful to you that I have Lindsay back. I'll never let her get away from me again."

"As soon as they'll let me out of this hospital bed, I'll go to the jail," Lucas said. "Despite what I said back there in Lindsay's house, I know I deserve to. Maybe you could help me by speaking in my behalf. I don't want to go to jail for the rest of my life. But right now, I'm safer in jail until Dwight's caught. He'll be after me. He'll either come himself or send Johnny. We're all in danger as long as they're out there. When Dwight hates someone, it's forever."

"Where can we find Johnny Redding?" Matt asked.

"I honestly don't know. However, I do know that like Dwight, he's the son of one of the ranchers somewhere in the state. I finally realized that he couldn't care less about wild animals. He's just out for revenge against the ranchers like Dwight is. I don't know why he feels he has to even the score, but he's full of bitterness."

"That brings us to one of the purposes of this visit. I was wondering if you could help us locate and arrest Dwight," Matt said.

"How could I do that?" Lucas asked, his eyes growing wide. "I can't even walk."

"You won't need to. Do you know how to make contact with him?" Matt asked.

"I think so, but I don't know if it would do any good. Why would you want me to do that anyway?"

"I was thinking that you might be able to convince him that you needed to talk to him. Make him think it's important. Pretend that you trust him, and only him, with the information you've come across. See if he'll meet you somewhere. Then we'll be there to bring him in."

"I'll try if I have your word that you won't let him get to me."

"You'll be safe, Lucas. I'll see to that. I do believe that this is our best chance of nabbing him. I'll bring you a cell phone you can use. If and when you arrange a meeting with him, give me a call. I'll take it from there. If we can get him right away, the prosecutor says he will cut you some slack."

"I'll try. That's all I can say," Lucas promised.

Matt and Lindsay headed for West Yellowstone to meet his sons and parents. Jimmy greeted them silently but snuggled into Lindsay's arms after clinging to his dad for a couple of minutes. Keith tearfully hugged Lindsay. They rented rooms for the night, deciding that it was best to remain there. The boys stayed in the room with Matt. Lindsay was in a room on one side of them, his parents on the other. At midnight Matt awoke to the ringing of his cell phone.

"Matt, this is Lucas. Dwight has agreed to meet me. Can you write this down? I'll give you an address."

Matt hurriedly dressed and slipped out of his room. Neither of his sons stirred. He tapped on Lindsay's door. She opened it so fast he wondered if she'd been sitting there waiting just in case something happened. "I've got to go. Dwight's agreed to meet Lucas," he said. "Hopefully this will all be over in a few hours."

"I'm coming," she said.

"No, you better—"

She cut him off midsentence. "Please, Matt. I can't bear to have you go off like this without me. I want to be with you. Anyway, Dwight is my brother."

"Okay. We'll leave in five minutes," he said softly. "I'll tell my parents we're going so they can watch Jimmy and Keith."

Four hours later, an old brown car pulled up outside a house in Great Falls. Law officers concealed nearby had been watching the building. Matt lifted a pair of powerful nighttime binoculars to his eyes. He watched for a moment, then whispered, "It's him."

Lindsay reached over, put her trembling arms around Matt, and began to sob. "I love you, Matt," she said between her tears. "I'll wait here. I can't watch."

26

Avenger's face was dark with anger. He glanced at the blinds covering the front window. Protector stood quietly, eagerly awaiting whatever orders his leader gave him. "I haven't heard from Guardian or Enforcer. They were to have found and silenced Defender, but they failed, and now it appears they don't have the courage to tell me. I'm afraid their usefulness has come to an end, but that little matter can be attended to later. I've also been trying to locate Harrier, Keeper, and Reactor, but it appears they've fled. Such idiots. They thought this was all about saving wolves and buffalo." Dwight gave an ugly laugh.

"I can find them and take care of them for you," Protector said.

"In time, in time," Avenger responded. "Traitors and fools can't be allowed to live. You and I are the only ones who've known all along what our real purpose was. The others have all helped, but they can't now. We'll find ways, you and me, to ruin the ranchers. We'll make them pay for the way they treated us. But first we have to deal with Defender."

Avenger turned toward the door in anticipation of Defender's arrival. He thought about how easily he and Protector had convinced the other members of their society to help them do serious damage to the ranchers they both despised. It was never about wild animals, but the ruse had worked well. Their recruits, all wolf lovers, were easy to propagandize. But he knew that kind of deception wouldn't work any longer. He and Protector hadn't introduced wolves to save the wolves. They meant only to financially cripple the ranchers.

"He should be here soon, the big fool. Defender doesn't even know he's in trouble with me. I gave him a perfectly clear assignment and he failed. My sister may still be alive. That is unacceptable."

"If she's alive, I'll deal with her myself. It will be a pleasure," Protector said.

Avenger impatiently waved an arm. "I know you will, if she's still alive. We'll know in a few minutes. Defender will tell us, and then he will die. He'll disappear forever."

Protector nodded in agreement. "I'll begin searching for the others and deal with each of them when I find them," he said.

"That's exactly what I want, but you can't be too careful. There's still a lot more to do. Hey, I think he's here. Protector, you slip into that bedroom and wait. I want to talk to Defender by myself for a moment. You come in when I give you the signal."

Protector quietly slipped from the room as Dwight moved toward the door, his hatred making him almost rigid. A forceful knock on the door broke the strained silence.

* * *

The light was fading fast as Matt watched and listened from his position behind a tree at the edge of the street. He was just a few feet from the house where Lucas had told him they would probably find Dwight that evening. The local police chief had insisted that he and his men would take the lead in Dwight's arrest. One of his officers had just knocked on the door. Two more stood on either side of the entrance, waiting either to go in behind the first officer when Dwight opened it or to break the door down if necessary.

Three other officers, including Sheriff Baker, were in positions similar to Matt's, and two more were covering the back door. For a moment, it was as if time had stopped. Then Matt heard someone call out, "Defender, is that you?" The voice was muffled by the door, but Matt was certain it was Dwight's.

The officer at the door stepped to one side, his sidearm drawn, and said, "Police. Open up!"

Nothing happened, and then the officer stepped rapidly in front of the door and delivered a powerful kick. The lock gave way, and the door swung open. The three officers rushed in. A moment later, as Matt rushed for the door, a barrage of shooting erupted in back of the house. Matt swerved to his left, running as hard as he could around the house. But before he reached the backyard, shooting began inside. Again he changed direction and ran to the front just in time to see someone flee from the house, firing behind him as he ran. He knew instantly that it was Dwight.

As Matt raised his weapon, an officer appeared in the doorway, his gun blazing. Suddenly, he flew backward, screaming in pain. Dwight also fell, but he leaped to his feet. Matt felt a stinging in his left hand as the gun in Dwight's hand bucked. Matt fired and Dwight went down once more. He looked rapidly around for other officers but saw no one. At that moment, he heard gunfire from behind the house again.

Matt approached Dwight's still figure. He was within ten feet when Dwight's hand shot up. Before Matt could fire again, he felt a bullet thud into his chest, knocking him backward. He lost his footing and fell, his pistol flying from his hand. Dazed, he looked around for a few moments to get his bearing. As he struggled to his knees, searching frantically for his pistol, he sensed the deadly quiet.

"Matt, are you okay?" The sheriff gripped his elbow.

"Yeah, I think so," he said. "Dwight's bullet hit my vest, and it knocked the wind out of me. Watch out for him!"

"He's under control. Let me help you up."

"He was down when he shot me," Matt said as he finally spotted his pistol lying four or five feet away. He twisted, trying to get to his gun.

"He's disarmed, Matt, and an officer is putting cuffs on him," the sheriff said as Matt scrambled for his gun. "And he's shot up pretty badly."

Matt stumbled to his feet and turned to where Dwight lay on the ground, an officer pressing a hand against a profusely bleeding stomach wound. "There are others," he said as he took his eyes off the pathetic figure of Lindsay's brother.

"Just one," the sheriff responded. "He's dead. But he put up a whale of a fight."

"The other officers—" Matt began.

"Two of them were injured, but ambulances are on the way. They'll live," the sheriff assured him. "Are you sure you're okay?"

Before he could answer, another voice called out, "Matt!" He turned his head as Lindsay tore across the street toward him. He started toward her, trying to create distance between him and her critically injured brother. "Are you hurt?" she cried.

"I'm fine," he said.

"You're bleeding!"

"I am?"

"Yes. Look at your arm."

He saw that his left hand was bloody, a little trickle oozing from a cut just above his thumb. Then he remembered feeling something sting his hand when Dwight first shot at him. He lifted his hand but could see that he was not seriously hurt. He shook off the blood that was pooling there.

"You fell. I saw you go down," Lindsay said, anguish still in her voice.

"My vest stopped his bullet," he said. "I'm okay."

"Oh, Matt, is that Dwight?" She had finally become aware of the crumpled figure lying thirty feet beyond them, the sheriff and another officer beside him.

"I'm afraid so. You shouldn't be here, Lindsay. You don't need to see him like this."

But Lindsay was already running toward Dwight. She dropped to her knees beside Sheriff Baker, her hand reaching for her brother's shoulder. As she touched him, Matt joined her, and Dwight's eyes opened. Sirens began to wail in the distance. Lindsay was sobbing softly. After a moment, she said, "Dwight, it's Lindsay."

Dwight groaned. Then moving his head slightly, he said, "He didn't kill you." He was silent for a moment, struggling for breath. Then he said, "Lucas was supposed to kill you, the traitor."

"Dwight, how could you?" she sobbed. "Dad and I never stopped loving you."

"The old man got his," he said with an iciness that made Matt shudder.

"Dwight, oh, Dwight," she said, sobbing. Then anger crept into her voice. "Whatever happened? What made you so hateful?"

Her brother had no answer. Instead he closed his eyes, his face grimacing in pain. Then he opened them again. "That you, Prescott?" he asked.

"Yes, it's me."

"Prescott, did that traitor Lucas tell you how to find me?"

Matt saw no harm in telling him the truth. If he survived, he would learn soon enough anyway. "He helped us, yes."

A chuckle gurgled from Dwight's throat. "You don't know, do you?" he finally asked.

"Know what?" Matt asked.

Dwight chuckled again, but there was no humor in it—the sound was ugly. An ambulance drew up, and two paramedics ran toward Dwight. With a great deal of effort, he spoke a few more words before they reached him.

Matt listened in shock to what Dwight had to say. Then he stumbled back, a scream of horror stuck in his throat. Lindsay also recoiled, and she threw her arms protectively around Matt as the paramedics tended to her brother.

* * *

Lindsay was cried out, and it was fully dark by the time Matt came to the truck. She'd gone back there shortly after Dwight had been taken in the ambulance. There, alone in her misery, she mourned the evil ways of her brother. Even more, she mourned the loss of her father, who would still be alive if it hadn't been for Dwight. Matt opened the door. His face was drawn and tired. "I'm sorry I was so long," he said.

"That's okay. I chose to come," she replied.

He nodded as he slid in beside her. "You shouldn't have," he said as he started the engine.

"I know. But I couldn't let you come without me."

He nodded again. Then he began to drive. "At least it's over. I'm sorry it had to end this way," he said. His voice sounded distant, distracted. She knew what he was thinking about, and it hurt.

As they rode south in anxious silence, Dwight's words kept running through her mind. She wondered what Matt was thinking and what he was going to do about Dwight's disclosure. It worried her.

She finally broke the silence. "It's not really over, is it?"

He glanced her way, his face unreadable. "There will be trials after Dwight gets well, and I think he will. However, I'm sure he'll spend the rest of his life in prison."

"I honestly hope so," she said. Then she paused for a moment. There was something else she had to say. Finally she found the words. "I'm sorry about Carol and Sarah."

Tears filled Matt's eyes. "He did it," Matt said with bitterness in his voice.

"I know," she agreed.

"I can't ignore it, Lindsay. I won't ignore it. It's his fault they're dead. It's his fault Jimmy can't talk. I know I shouldn't feel this way, but I am so angry."

She wished he could ignore it, and yet she couldn't blame him.

"Please don't forget what else he did," she said softly.

Again he looked at her, but he said nothing. Anger filled his eyes. She almost hated Dwight right then. Why did he have to do what he did and say what he said? He took such pleasure in hurting others. Why couldn't he have done one decent thing and simply not spoken the words he knew would cause so much more pain and anger?

She would probably never know.

* * *

It was late when Matt and Lindsay reached the sheriff's office where Lindsay's truck was parked. His boys were with his parents at their home. They had driven back from West Yellowstone immediately after Matt called to tell them they were safe. Lindsay offered to go with Matt to take care of something he felt he had to do that night. But he insisted he needed to go alone. She was tearful as she drove away from him.

Matt knew he probably should have waited until morning. The middle of the night wasn't the best time to be visiting the hospital. He moved, robotlike, to the room Lucas Mallory still occupied. The officer at the door stood up. "Kind of late, isn't it?" he said.

Matt nodded. "This won't wait," he said before pushing the door open and entering the room.

He flipped on the light and stepped toward the bed. Lucas's eyes opened and he looked up at Matt in surprise. Matt said nothing.

"Did you arrest him?" Lucas asked.

Matt just stared at the man. He wasn't sure how to begin.

"What's wrong, Sergeant? Did Dwight get away? Wasn't he there? What's the matter?"

Matt finally spoke. "Dwight's badly injured and under arrest, Lucas. Protector is dead."

A look of relief came across Lucas's face. "So I'm out of danger," he said.

Matt nodded. "You're safe."

"So what happened?" Lucas asked.

"You'll learn soon enough," Matt said as he continued to fight the anger that filled him, that almost consumed him.

"What's botherin' you, Matt? Was someone else hurt? Oh, no, not Lindsay. Lindsay's not hurt, is she?" Lucas asked.

"Lindsay's fine," Matt said. Then he took a deep breath. "Answer one question, will you Lucas?"

"Sure, what's the question?"

"Why did you do it?"

Lucas looked stunned. For a moment, he didn't speak. Then he said, "Do what?"

"Okay, let me ask this. My dog, Claw, was your dog, wasn't he?"

The blood drained from Lucas's face. "I'm sorry," he said as tears suddenly filled his eyes.

"So why did you do it, Lucas? Why did you kill my wife and daughter?"

Lucas tried to sit up. Matt reached down and pushed him firmly back onto his pillow. "Talk, Lucas. I'm listening."

"It was an accident," the big man said. "I didn't mean it. The road was slick. It was dark. How'd you know?"

"Dwight told me. It was his last little 'gift' to me before the paramedics took him away."

Lucas groaned. "You aren't going to back out on your promise, are you?" he begged. "I didn't mean to hurt you or your family. I'm sorry, Matt. I am so terribly sorry."

For a long time, Matt looked Lucas in the eye. His anger slowly turned to pity. Finally, he said, "A deal's a deal. But after the court proceedings are over, I don't want to see you again, Lucas. Not ever."

"I said I was sorry," the big man said. Unexpectedly, his eyes filled with tears.

"I heard you. But that doesn't bring back Carol and Sarah. And it doesn't help my little boy to talk. At least I know now why he went into his shell again the day you ran over Lindsay's dog. Seeing you again brought it all back to him."

"If I could see him again, maybe I could explain to him," Lucas said.

"No!" Matt exploded. "I don't want that boy to ever lay eyes on you again." The two men locked eyes once more. Despite himself, Matt had to admit that there was genuine regret on Lucas's face. When Matt spoke again, it was with sadness. "I've got to go take care of my boy. I hope you can get a grip on your life. Good-bye, Lucas."

EPILOGUE

Two Weeks Later

The lights were low in the restaurant. Lindsay and Matt sat at a solitary table in a private corner of the room. The air-conditioning was humming, fighting the intense heat of the summer evening. For the first time since the day Dwight's words had brought back all the pain of Matt's loss the previous year, Matt and Lindsay were together. Lindsay had felt awkward knowing that Matt's mind was on what Lucas had done to his family. She wasn't even sure what the fresh hurt would mean to their future. She had hoped her phone would ring as she worked hard on the ranch each day, trying to erase the aching in her own heart. But Matt hadn't called until that morning.

When he had, he simply said, "Are you free for dinner this evening?"

She responded that she was, wondering what was going to happen. She was so afraid that she had lost him, that she would always be a reminder of his pain. Or maybe he had decided it would be easier just to go on with his life without her in it. At the door, when he'd come to pick her up, he'd greeted her with a smile, but she could still see traces of sadness lingering in his eyes. And she knew that he could see the same in hers.

"You look nice," he said.

"Thank you," she responded. She didn't tell him how incredibly good he looked to her. She didn't dare. And he made no attempt to explain the past two weeks.

On the way to town, Matt talked about Jimmy. He explained how, armed with an explanation for what had caused Jimmy's serious relapse, Dr. Lubek was able to make progress with the boy. He smiled when he said, "Jimmy said a complete sentence this morning at breakfast. Dr. Lubek is great. And with Lucas out of the way, I think we'll find things improving at a steadier rate now. I'm so grateful to her and to the Lord."

"Oh, Matt, that's such good news. I'm so happy to hear he's doing better," she said. "I've been worried about him."

"I'm sorry I haven't called," he told her, although he still offered no explanation. Instead, he asked her how the ranch was doing. They talked about that and other minutia the rest of the way to town.

Now, in the semidarkness of the restaurant, they gave the waitress their order. As the young woman walked away, Matt said, "Are you okay?"

"Sure, why wouldn't I be?" she asked, knowing there were plenty of reasons.

"Because of the way I've treated you," he said. "I should have called. I'm sorry about that. I wanted to, but I've been, well, torn, I guess."

"About us?" she asked, not sure she wanted to hear his answer.

"Yes, that, but also a lot of other things. It's been hard. I wasn't very kind to Lucas."

"It wasn't right what he did to you and your family," she said.

"Actually, it was criminal of him," Matt corrected her. "It's been so hard these past few days, just thinking about it, about them, about Lucas. But I know I've got to put it behind me."

Lindsay nodded. "Like I've got to put what Dwight did to me and my father behind me."

"Yes, like that. Lindsay, I've spent so much time lately just thinking—and feeling. I know I've never told you about my ranch and how my father was cheated out of a great deal more land by his own brother and how that's why the ranch is so small. Dad let go of his bitterness years ago, but I think I've held on to his share even though I've never been told the whole story. I finally realized that Dad is happy and successful and has no regrets about the turns his life has taken. And that's because the past no longer has a hold on him. Lindsay, I want to be like Dad. I'm ready to throw away my bitterness toward Uncle Thomas and my anger against Lucas. I want to get rid of those heavy weights. They've dragged me down long enough."

Matt looked closely at her in the dim light. "You are beautiful, Lindsay," he said.

"Thank you." She was a little stunned by the suddenness of his tender words.

"You need to know that I love you, Lindsay. In fact, I love you more than ever. Can you forgive me for the past two weeks?"

Her heart soared. "I can, and I do. But I don't think there's anything to forgive. I love you, and I've been trying to understand what you've been going through. Now I think I do."

Matt reached across the table and took her hand in his. "I wasn't sure I was going to be able to eat. My stomach has been churning all day. I've missed you so much."

She smiled. "And I've missed you."

"Then are we ready to put the pain from our pasts behind us and start looking toward the future?" he asked.

"Yes," was all she could say.

It was all she needed to say.

ABOUT THE AUTHOR

Clair M. Poulson was born and raised in Duchesne, Utah; he spent many years patrolling the highways and enforcing the law in Duchesne County as a highway patrolman and deputy sheriff, followed by two years of service in the U.S. Army Military Police Corps. He completed his twenty-year law enforcement career with eight years as Duchesne County Sheriff. For the past fifteen years, Clair has served as a justice court judge in Duchesne County.

Clair also does a little farming. His main interest is horses, although he has raised a variety of other livestock, including cattle, pigs, and sheep. Both Clair and his wife currently help their oldest son run Al's Foodtown, the grocery store in Duchesne.

He met his wife, Ruth, while they were both attending Snow College. They are the parents of five married children and grand-parents of twelve. Ruth has been a great support to Clair in all of his endeavors and now assists him with his writing by proofreading and making suggestions.

Clair has always been an avid reader, but his interest in creating fiction found its beginning many years ago when he told bedtime stories to his small children. They would beg for just one more story before going to sleep. He still practices that hobby with his grandchildren. He uses his life's experiences in law enforcement and the judicial arena to help him develop plots for his novels.